Leave it to PET!

The Misadventures of a recycled Super Robot

3

Help me!
PET-kun!

Story and Art by
Kenji Sonishi

Leave It to PET Vol. 3

STORY & ART BY Kenji Sonishi

Translation/Katherine Schilling
Touch-up Art & Lettering/John Hunt
Cover & Book Design/Frances O. Liddell
Editor/Traci N. Todd

VP, Production/Alvin Lu
VP, Publishing Licensing/Rika Inouye
VP, Sales & Product Marketing/Gonzalo Ferreyra
VP, Creative/ Linda Espinosa
Publisher/Hyoe Narita

MAKASETE PET KUN Vol. 3
© Kenji Sonishi 2005
All rights reserved. Original Japanese edition published by POPLAR Publishing Co., Ltd., Tokyo. English translation rights directly arranged with POPLAR Publishing Co., Ltd., Tokyo.

Printed in the U.S.A.

Published by VIZ Media, LLC
P.O. Box 77010
San Francisco, CA 94107

10 9 8 7 6 5 4 3 2 1
First printing, October 2009

www.vizkids.com

Contents:

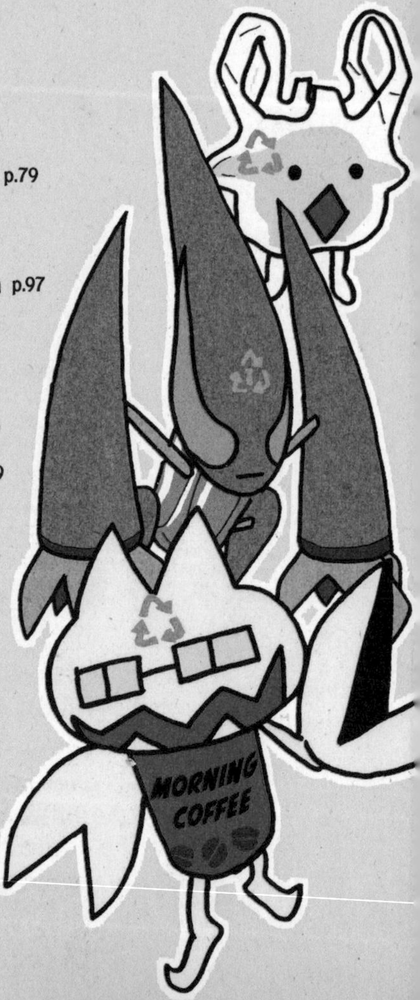

MORNING COFFEE

Leave it to PET!

The Misadventures of a recycled Super Robot

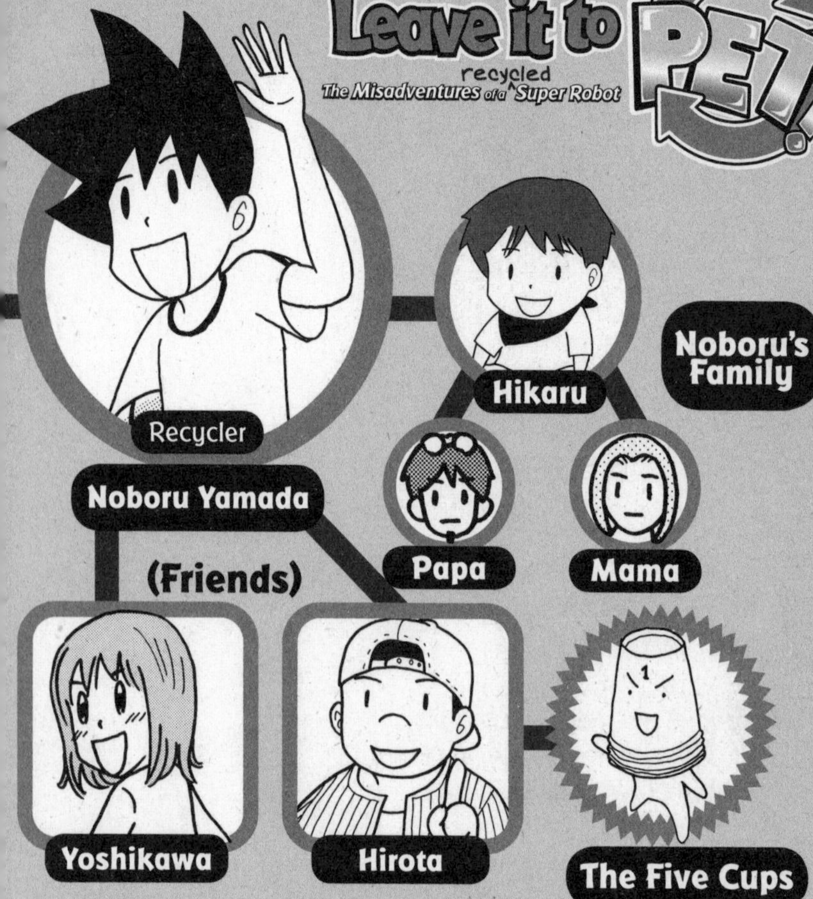
Recycler
Noboru Yamada
Hikaru
Noboru's Family
Papa
Mama
(Friends)
Yoshikawa
Hirota
The Five Cups

The Story

A plastic bottle gets recycled and comes back as a helpful robot!

Meet Noboru, your average Japanese elementary school student. One day he finds a plastic bottle in the park and recycles it. Then the bottle comes back as the robot "**PET**"! **PET** can transform, combine with other robots, and use special **PET** gadgets! Together with his sister, **Alu**, and friend, **Plaz**, **PET** saves Noboru from all kinds of trouble... At least that's the idea.

Who's Who

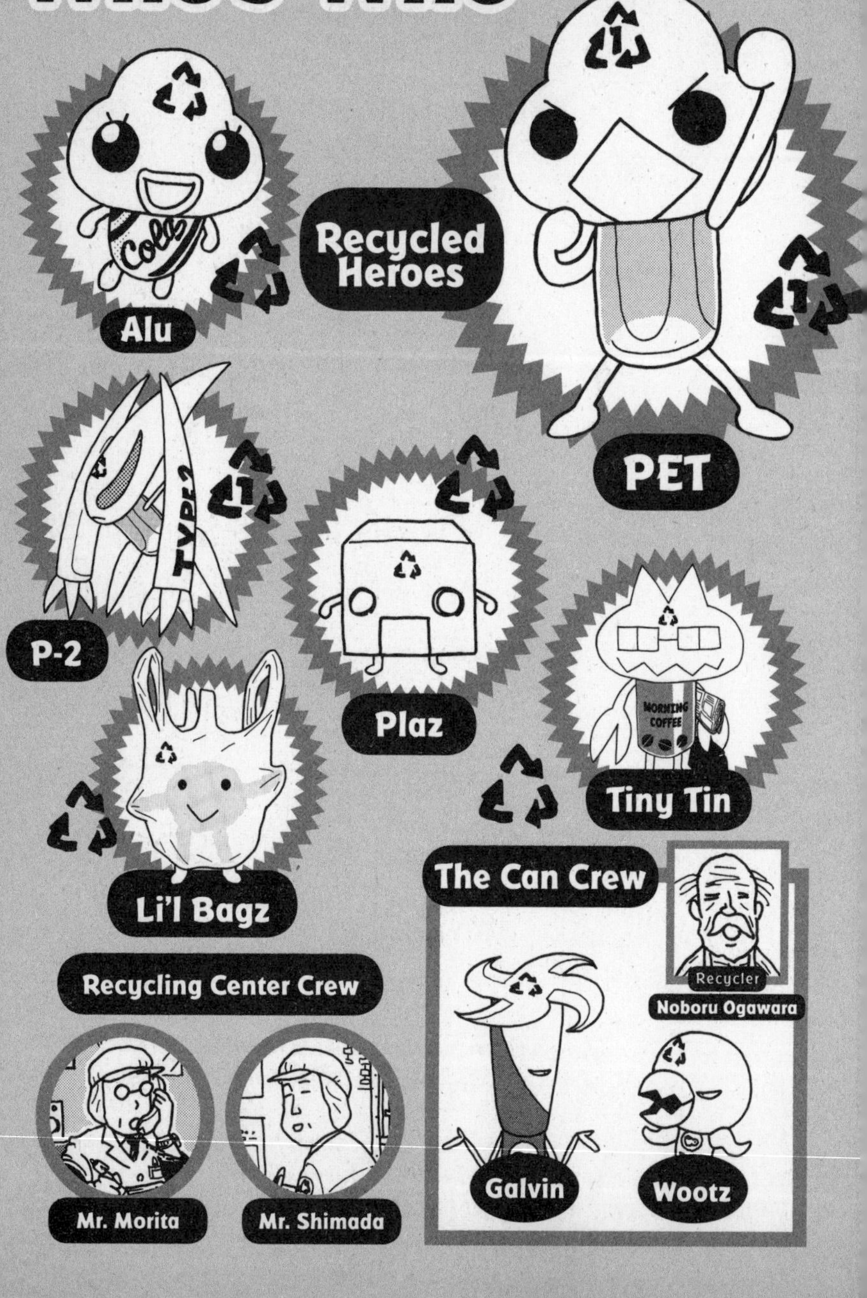
Recycled Heroes
PET
Alu
Cola
P-2
TYPE2
Plaz
Tiny Tin
MORNING COFFEE
Li'l Bagz
The Can Crew
Recycler
Noboru Ogawara
Galvin
Wootz
Recycling Center Crew
Mr. Morita
Mr. Shimada

PET's Haiku*

RECYCLING IS GOOD
SO IS SITTING QUIETLY
RECYCLING YOUR THOUGHTS.

PET

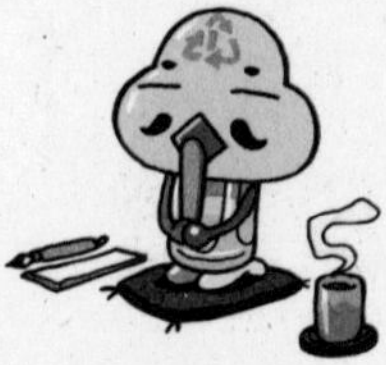

*A haiku is a type of Japanese poem that is three lines long. The first line has five syllables, the second has seven, and the third has five again.

CHAPTER 1

Quoth the PET: "Nevermore!"

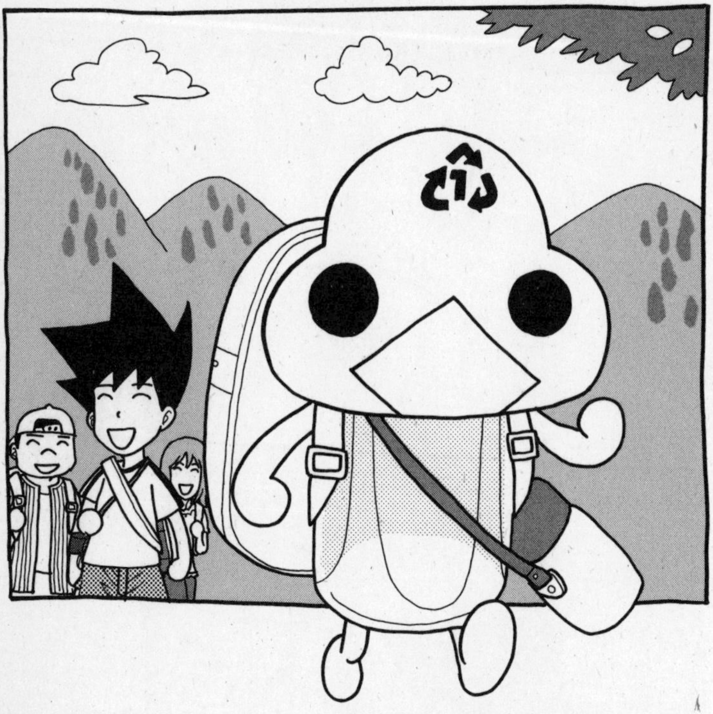

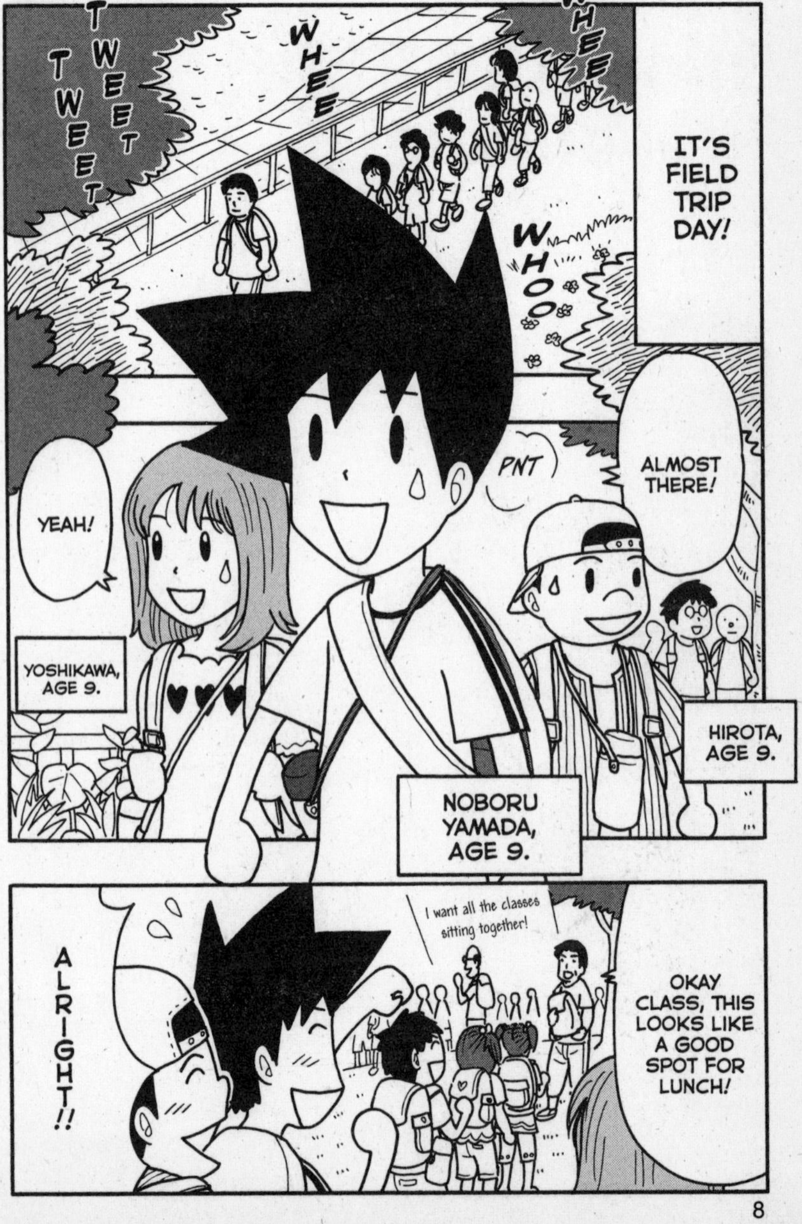
IT'S FIELD TRIP DAY!
WHEE
WHEE
TWEET TWEET
WHOO
ALMOST THERE!
PNT
YEAH!
HIROTA, AGE 9.
NOBORU YAMADA, AGE 9.
YOSHIKAWA, AGE 9.
OKAY CLASS, THIS LOOKS LIKE A GOOD SPOT FOR LUNCH!
I want all the classes sitting together!
ALRIGHT!!

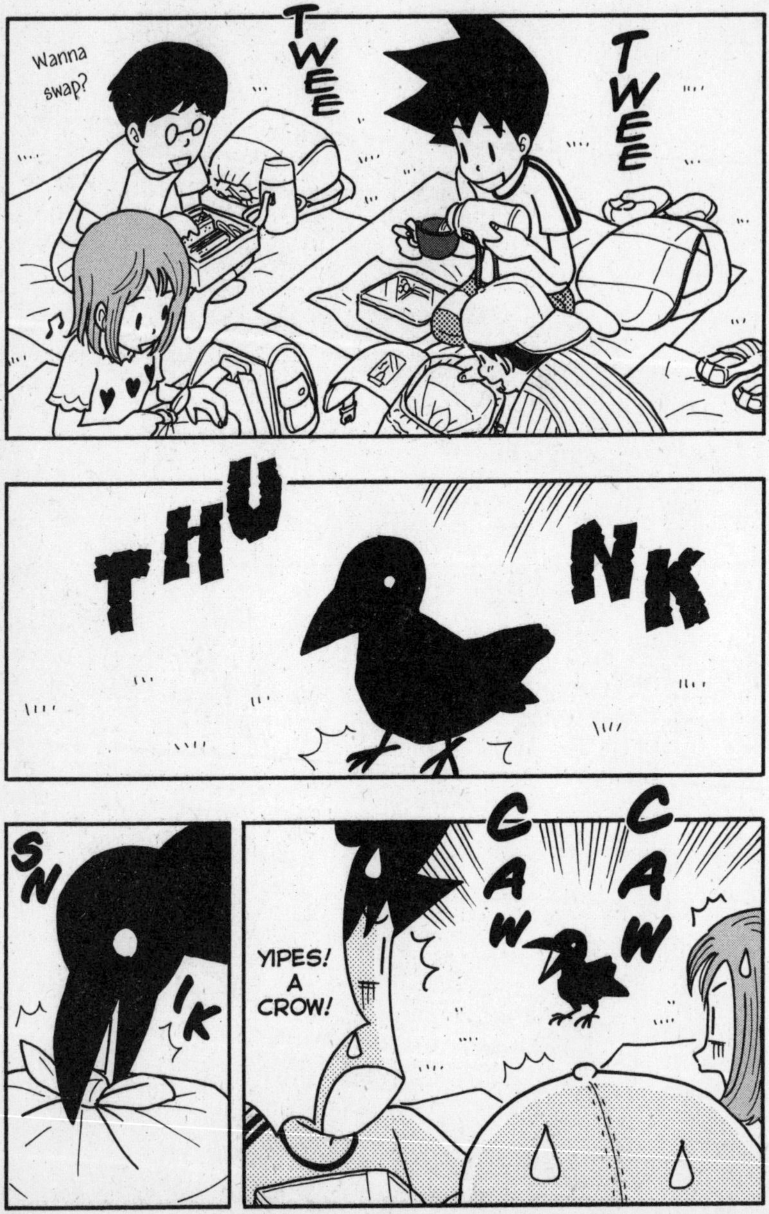
TWEE
TWEE
Wanna swap?
THUNK
C CAW
C CAW
YIPES! A CROW!
SNIK

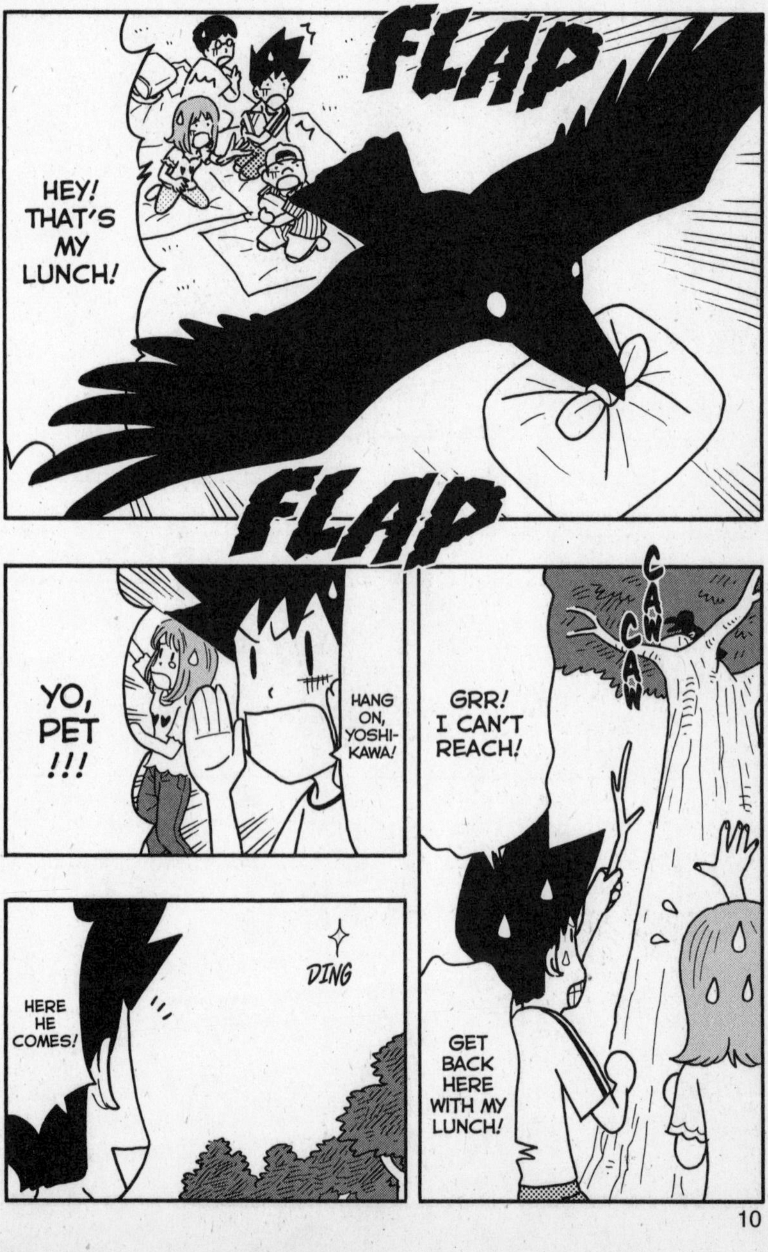
FLAP
HEY! THAT'S MY LUNCH!
FLAP
CAW CAW
GRR! I CAN'T REACH!
GET BACK HERE WITH MY LUNCH!
HANG ON, YOSHI-KAWA!
YO, PET!!!
DING
HERE HE COMES!

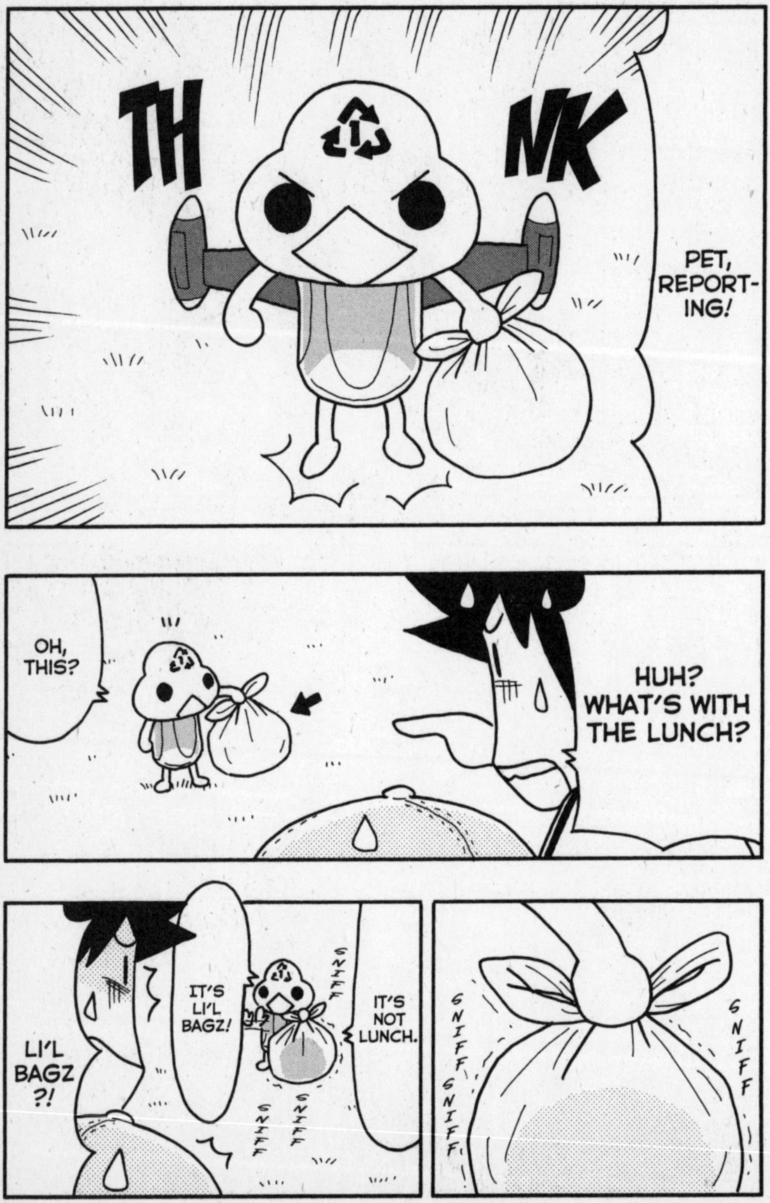
TH NK
PET, REPORTING!
HUH? WHAT'S WITH THE LUNCH?
OH, THIS?
SNIFF
SNIFF
SNIFF
IT'S NOT LUNCH.
SNIFF
IT'S LI'L BAGZ!
SNIFF
SNIFF
LI'L BAGZ?!

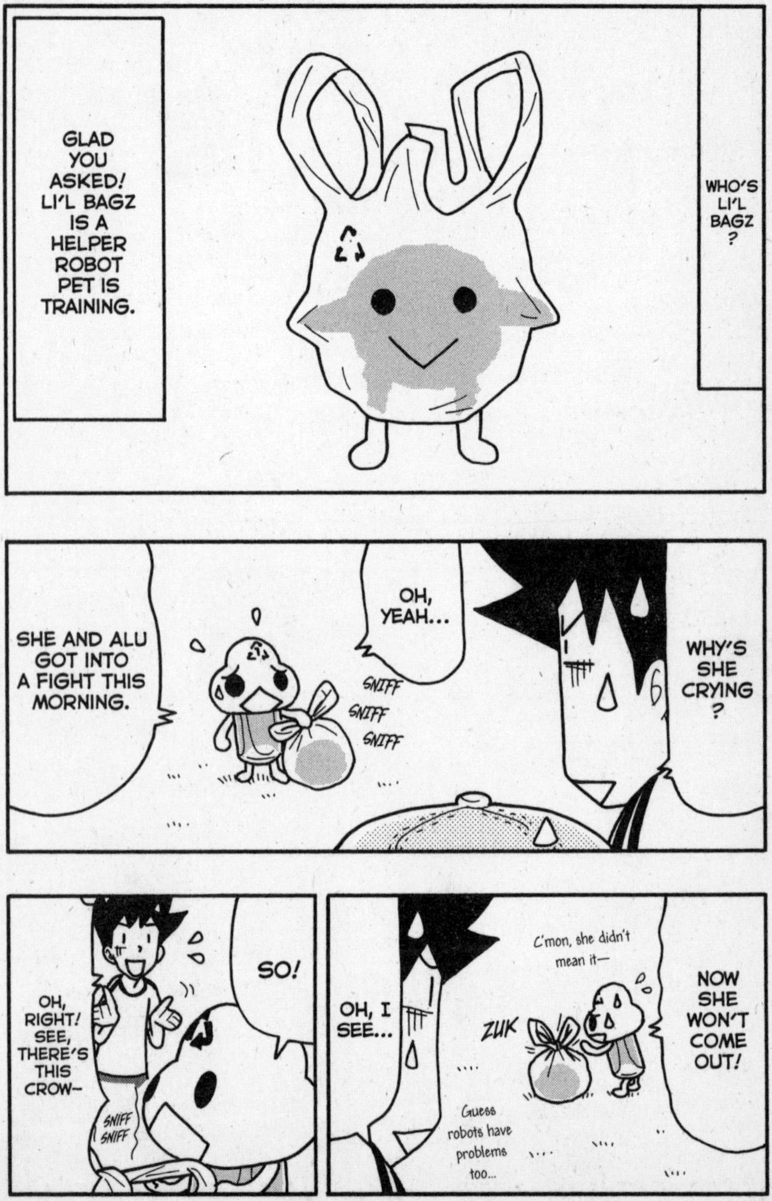
WHO'S LI'L BAGZ?
GLAD YOU ASKED! LI'L BAGZ IS A HELPER ROBOT PET IS TRAINING.
WHY'S SHE CRYING?
OH, YEAH...
SNIFF
SNIFF
SNIFF
SHE AND ALU GOT INTO A FIGHT THIS MORNING.
NOW SHE WON'T COME OUT!
C'mon, she didn't mean it—
ZUK
OH, I SEE...
Guess robots have problems too...
SO!
OH, RIGHT! SEE, THERE'S THIS CROW—
SNIFF SNIFF

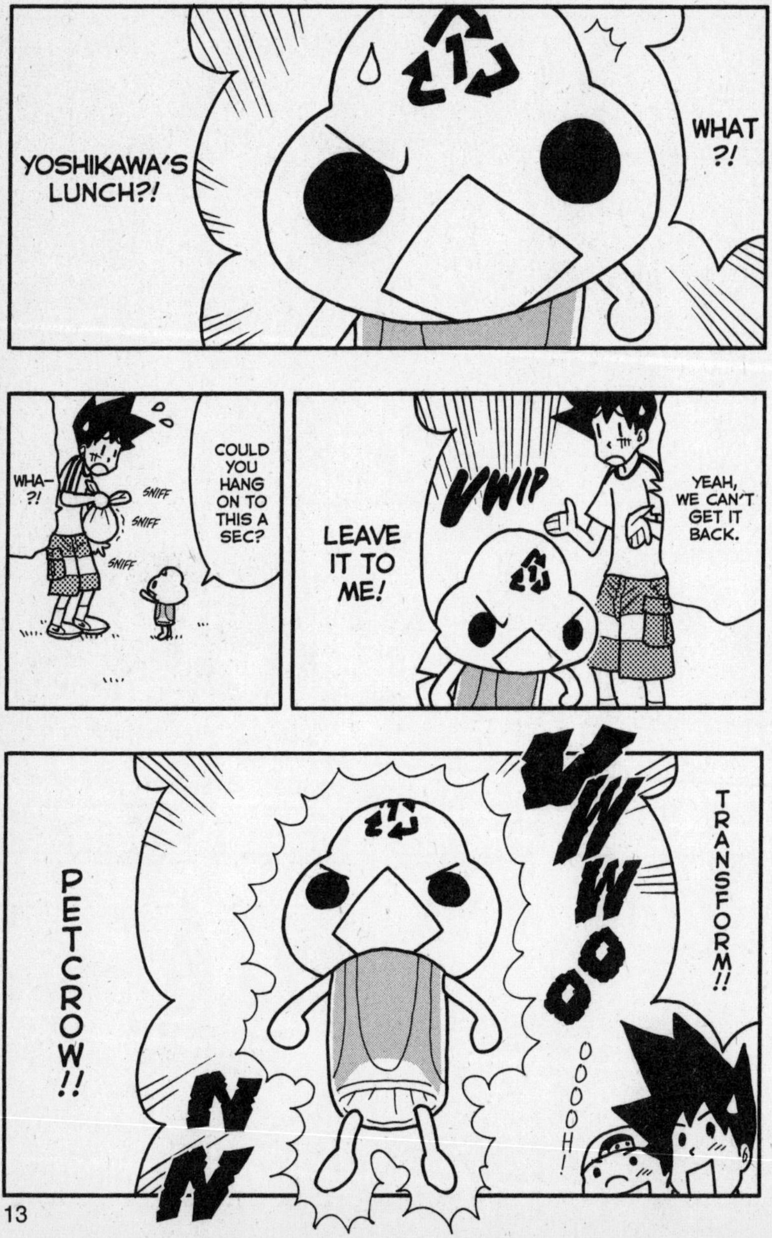
WHAT ?!
YOSHIKAWA'S LUNCH?!
YEAH, WE CAN'T GET IT BACK.
VWIP
LEAVE IT TO ME!
COULD YOU HANG ON TO THIS A SEC?
WHA— ?!
SNIFF
SNIFF
SNIFF
TRANSFORM!!
VWWOO
OOOOH!
PETCROW!!
NN

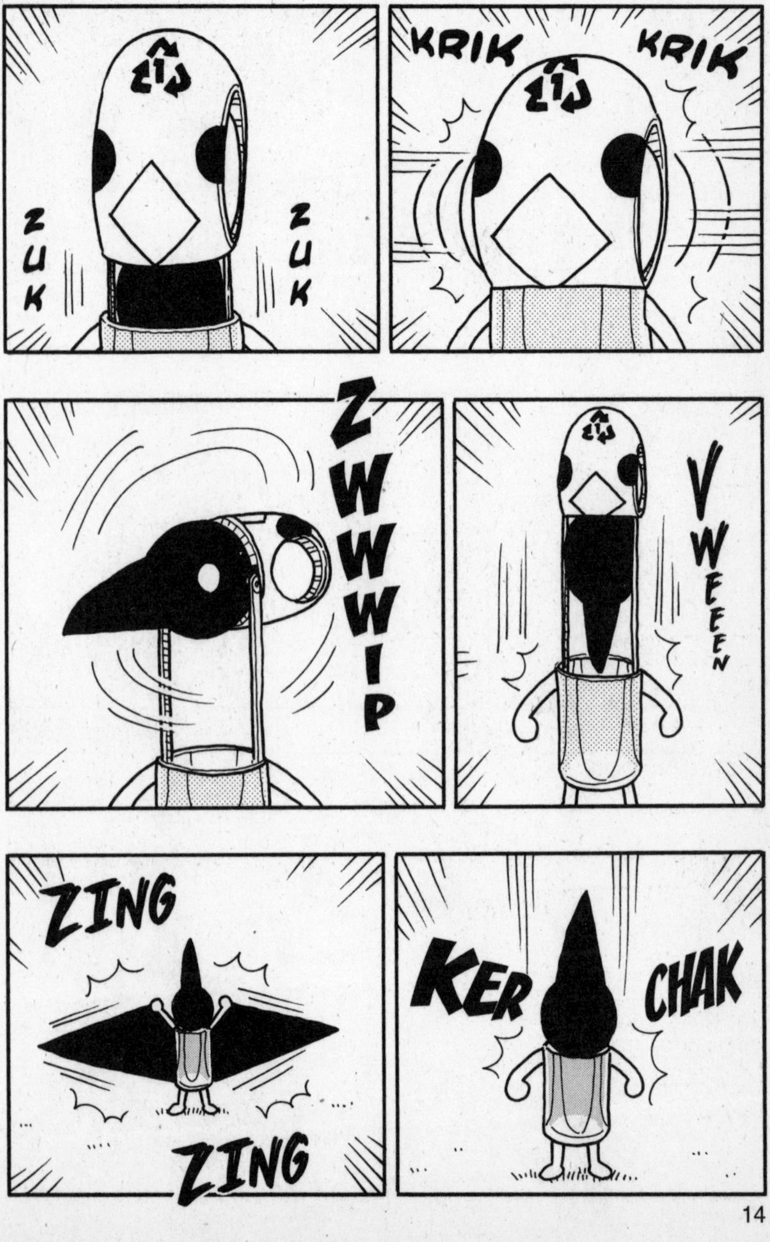
KRIK KRIK
ZUK ZUK
VWEEEN
ZWWWIP
KERCHAK
ZING
ZING

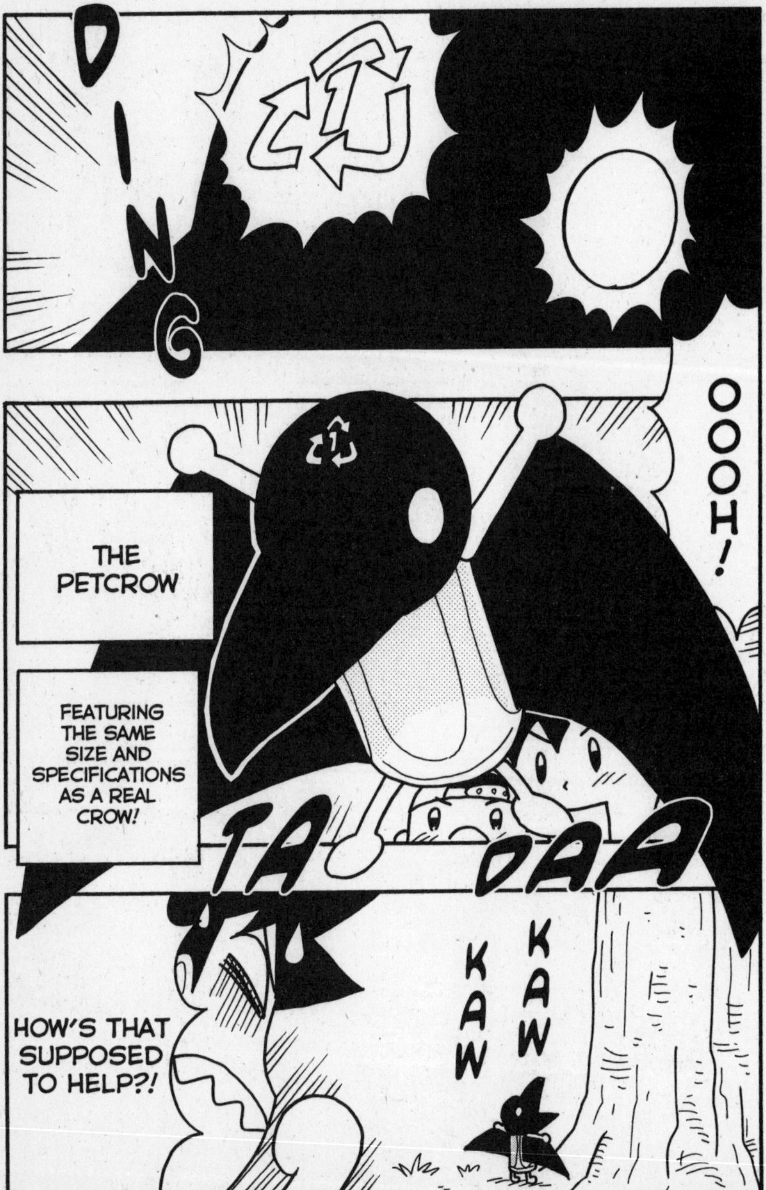
DING
OOOH!
THE PETCROW
FEATURING THE SAME SIZE AND SPECIFICATIONS AS A REAL CROW!
TA DAA
KAW
KAW
HOW'S THAT SUPPOSED TO HELP?!

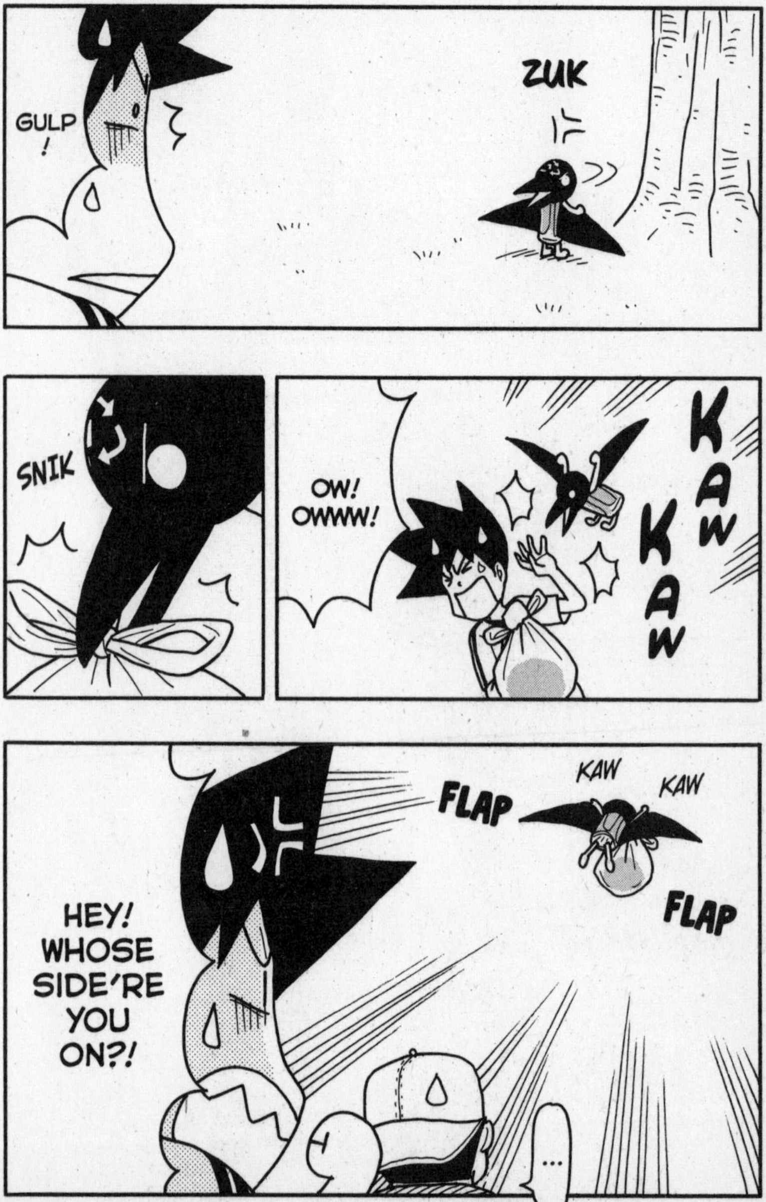
ZUK
GULP!
KAW KAW
KAW KAW
OW! OWWW!
SNIK
KAW
KAW
FLAP
FLAP
HEY! WHOSE SIDE'RE YOU ON?!
...

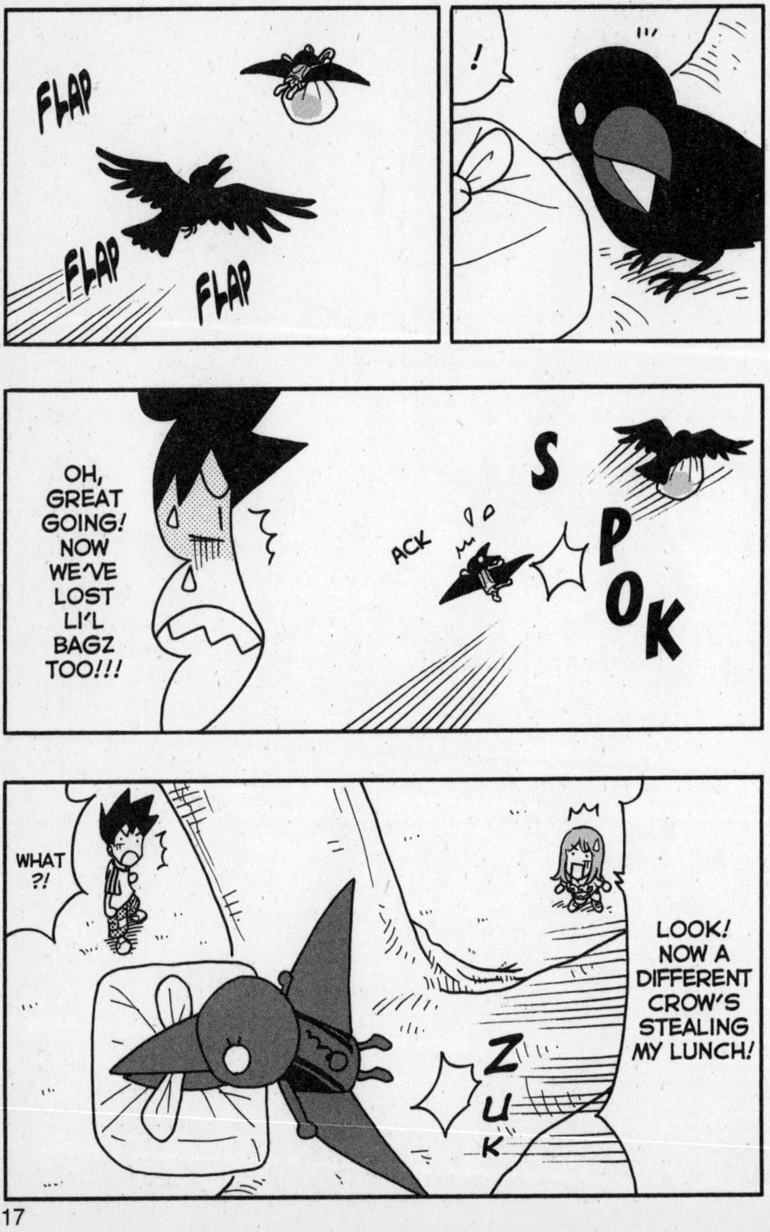
!
FLAP
FLAP
FLAP
SPOK
ACK
OH, GREAT GOING! NOW WE'VE LOST LI'L BAGZ TOO!!!
LOOK! NOW A DIFFERENT CROW'S STEALING MY LUNCH!
ZUK
WHAT?!

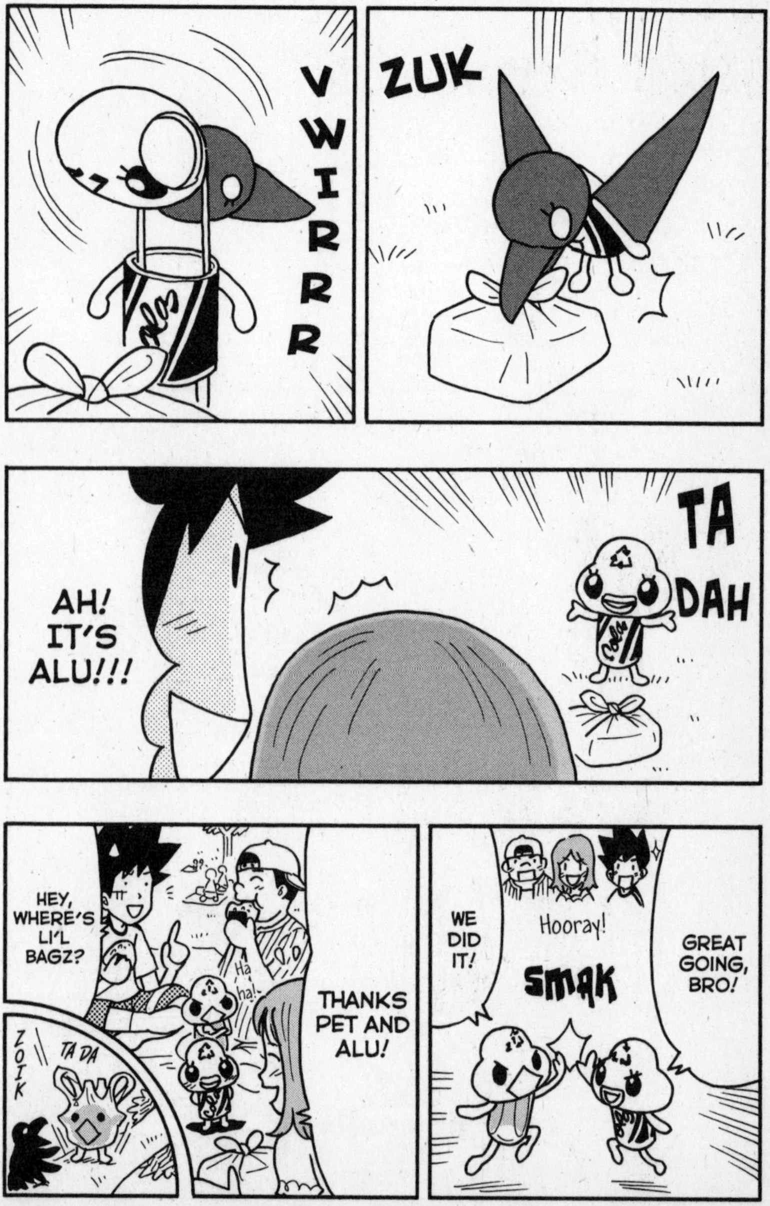
ZUK
VWIRRR
TA DAH
AH! IT'S ALU!!!
Hooray!
GREAT GOING, BRO!
WE DID IT!
SMAK
THANKS PET AND ALU!
HEY, WHERE'S LI'L BAGZ?
Ha ha!
TA DA
ZOIK

CHAPTER 2
Alu's Gadgets

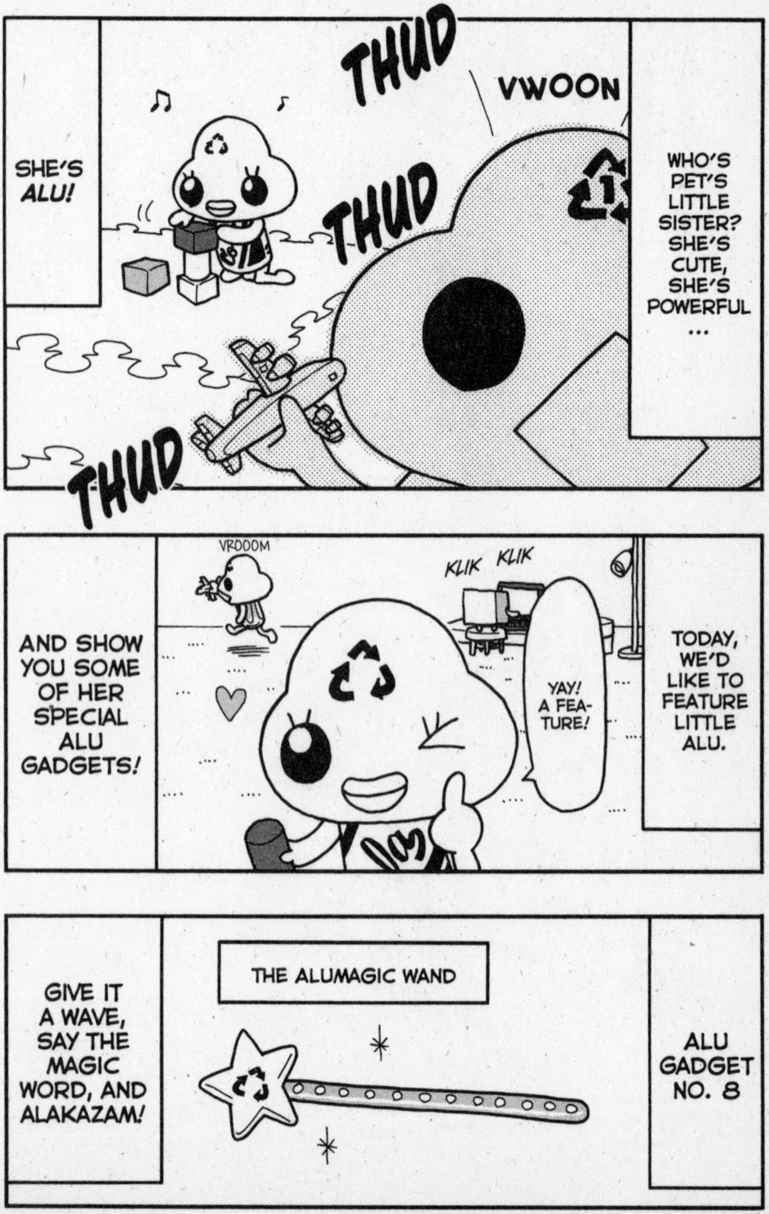
WHO'S PET'S LITTLE SISTER? SHE'S CUTE, SHE'S POWERFUL ...
VWOON
THUD
THUD
THUD
SHE'S ALU!
TODAY, WE'D LIKE TO FEATURE LITTLE ALU.
YAY! A FEA-TURE!
KLIK KLIK
VROOOM
AND SHOW YOU SOME OF HER SPECIAL ALU GADGETS!
ALU GADGET NO. 8
THE ALUMAGIC WAND
GIVE IT A WAVE, SAY THE MAGIC WORD, AND ALAKAZAM!

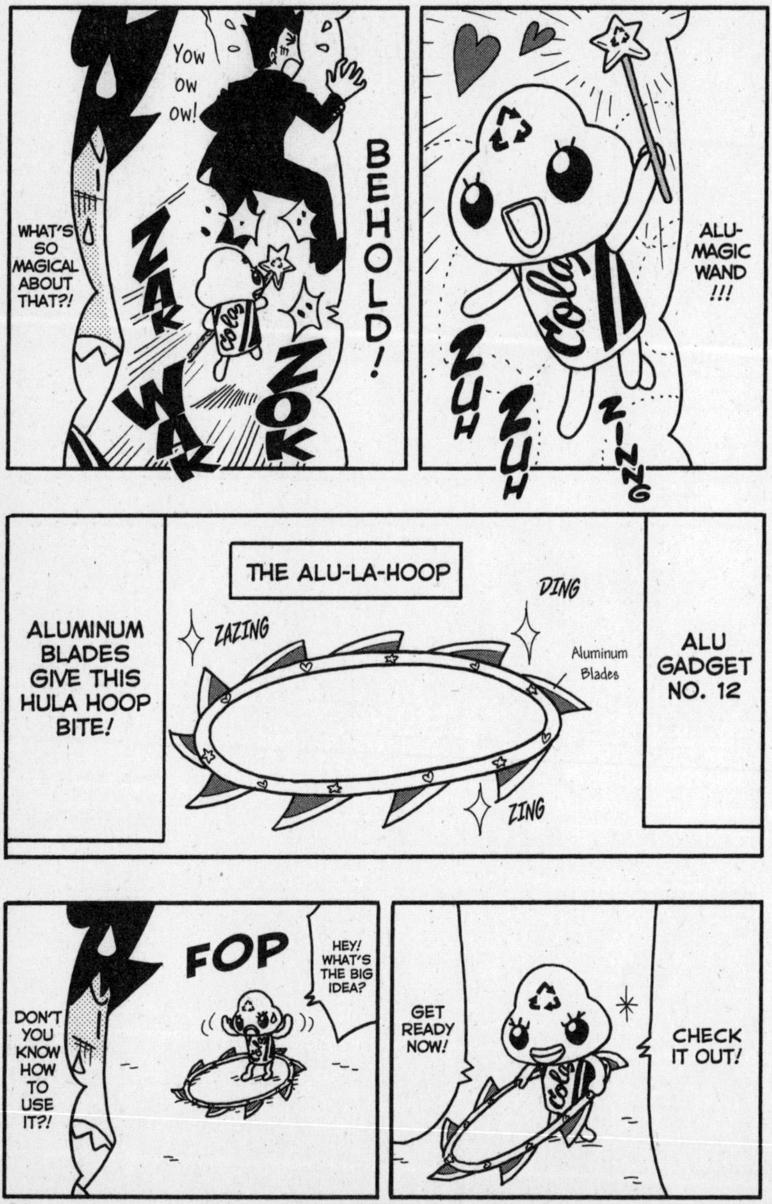
ALU-MAGIC WAND!!!
ZUH
ZUH
ZING
BEHOLD!
YOW OW OW!
ZAK
WAK
ZOK
WHAT'S SO MAGICAL ABOUT THAT?!
ALU GADGET NO. 12
THE ALU-LA-HOOP
DING
Aluminum Blades
ZAZING
ZING
ALUMINUM BLADES GIVE THIS HULA HOOP BITE!
CHECK IT OUT!
GET READY NOW!
HEY! WHAT'S THE BIG IDEA?
FOP
DON'T YOU KNOW HOW TO USE IT?!

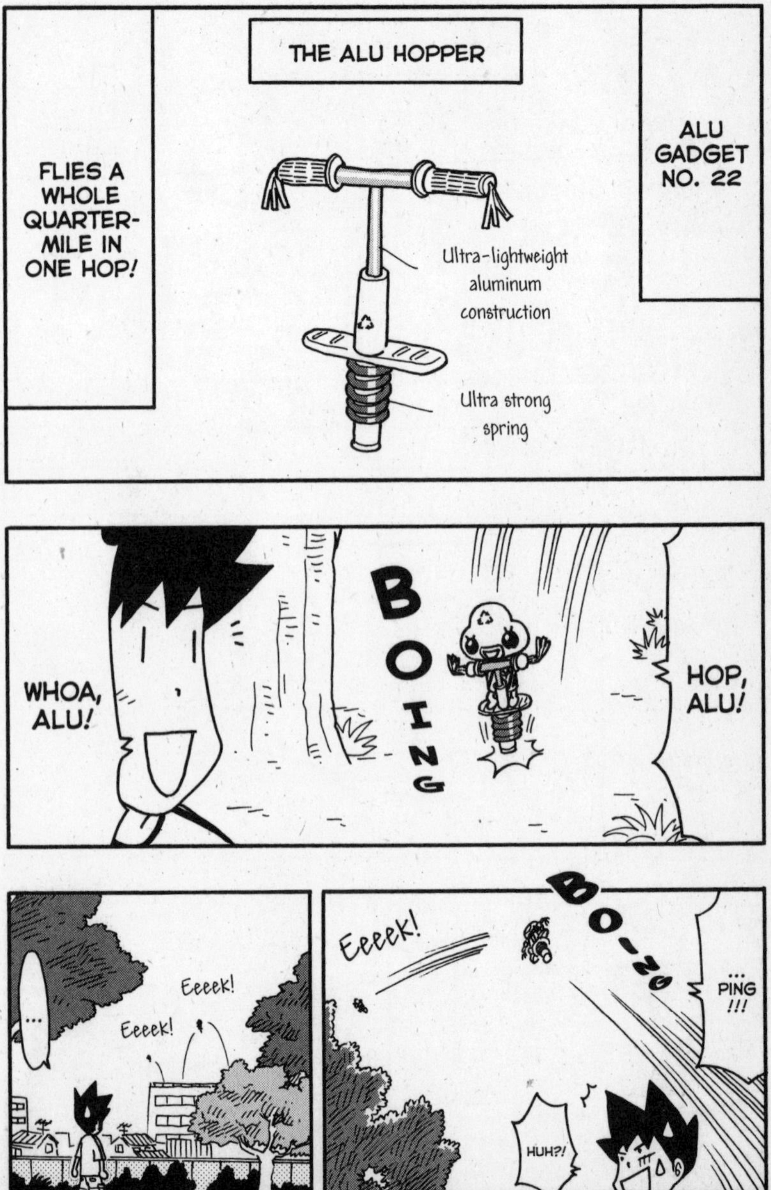
ALU GADGET NO. 22
THE ALU HOPPER
Ultra-lightweight aluminum construction
Ultra strong spring
FLIES A WHOLE QUARTER-MILE IN ONE HOP!
HOP, ALU!
BOING
WHOA, ALU!
BO-ING
...PING!!!
Eeeek!
HUH?!
Eeeek!
Eeeek!
...

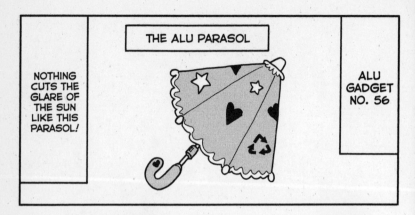

THE ALU PARASOL
NOTHING CUTS THE GLARE OF THE SUN LIKE THIS PARASOL!
ALU GADGET NO. 56
IT'S ALL ABOUT THE LOOK!
ZZUP
BUT YOU'RE A ROBOT. YOU DON'T HAVE TO WORRY ABOUT THE SUN!
THAT'S IT...
THAT'S IT?!
TIME TO GO, ALU!
VWEE
VWEE
VWIP
OKAY!!
THE ALU HANDBAG
NEVER LEAVE HOME WITHOUT IT!
ALU GADGET NO. 72
Holds everything you need for a day on the town!

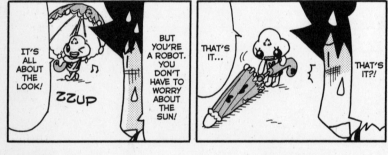

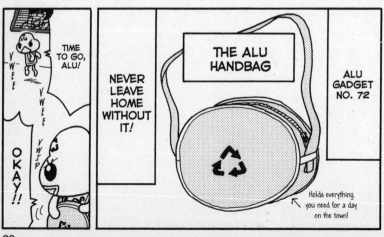

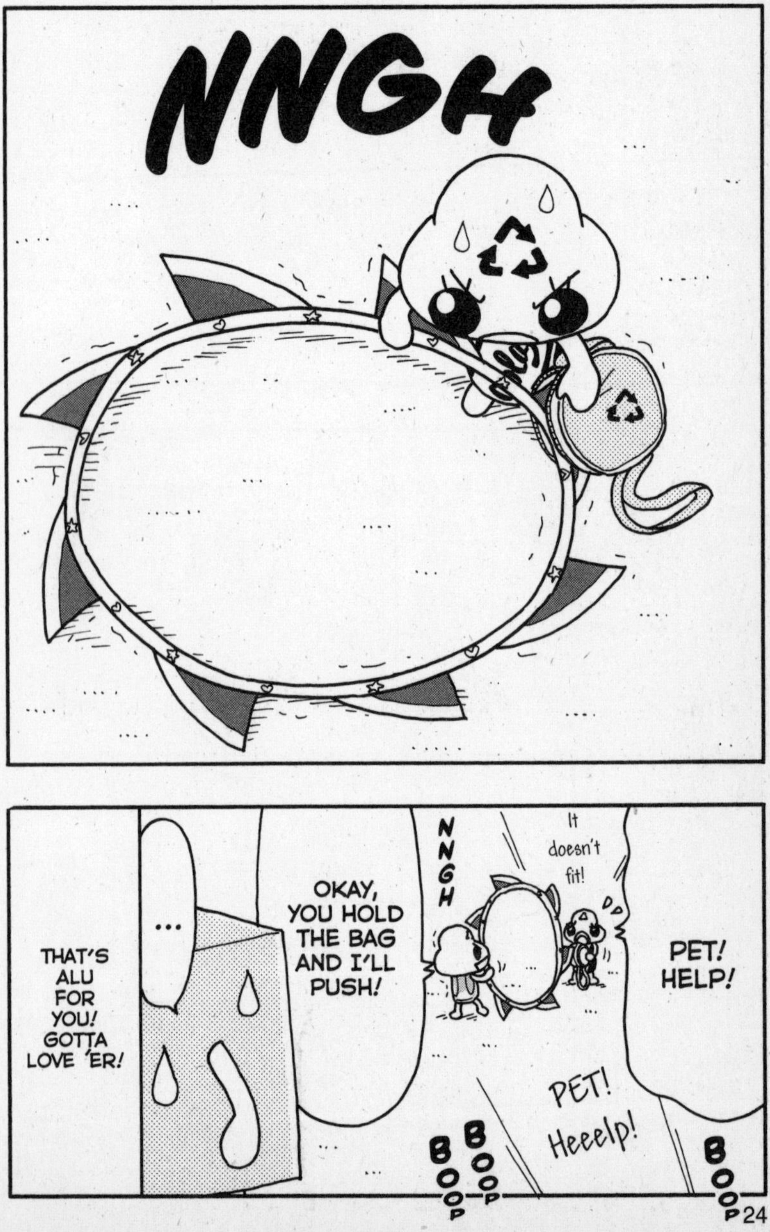
NNGH
It doesn't fit!
PET! HELP!
NNGH
OKAY, YOU HOLD THE BAG AND I'LL PUSH!
...
THAT'S ALU FOR YOU! GOTTA LOVE 'ER!
PET! Heeelp!
BOOOP
BOOOP
BOOOP

CHAPTER 3 Power-Up, PET!

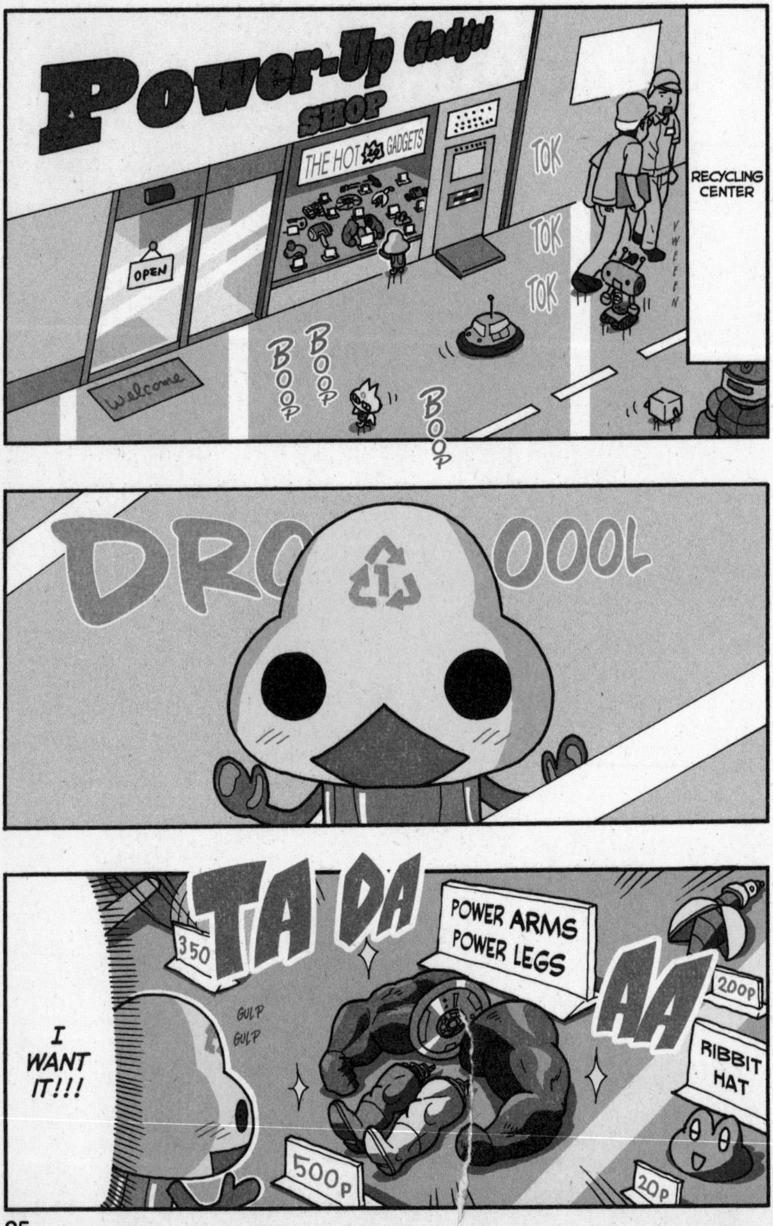
RECYCLING CENTER
Power-Up Gadget SHOP
THE HOT GADGETS
TOK
TOK
TOK
VWEEEN
OPEN
BOOP
BOOP
BOOP
Welcome
DRO
OOOL
POWER ARMS
POWER LEGS
200P
RIBBIT HAT
TA DA
AA
350
I WANT IT!!!
GULP
GULP
20P
500P

CHAPTER 3
Power-Up, PET!

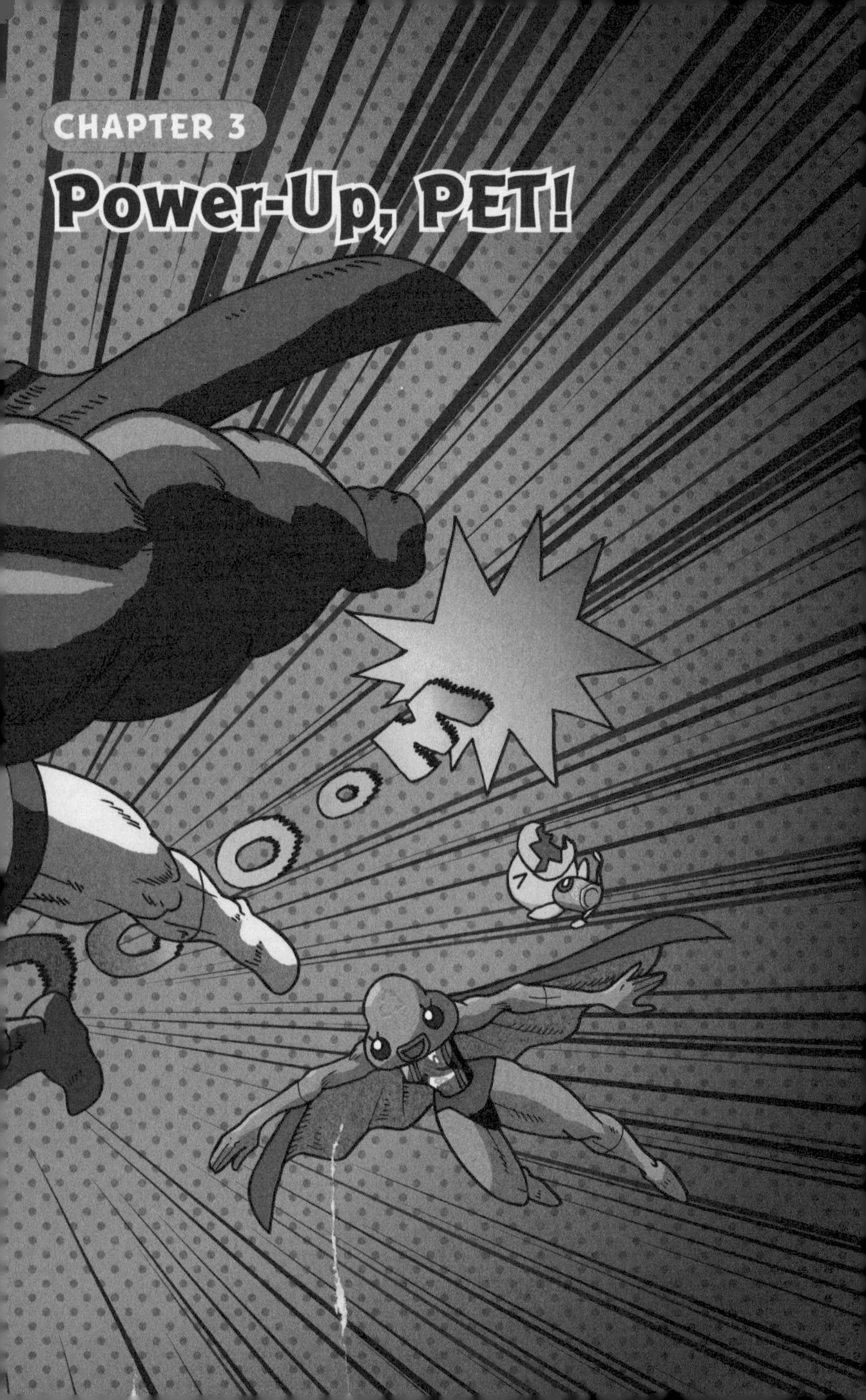

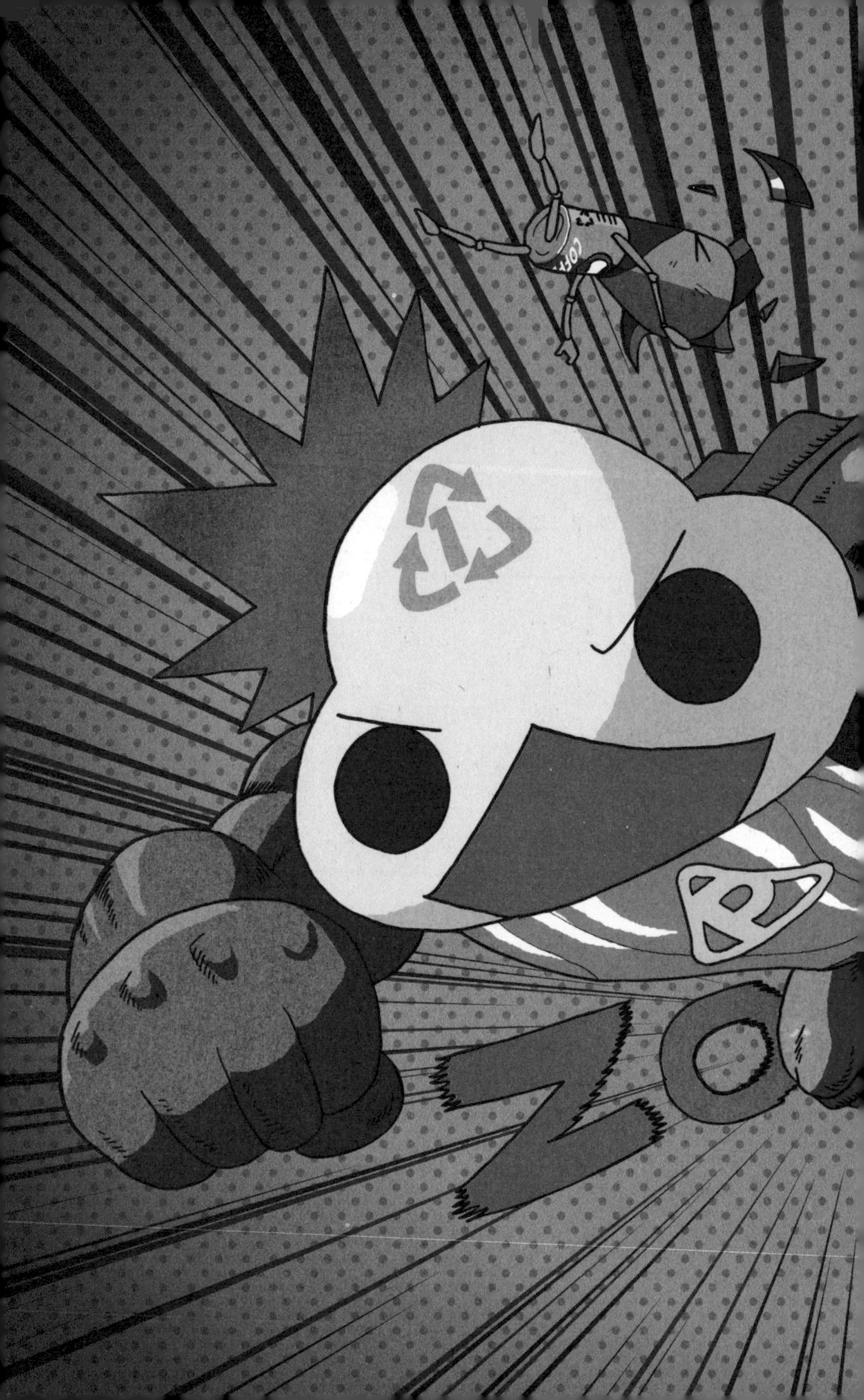

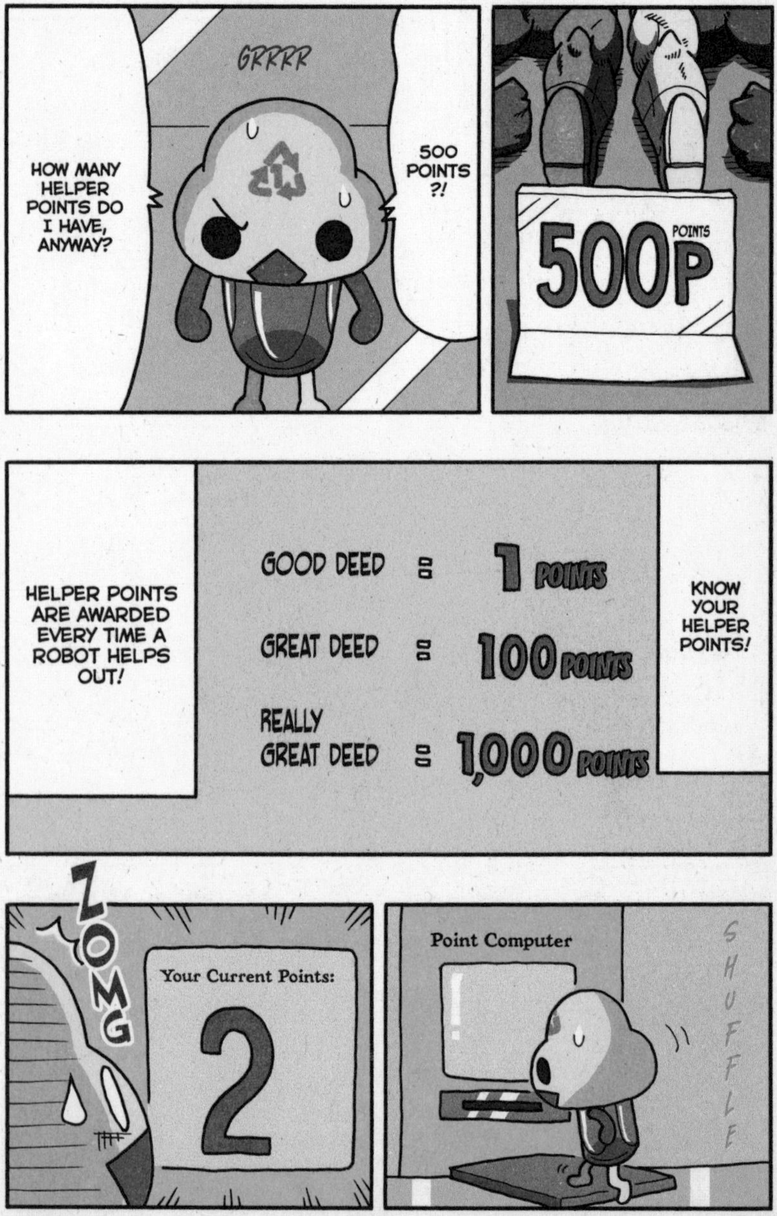
POINTS
500P
GRRRR
500 POINTS ?!
HOW MANY HELPER POINTS DO I HAVE, ANYWAY?
KNOW YOUR HELPER POINTS!
GOOD DEED = 1 POINTS
GREAT DEED = 100 POINTS
REALLY GREAT DEED = 1,000 POINTS
HELPER POINTS ARE AWARDED EVERY TIME A ROBOT HELPS OUT!
SHUFFLE
Point Computer
ZOMG
Your Current Points:
2

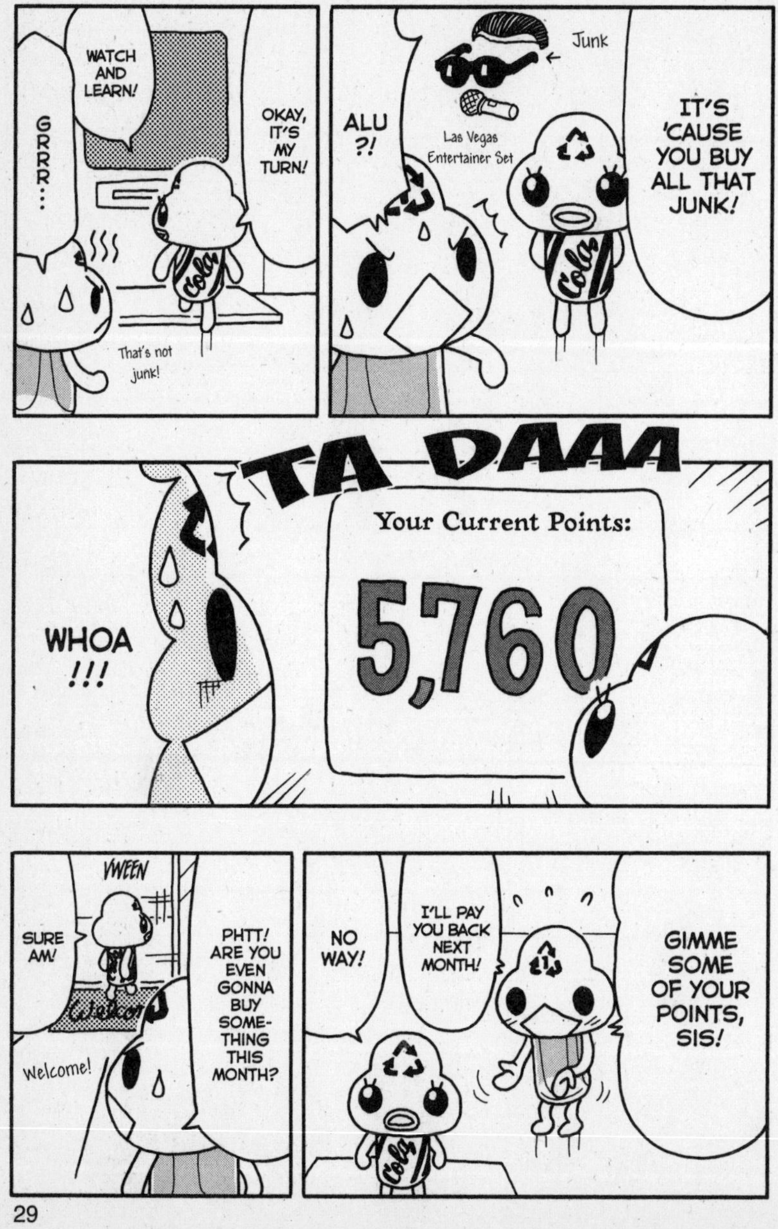
IT'S 'CAUSE YOU BUY ALL THAT JUNK!
Junk
Las Vegas Entertainer Set
ALU ?!
OKAY, IT'S MY TURN!
WATCH AND LEARN!
GRRR...
That's not junk!
TA DAAA
Your Current Points:
5,760
WHOA !!!
GIMME SOME OF YOUR POINTS, SIS!
I'LL PAY YOU BACK NEXT MONTH!
NO WAY!
PHTT! ARE YOU EVEN GONNA BUY SOME-THING THIS MONTH?
VWEEN
SURE AM!
Welcome!

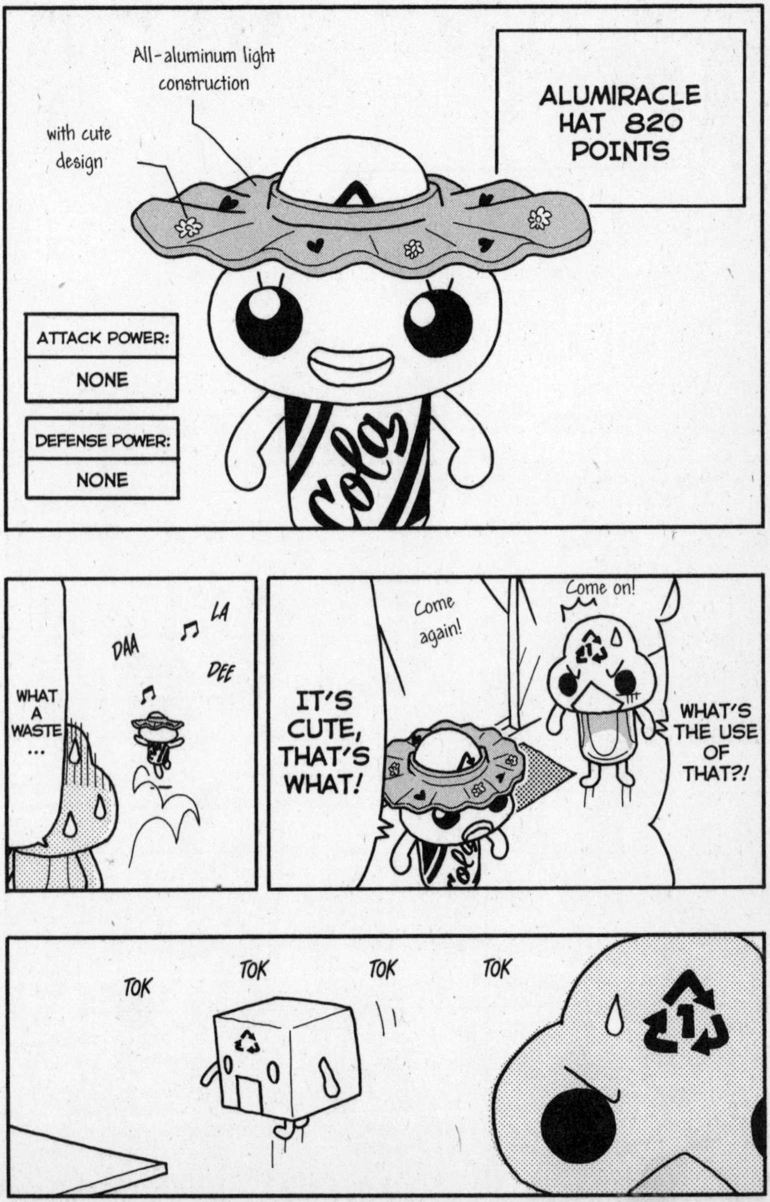
ALUMIRACLE HAT 820 POINTS
All-aluminum light construction
with cute design
ATTACK POWER:
NONE
DEFENSE POWER:
NONE
Come on!
WHAT'S THE USE OF THAT?!
Come again!
IT'S CUTE, THAT'S WHAT!
LA
DEE
DAA
WHAT A WASTE...
TOK
TOK
TOK
TOK

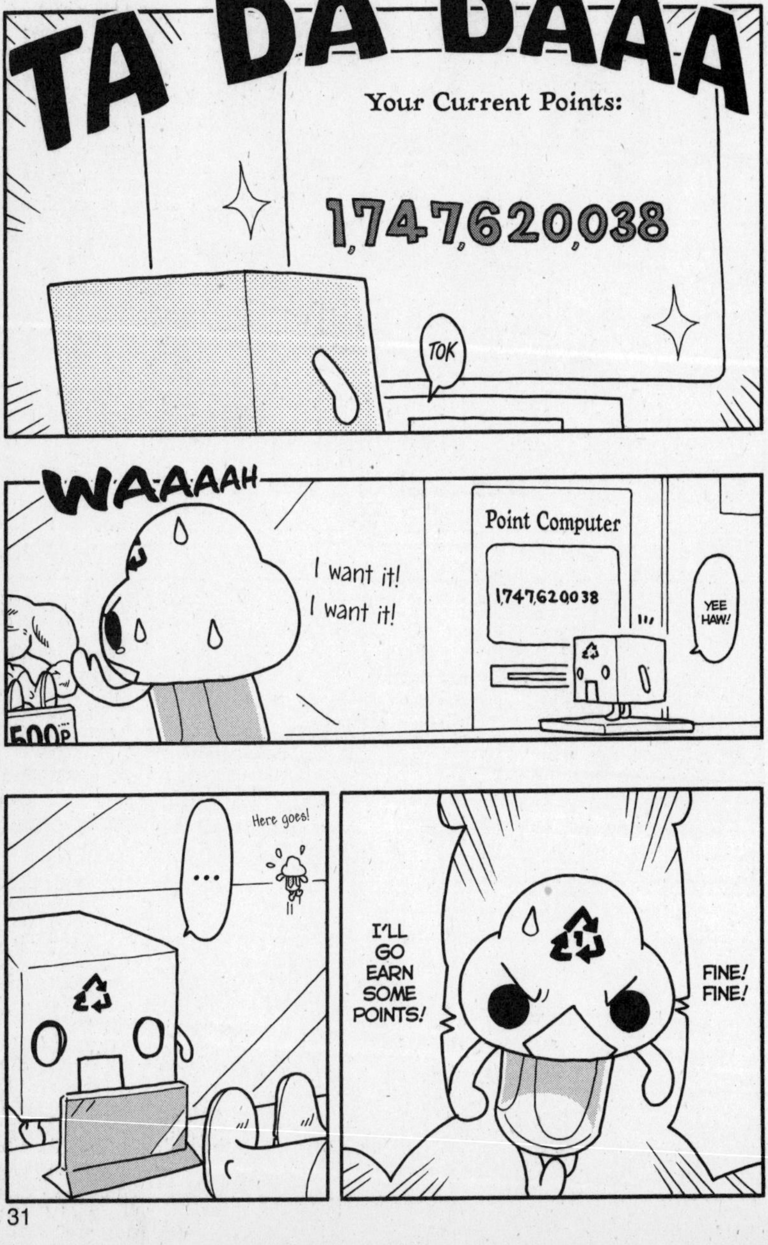
TA DA DAAAA
Your Current Points:
1,747,620,038
TOK
Point Computer
1,747,620,038
YEE HAW!
WAAAAH
I want it! I want it!
500P
FINE! FINE!
I'LL GO EARN SOME POINTS!
Here goes!
...

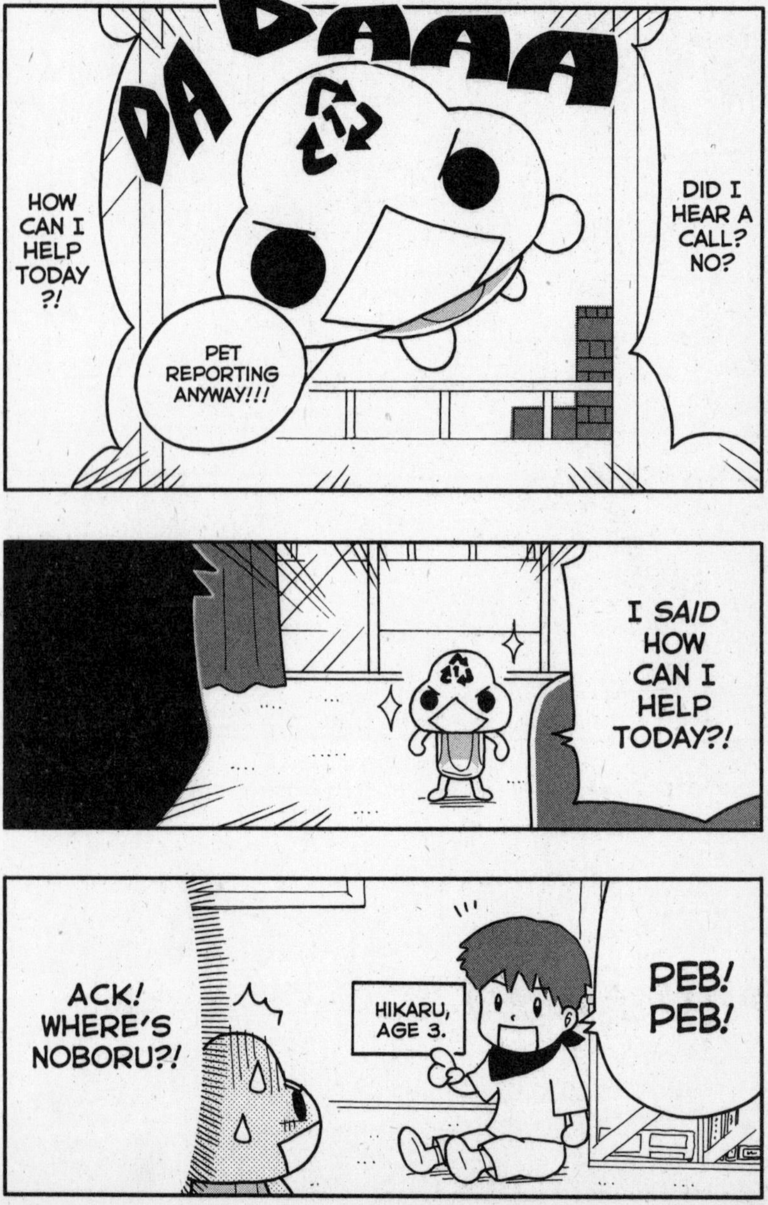
DADAAA
DID I HEAR A CALL? NO?
PET REPORTING ANYWAY!!!
HOW CAN I HELP TODAY?!
I SAID HOW CAN I HELP TODAY?!
PEB! PEB!
HIKARU, AGE 3.
ACK! WHERE'S NOBORU?!

WHEEE!
ZAK
GRRRRRK
UNH... WHERE'S YOUR BROTHER?
YOW YOW YOW.
BUDDER?
VWRRK
YEAH!
HEEEELP!
MY BUDDER?
BY MUDDER?
MUGGER!
HUH?
MUGGER!
GAK
WHAAA—?!

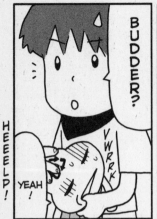

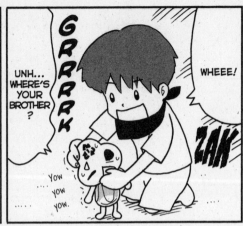

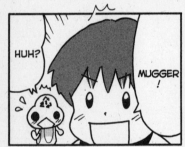

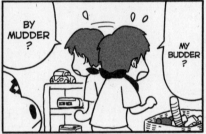

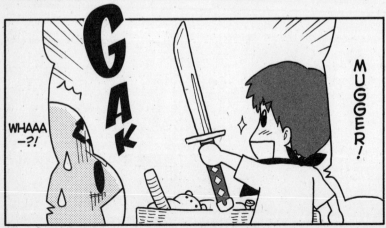

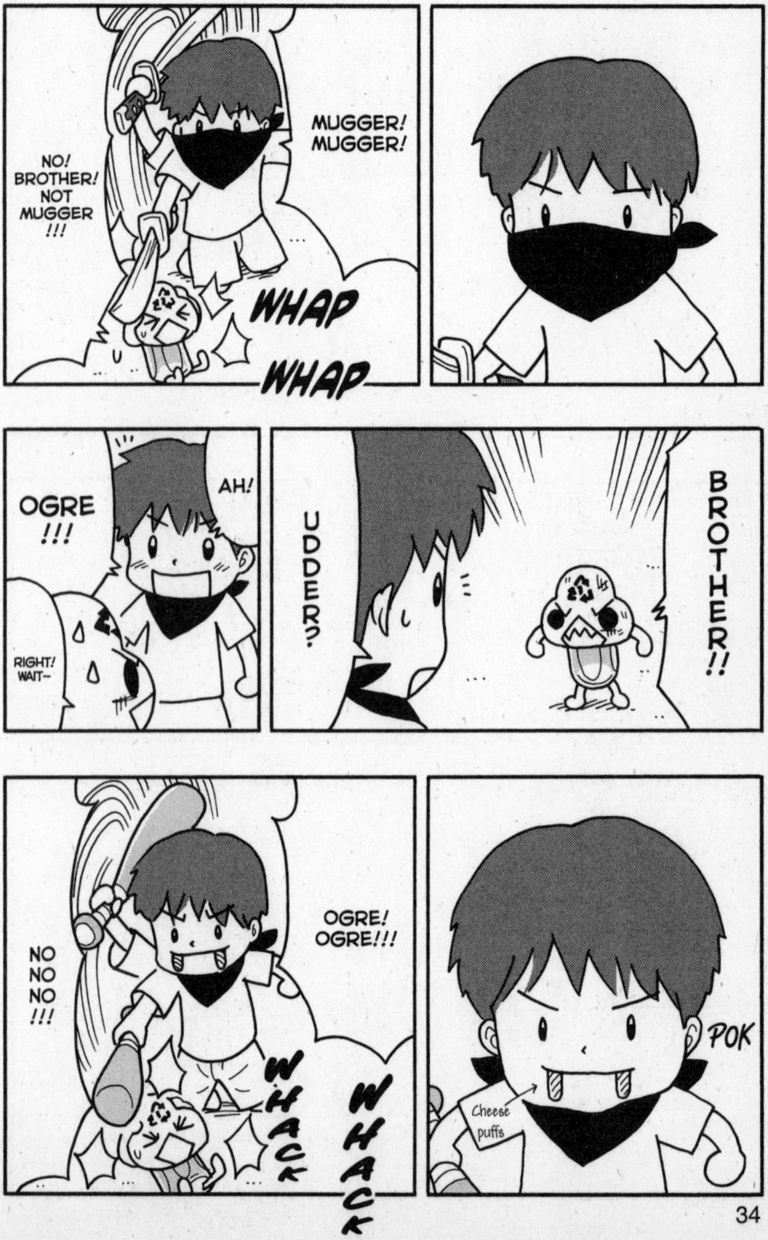
MUGGER! MUGGER!
NO! BROTHER! NOT MUGGER!!!
...
WHAP
WHAP
BROTHER!!
UDDER?
AH!
OGRE!!!
RIGHT! WAIT–
POK
Cheese puffs
OGRE! OGRE!!!
NO NO NO!!!
WHACK
WHACK

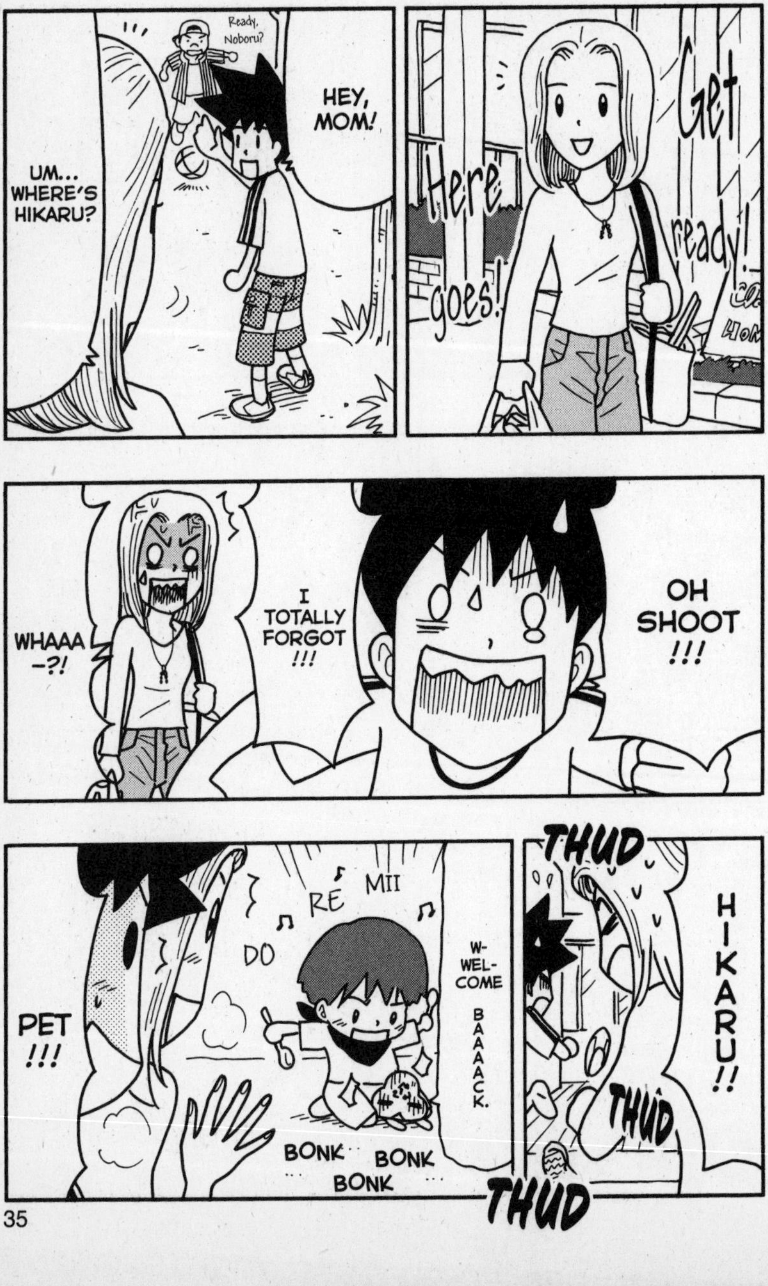
Get ready!
Here goes!
Ready, Noboru?
HEY, MOM!
UM... WHERE'S HIKARU?
OH SHOOT!!!
I TOTALLY FORGOT!!!
WHAAA-?!
THUD
HIKARU!!
THUD
THUD
W-WELCOME BAAAACK.
MII
RE
DO
BONK... BONK... BONK...
PET!!!

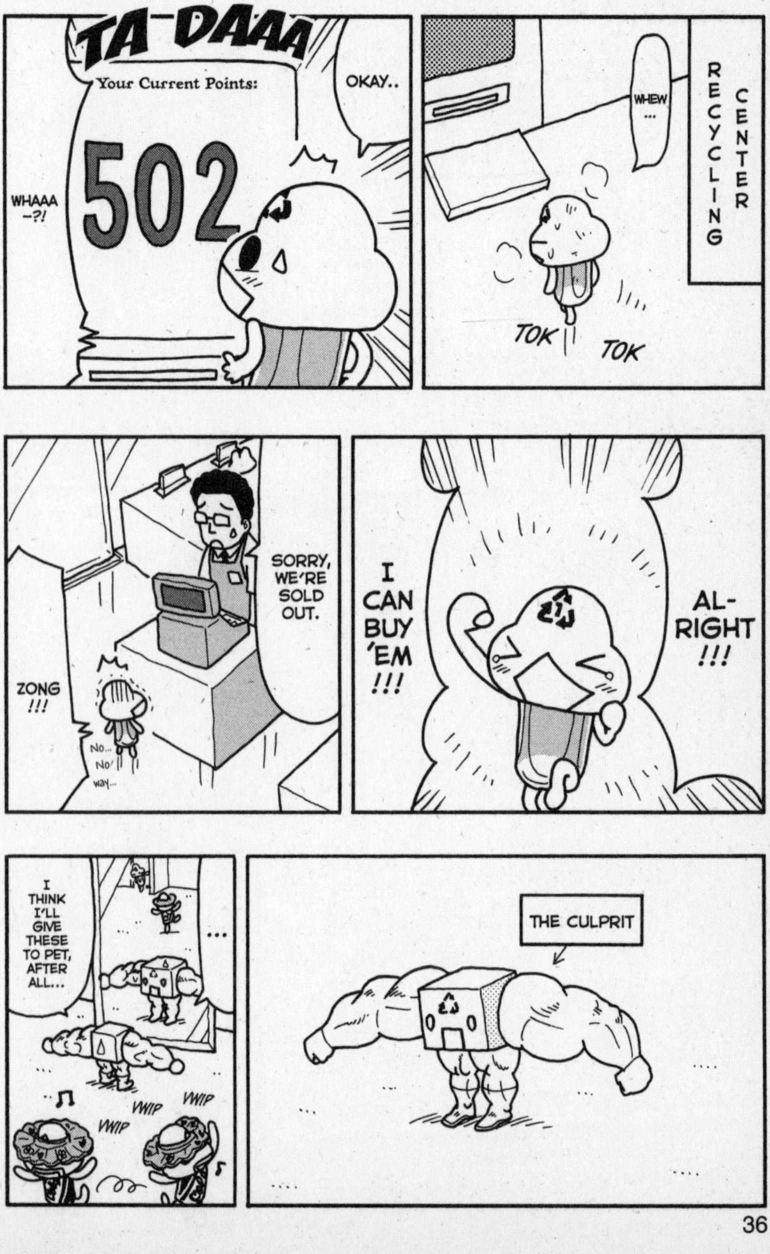
RECYCLING CENTER
WHEW...
TOK
TOK
TA-DAAA
Your Current Points:
502
OKAY..
WHAAA-?!
AL-RIGHT!!!
I CAN BUY 'EM!!!
SORRY, WE'RE SOLD OUT.
ZONG!!!
No... No! way...
THE CULPRIT
I THINK I'LL GIVE THESE TO PET, AFTER ALL...
...
VWIP
VWIP
VWIP

CHAPTER 4
Power-Up, Alu!

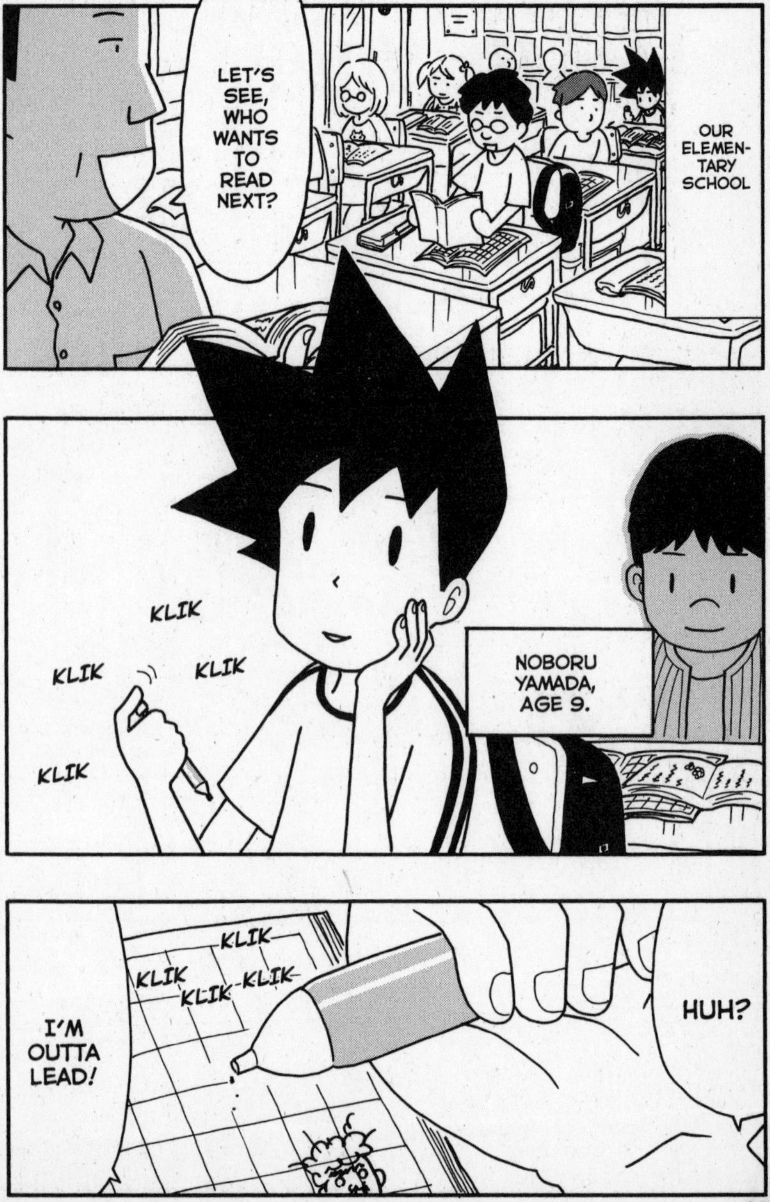
OUR ELEMENTARY SCHOOL
LET'S SEE, WHO WANTS TO READ NEXT?
NOBORU YAMADA, AGE 9.
KLIK
KLIK
KLIK
KLIK
HUH?
KLIK
KLIK
KLIK
KLIK
I'M OUTTA LEAD!

TOK
HB 0.5
TOK
TOK
ACK!
DOWN TO MY LAST ONE!
GULP...
CAREFUL... CAREFUL!
TREMBL
TREMBL
TREMBL
YOU'RE UP, YAMADA!
HUH ?!
ZOIK
OH NO!
POK

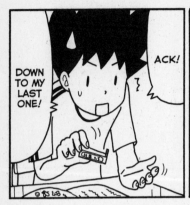

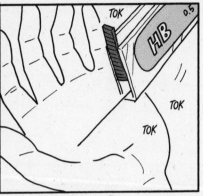

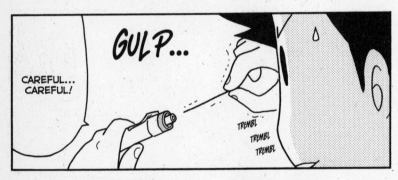

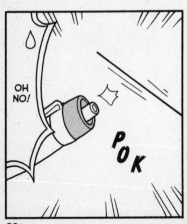

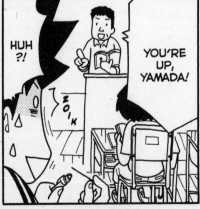

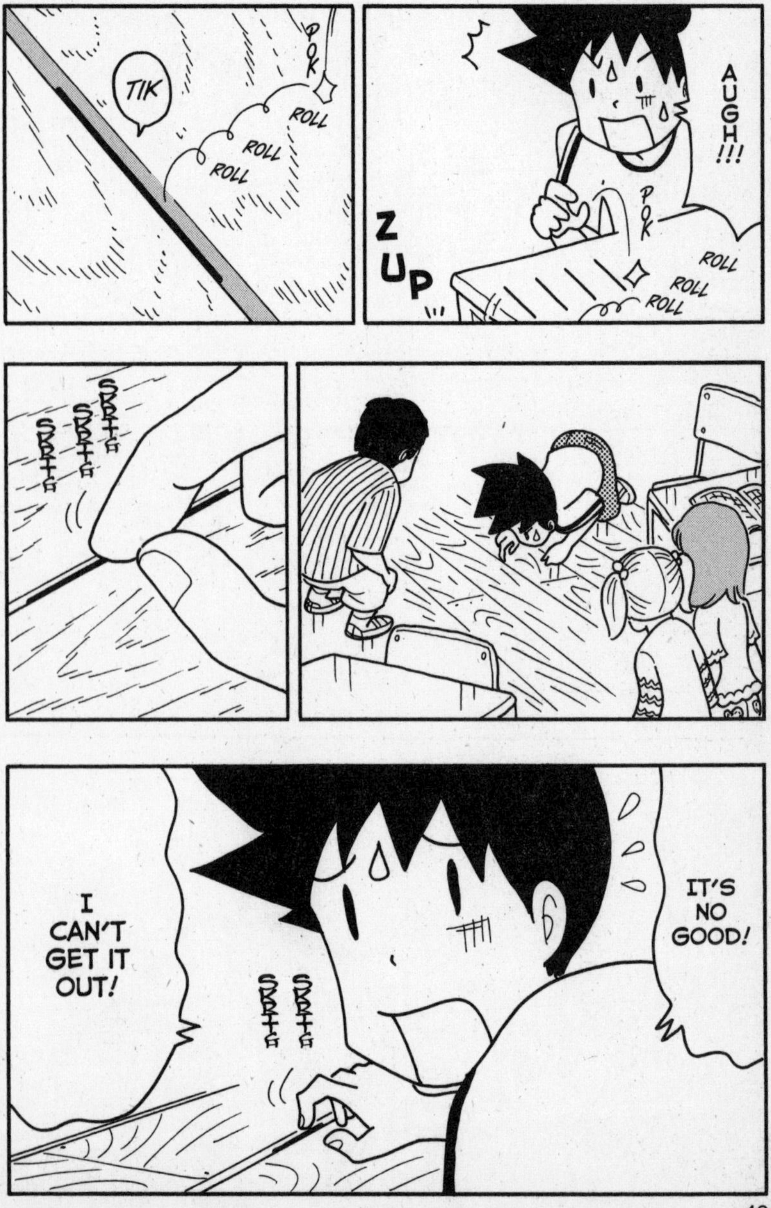
AUGH!!!
POK
ROLL
ROLL
ROLL
ZUP
POK
TIK
ROLL
ROLL
ROLL
IT'S NO GOOD!
I CAN'T GET IT OUT!

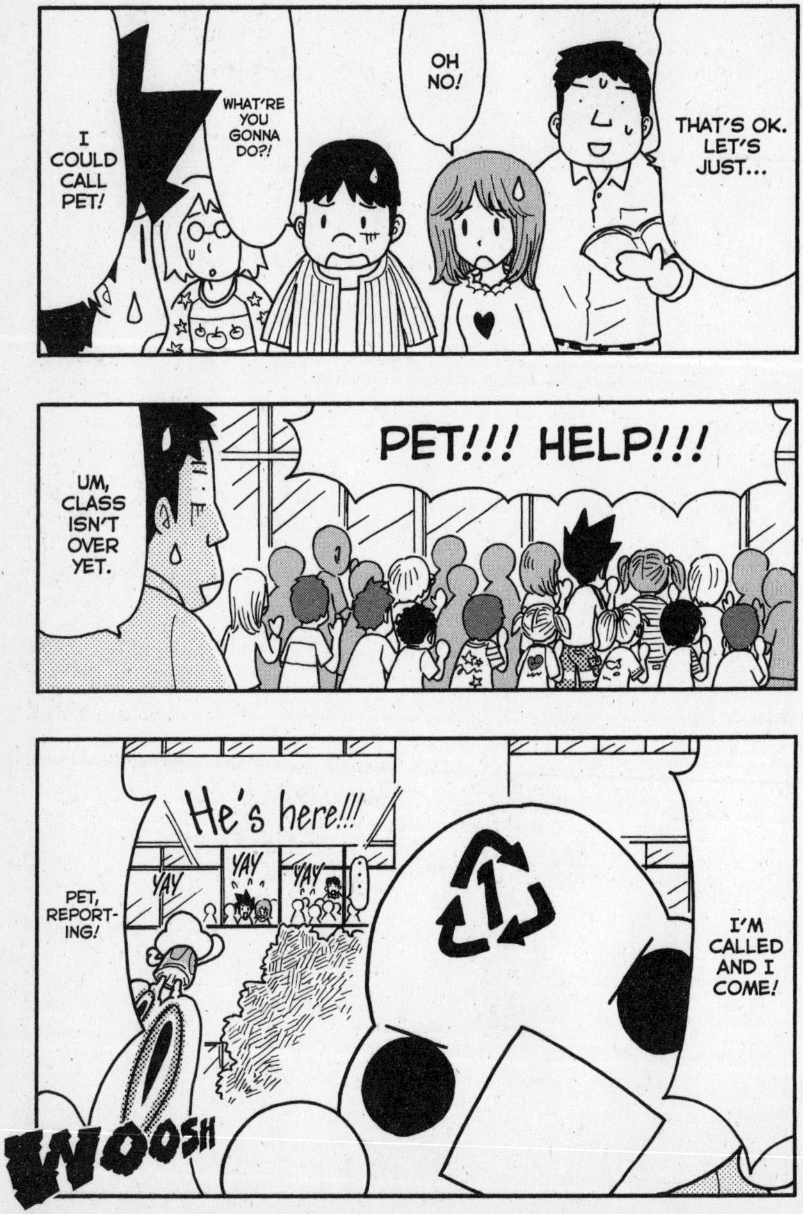
THAT'S OK. LET'S JUST...
OH NO!
WHAT'RE YOU GONNA DO?!
I COULD CALL PET!
PET!!! HELP!!!
UM, CLASS ISN'T OVER YET.
I'M CALLED AND I COME!
He's here!!!
YAY
YAY
YAY
PET, REPORTING!
WOOSH

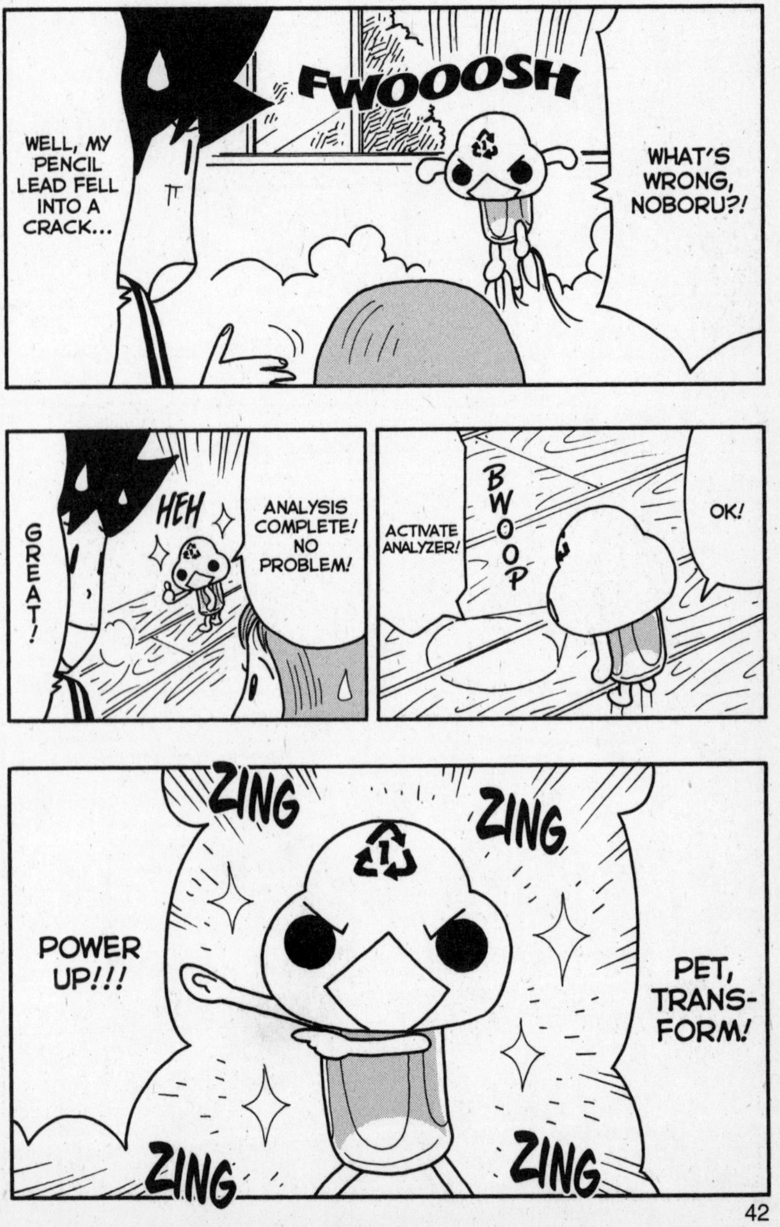
WHAT'S WRONG, NOBORU?!
FWOOOSH
WELL, MY PENCIL LEAD FELL INTO A CRACK...
OK!
BWOOP
ACTIVATE ANALYZER!
ANALYSIS COMPLETE! NO PROBLEM!
HEH
GREAT!
PET, TRANSFORM!
ZING
ZING
POWER UP!!!
ZING
ZING

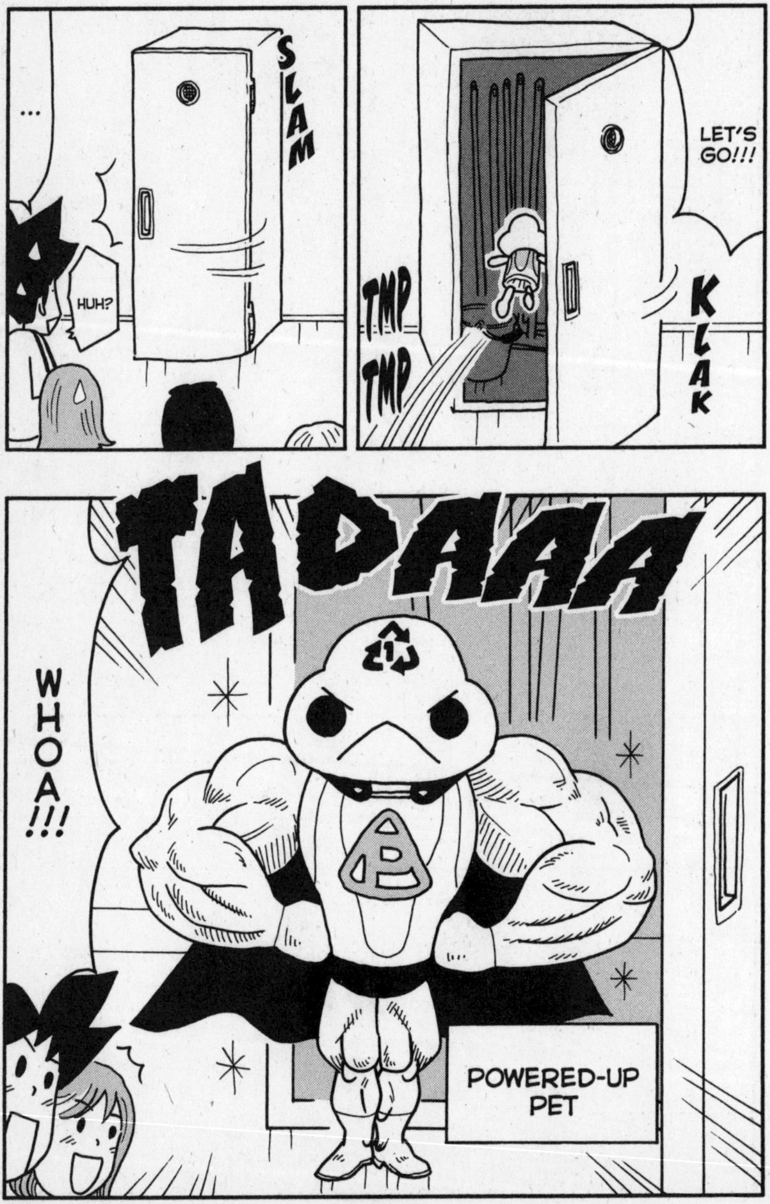
LET'S GO!!!
KLAK
TMP TMP
SLAM
...
HUH?
TADAAA
WHOA!!!
POWERED-UP PET

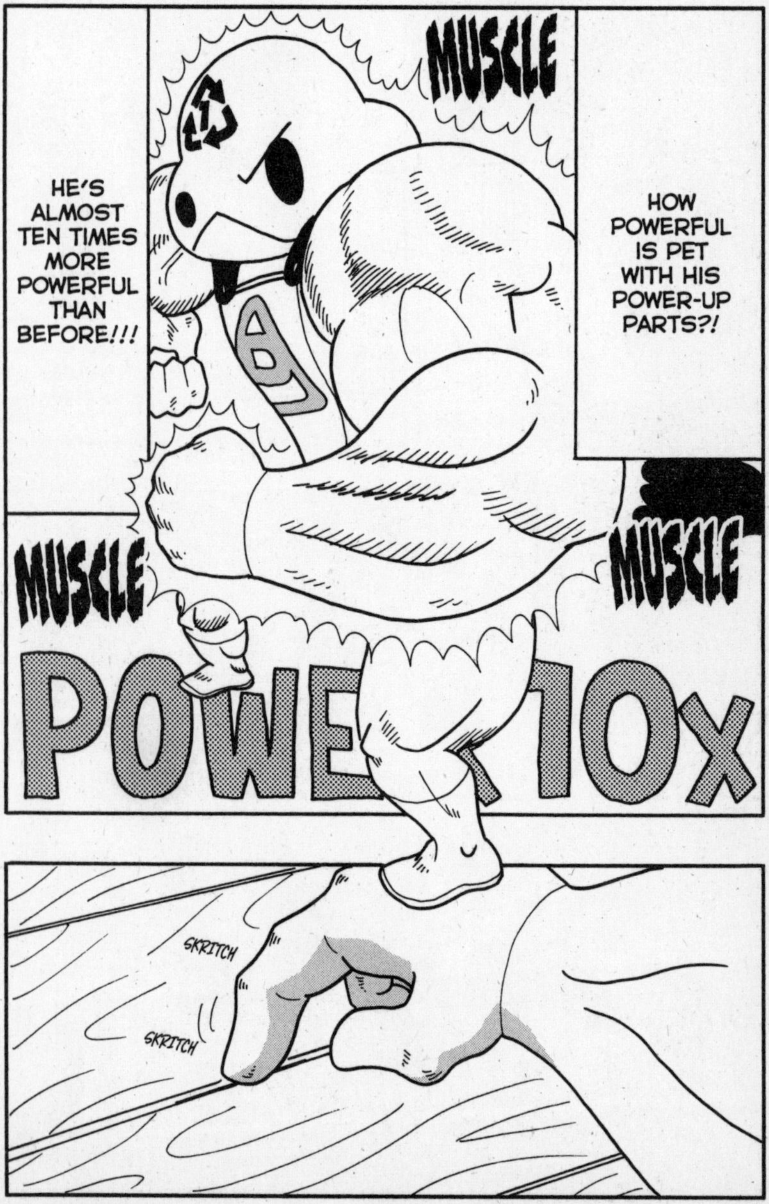
HOW POWERFUL IS PET WITH HIS POWER-UP PARTS?!
MUSCLE
HE'S ALMOST TEN TIMES MORE POWERFUL THAN BEFORE!!!
MUSCLE
MUSCLE
POWE 10x
SKRITCH
SKRITCH

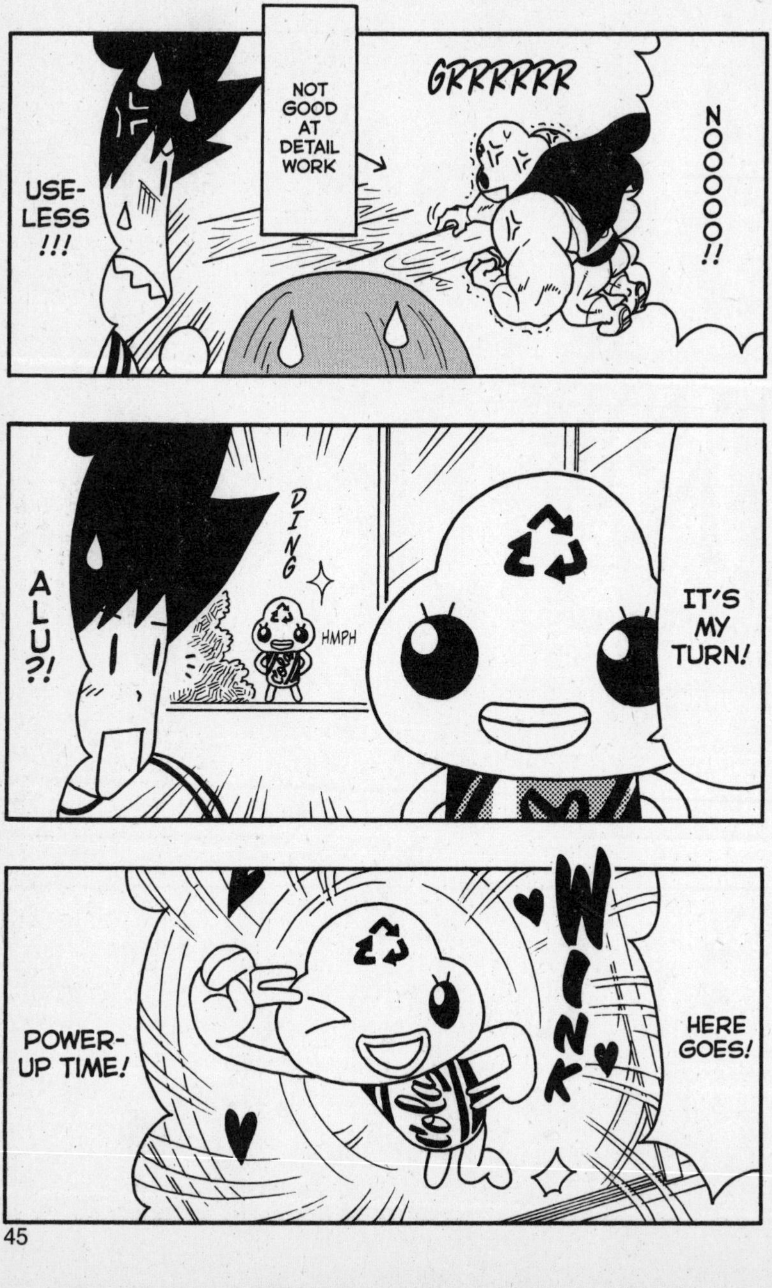
NOOOOO!!
GRRRRRR
NOT GOOD AT DETAIL WORK
USE-LESS!!!
IT'S MY TURN!
HMPH
DING
ALU?!
HERE GOES!
WINK
POWER-UP TIME!

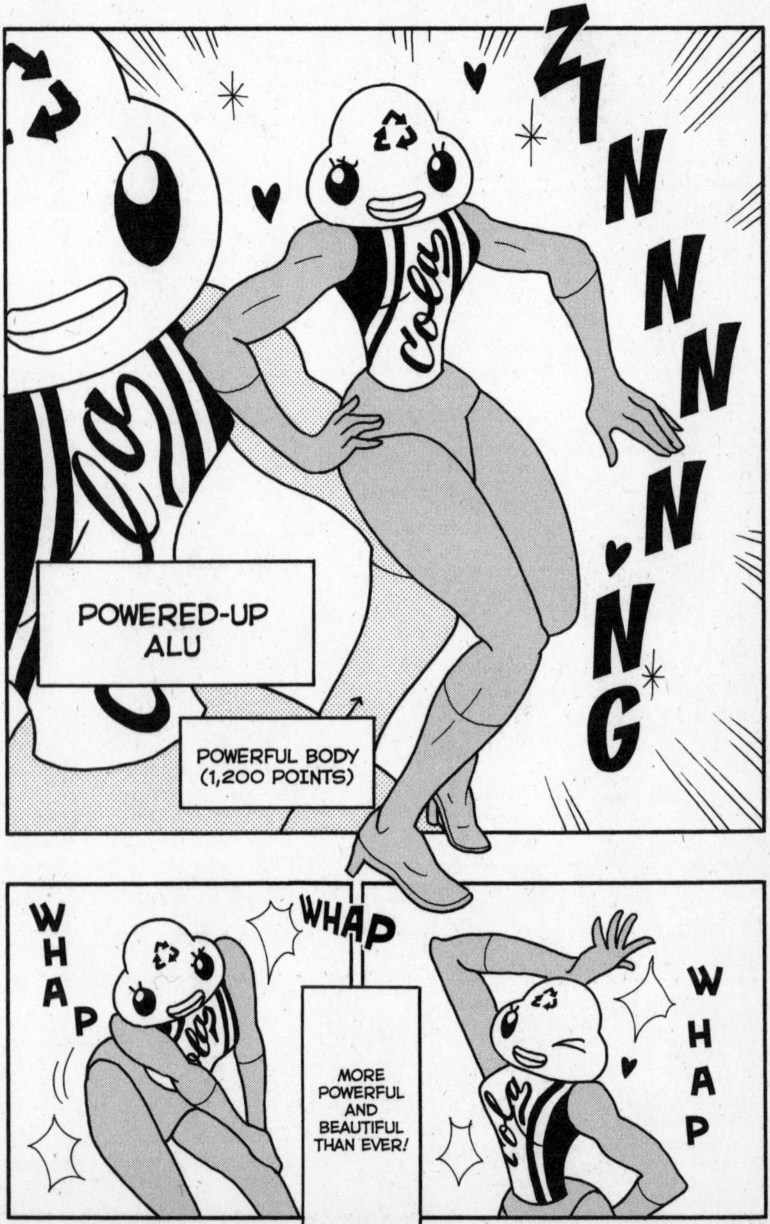
ZNNNNNG
POWERED-UP ALU
POWERFUL BODY (1,200 POINTS)
WHAP
MORE POWERFUL AND BEAUTIFUL THAN EVER!
WHAP
WHAP

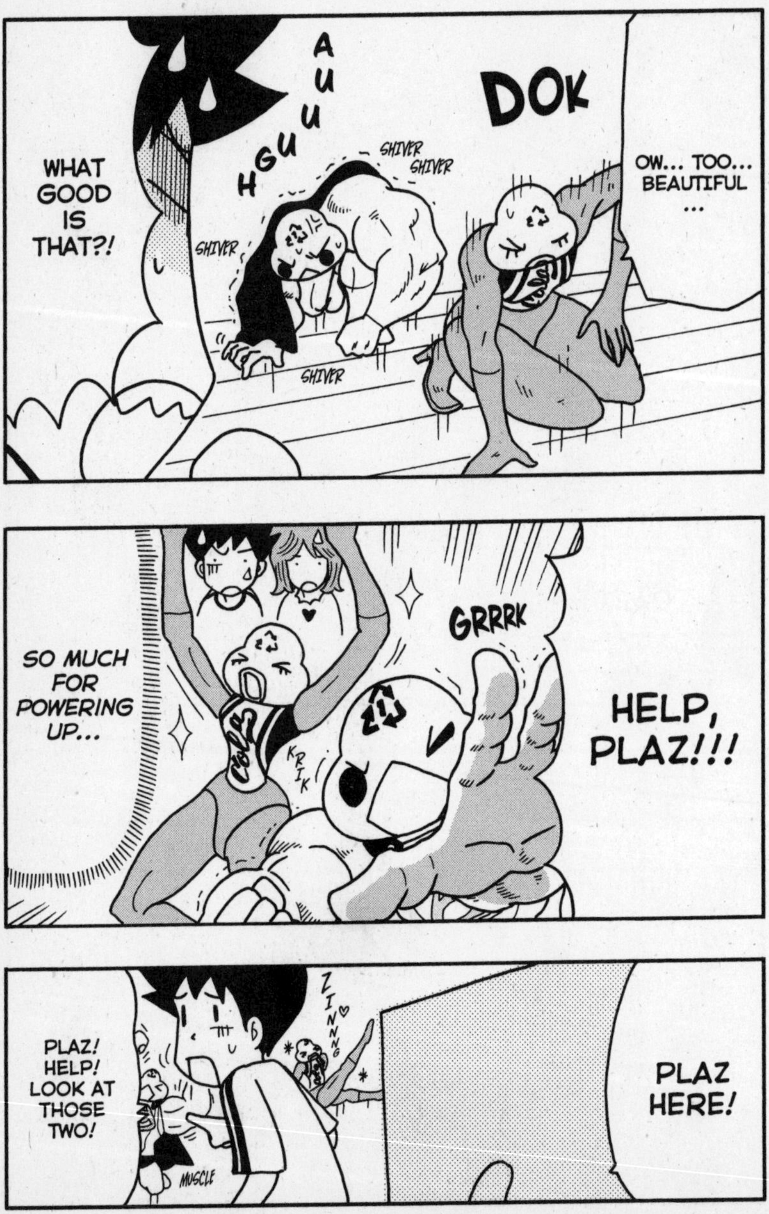
DOK
OW... TOO... BEAUTIFUL ...
HGUUUA
SHIVER SHIVER
SHIVER
SHIVER
WHAT GOOD IS THAT?!
HELP, PLAZ!!!
GRRRK
KRIK
SO MUCH FOR POWERING UP...
PLAZ HERE!
ZINNNG
PLAZ! HELP! LOOK AT THOSE TWO!
MUSCLE

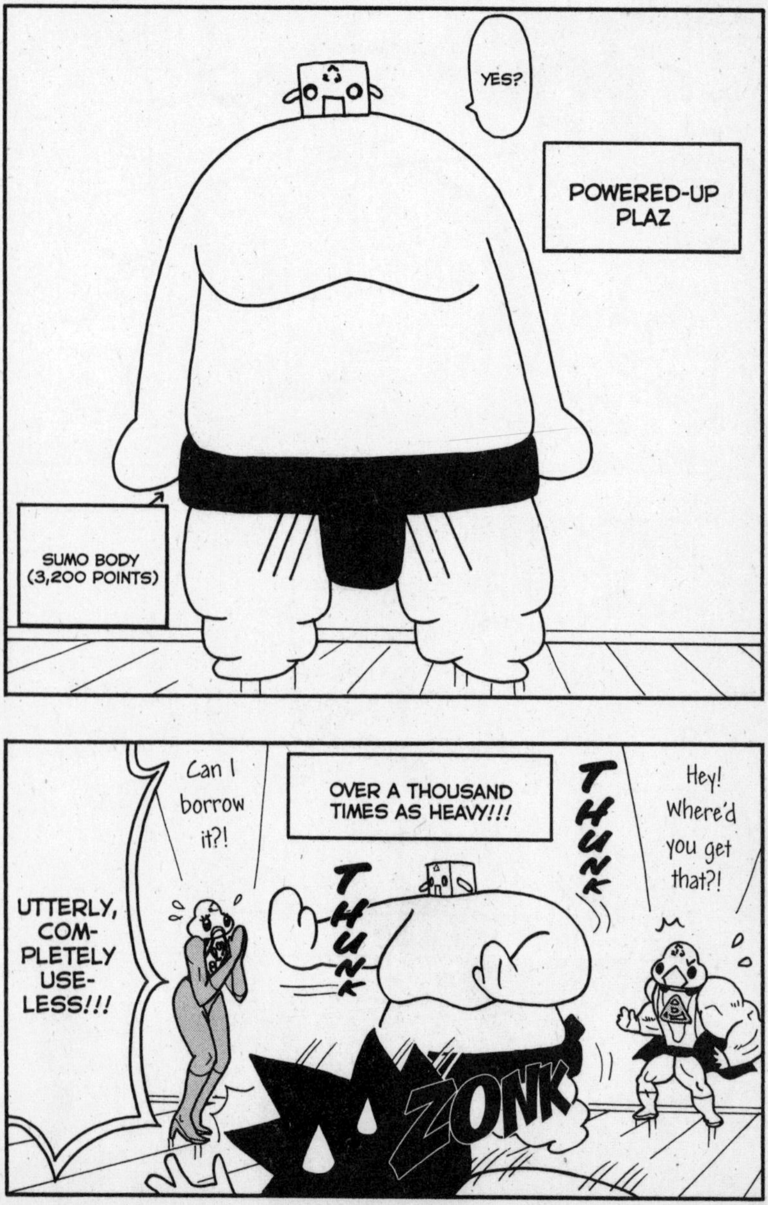
YES?
POWERED-UP PLAZ
SUMO BODY (3,200 POINTS)
Hey! Where'd you get that?!
THUNK
OVER A THOUSAND TIMES AS HEAVY!!!
THUNK
Can I borrow it?!
UTTERLY, COM- PLETELY USE- LESS!!!
ZONK

CHAPTER 5

Act Now, PET!

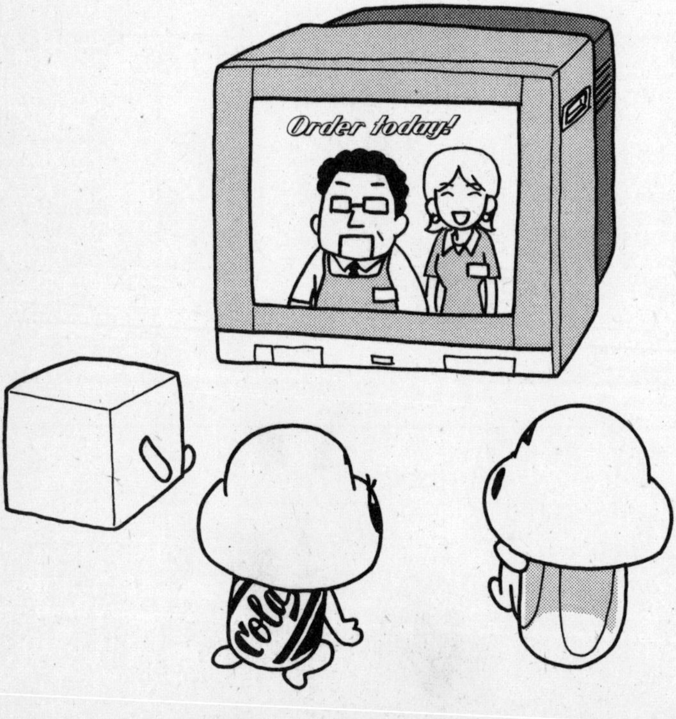
Order today!
cola

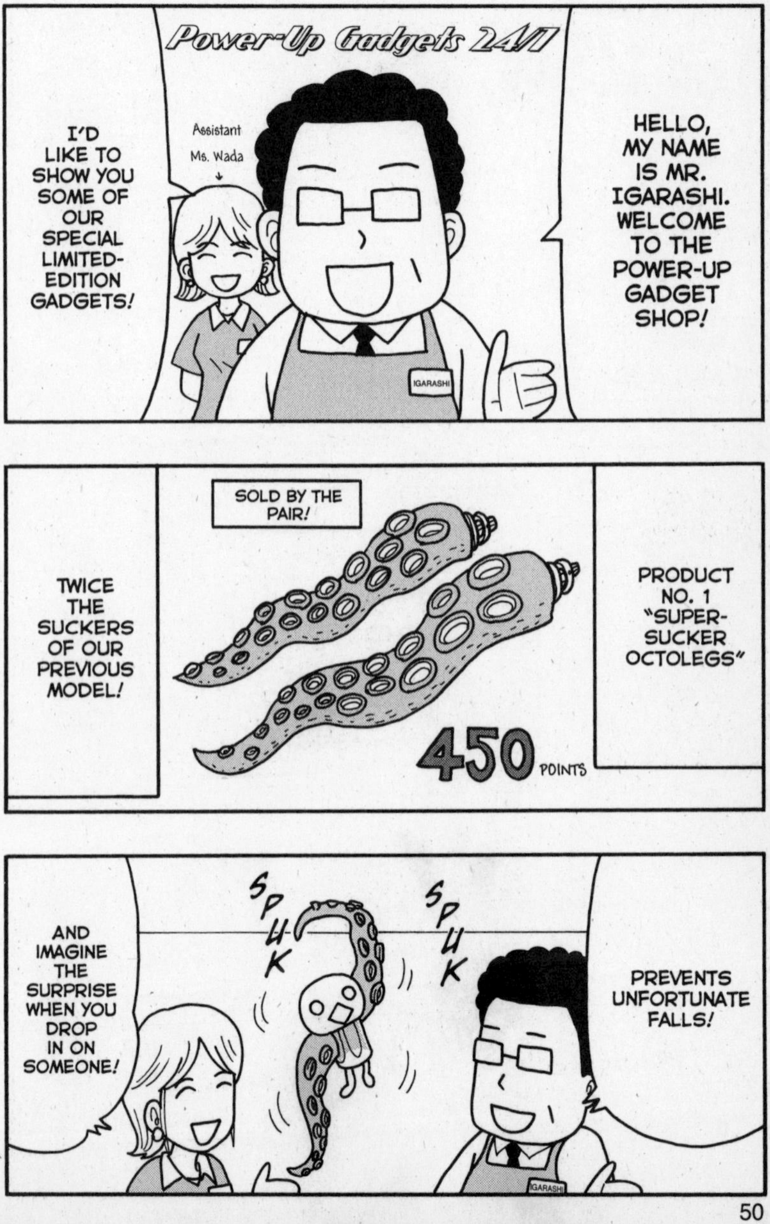
Power-Up Gadgets 24/7
HELLO, MY NAME IS MR. IGARASHI. WELCOME TO THE POWER-UP GADGET SHOP!
IGARASHI
Assistant Ms. Wada
I'D LIKE TO SHOW YOU SOME OF OUR SPECIAL LIMITED-EDITION GADGETS!
PRODUCT NO. 1 "SUPER-SUCKER OCTOLEGS"
SOLD BY THE PAIR!
450 POINTS
TWICE THE SUCKERS OF OUR PREVIOUS MODEL!
PREVENTS UNFORTUNATE FALLS!
IGARASHI
SPUK
SPUK
AND IMAGINE THE SURPRISE WHEN YOU DROP IN ON SOMEONE!

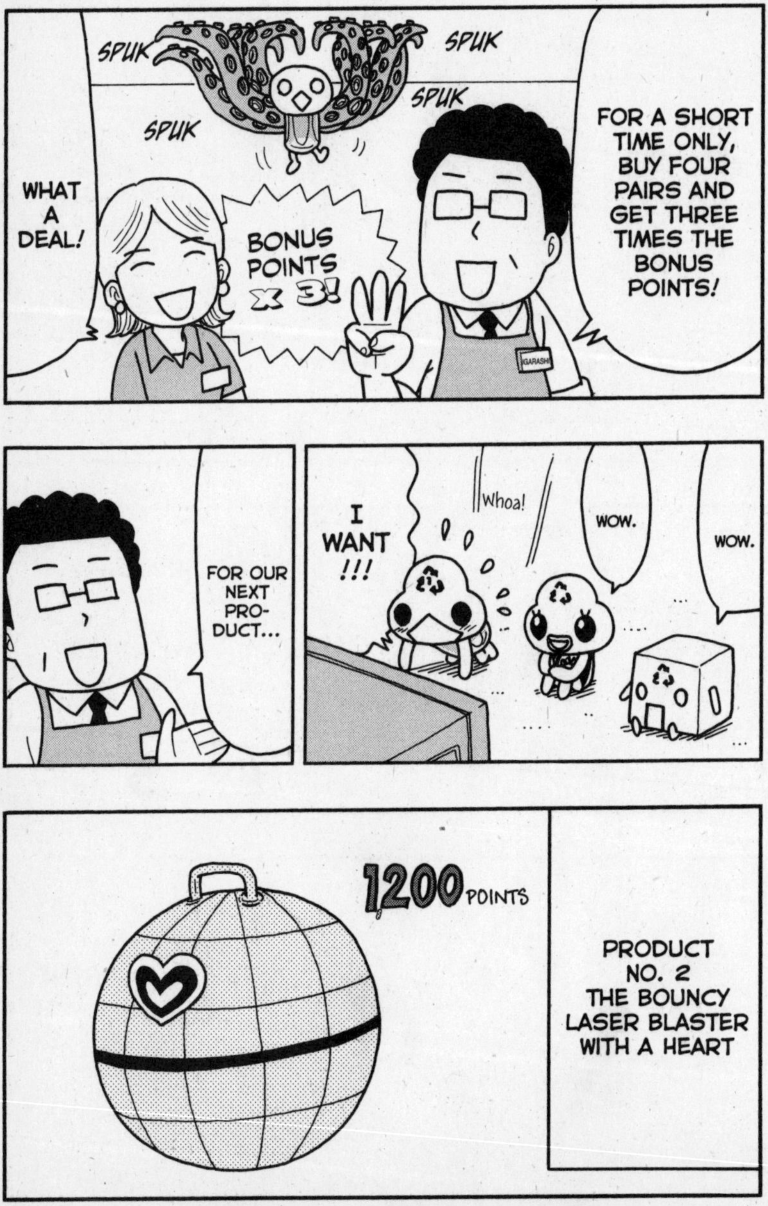
FOR A SHORT TIME ONLY, BUY FOUR PAIRS AND GET THREE TIMES THE BONUS POINTS!
SPUK
SPUK
SPUK
SPUK
BONUS POINTS x 3!
WHAT A DEAL!
IGARASHI
WOW.
WOW.
Whoa!
I WANT!!!
FOR OUR NEXT PRO-DUCT...
PRODUCT NO. 2 THE BOUNCY LASER BLASTER WITH A HEART
1,200 POINTS

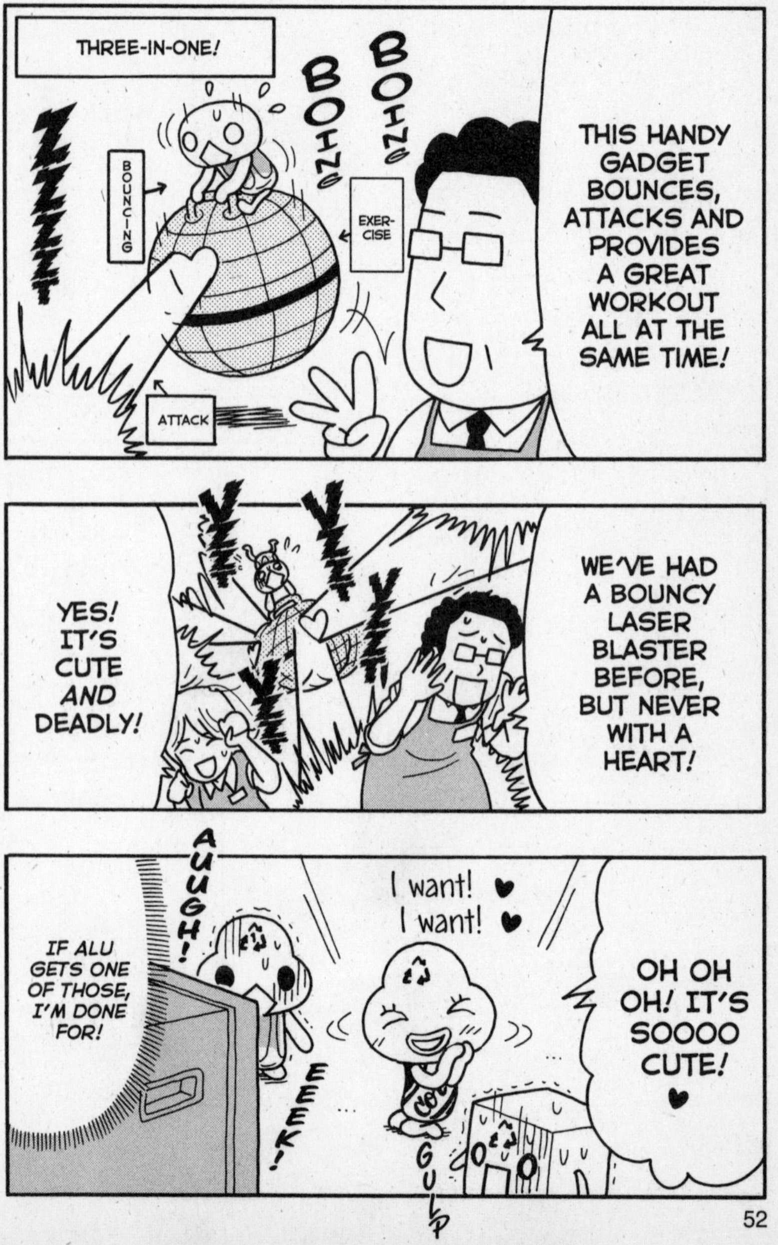
THIS HANDY GADGET BOUNCES, ATTACKS AND PROVIDES A GREAT WORKOUT ALL AT THE SAME TIME!
BOING
BOING
THREE-IN-ONE!
EXER-CISE
BOUNCING
ZZZZZT
ATTACK
WE'VE HAD A BOUNCY LASER BLASTER BEFORE, BUT NEVER WITH A HEART!
YES! IT'S CUTE AND DEADLY!
OH OH OH! IT'S SOOOO CUTE!
I want! I want!
AUUGH!
IF ALU GETS ONE OF THOSE, I'M DONE FOR!
EEEEK!
GULP

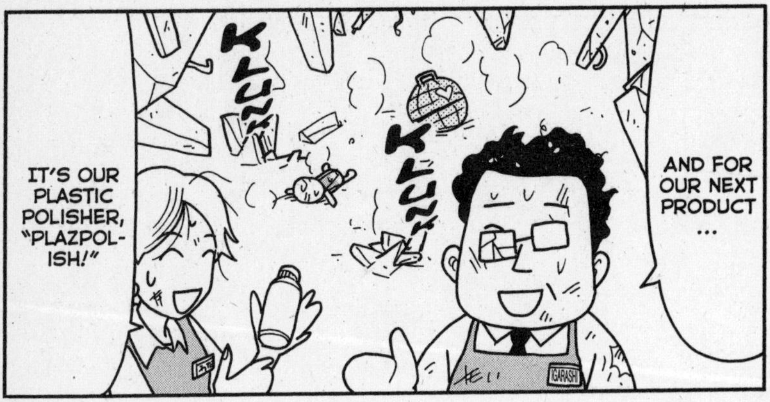
AND FOR OUR NEXT PRODUCT ...
KLUNK
KLUNK
IGARASHI
IT'S OUR PLASTIC POLISHER, "PLAZPOL-ISH!"

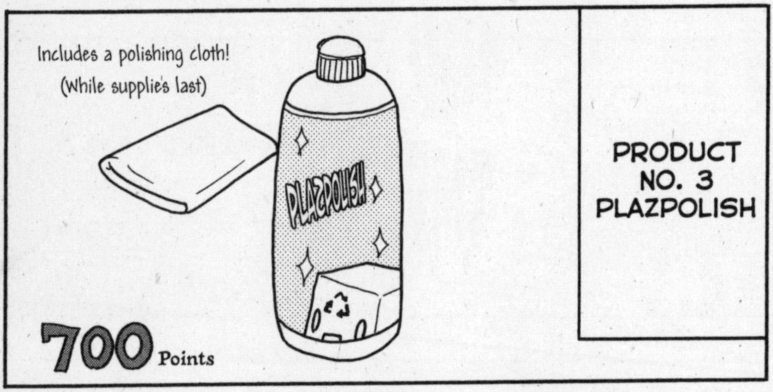
PRODUCT NO. 3 PLAZPOLISH
Includes a polishing cloth!
(While supplie's last)
PLAZPOLISH
700 Points

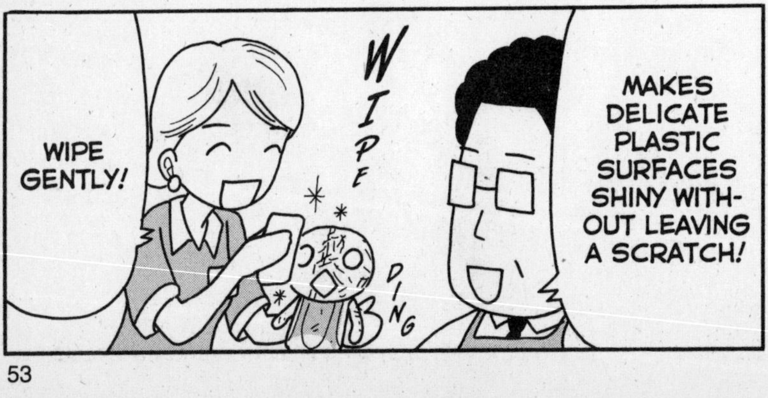
MAKES DELICATE PLASTIC SURFACES SHINY WITH-OUT LEAVING A SCRATCH!
WIPE
DING
WIPE GENTLY!

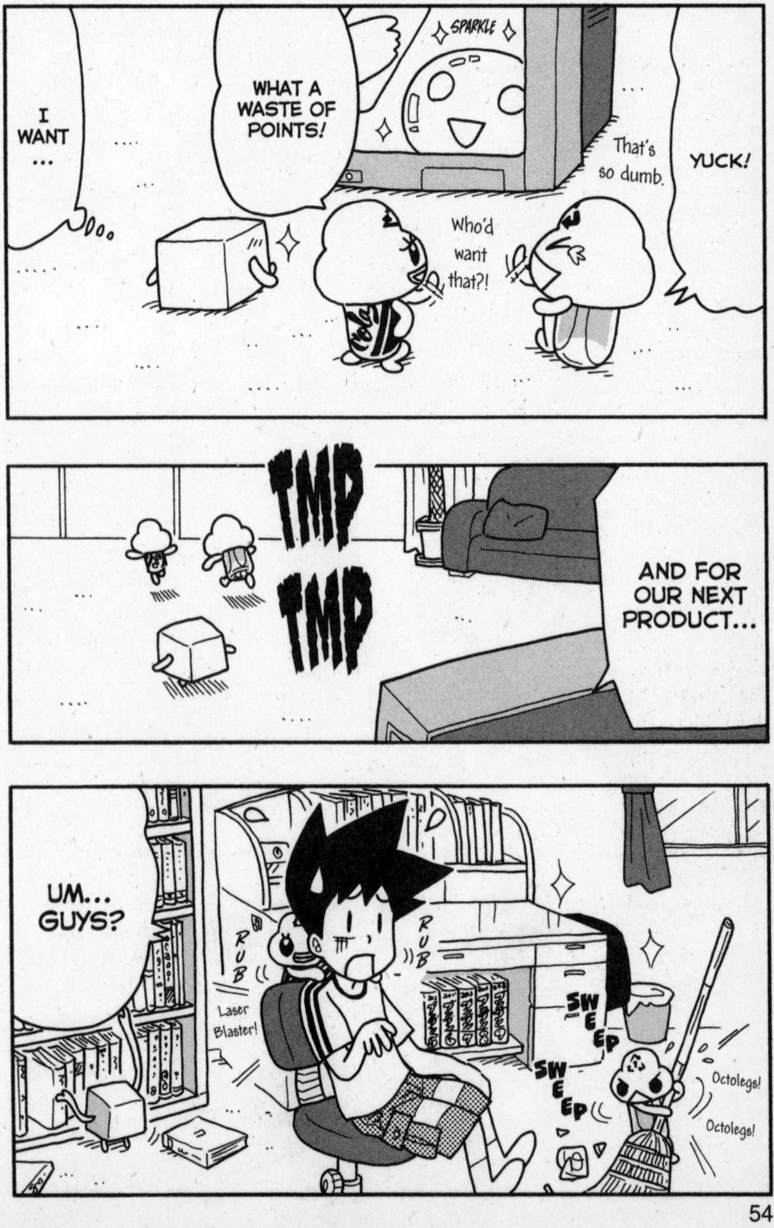
YUCK!
That's so dumb.
SPARKLE
WHAT A WASTE OF POINTS!
Who'd want that?!
I WANT...
Dooo
AND FOR OUR NEXT PRODUCT...
TMP
TMP
Octolegs!
Octolegs!
SWEEP
SWEEP
RUB
RUB
Laser Blaster!
UM... GUYS?

CHAPTER 6 Calling Dr. PET!

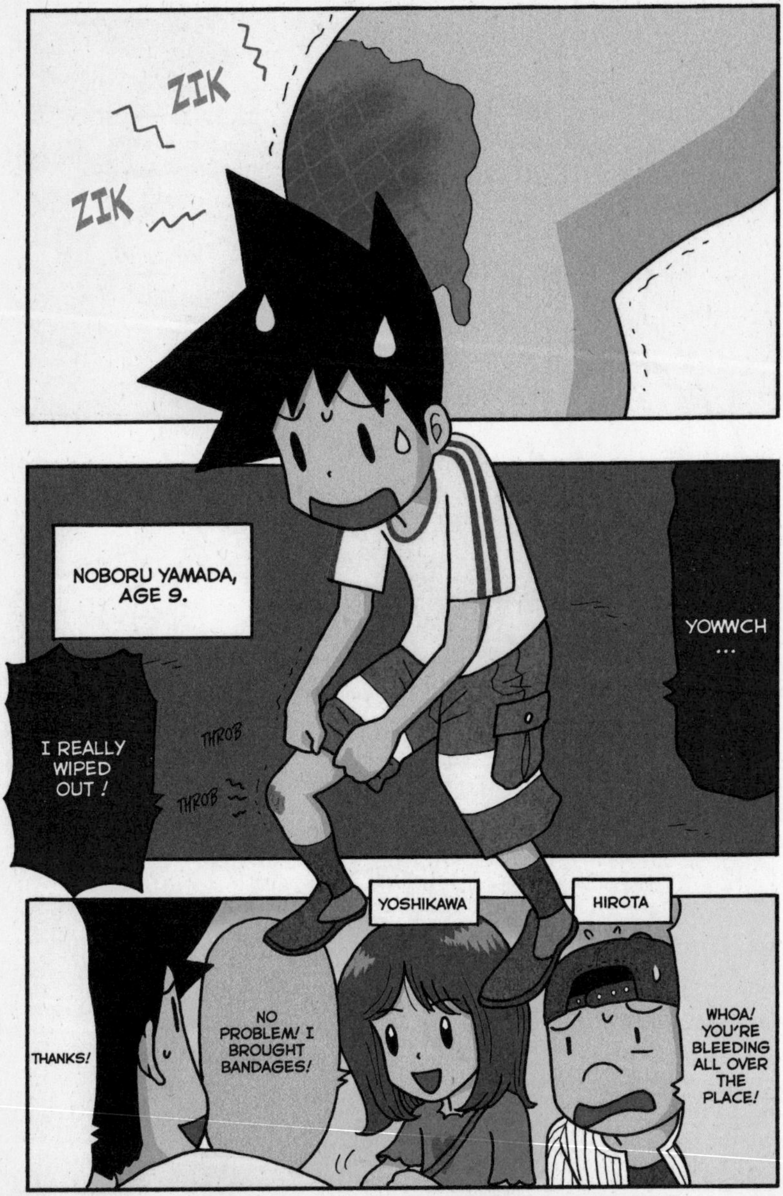
ZIK
ZIK
YOWWCH ...
NOBORU YAMADA, AGE 9.
I REALLY WIPED OUT!
THROB
THROB
HIROTA
YOSHIKAWA
WHOA! YOU'RE BLEEDING ALL OVER THE PLACE!
NO PROBLEM! I BROUGHT BANDAGES!
THANKS!

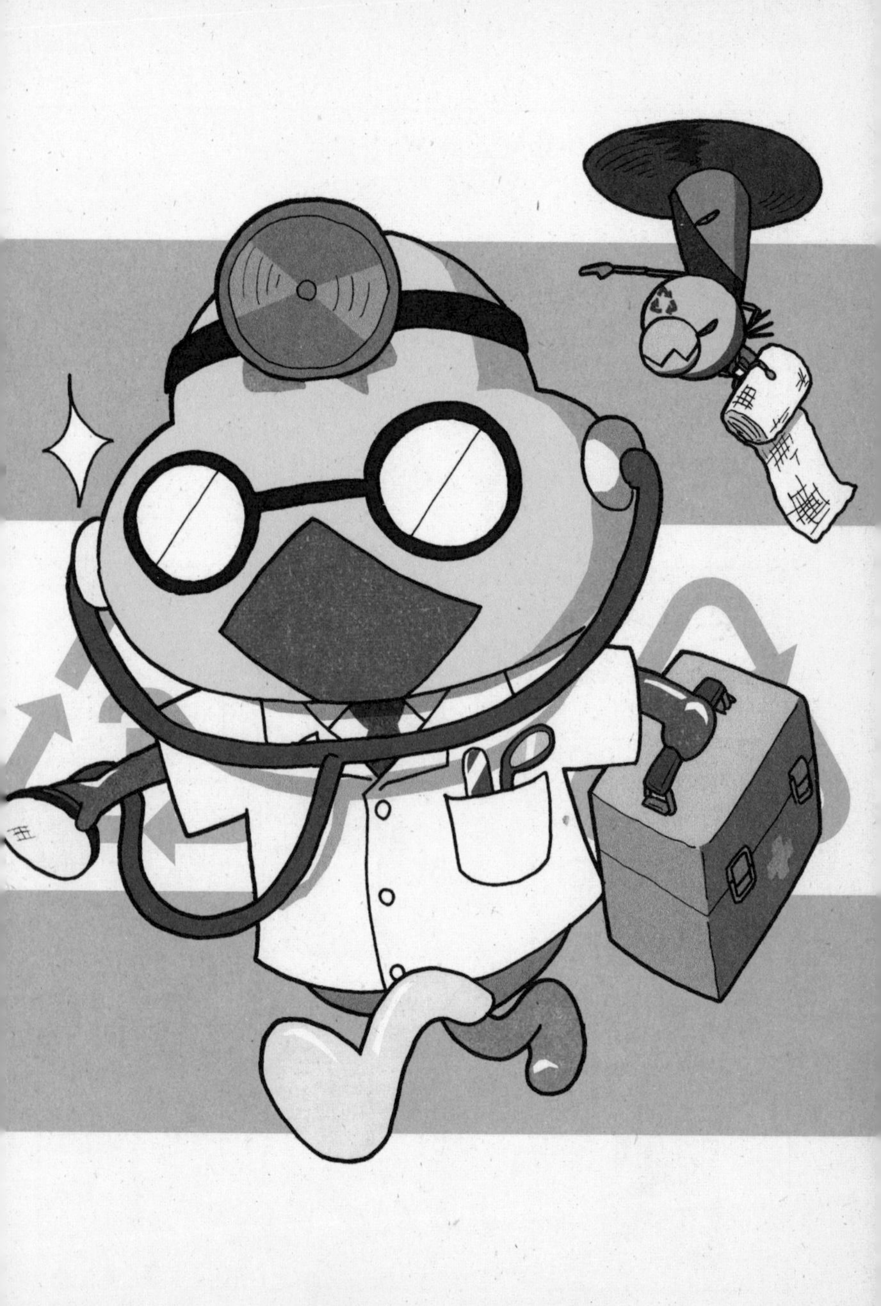

CHAPTER 6

Calling Dr. PET!

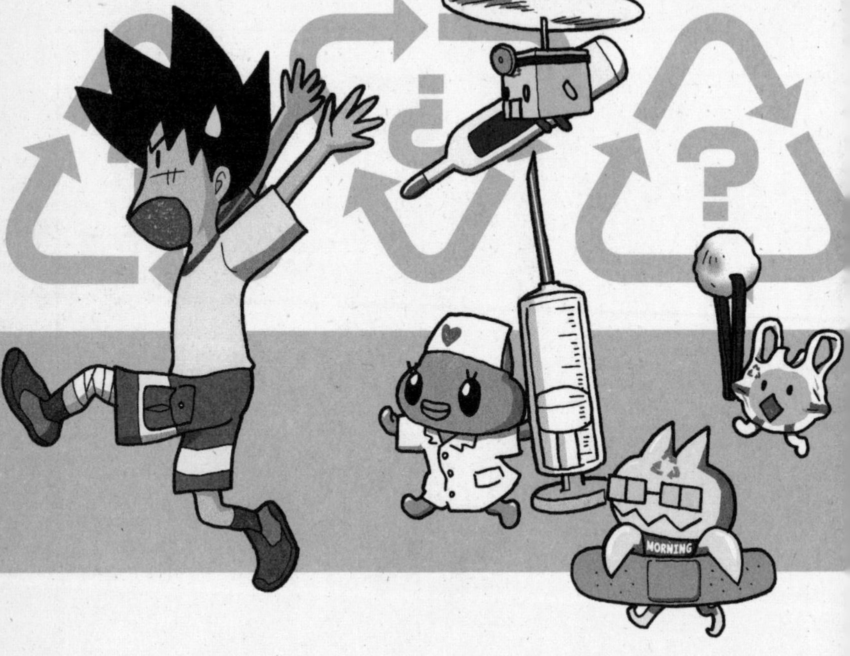
MORNING

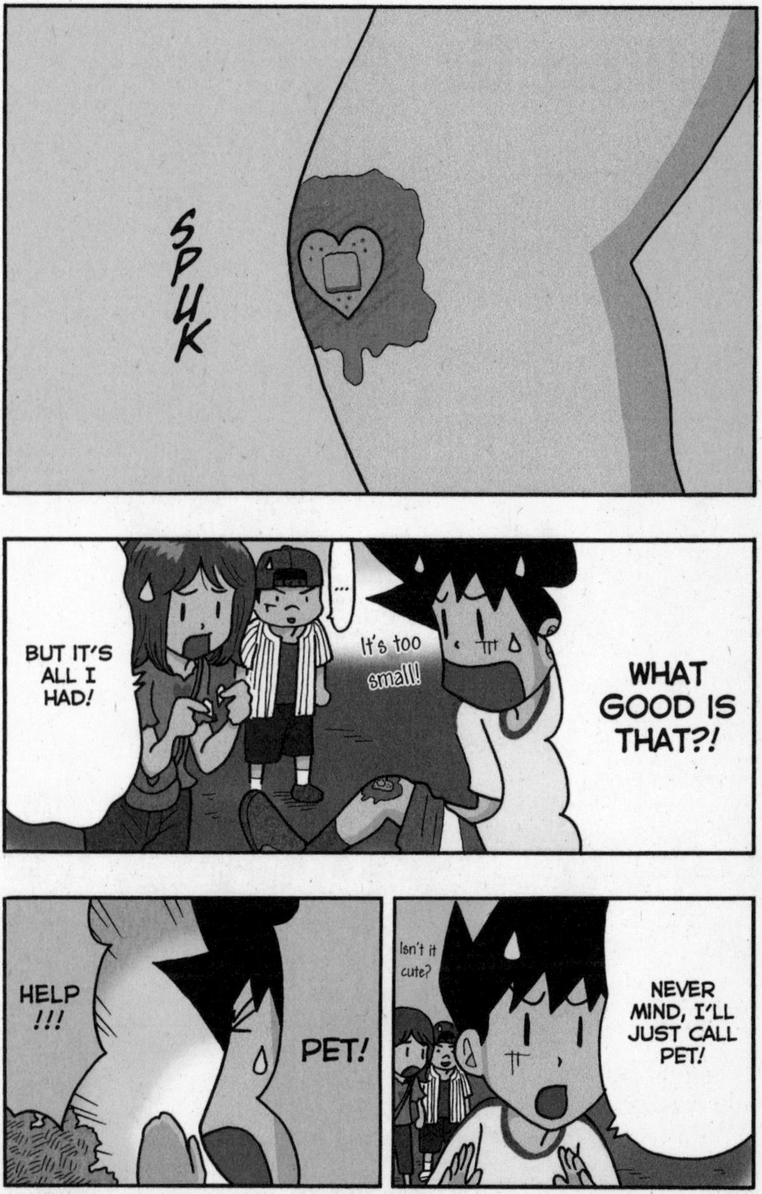
SPUK
WHAT GOOD IS THAT?!
It's too small!
...
BUT IT'S ALL I HAD!
NEVER MIND, I'LL JUST CALL PET!
Isn't it cute?
PET!
HELP !!!

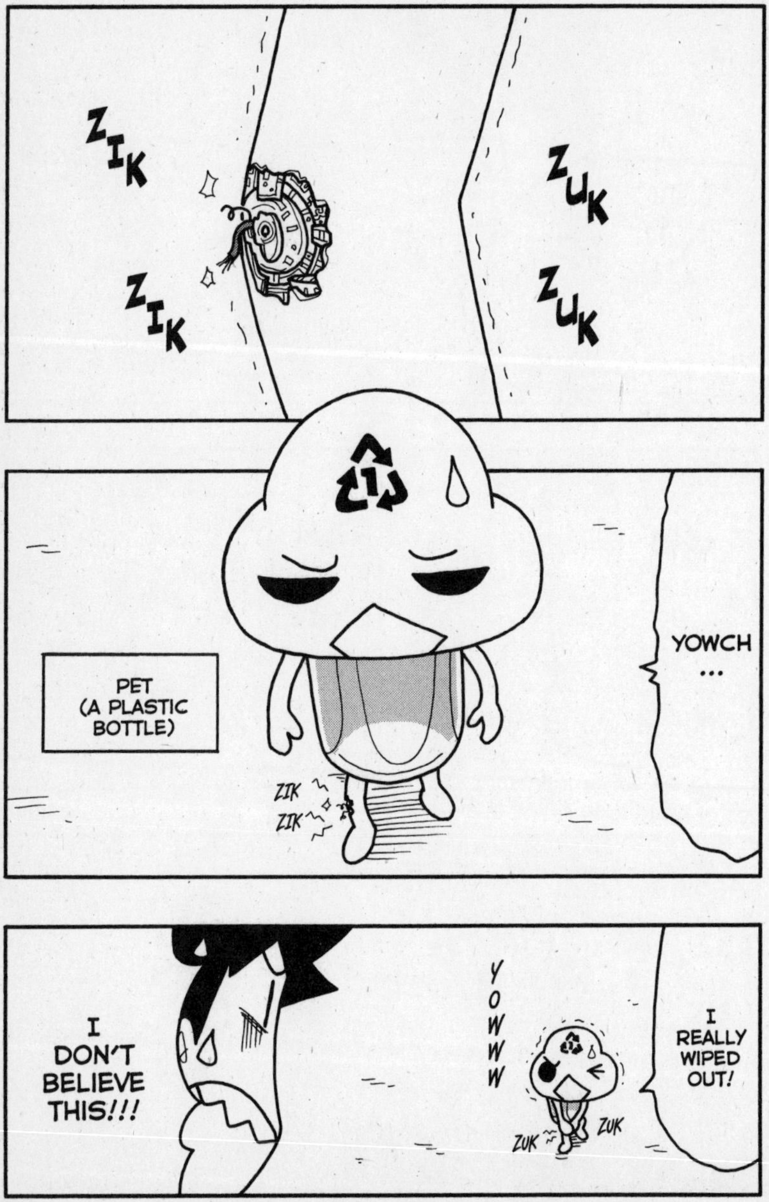
ZUK
ZUK
ZIK
ZIK
YOWCH ...
PET (A PLASTIC BOTTLE)
ZIK
ZIK
I REALLY WIPED OUT!
YOWWW
ZUK
ZUK
I DON'T BELIEVE THIS!!!

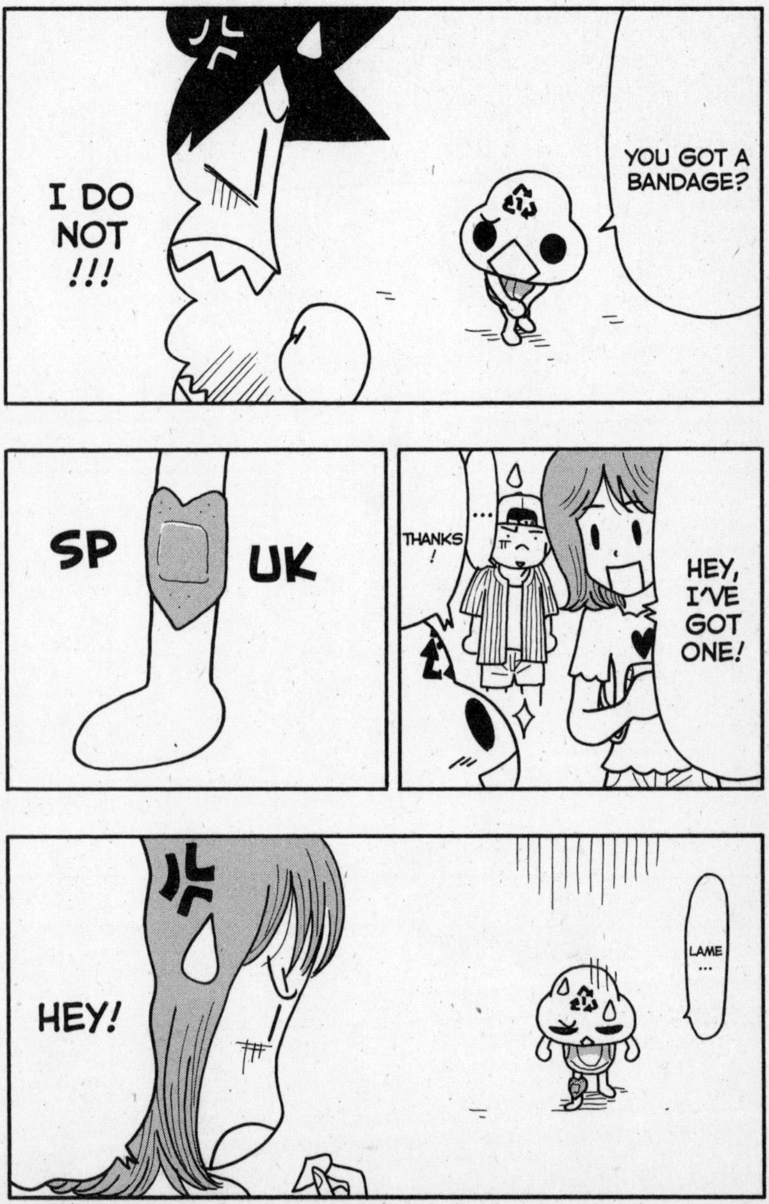
YOU GOT A BANDAGE?
I DO NOT!!!
HEY, I'VE GOT ONE!
...
THANKS!
SP
UK
LAME...
HEY!

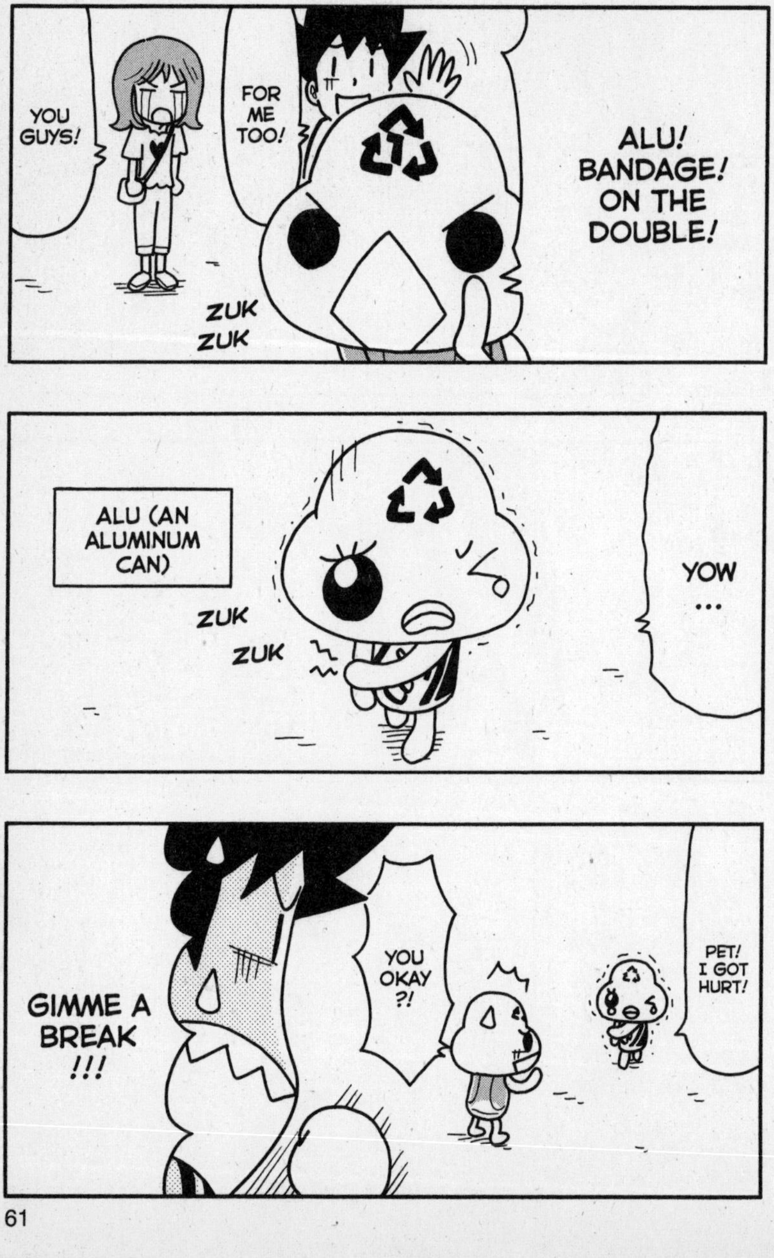
ALU! BANDAGE! ON THE DOUBLE!
FOR ME TOO!
YOU GUYS!
ZUK ZUK
YOW ...
ALU (AN ALUMINUM CAN)
ZUK ZUK
PET! I GOT HURT!
YOU OKAY ?!
GIMME A BREAK !!!

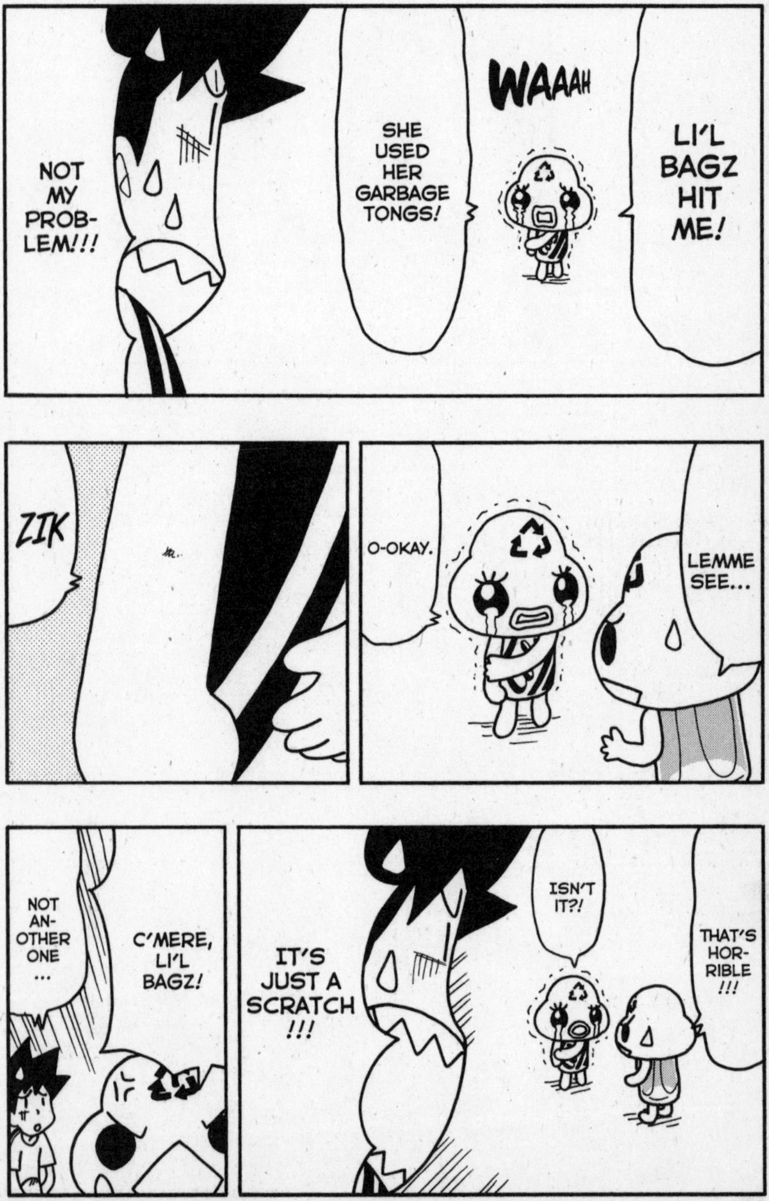
LI'L BAGZ HIT ME!
WAAAH
SHE USED HER GARBAGE TONGS!
NOT MY PROB-LEM!!!
LEMME SEE...
O-OKAY.
ZIK
THAT'S HOR-RIBLE!!!
ISN'T IT?!
IT'S JUST A SCRATCH!!!
C'MERE, LI'L BAGZ!
NOT AN-OTHER ONE ...

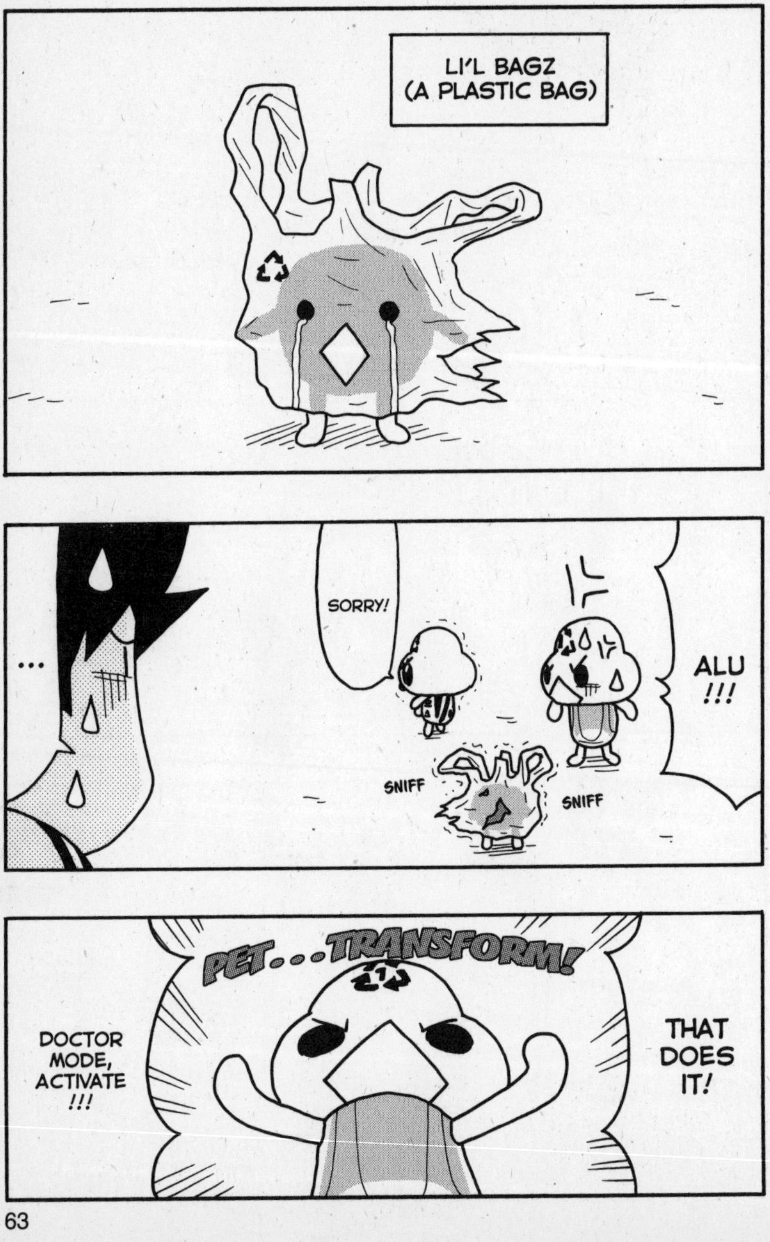
LI'L BAGZ (A PLASTIC BAG)
ALU !!!
SNIFF
SNIFF
SORRY!
...
THAT DOES IT!
PET...TRANSFORM!
DOCTOR MODE, ACTIVATE !!!

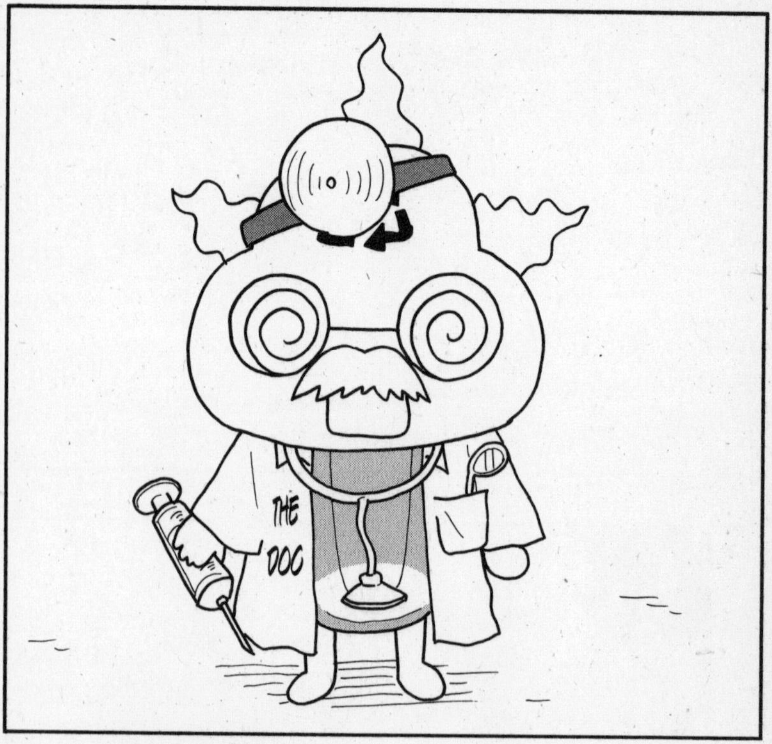
THE DOC

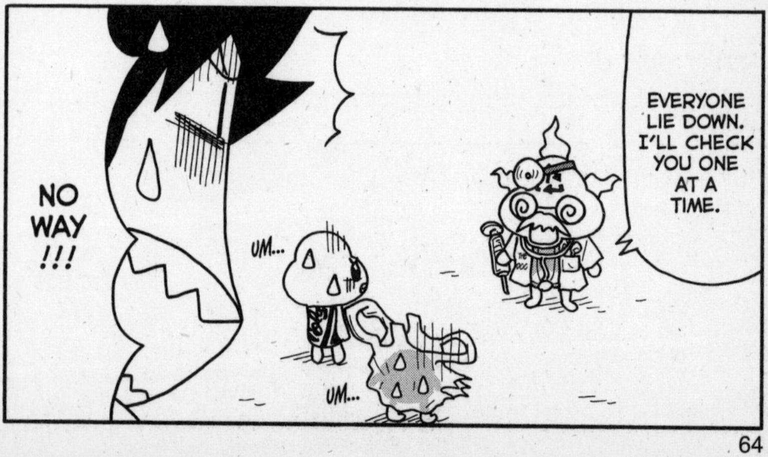
EVERYONE LIE DOWN. I'LL CHECK YOU ONE AT A TIME.
UM...
UM...
NO WAY !!!

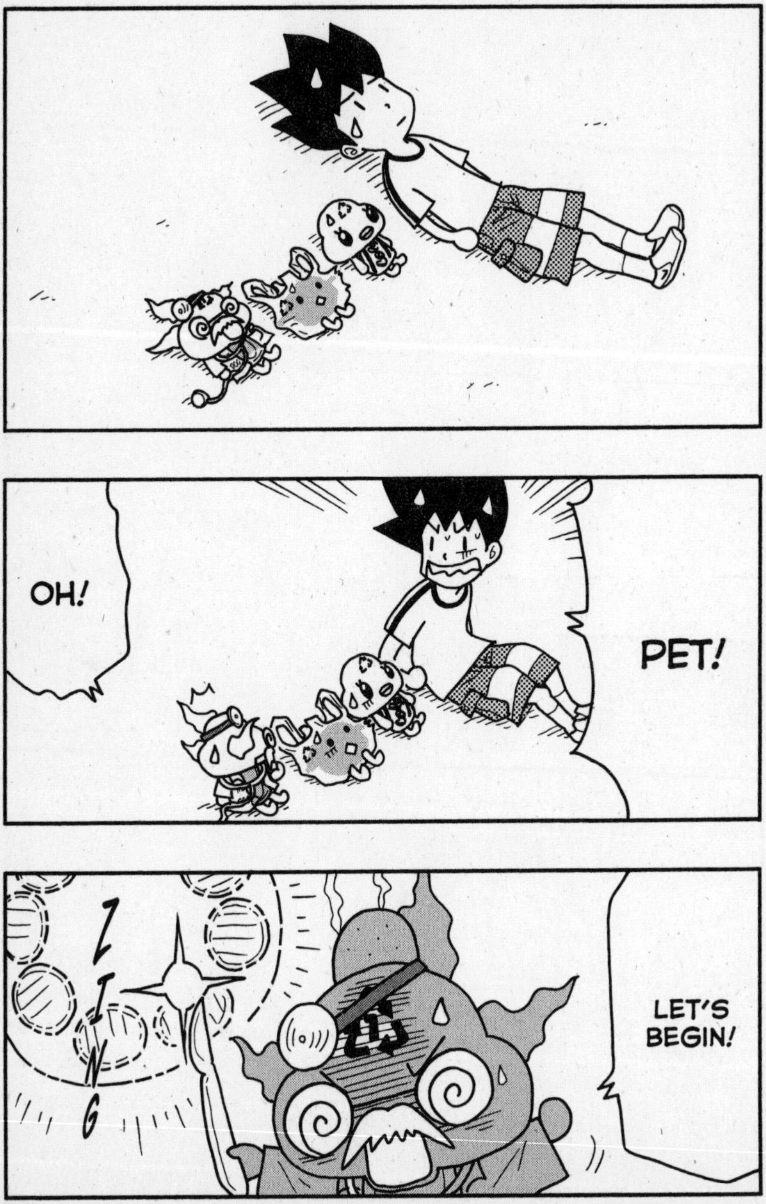
PET!
OH!
LET'S BEGIN!
ZING

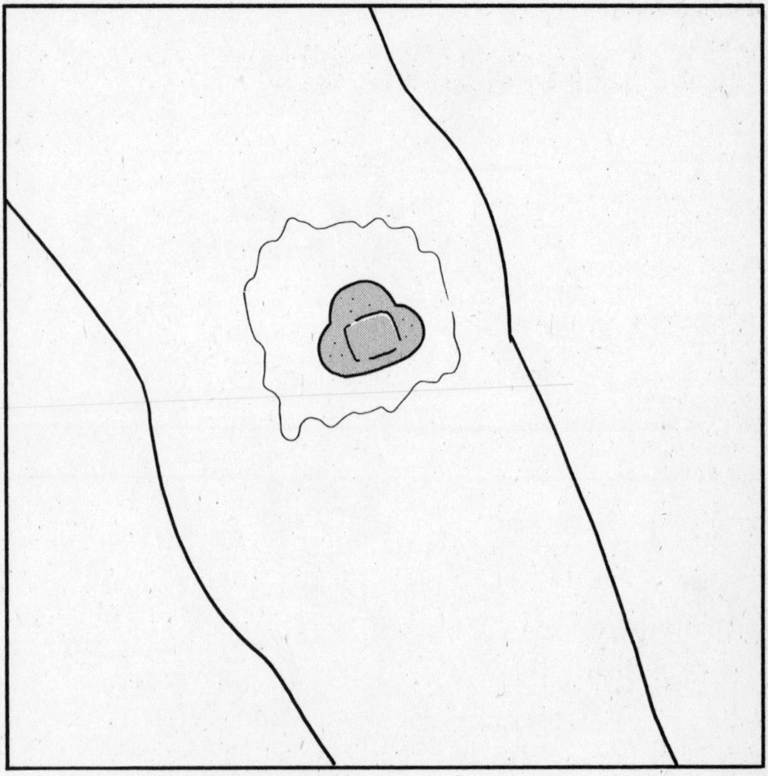

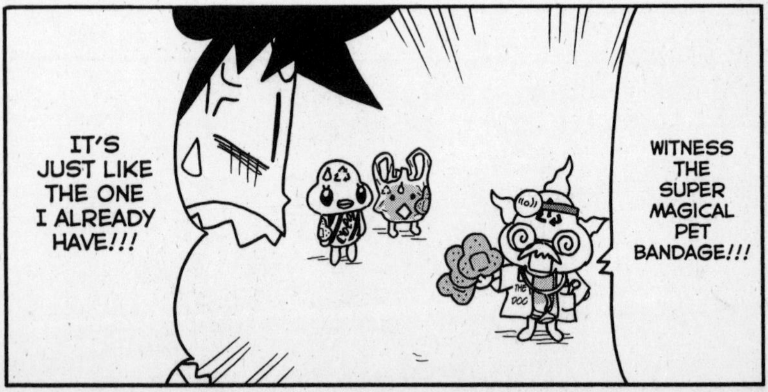
WITNESS THE SUPER MAGICAL PET BANDAGE!!!
THE DOC
IT'S JUST LIKE THE ONE I ALREADY HAVE!!!

PET Looks It Up

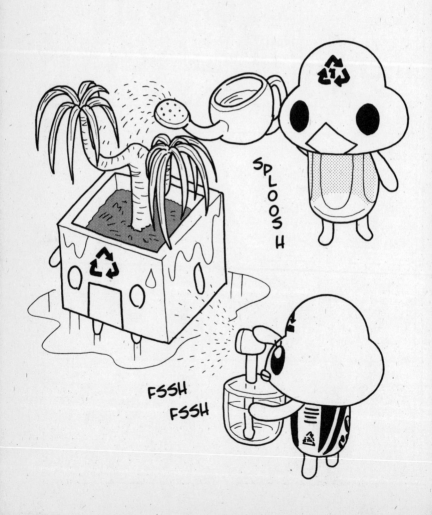

SPLOOSH

FSSH
FSSH

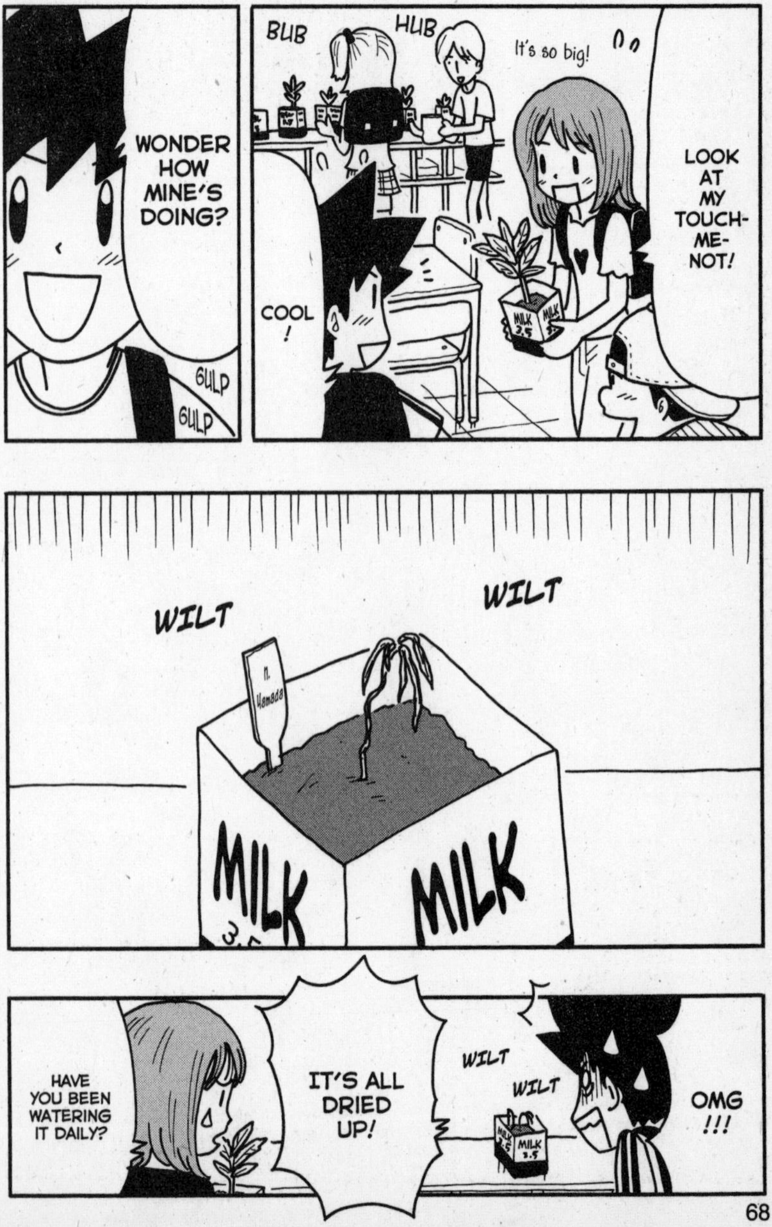
LOOK AT MY TOUCH-ME-NOT!
It's so big!
HUB
BUB
COOL!
WONDER HOW MINE'S DOING?
GULP
GULP
WILT
WILT
MILK
MILK
OMG!!!
WILT
WILT
IT'S ALL DRIED UP!
HAVE YOU BEEN WATERING IT DAILY?

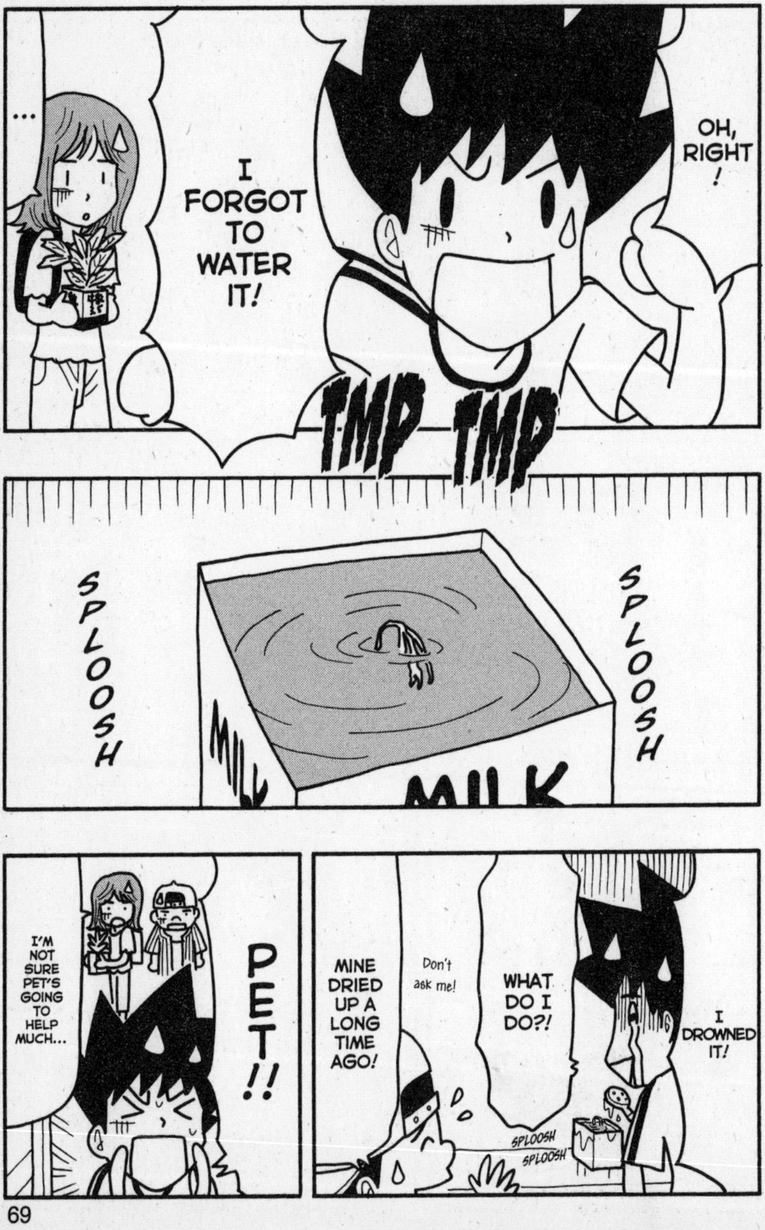
OH, RIGHT!
I FORGOT TO WATER IT!
...
TMP TMP
SPLOOSH
SPLOOSH
MILK
MILK
I DROWNED IT!
WHAT DO I DO?!
Don't ask me!
MINE DRIED UP A LONG TIME AGO!
SPLOOSH
SPLOOSH
PET!!
I'M NOT SURE PET'S GOING TO HELP MUCH...

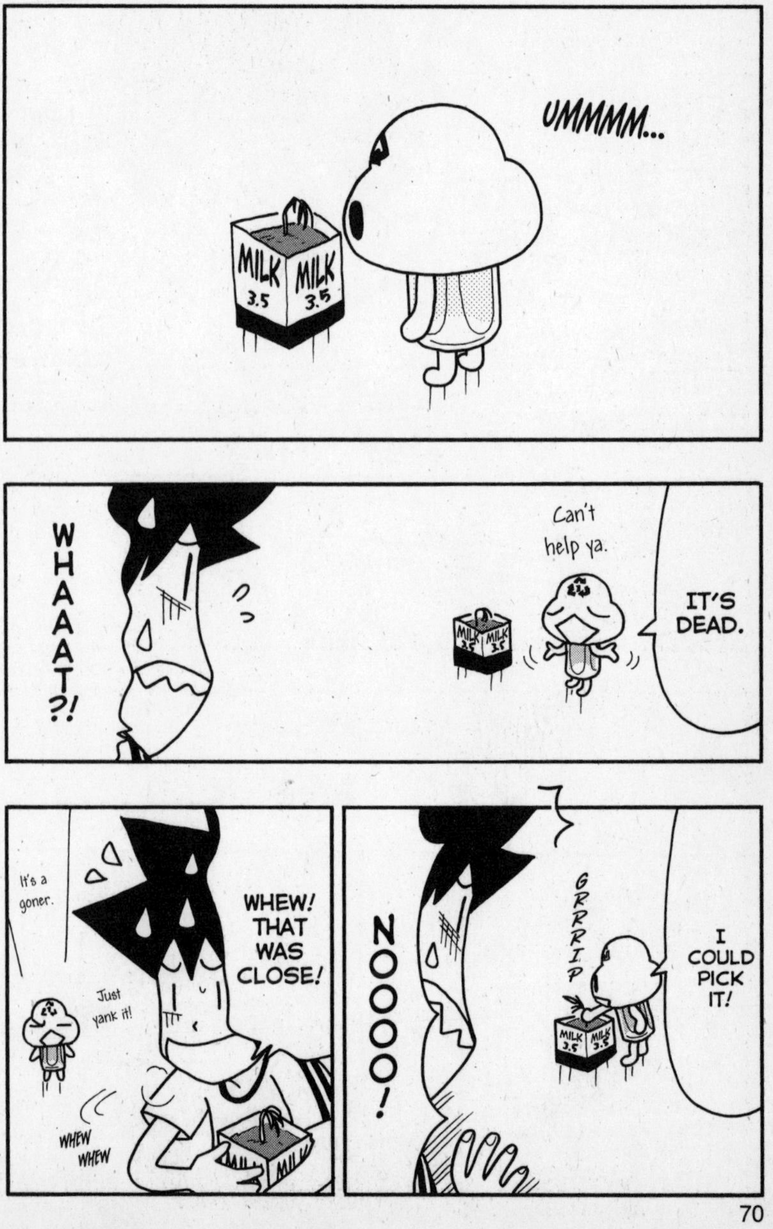
UMMMM...
IT'S DEAD.
Can't help ya.
WHAAAT?!
I COULD PICK IT!
GRRRIP
NOOOO!
WHEW! THAT WAS CLOSE!
It's a goner.
Just yank it!
WHEW WHEW

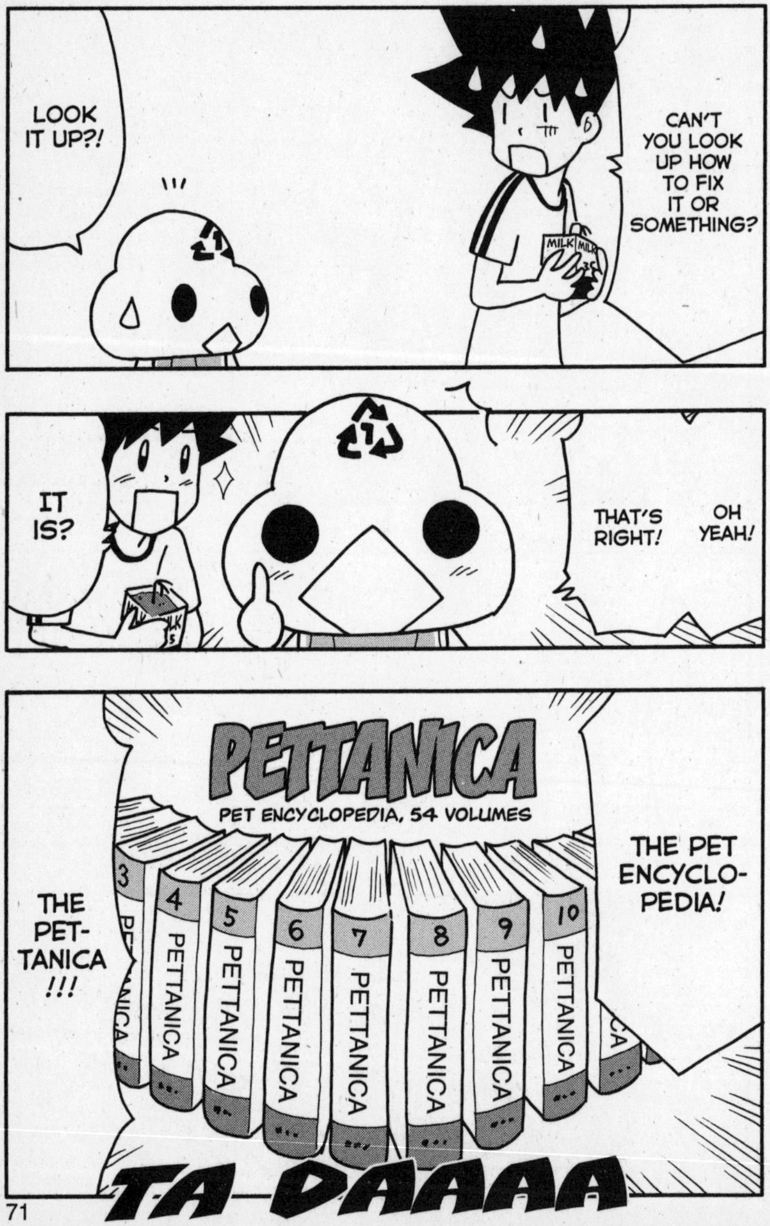
CAN'T YOU LOOK UP HOW TO FIX IT OR SOMETHING?
MILK
LOOK IT UP?!
OH YEAH!
THAT'S RIGHT!
IT IS?
THE PET ENCYCLOPEDIA!
PETTANICA
PET ENCYCLOPEDIA, 54 VOLUMES
PETTANICA
THE PET-TANICA!!!
TA-DAAAA

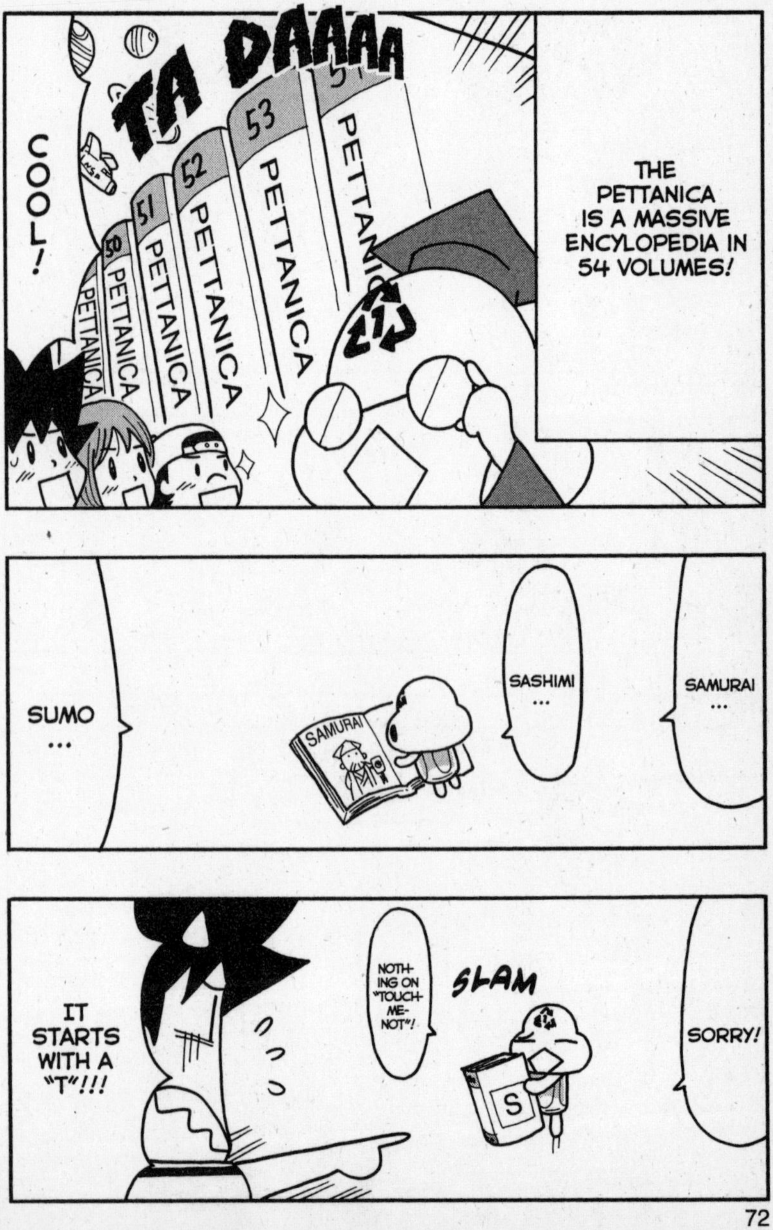
THE PETTANICA IS A MASSIVE ENCYCLOPEDIA IN 54 VOLUMES!
TA DAAAA
53 PETTANICA
52 PETTANICA
51 PETTANICA
50 PETTANICA
COOL!
SAMURAI ...
SASHIMI ...
SAMURAI
SUMO ...
SORRY!
SLAM
NOTHING ON "TOUCH-ME-NOT"!
IT STARTS WITH A "T"!!!

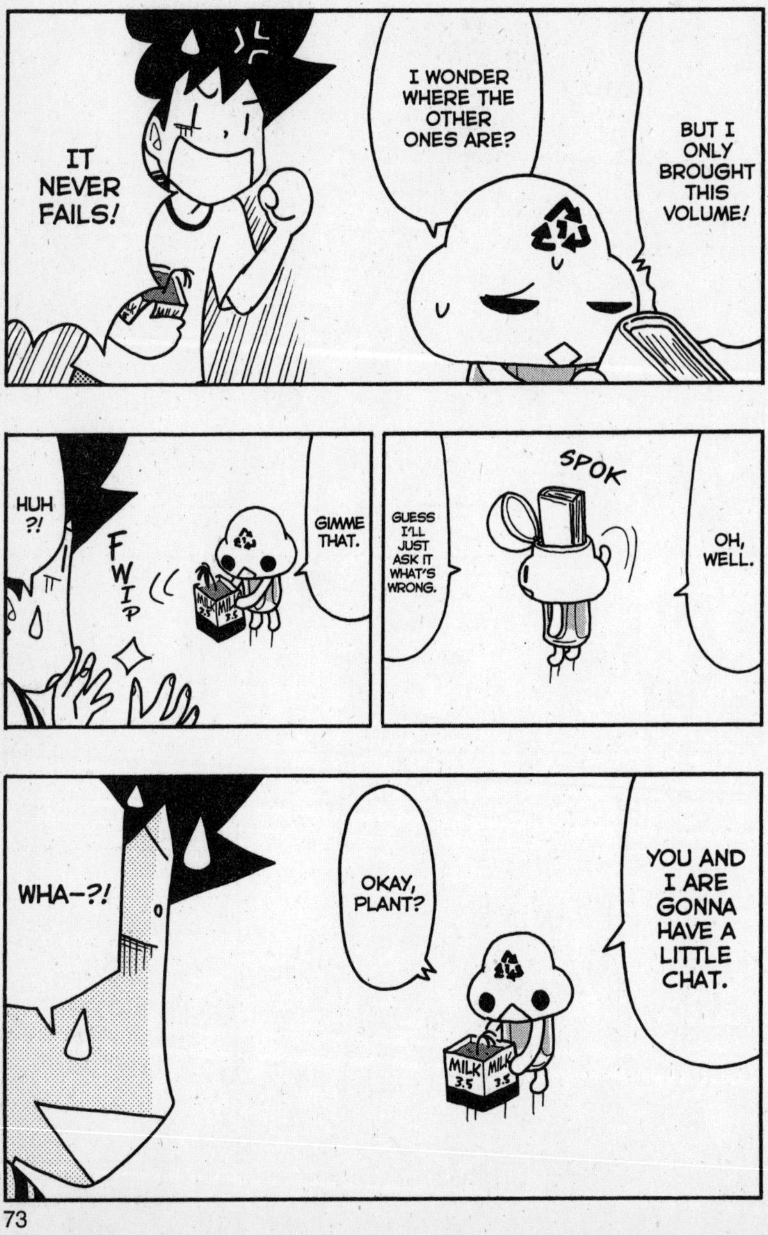
BUT I ONLY BROUGHT THIS VOLUME!
I WONDER WHERE THE OTHER ONES ARE?
IT NEVER FAILS!
OH, WELL.
SPOK
GUESS I'LL JUST ASK IT WHAT'S WRONG.
GIMME THAT.
FWIP
HUH?!
YOU AND I ARE GONNA HAVE A LITTLE CHAT.
OKAY, PLANT?
WHA-?!

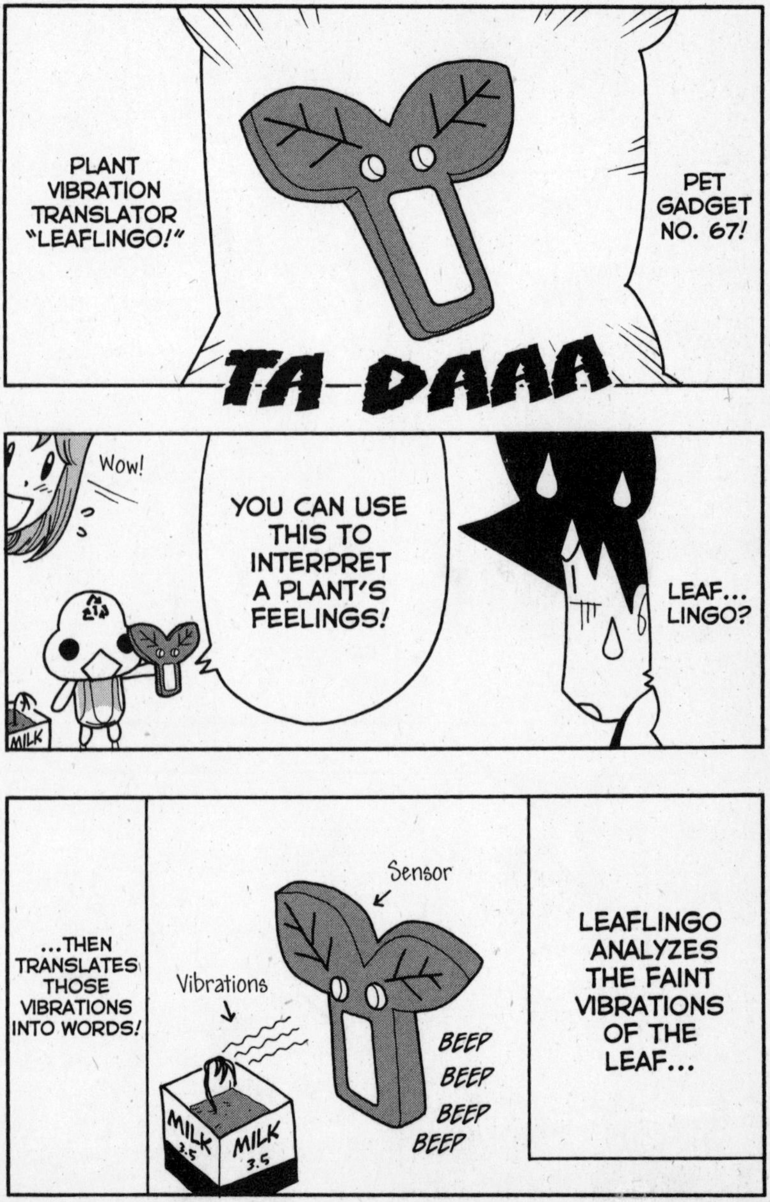

PET GADGET NO. 67!
PLANT VIBRATION TRANSLATOR "LEAFLINGO!"
TA DAAA
LEAF... LINGO?
YOU CAN USE THIS TO INTERPRET A PLANT'S FEELINGS!
Wow!
LEAFLINGO ANALYZES THE FAINT VIBRATIONS OF THE LEAF...
Sensor
BEEP BEEP BEEP BEEP
Vibrations
MILK 3.5
MILK 3.5
...THEN TRANSLATES THOSE VIBRATIONS INTO WORDS!
MILK

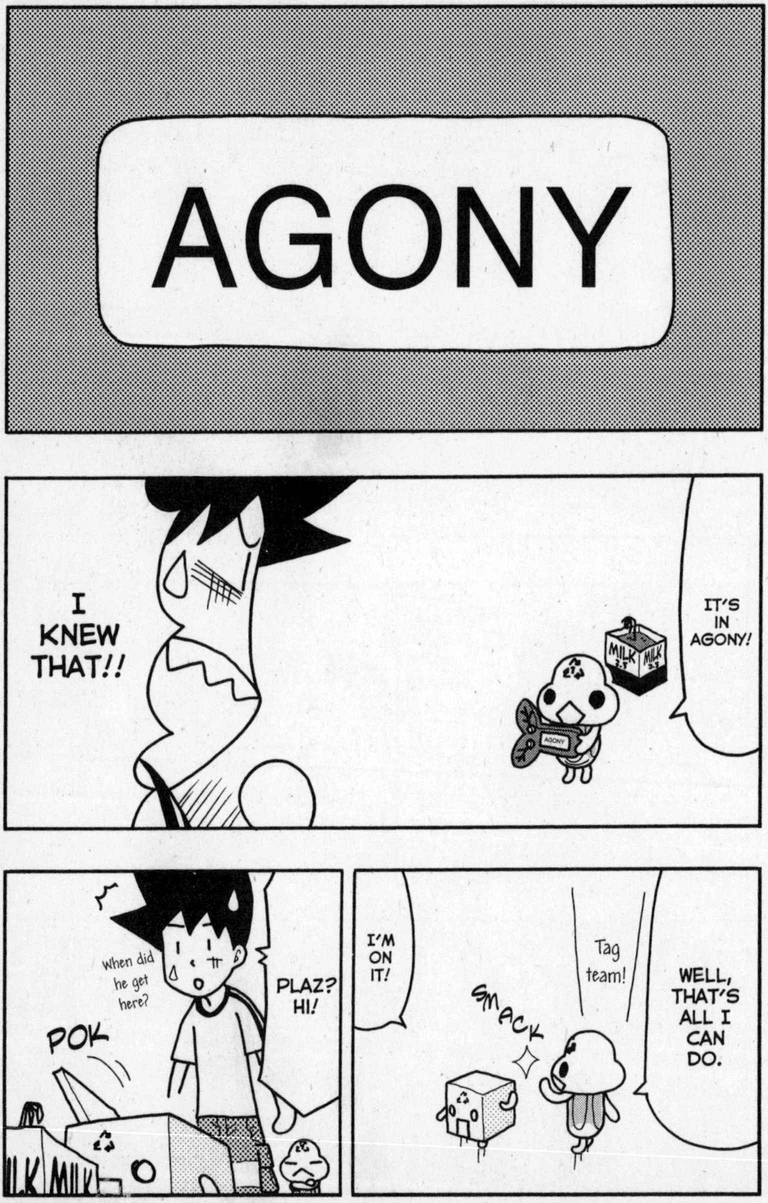
AGONY
IT'S IN AGONY!
MILK
MILK
AGONY
I KNEW THAT!!
WELL, THAT'S ALL I CAN DO.
Tag team!
SMACK
I'M ON IT!
PLAZ? HI!
when did he get here?
POK

PLAZ IS A GARDENING SPECIALIST!
ZUK
ZUK
ZUK
WOP
WOP
Liner
Plant Soil
FERTILIZER
GROW
MILK 3.5
MILK 3.5
ZUK
ZUK
MILK
ZHUP
ZIP
ZAP
ZUP
ZUP
PAT
I'll help!
PAT
WOW!
MILK 3.5
MILK 3.5

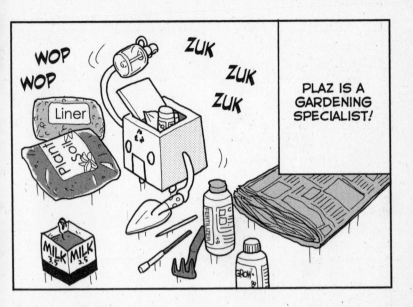

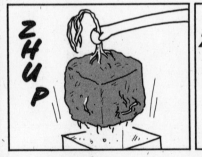

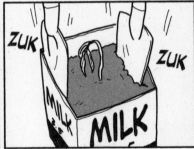

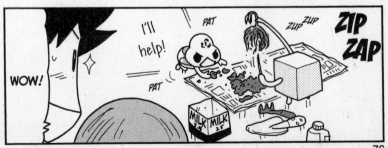

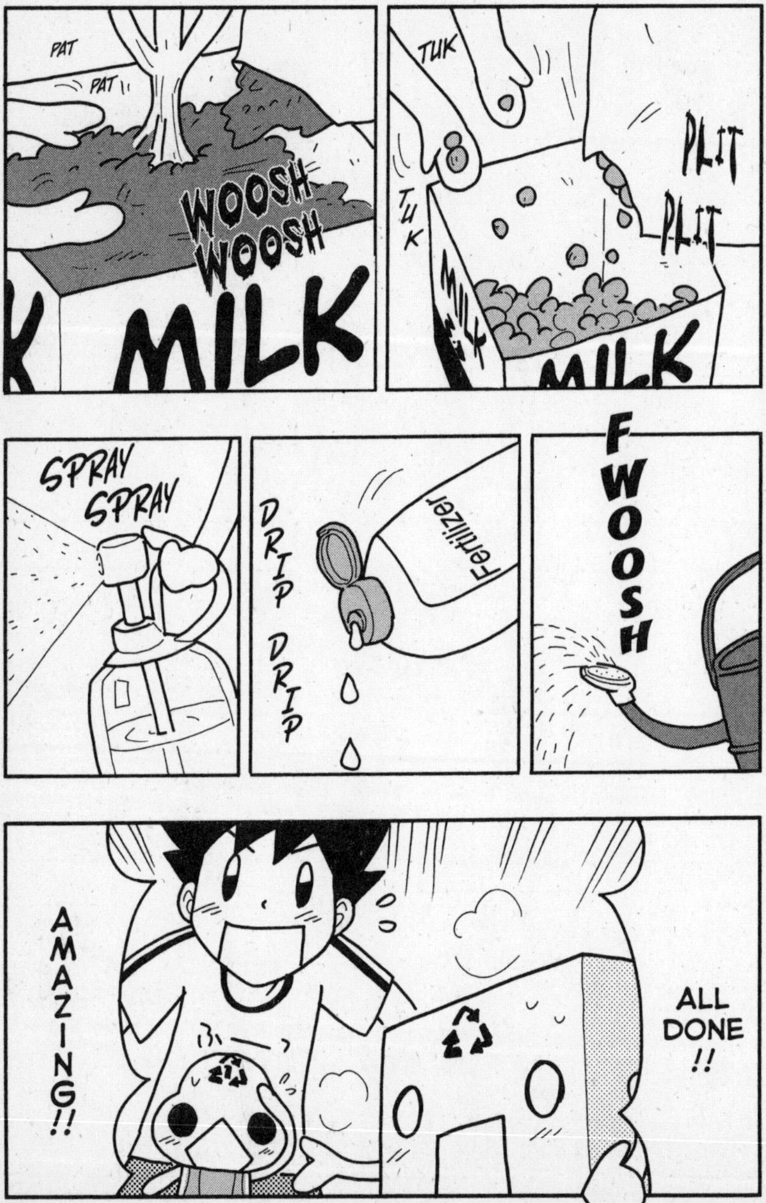
TUK
TUK
PLIT
PLIT
MILK
MILK
PAT
PAT
WOOSH
WOOSH
MILK
FWOOSH
Fertilizer
DRIP
DRIP
SPRAY
SPRAY
ALL DONE!!
AMAZING!!
ふーっ

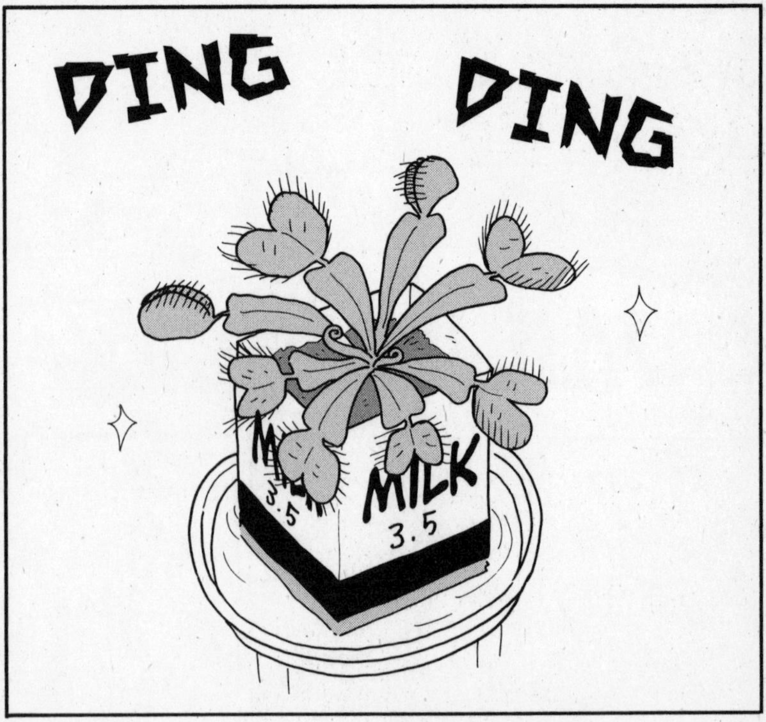
DING
DING
MILK
3.5

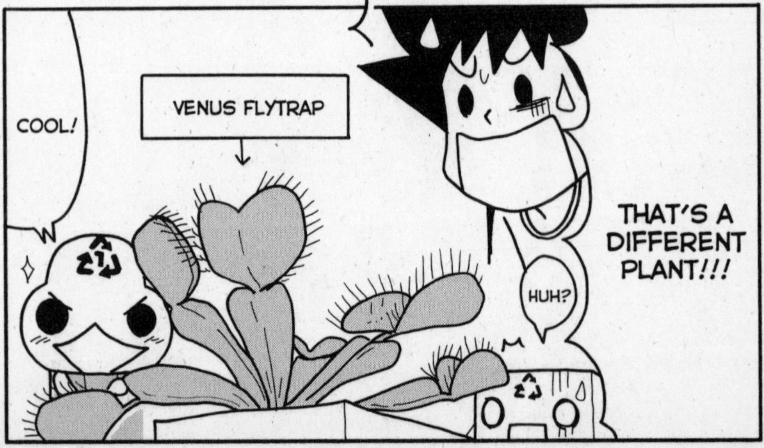
THAT'S A DIFFERENT PLANT!!!
HUH?
VENUS FLYTRAP
COOL!

CHAPTER 8

The Can Crew Cleans Up

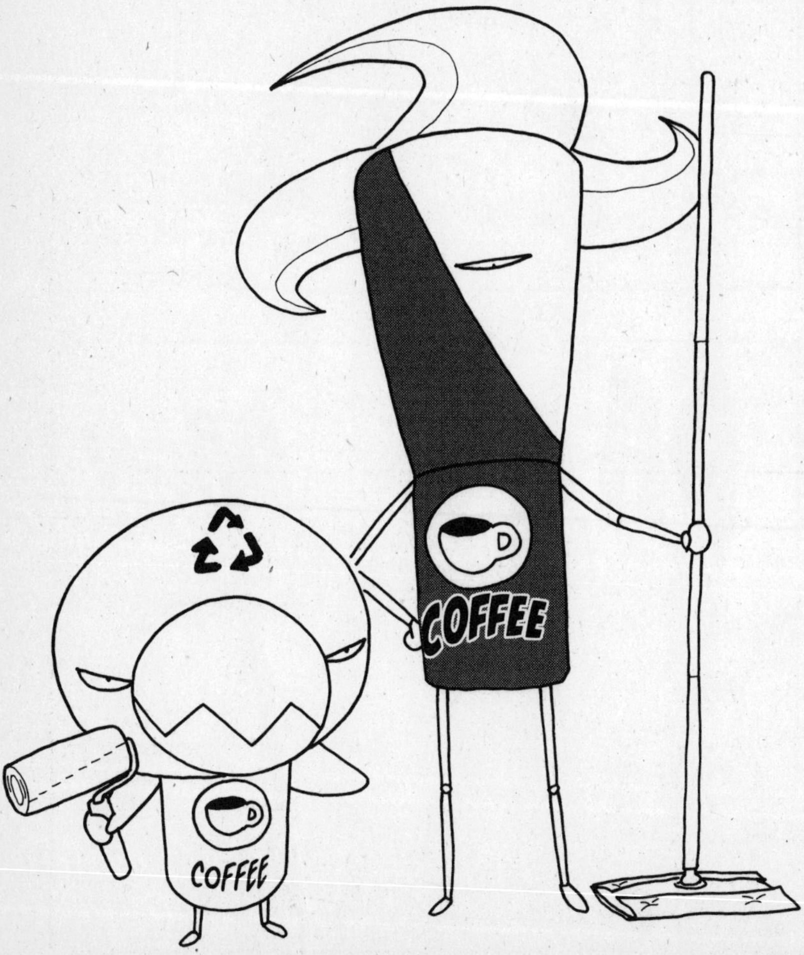
COFFEE
COFFEE

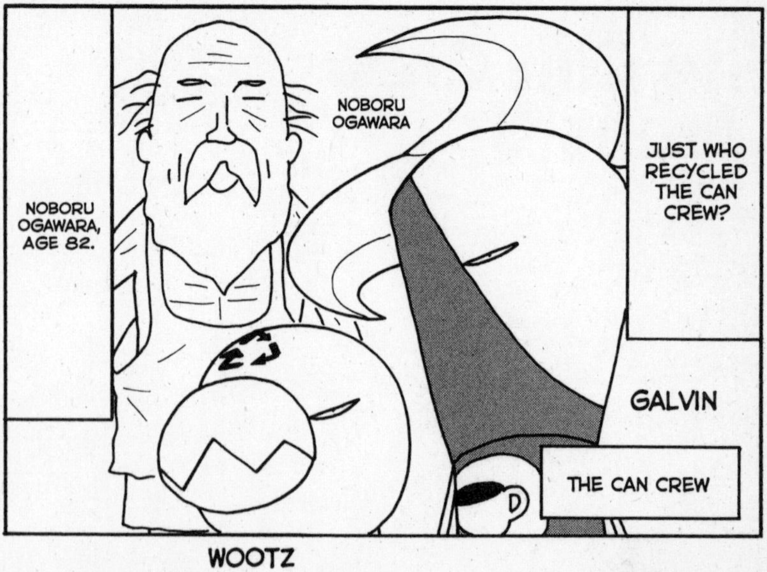
JUST WHO RECYCLED THE CAN CREW?
NOBORU OGAWARA
NOBORU OGAWARA, AGE 82.
GALVIN
THE CAN CREW
WOOTZ

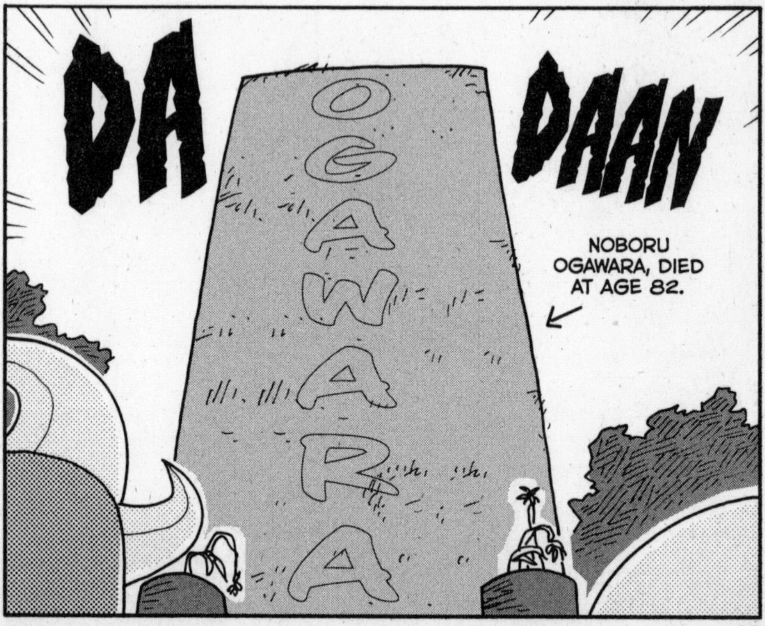
DA DAAN
NOBORU OGAWARA, DIED AT AGE 82.
OGAWARA

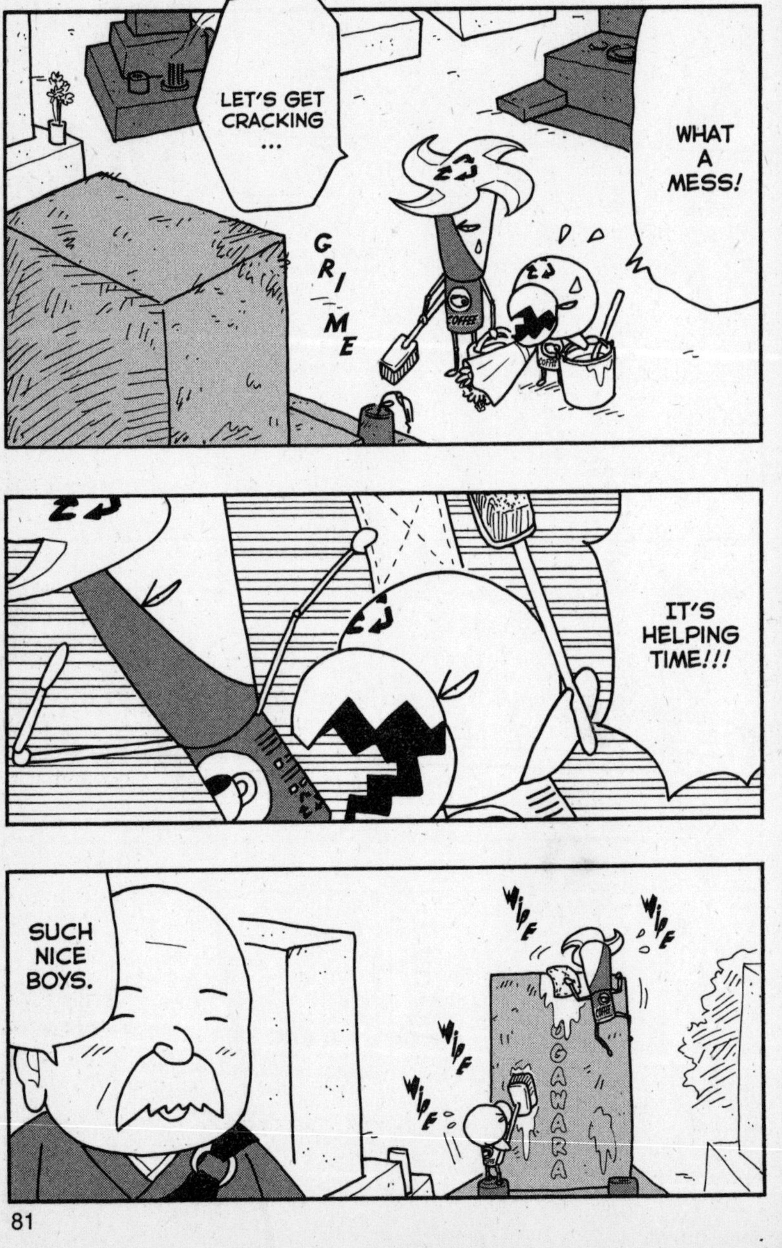
WHAT A MESS!
LET'S GET CRACKING ...
GRIME
IT'S HELPING TIME!!!
WIPE
WIPE
OGAWARA
WIPE
WIPE
SUCH NICE BOYS.

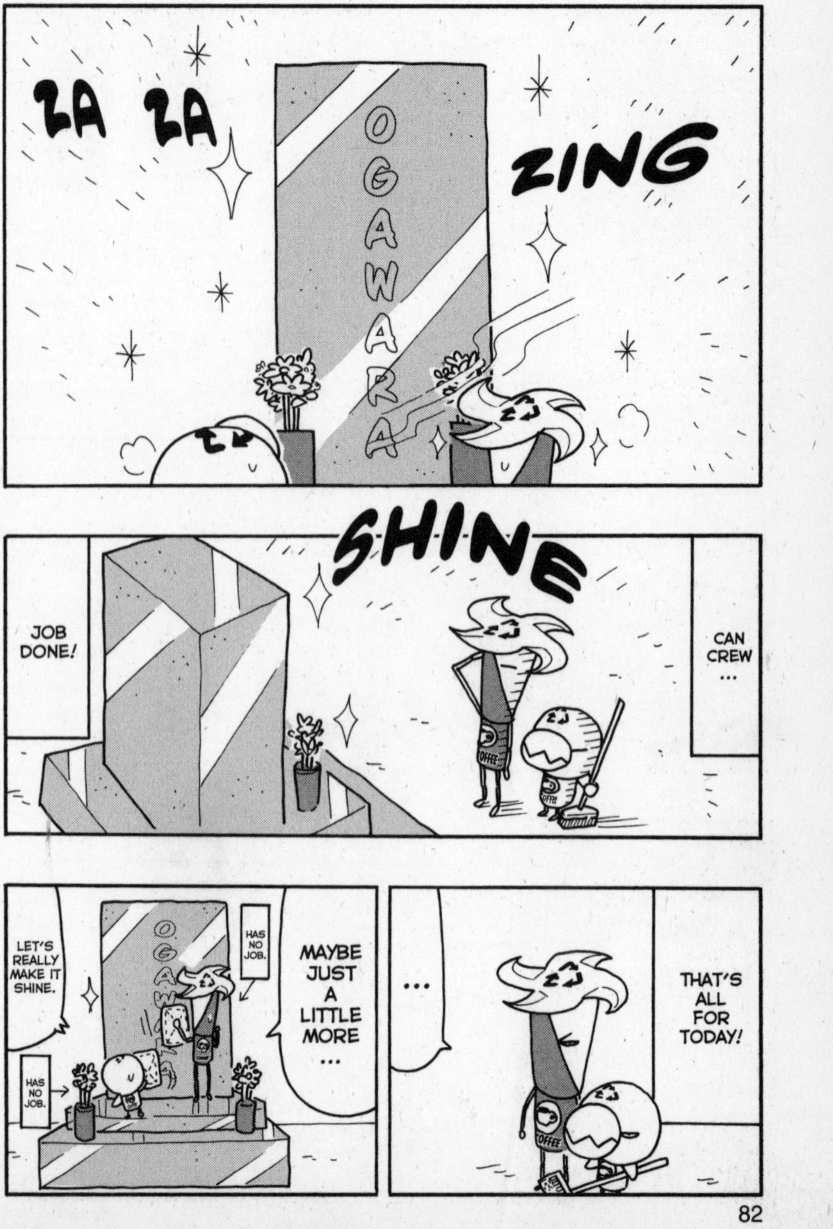
ZING
OGAWARA
ZA ZA
SHINE
CAN CREW ...
JOB DONE!
THAT'S ALL FOR TODAY!
...
MAYBE JUST A LITTLE MORE ...
HAS NO JOB.
OGAW
LET'S REALLY MAKE IT SHINE.
HAS NO JOB.

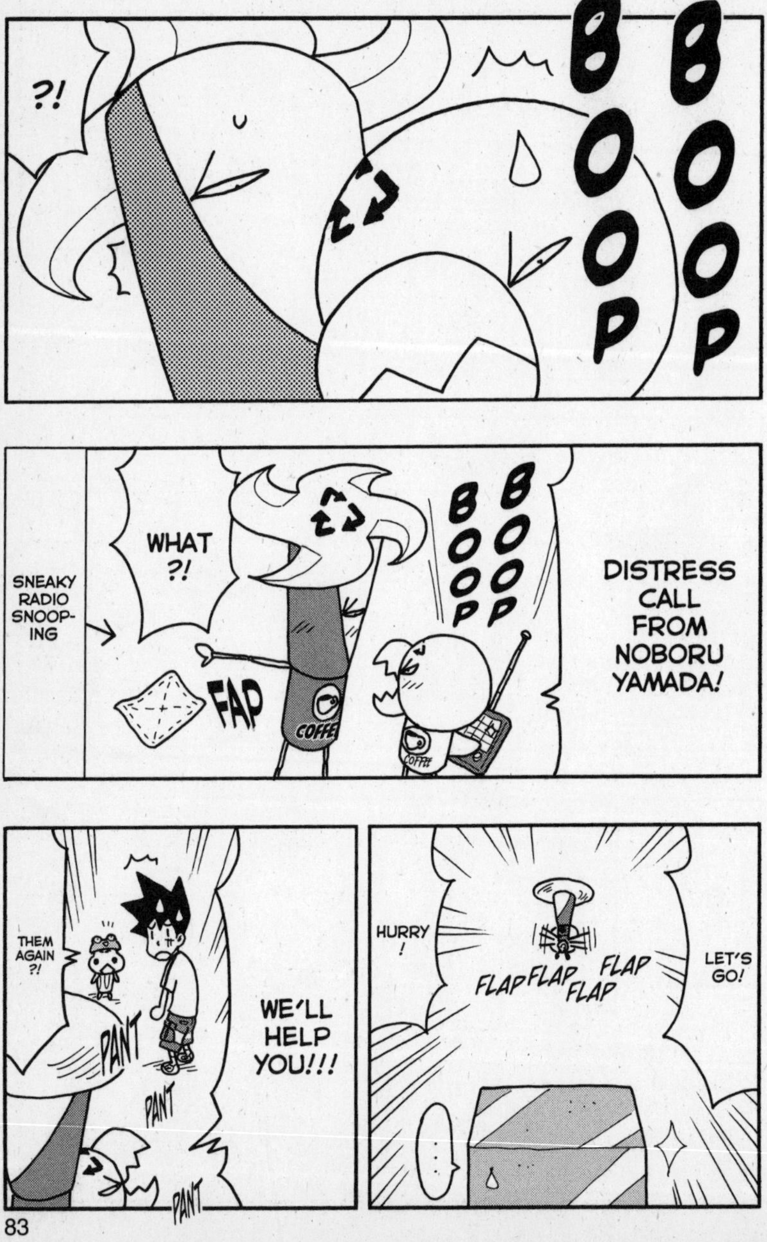
BOOP
BOOP
?!
DISTRESS CALL FROM NOBORU YAMADA!
BOOP
BOOP
WHAT?!
FAP
SNEAKY RADIO SNOOP-ING
LET'S GO!
FLAP FLAP FLAP FLAP
HURRY!
…
WE'LL HELP YOU!!!
THEM AGAIN?!
PANT
PANT
PANT

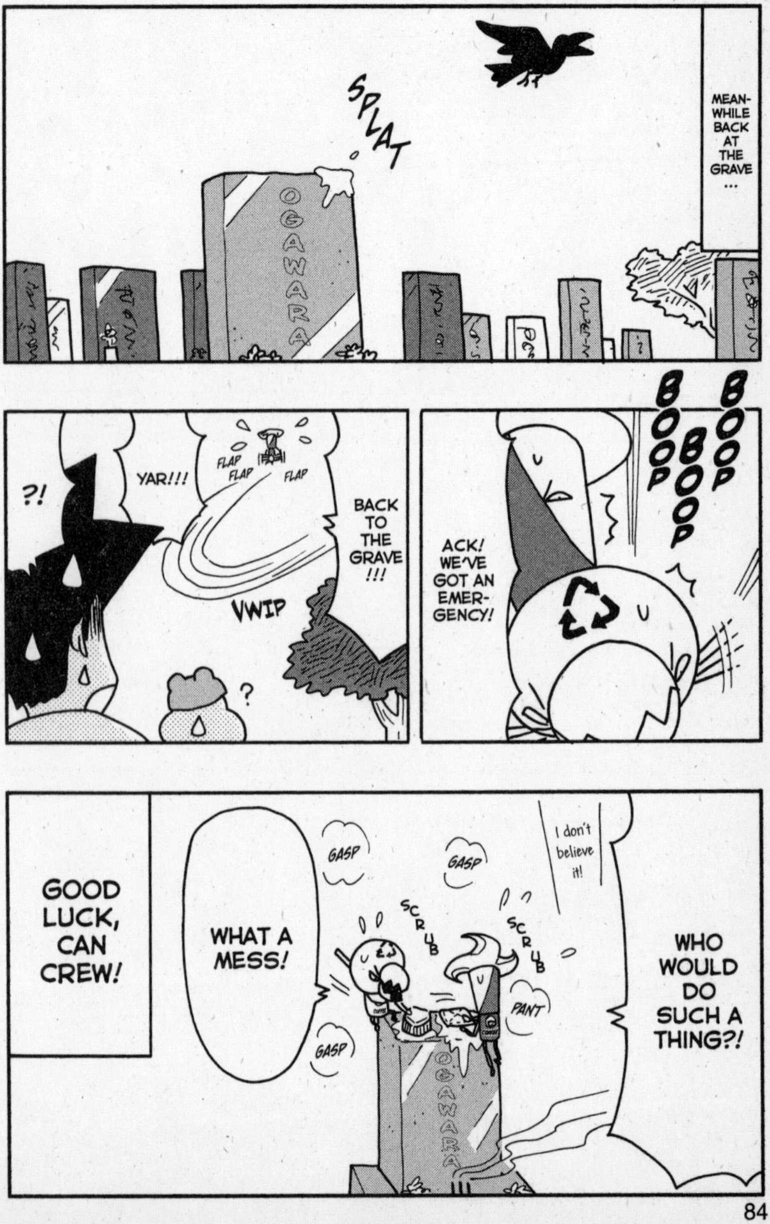
MEAN-WHILE BACK AT THE GRAVE...
SPLAT
OGAWARA
BOOP BOOP BOOP BOOP
ACK! WE'VE GOT AN EMERGENCY!
BACK TO THE GRAVE!!!
FLAP FLAP FLAP
YAR!!!
?!
VWIP
?
WHO WOULD DO SUCH A THING?!
I don't believe it!
GASP
SCRUB
SCRUB
PANT
GASP
GASP
WHAT A MESS!
OGAWARA
GOOD LUCK, CAN CREW!

CHAPTER 9

It's a Miracle?

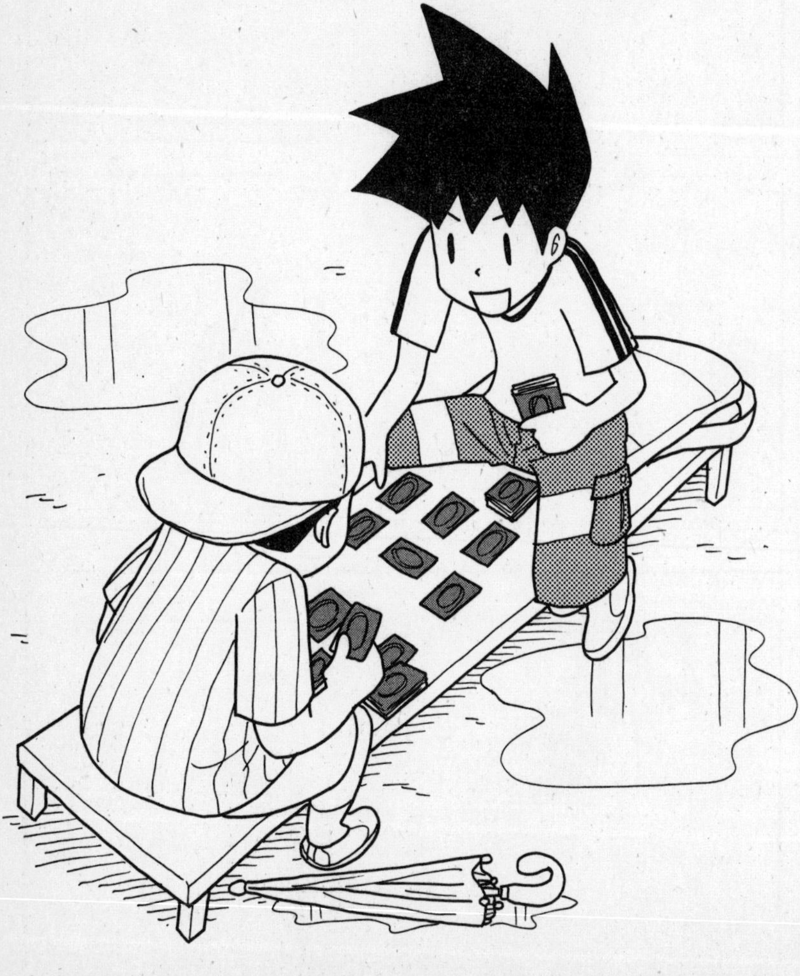

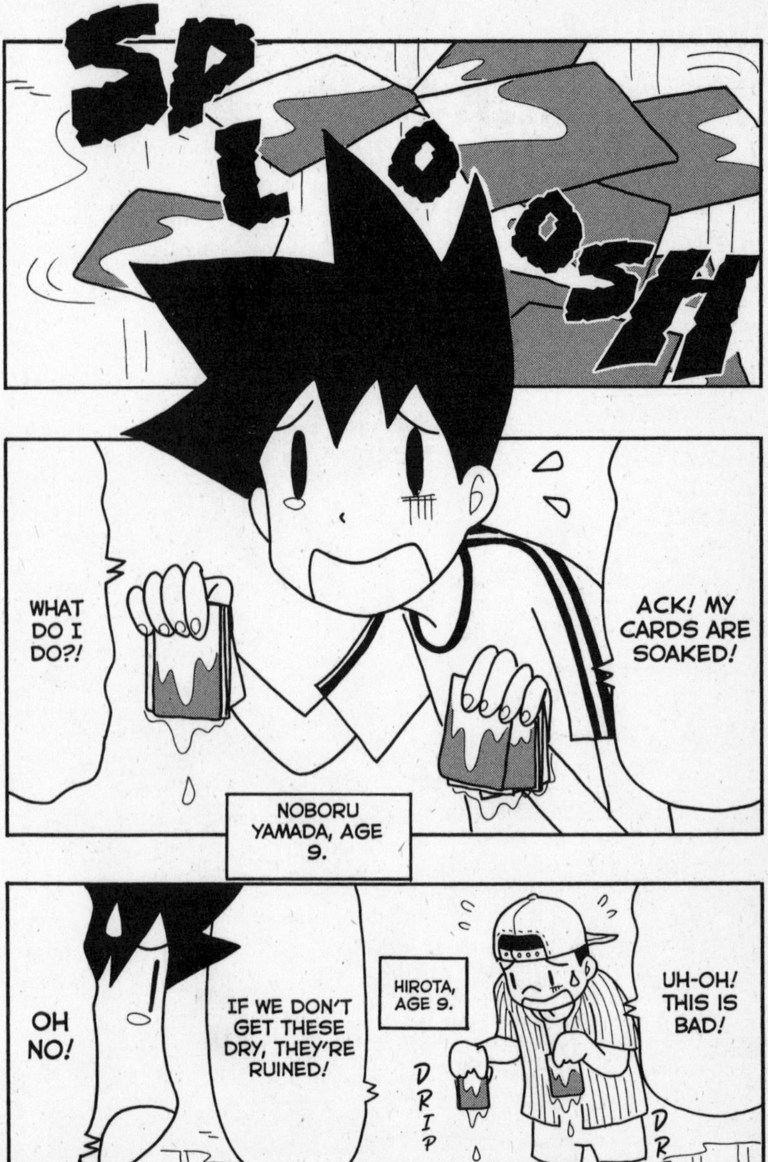
SPLOOSH
ACK! MY CARDS ARE SOAKED!
WHAT DO I DO?!
NOBORU YAMADA, AGE 9.
UH-OH! THIS IS BAD!
DRIP
HIROTA, AGE 9.
DRIP
IF WE DON'T GET THESE DRY, THEY'RE RUINED!
OH NO!

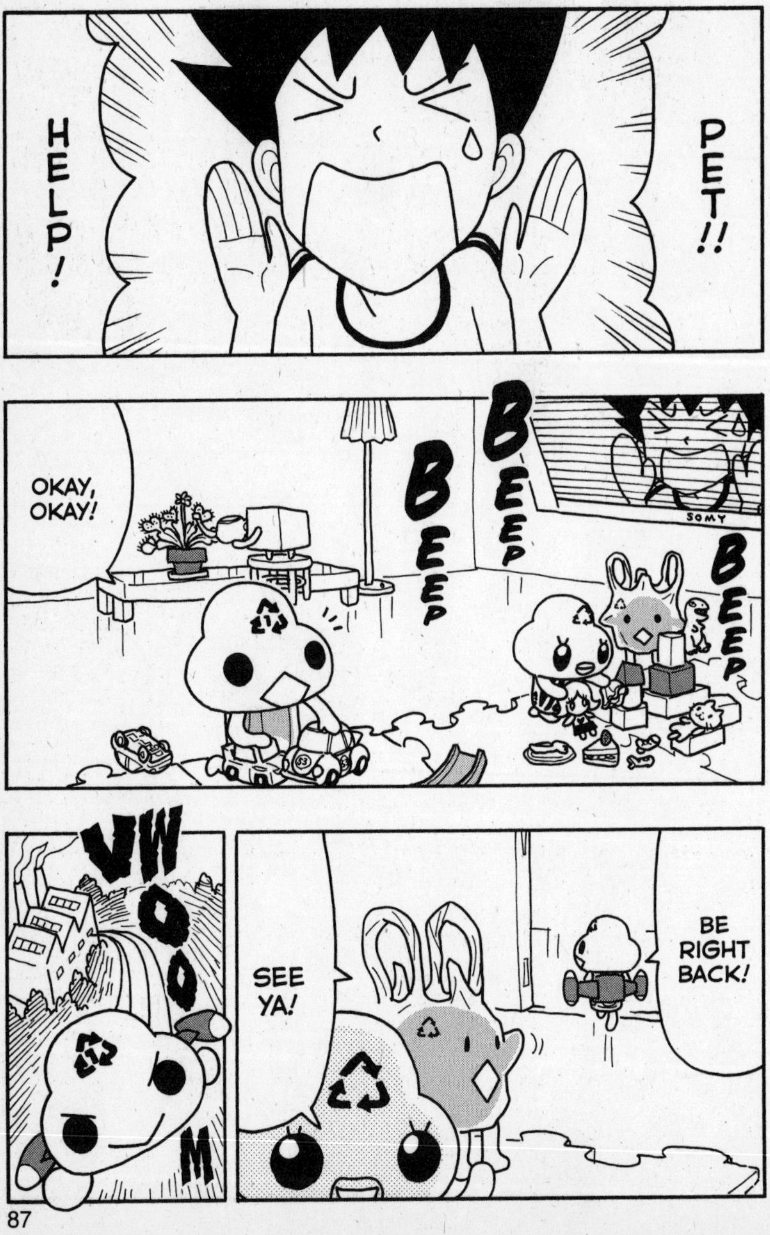
PET!!
HELP!
BEEP
BEEP
BEEP
OKAY, OKAY!
BE RIGHT BACK!
SEE YA!
VWOOOM

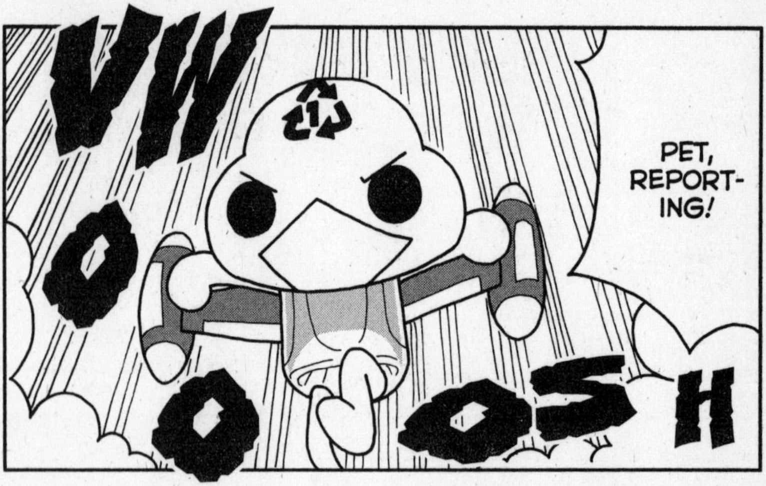
PET, REPORT-ING!
VWOOOOSH

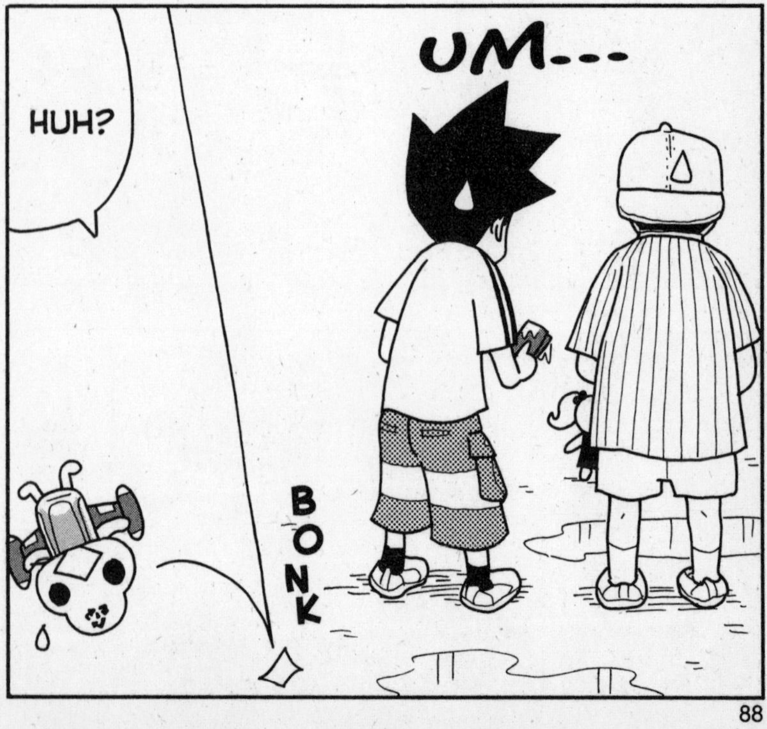
UM...
HUH?
BONK

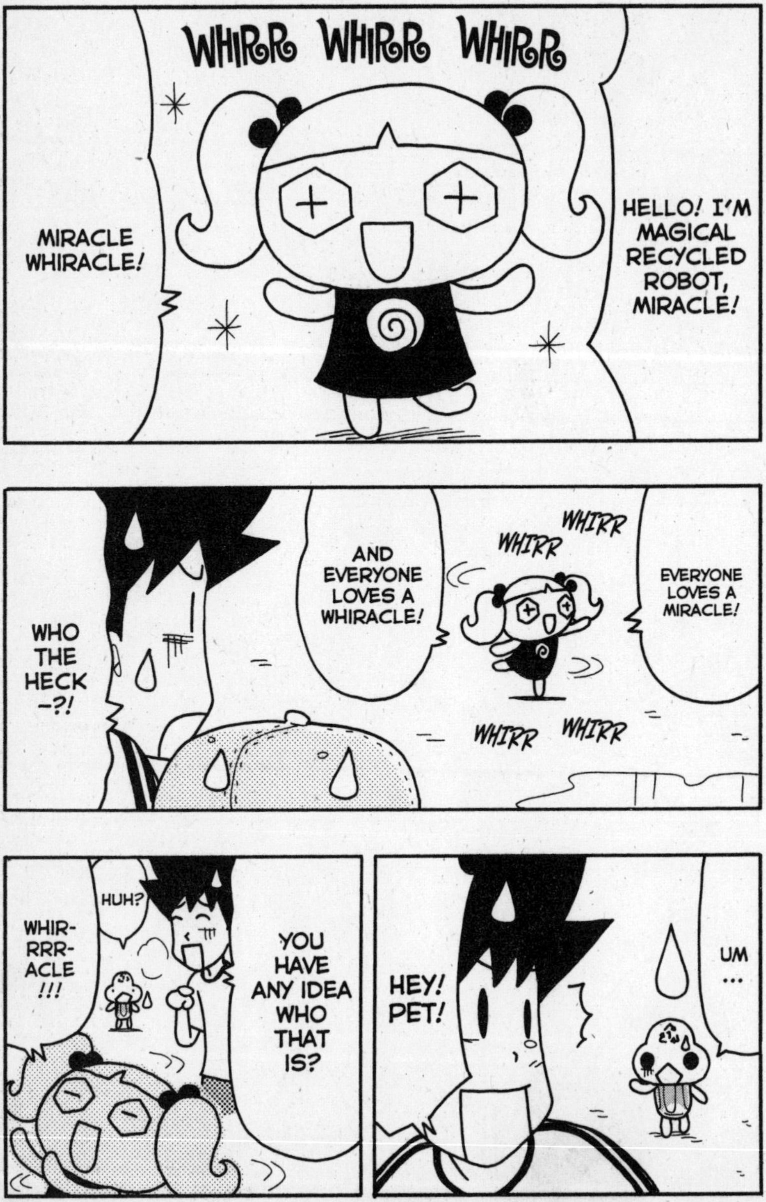
WHIRR WHIRR WHIRR
HELLO! I'M MAGICAL RECYCLED ROBOT, MIRACLE!
MIRACLE WHIRACLE!
EVERYONE LOVES A MIRACLE!
WHIRR
WHIRR
AND EVERYONE LOVES A WHIRACLE!
WHIRR
WHIRR
WHO THE HECK —?!
UM ...
HEY! PET!
YOU HAVE ANY IDEA WHO THAT IS?
HUH?
WHIR-RRR-ACLE !!!

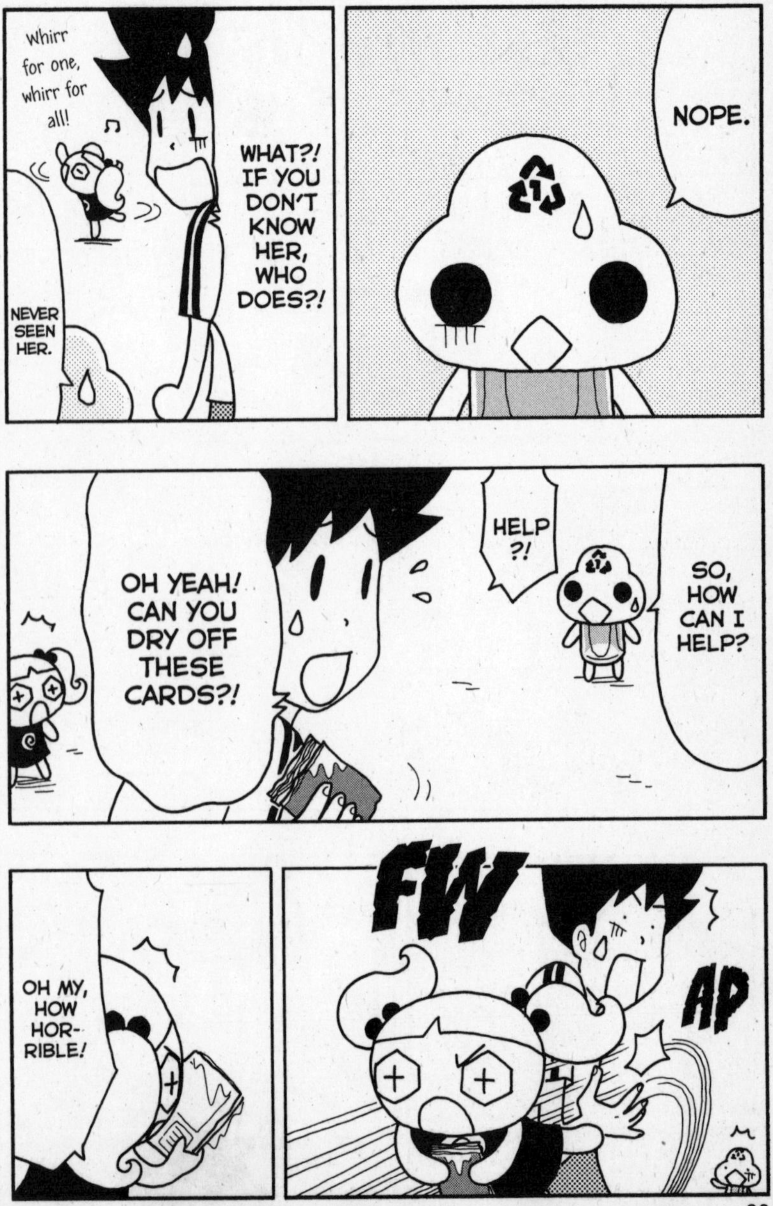
NOPE.
WHAT?! IF YOU DON'T KNOW HER, WHO DOES?!
whirr for one, whirr for all!
NEVER SEEN HER.
SO, HOW CAN I HELP?
HELP?!
OH YEAH! CAN YOU DRY OFF THESE CARDS?!
FW
AP
OH MY, HOW HOR-RIBLE!

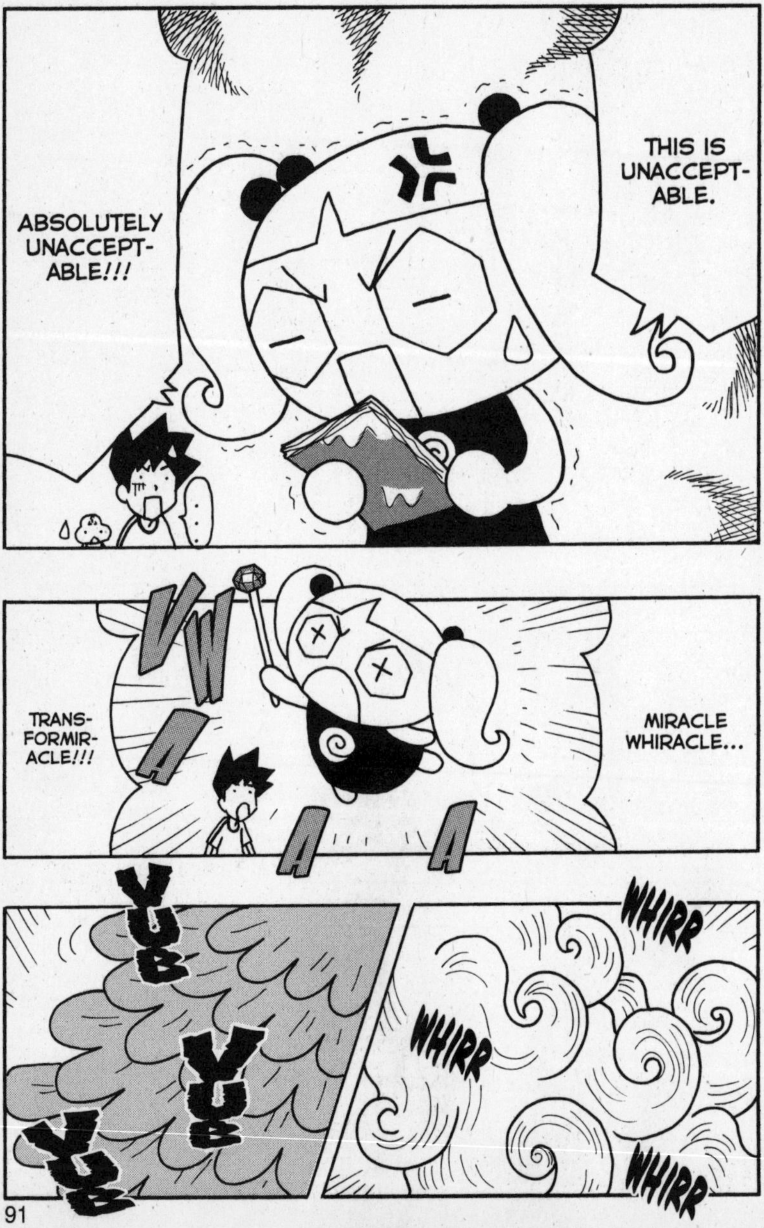
THIS IS UNACCEPT-ABLE.
ABSOLUTELY UNACCEPT-ABLE!!!
MIRACLE WHIRACLE...
TRANS-FORMIR-ACLE!!!
VWAAAA
WHIRR
WHIRR
WHIRR
YUB
YUB
YUB

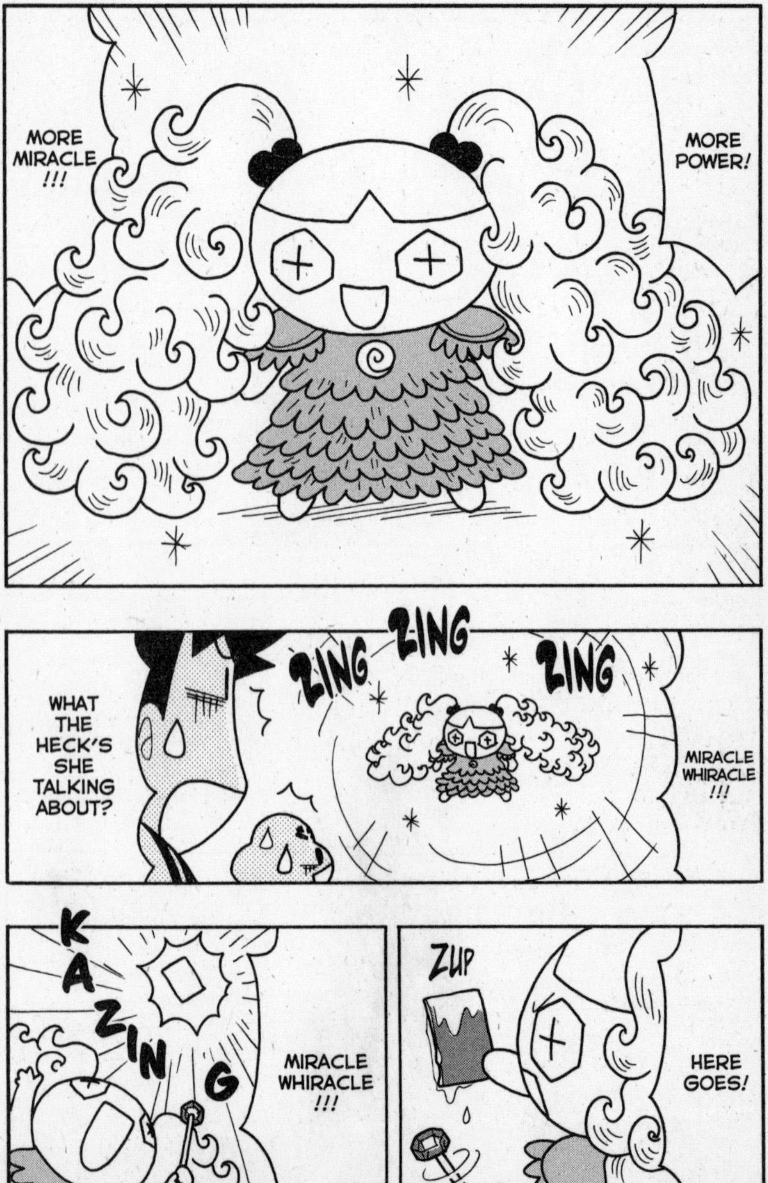
MORE POWER!
MORE MIRACLE!!!
ZING
ZING
ZING
MIRACLE WHIRACLE!!!
WHAT THE HECK'S SHE TALKING ABOUT?
HERE GOES!
ZUP
MIRACLE WHIRACLE!!!
KAZING

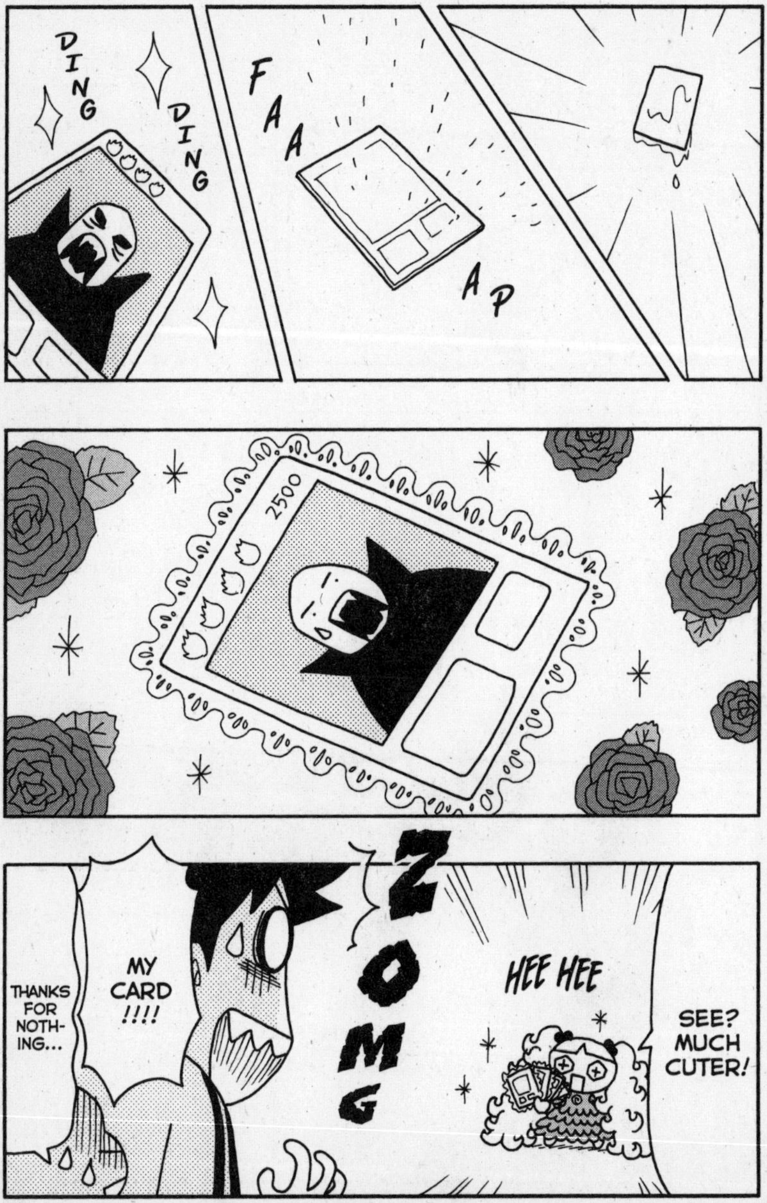
FAAAP
DING
DING
2500
SEE? MUCH CUTER!
HEE HEE
ZOMG
MY CARD!!!!
THANKS FOR NOTHING...

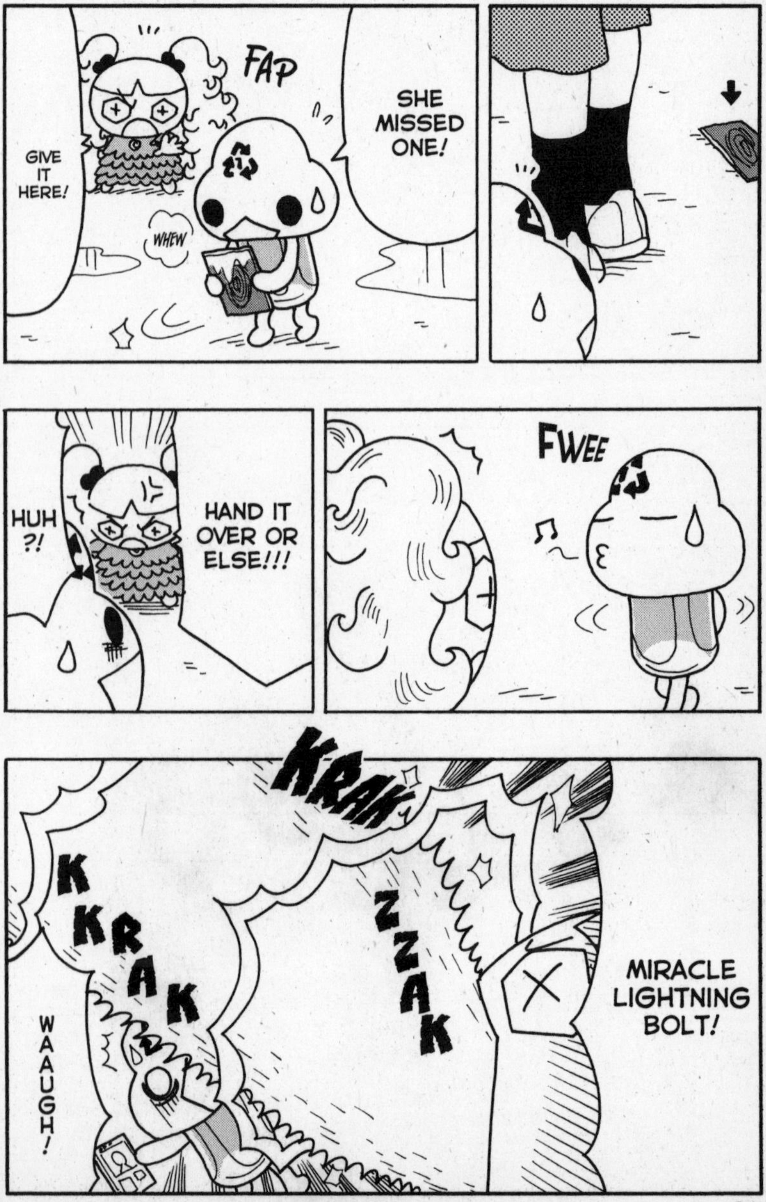
SHE MISSED ONE!
FAP
GIVE IT HERE!
WHEW
FWEE
HAND IT OVER OR ELSE!!!
HUH ?!
MIRACLE LIGHTNING BOLT!
KRAK
ZZAK
K KRAK
WAAAUGH!

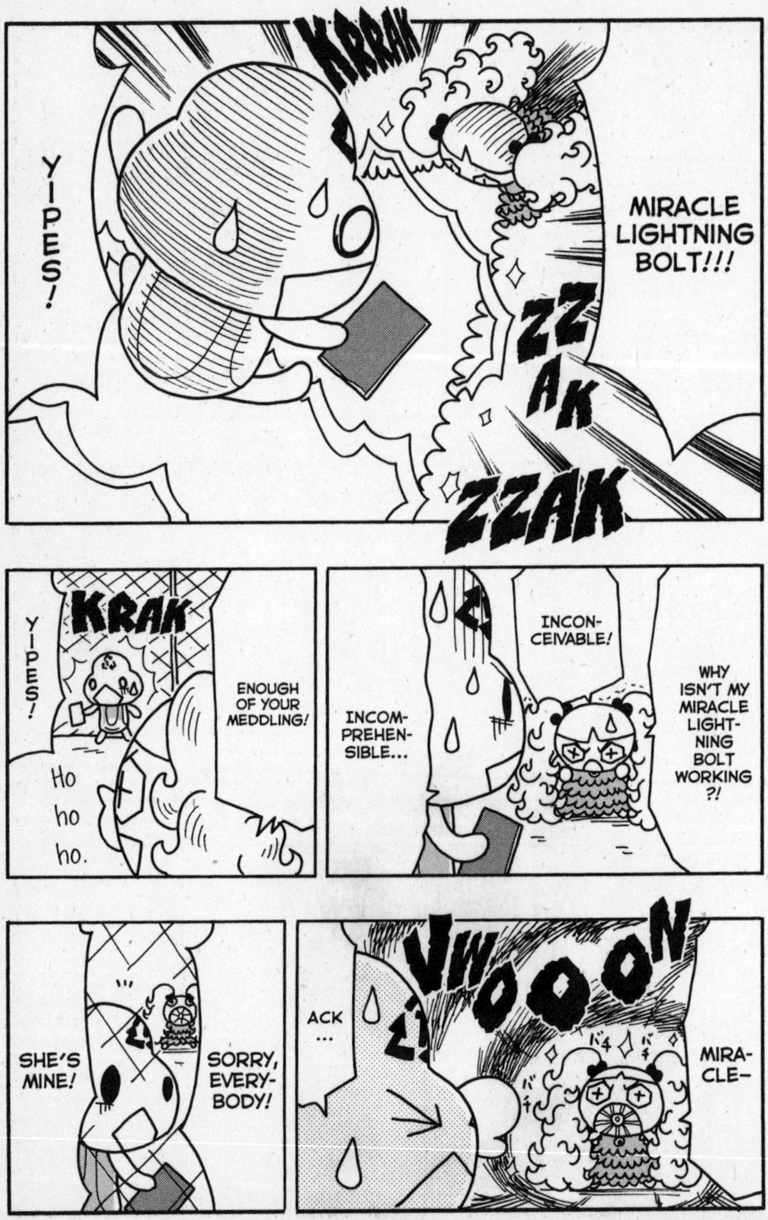
KRRAK
MIRACLE LIGHTNING BOLT!!!
ZZAK
ZZAK
YIPES!
INCONCEIVABLE!
WHY ISN'T MY MIRACLE LIGHTNING BOLT WORKING?!
INCOMPREHENSIBLE...
ENOUGH OF YOUR MEDDLING!
KRAK
YIPES!
Ho ho ho.
VWOOOON
MIRACLE—
ACK...
SORRY, EVERYBODY!
SHE'S MINE!

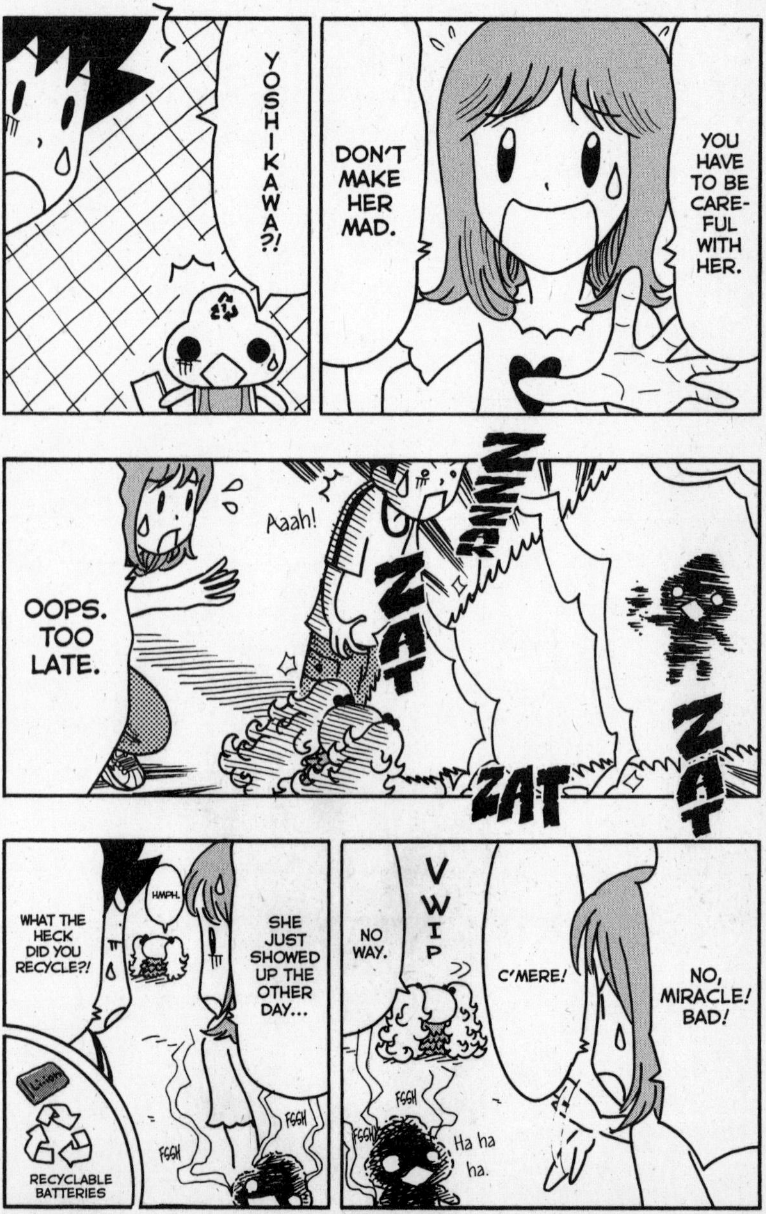
YOU HAVE TO BE CARE-FUL WITH HER.
DON'T MAKE HER MAD.
YOSHIKAWA?!
ZAT
Aaah!
OOPS. TOO LATE.
ZAT
ZAT
NO, MIRACLE! BAD!
C'MERE!
VWIP
NO WAY.
FSSH
FSSH
Ha ha ha.
SHE JUST SHOWED UP THE OTHER DAY...
HMPH.
WHAT THE HECK DID YOU RECYCLE?!
FSSH
FSSH
RECYCLABLE BATTERIES

CHAPTER 10

Making Miracles Happen

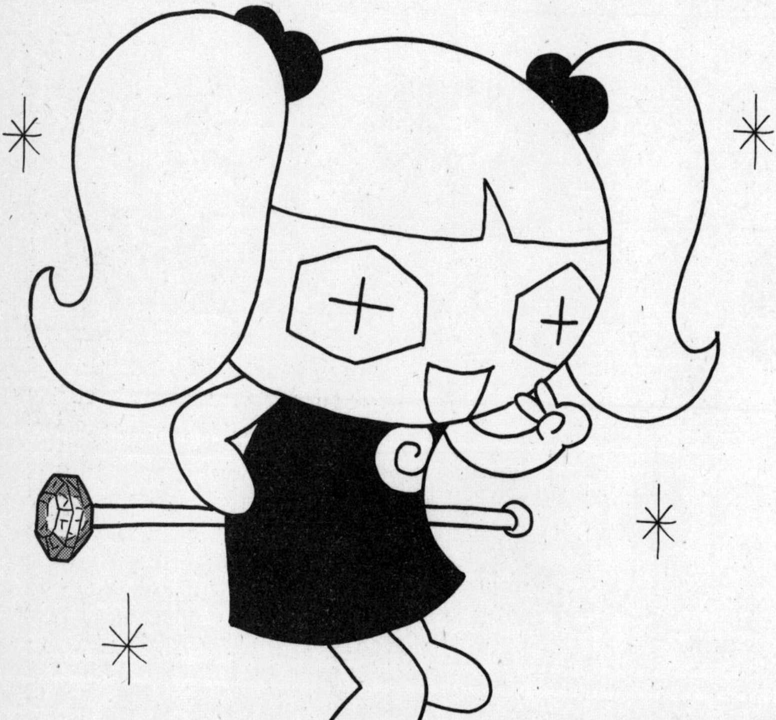

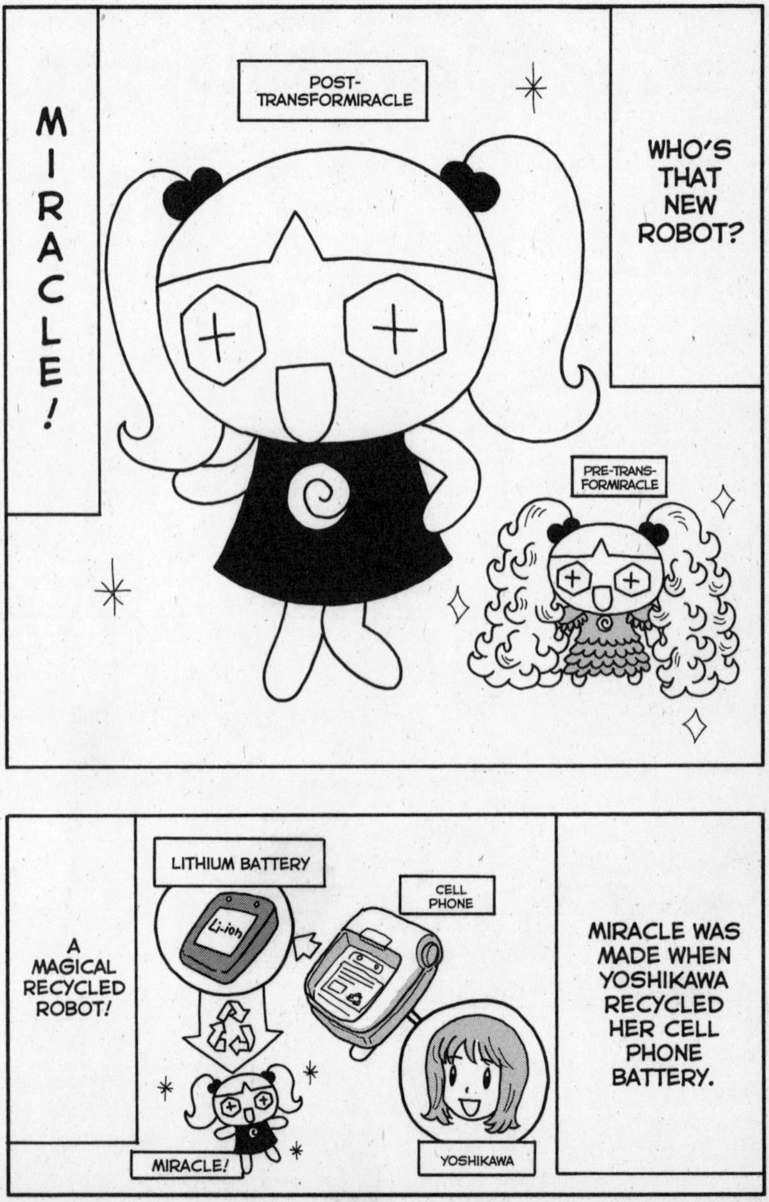

WHO'S THAT NEW ROBOT?
POST-TRANSFORMIRACLE
PRE-TRANS-FORMIRACLE
MIRACLE!
MIRACLE WAS MADE WHEN YOSHIKAWA RECYCLED HER CELL PHONE BATTERY.
CELL PHONE
LITHIUM BATTERY
Li-ion
YOSHIKAWA
MIRACLE!
A MAGICAL RECYCLED ROBOT!

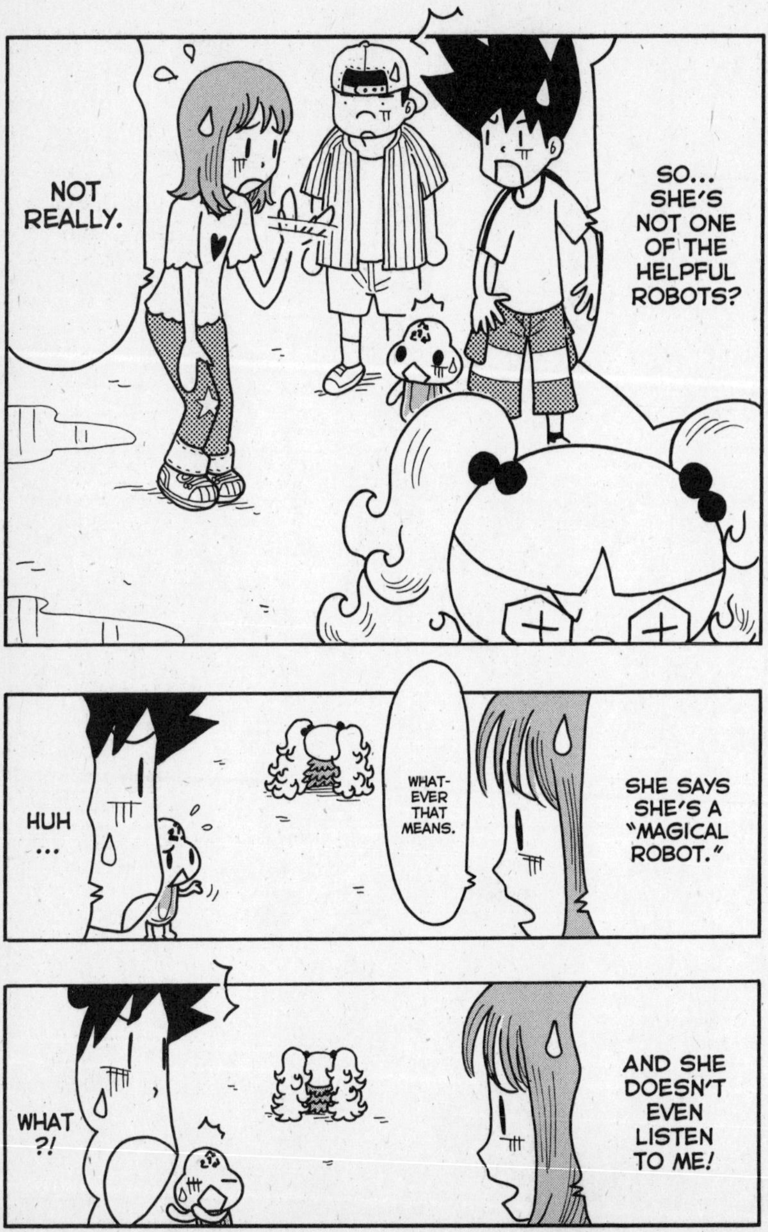
SO... SHE'S NOT ONE OF THE HELPFUL ROBOTS?
NOT REALLY.
SHE SAYS SHE'S A "MAGICAL ROBOT."
WHAT-EVER THAT MEANS.
HUH ...
AND SHE DOESN'T EVEN LISTEN TO ME!
WHAT ?!

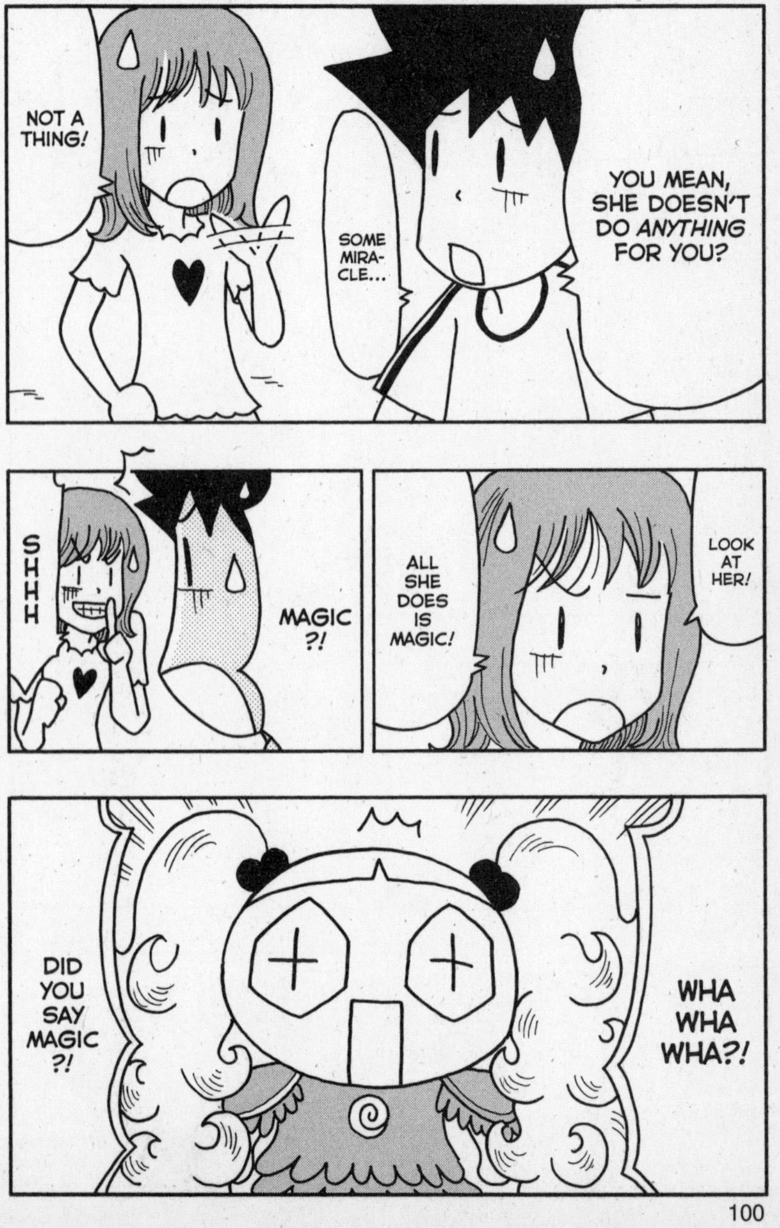
YOU MEAN, SHE DOESN'T DO *ANYTHING* FOR YOU?
SOME MIRACLE...
NOT A THING!
LOOK AT HER!
ALL SHE DOES IS MAGIC!
MAGIC?!
SHHH
WHA WHA WHA?!
DID YOU SAY MAGIC?!

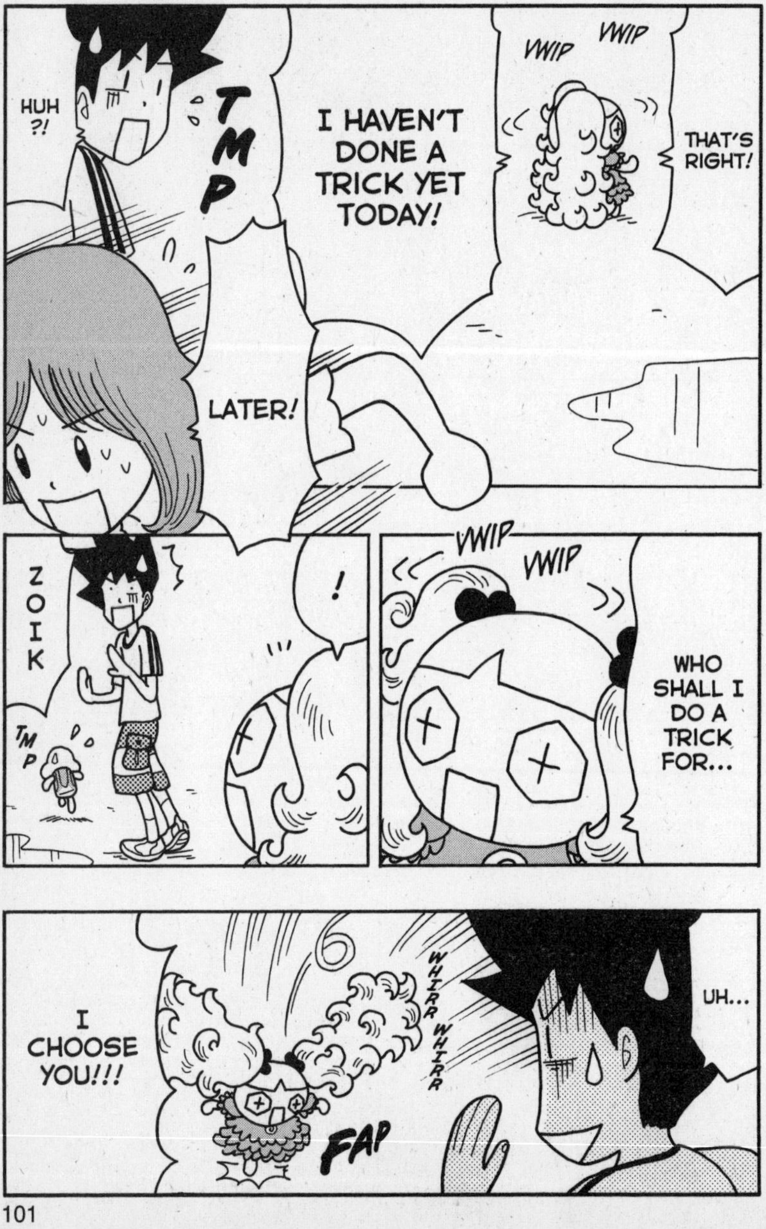
VWIP
VWIP
THAT'S RIGHT!
I HAVEN'T DONE A TRICK YET TODAY!
TMP
HUH ?!
LATER!
VWIP
VWIP
WHO SHALL I DO A TRICK FOR...
!
ZOIK
TMP
UH...
WHIRR WHIRR
FAP
I CHOOSE YOU!!!

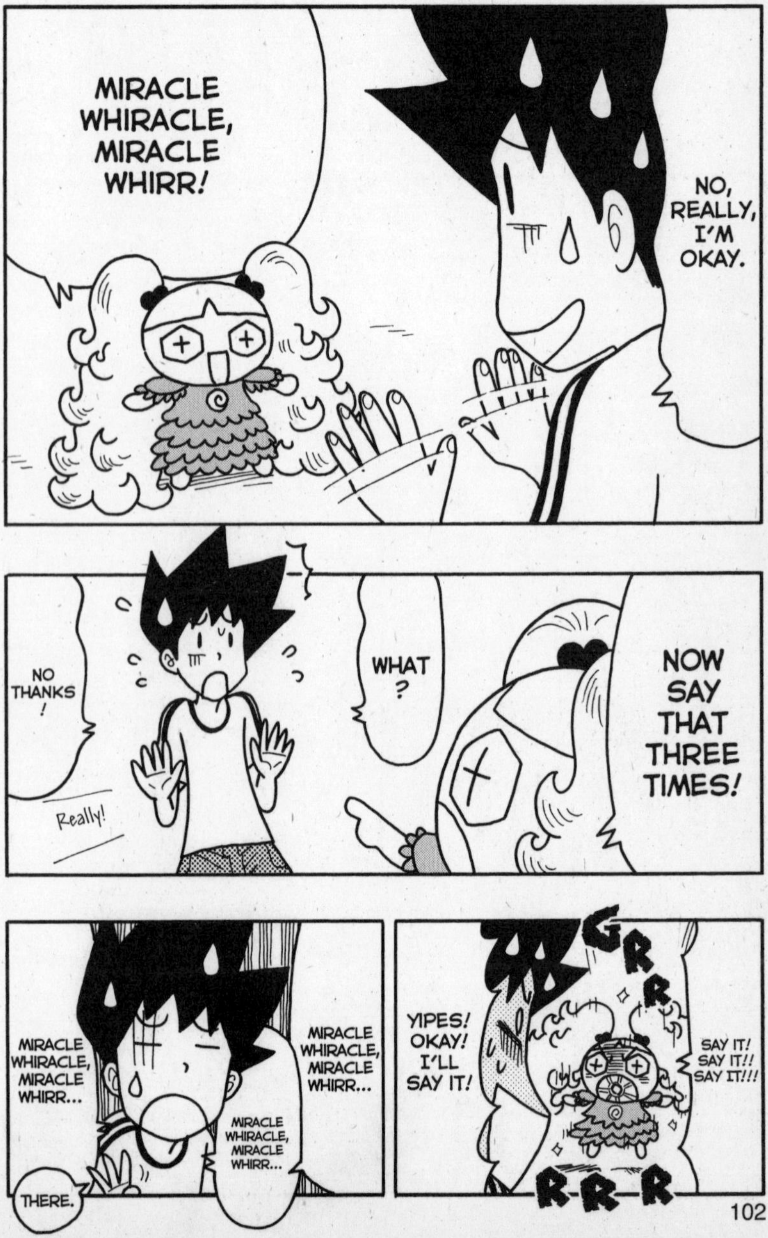
NO, REALLY, I'M OKAY.
MIRACLE WHIRACLE, MIRACLE WHIRR!
NOW SAY THAT THREE TIMES!
WHAT?
NO THANKS!
Really!
SAY IT! SAY IT!! SAY IT!!!
GRRR
RRR
YIPES! OKAY! I'LL SAY IT!
MIRACLE WHIRACLE, MIRACLE WHIRR...
MIRACLE WHIRACLE, MIRACLE WHIRR...
MIRACLE WHIRACLE, MIRACLE WHIRR...
THERE.

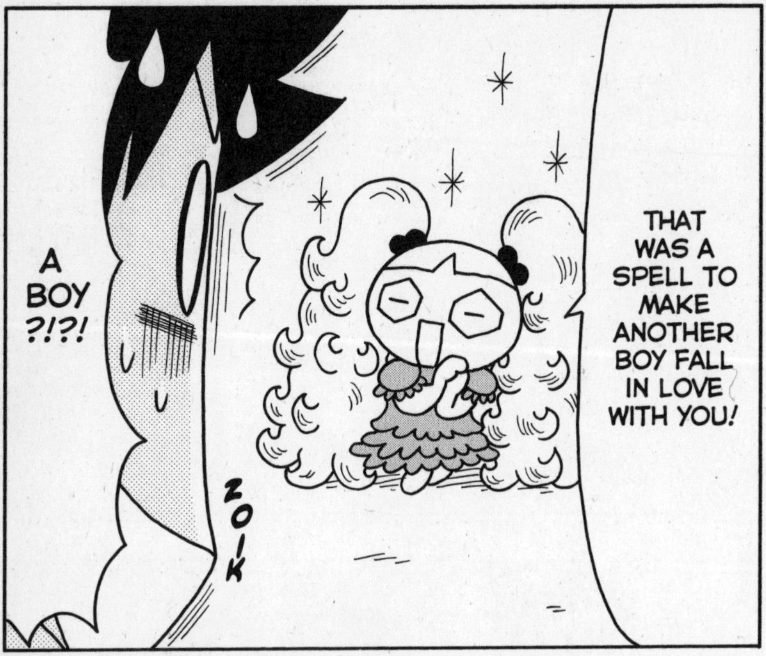
THAT WAS A SPELL TO MAKE ANOTHER BOY FALL IN LOVE WITH YOU!
ZOIK
A BOY ?!?!

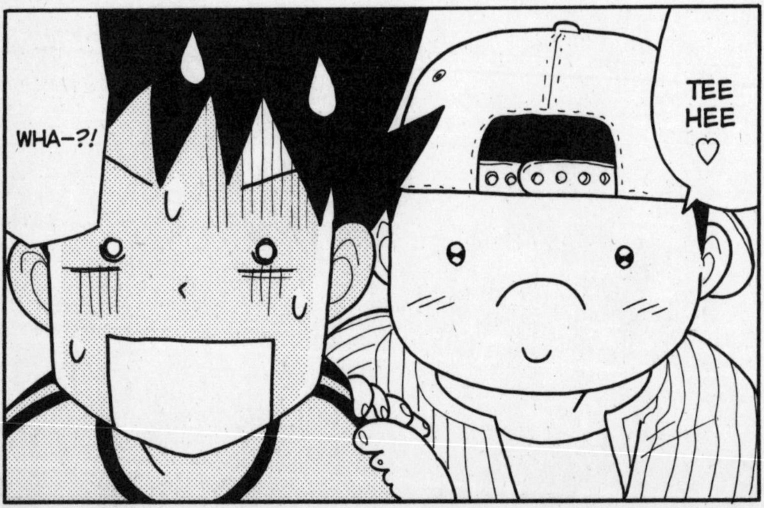
TEE HEE ♡
WHA-?!

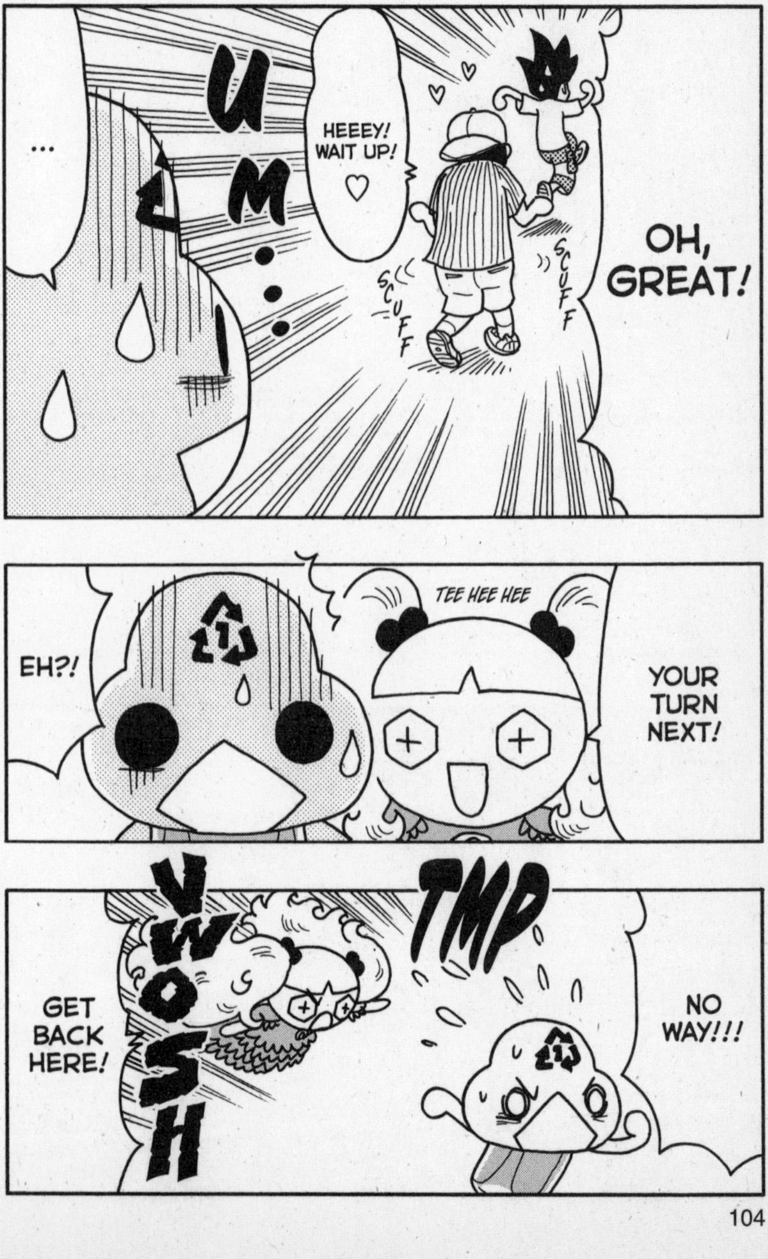
OH, GREAT!
HEEEY! WAIT UP! ♡
SCUFF
SCUFF
UM...
...
TEE HEE HEE
YOUR TURN NEXT!
EH?!
TMP
NO WAY!!!
VWOOSH
GET BACK HERE!

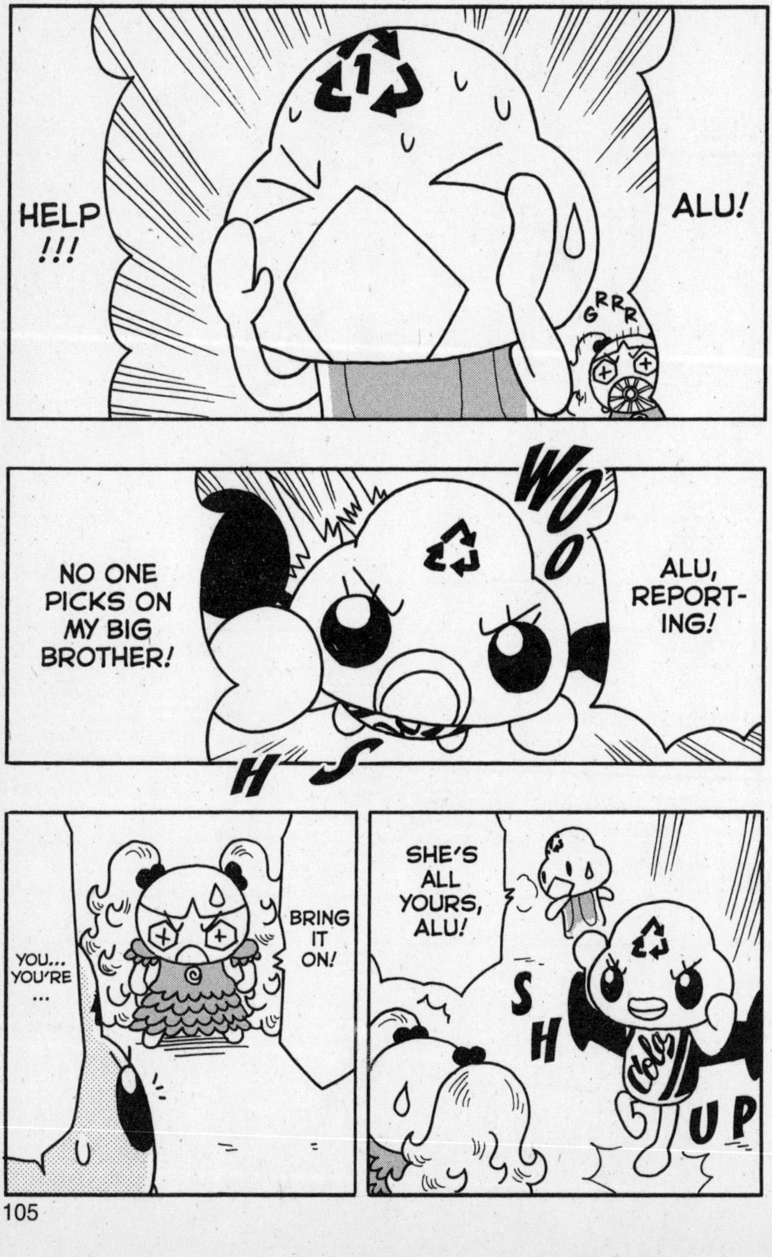
ALU!
HELP!!!
GRRR
WOOSH
ALU, REPORTING!
NO ONE PICKS ON MY BIG BROTHER!
SHE'S ALL YOURS, ALU!
SHUP
BRING IT ON!
YOU... YOU'RE ...

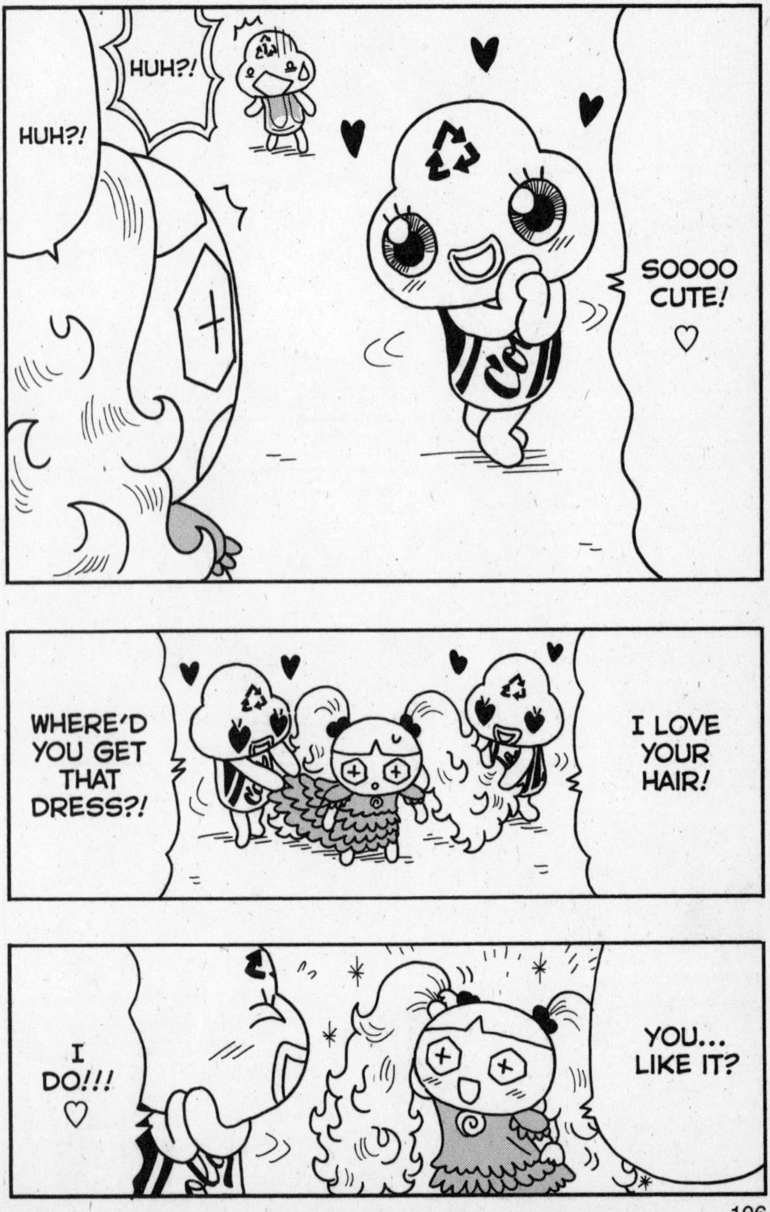
SOOOO CUTE! ♡
HUH?!
HUH?!
I LOVE YOUR HAIR!
WHERE'D YOU GET THAT DRESS?!
YOU... LIKE IT?
I DO!!! ♡

THEN I'LL GIVE YOU ONE TOO!
KRAK
KRAK
MIRACLE WHIRACLE!
KRAK
KRAK
LOOK LIKE ME!!!
VZZZ
!!
TA
VWIP
VWIP
VWIP
VWIP
POOF
POOF
POOF

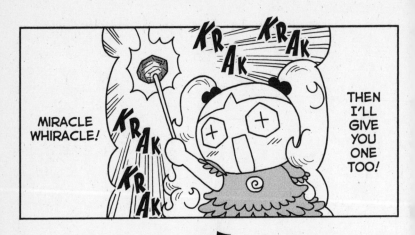

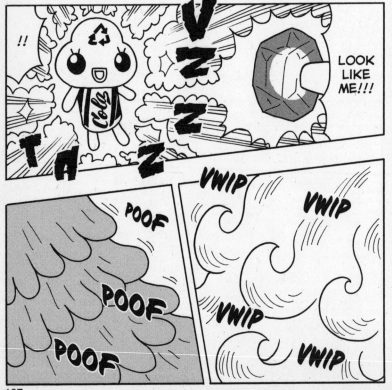

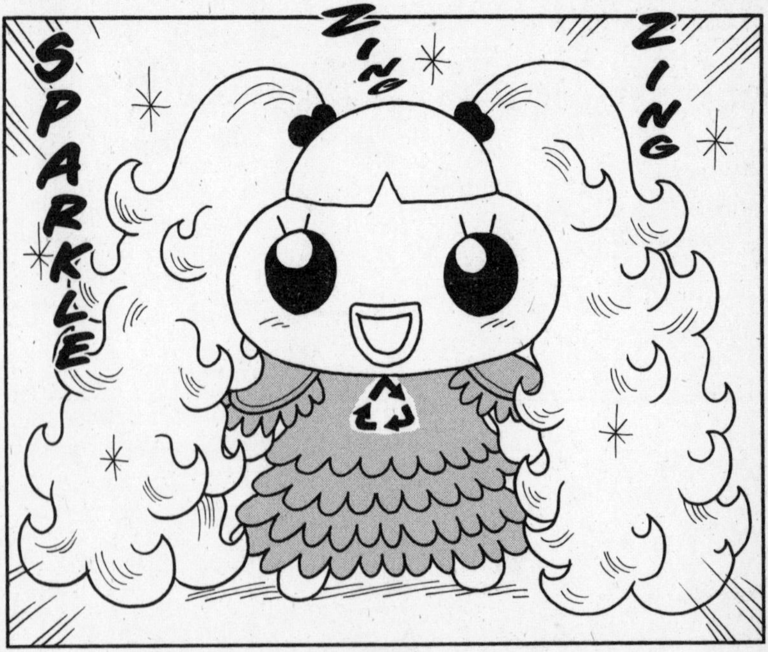
ZING
ZING
SPARKLE

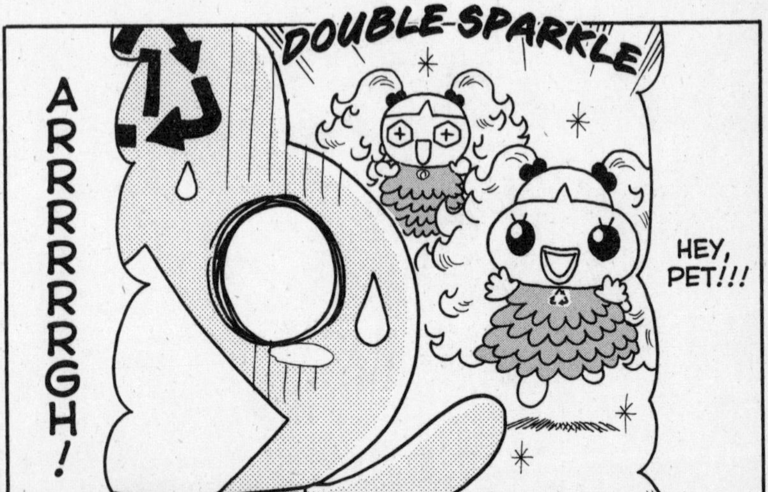
DOUBLE-SPARKLE
HEY, PET!!!
ARRRRRRGH!

CHAPTER 11

Miracles All Around

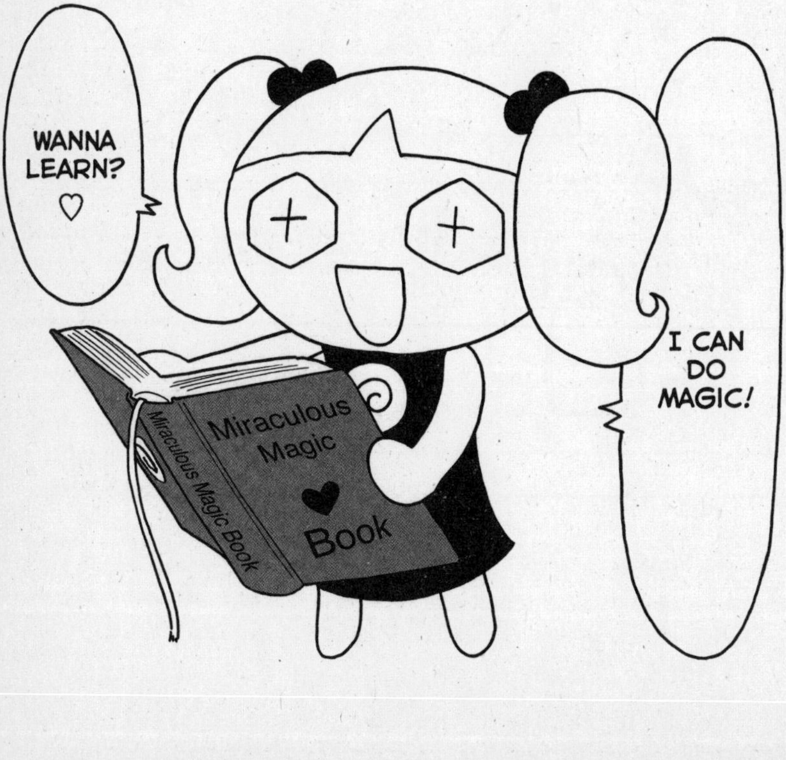
I CAN DO MAGIC!
WANNA LEARN? ♡
Miraculous Magic ♥ Book
Miraculous Magic Book

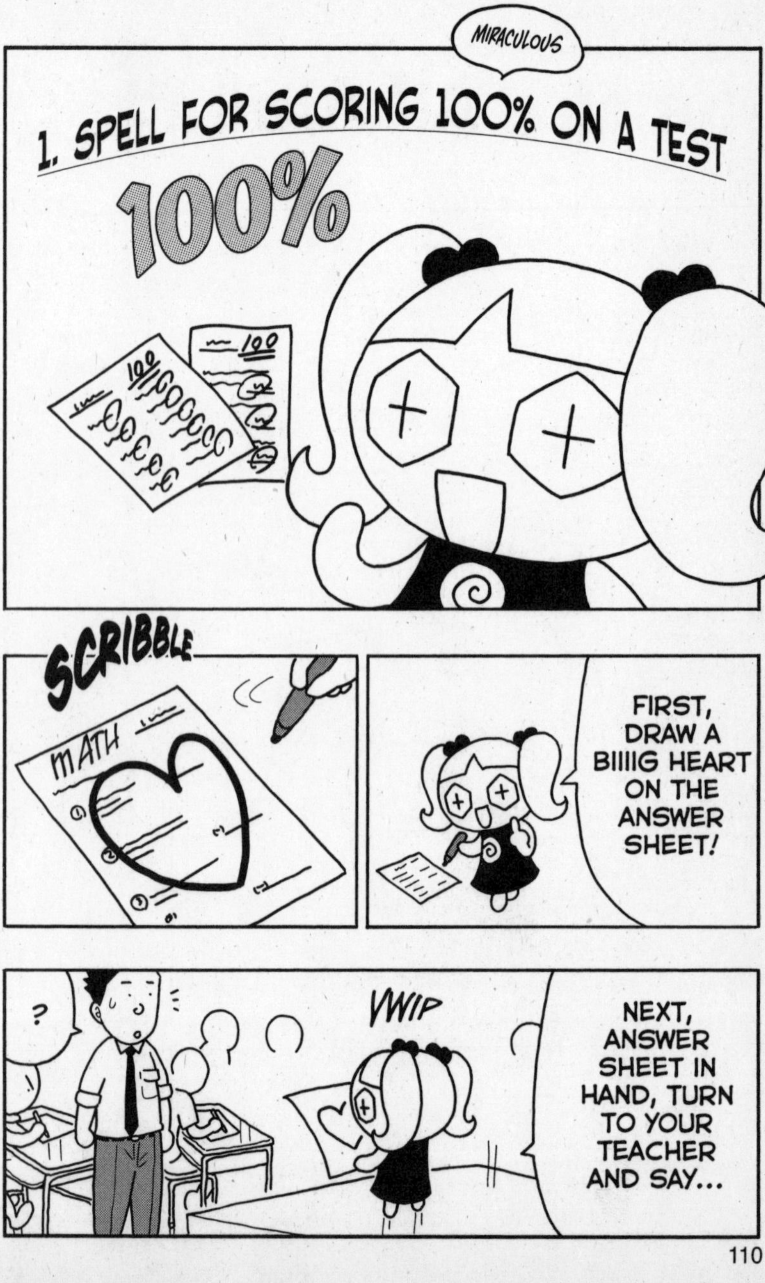
MIRACULOUS
1. SPELL FOR SCORING 100% ON A TEST
100%
FIRST, DRAW A BIIIIG HEART ON THE ANSWER SHEET!
SCRIBBLE
MATH
NEXT, ANSWER SHEET IN HAND, TURN TO YOUR TEACHER AND SAY...
VWIP
?

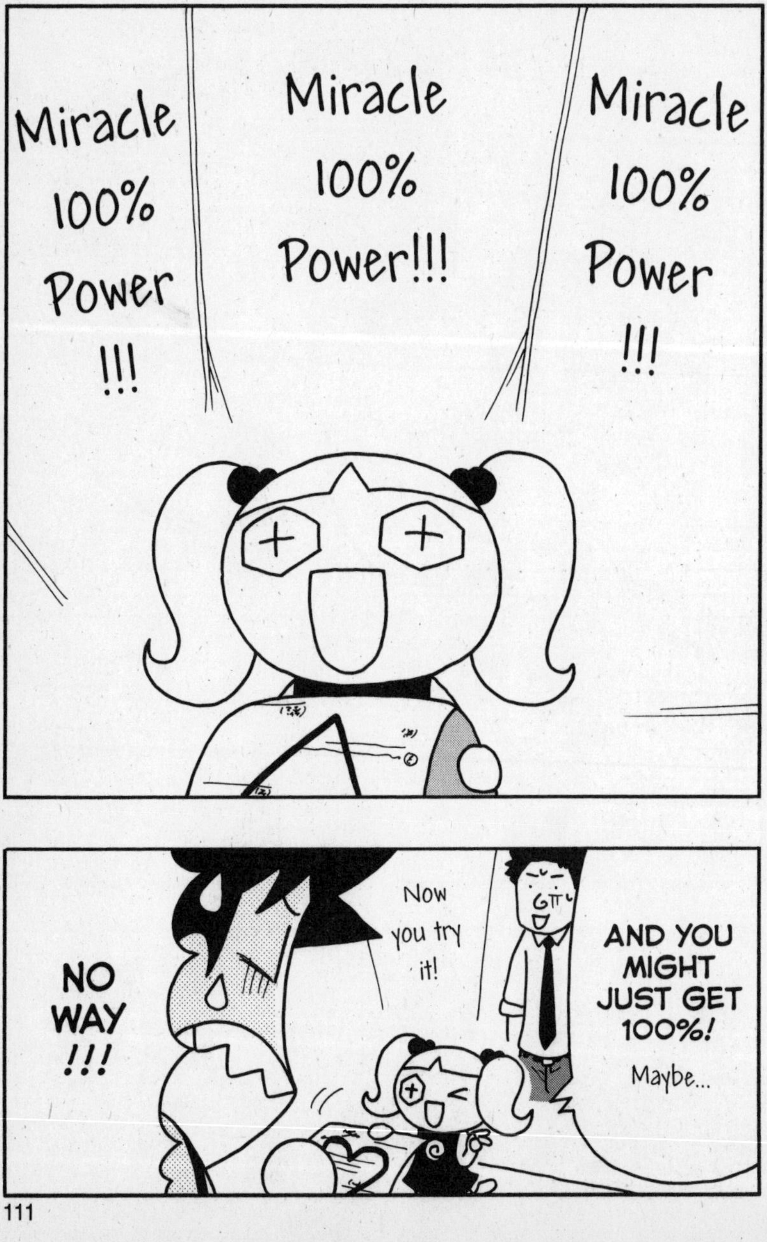
Miracle 100% Power !!!
Miracle 100% Power!!!
Miracle 100% Power !!!
Now you try it!
AND YOU MIGHT JUST GET 100%!
Maybe...
NO WAY !!!

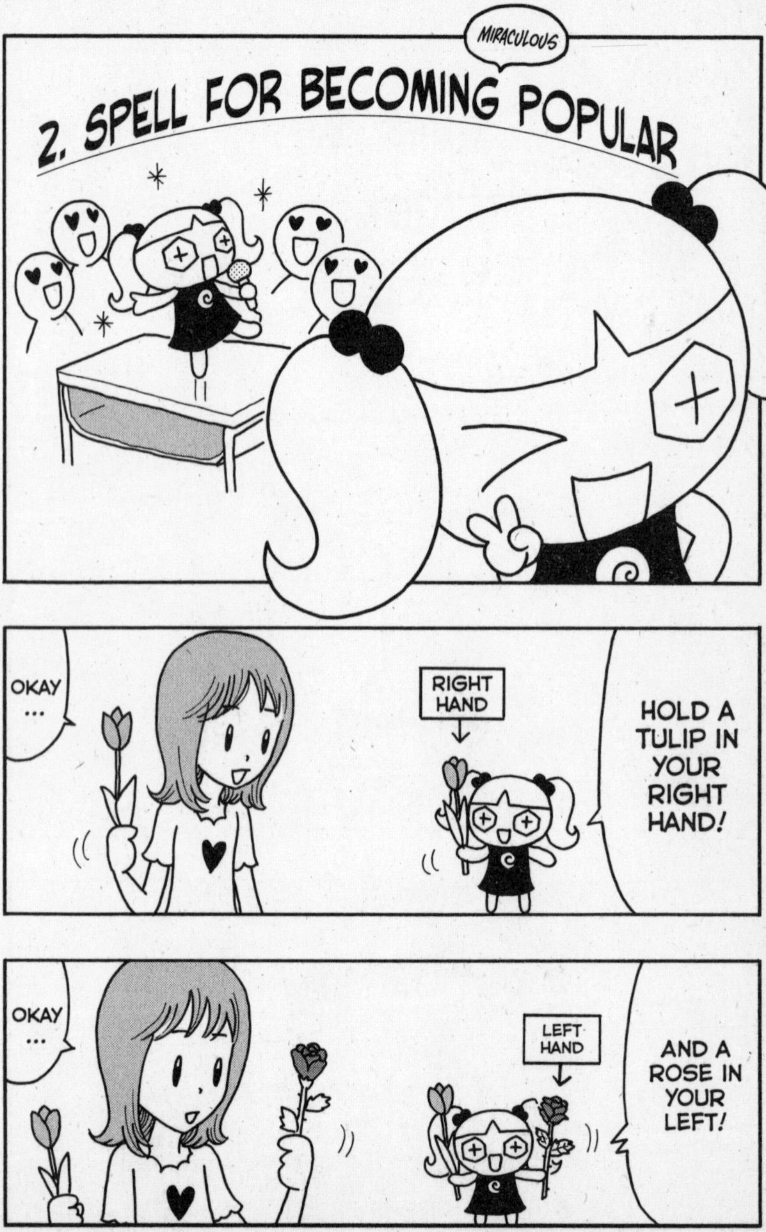
MIRACULOUS
2. SPELL FOR BECOMING POPULAR
HOLD A TULIP IN YOUR RIGHT HAND!
RIGHT HAND
OKAY ...
AND A ROSE IN YOUR LEFT!
LEFT HAND
OKAY ...

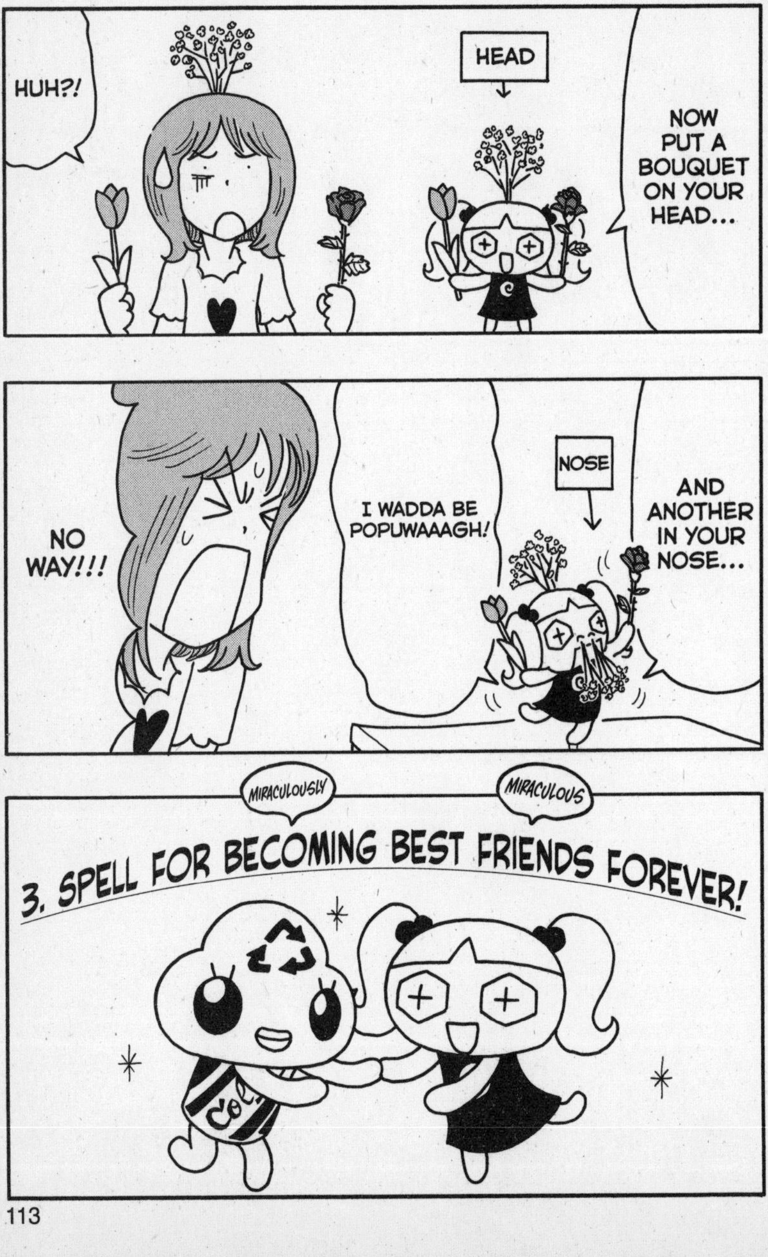
NOW PUT A BOUQUET ON YOUR HEAD...
HEAD
HUH?!
AND ANOTHER IN YOUR NOSE...
NOSE
I WADDA BE POPUWAAAGH!
NO WAY!!!
MIRACULOUS
MIRACULOUSLY
3. SPELL FOR BECOMING BEST FRIENDS FOREVER!

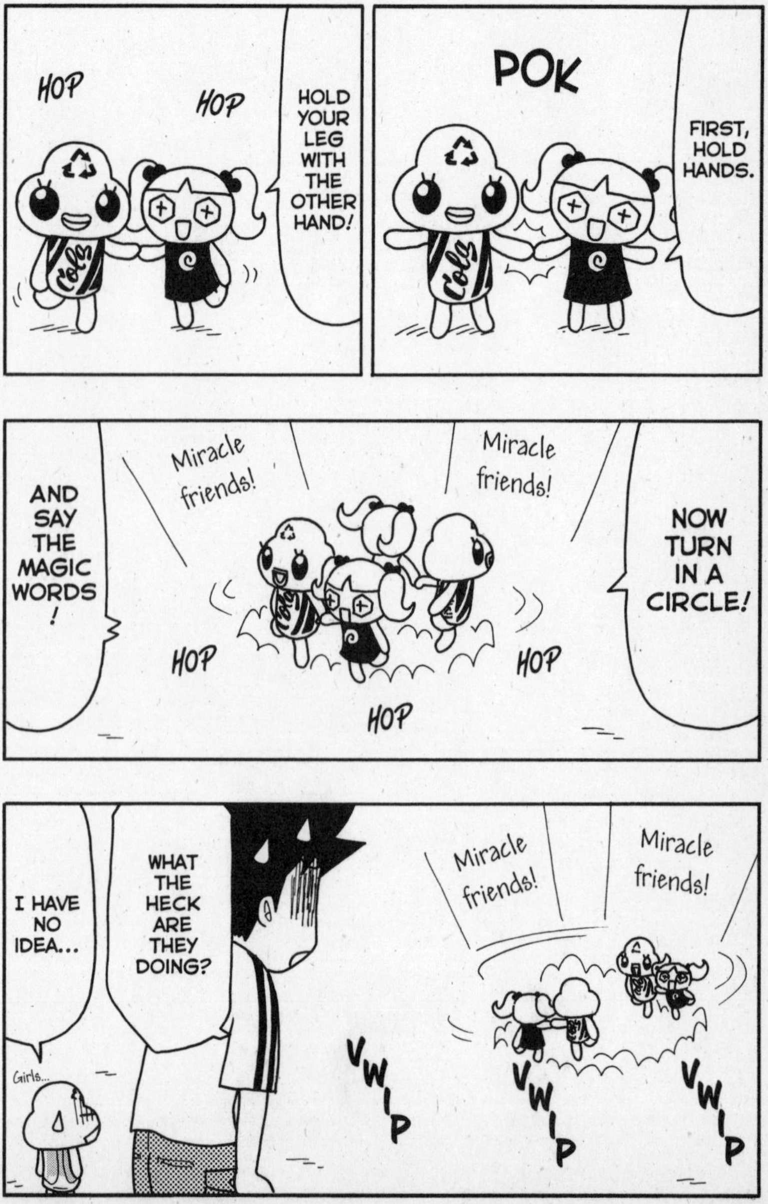
POK
FIRST, HOLD HANDS.
HOLD YOUR LEG WITH THE OTHER HAND!
HOP
HOP
NOW TURN IN A CIRCLE!
Miracle friends!
Miracle friends!
AND SAY THE MAGIC WORDS!
HOP
HOP
HOP
Miracle friends!
Miracle friends!
VWIP
VWIP
VWIP
WHAT THE HECK ARE THEY DOING?
I HAVE NO IDEA...
Girls...

CHAPTER 12 That's Not Punny!

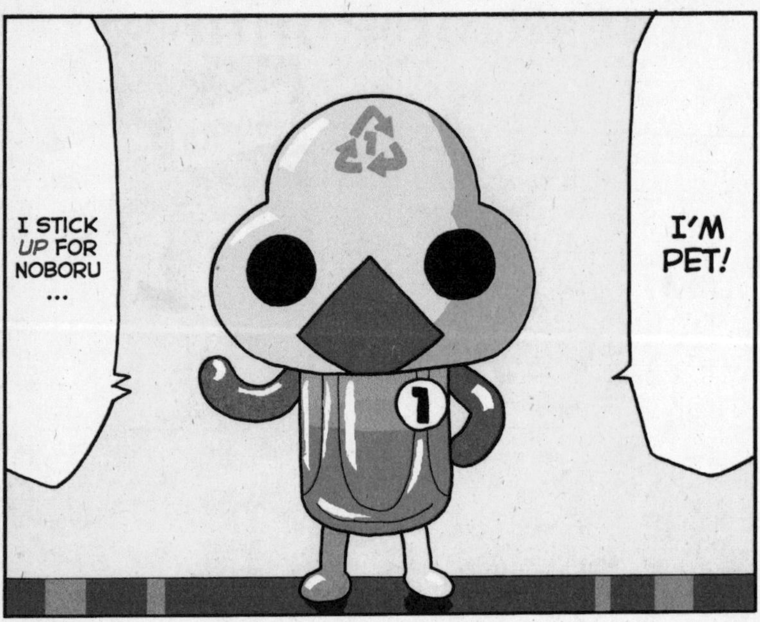
I'M PET!
I STICK *UP* FOR NOBORU ...

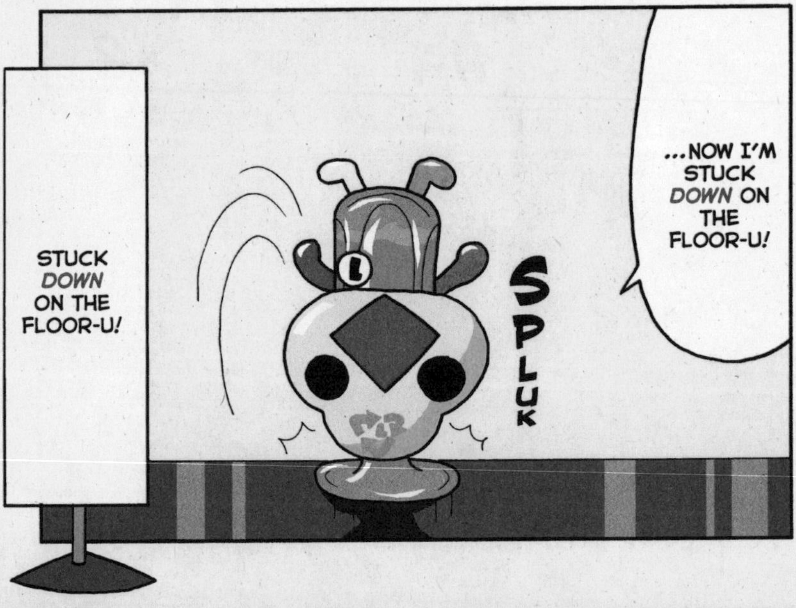
...NOW I'M STUCK *DOWN* ON THE FLOOR-U!
SPLUK
STUCK *DOWN* ON THE FLOOR-U!

CHAPTER 12
That's Not Punny!

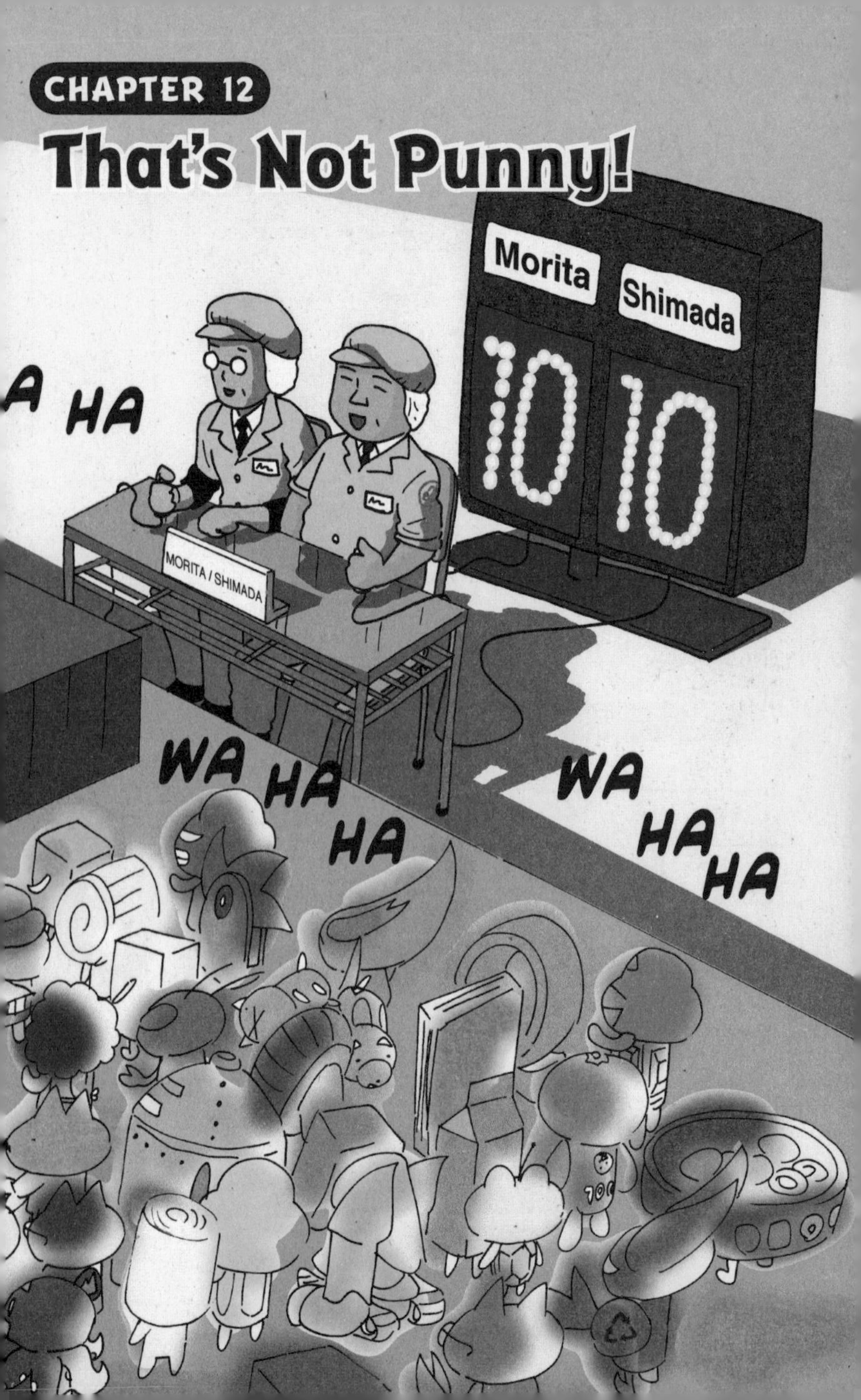
Morita
Shimada
10
10
MORITA / SHIMADA
WA HA HA
WA HA HA
A HA

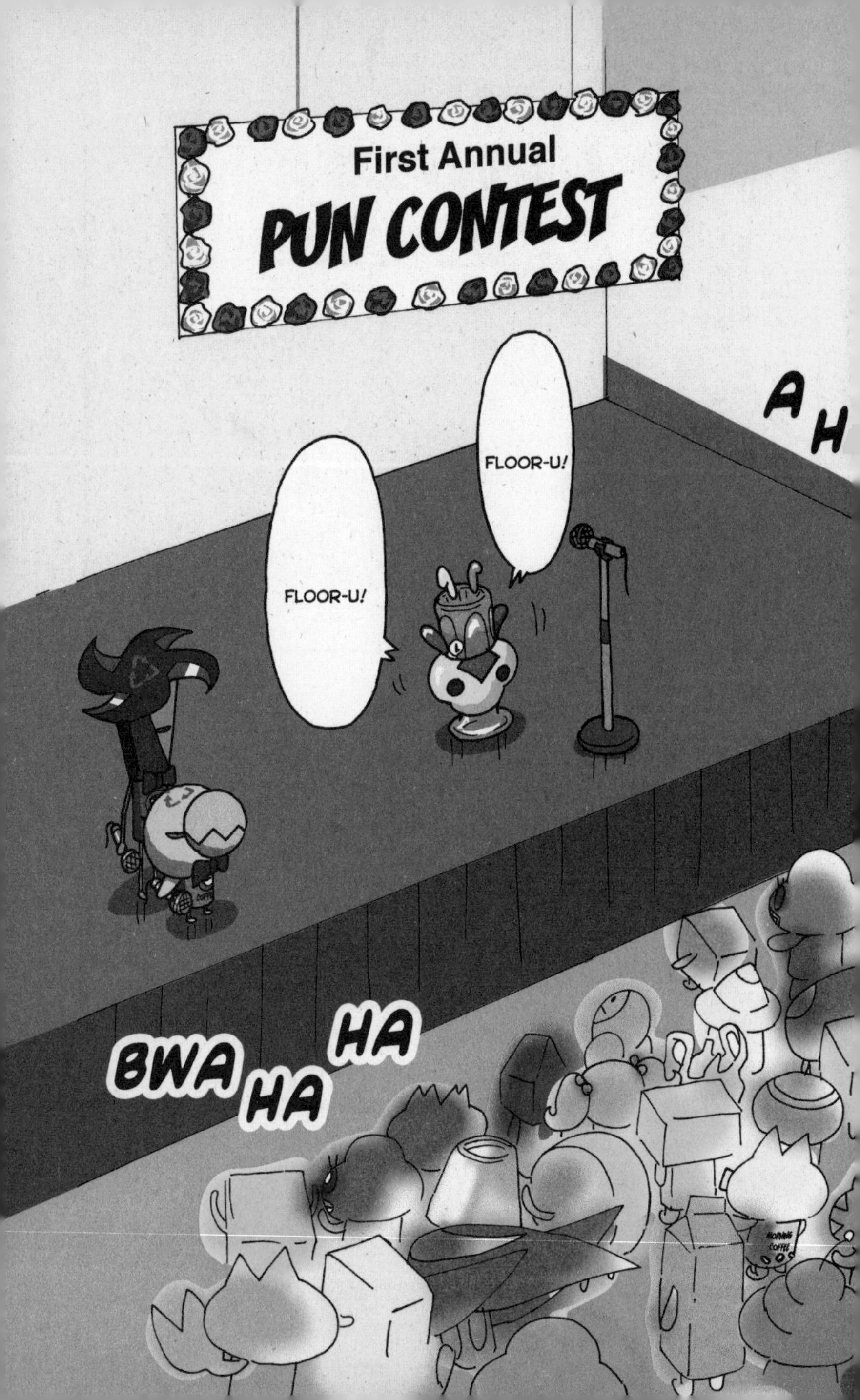
First Annual
PUN CONTEST
AH
FLOOR-U!
FLOOR-U!
BWA HA HA

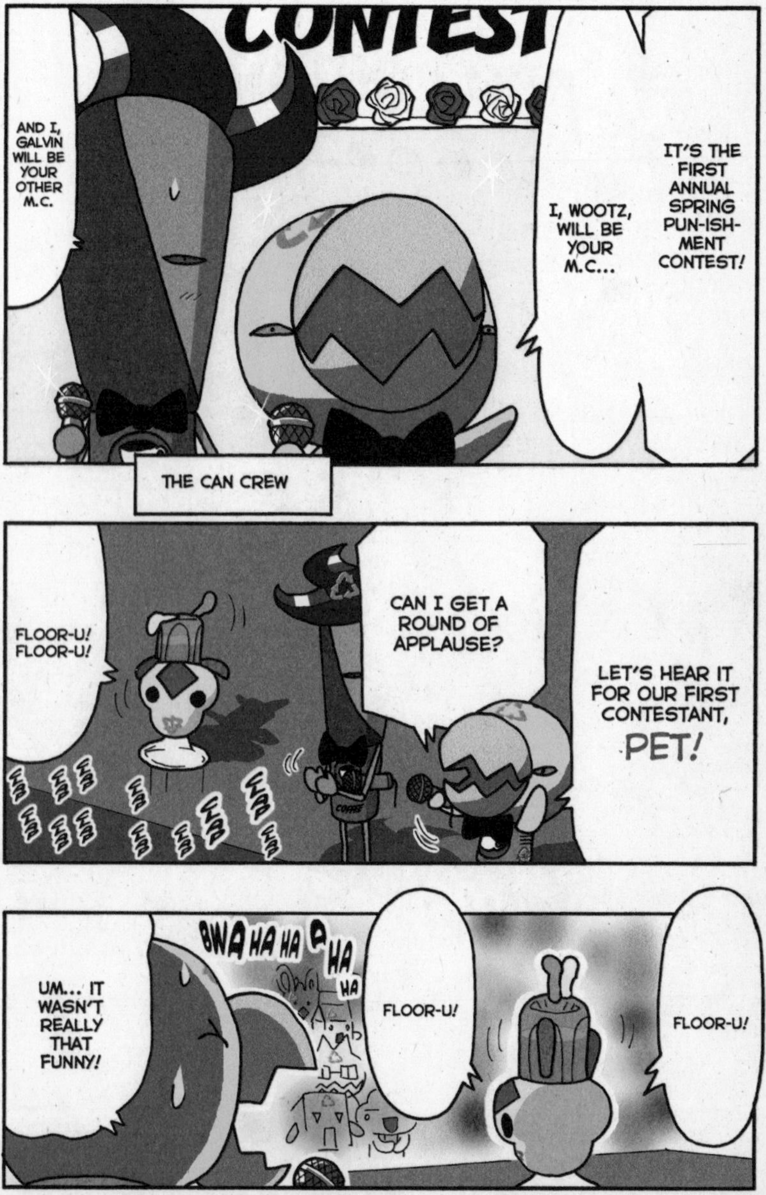
CONTEST
IT'S THE FIRST ANNUAL SPRING PUN-ISH-MENT CONTEST!
I, WOOTZ, WILL BE YOUR M.C...
AND I, GALVIN WILL BE YOUR OTHER M.C.
THE CAN CREW
LET'S HEAR IT FOR OUR FIRST CONTESTANT, PET!
CAN I GET A ROUND OF APPLAUSE?
FLOOR-U! FLOOR-U!
FLOOR-U!
FLOOR-U!
BWA HA HA A HA HA
UM... IT WASN'T REALLY THAT FUNNY!

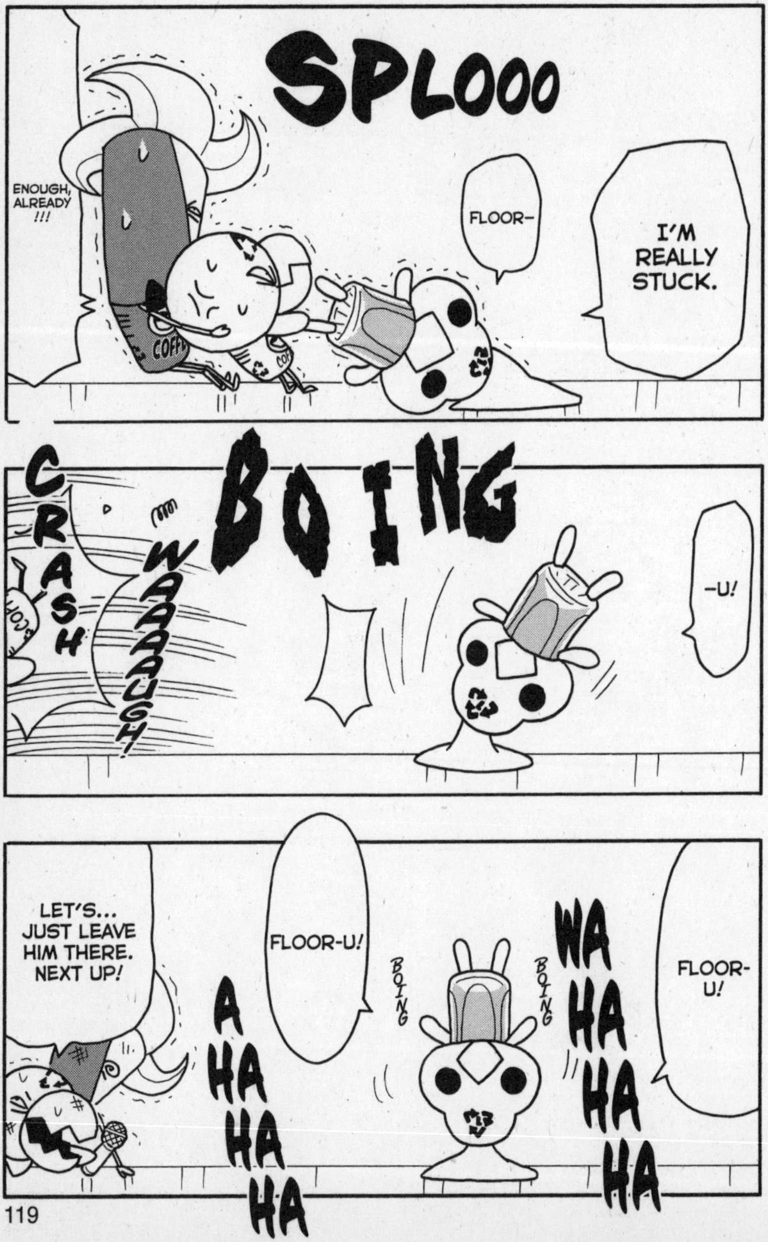
SPLOOO
I'M REALLY STUCK.
FLOOR-
ENOUGH, ALREADY!!!
-U!
BOING
WAAAAAUGH!
CRASH
FLOOR-U!
WA HA HA HA HA
BOING
FLOOR-U!
BOING
A HA HA HA HA
LET'S... JUST LEAVE HIM THERE. NEXT UP!

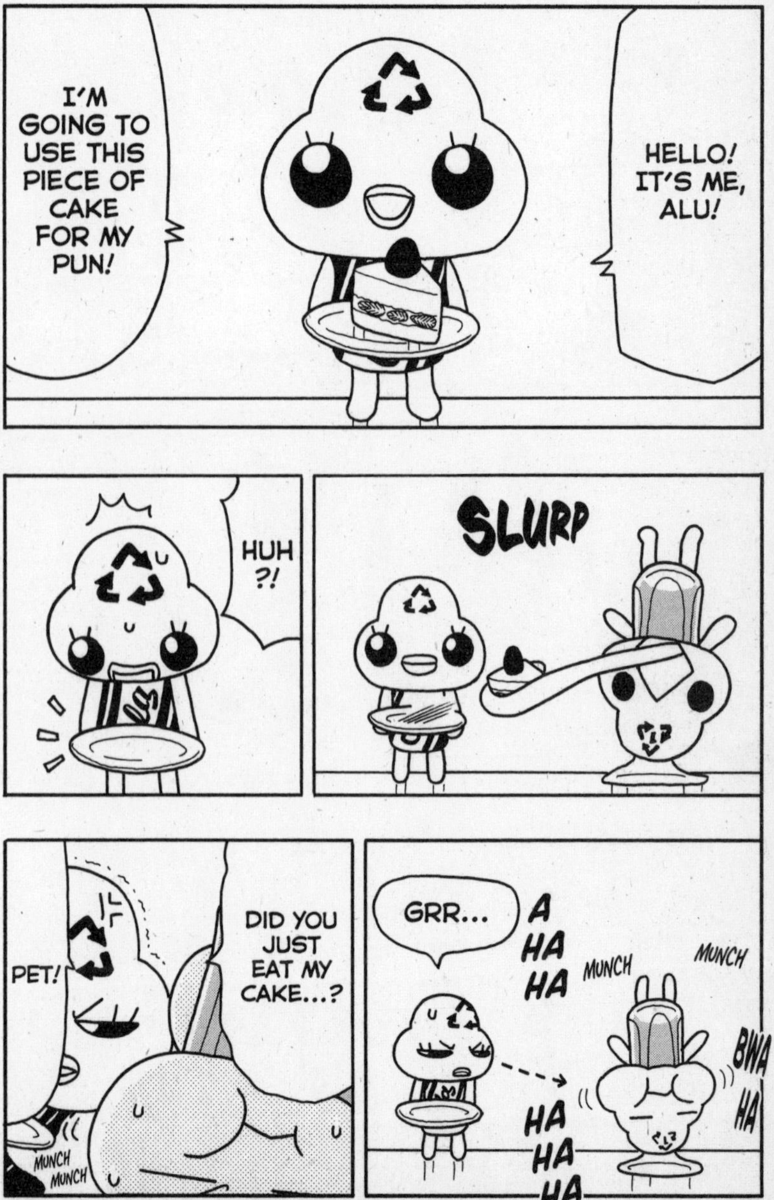
HELLO! IT'S ME, ALU!
I'M GOING TO USE THIS PIECE OF CAKE FOR MY PUN!
SLURP
HUH ?!
MUNCH
GRR...
A HA HA
MUNCH
BWA HA
HA HA HA
DID YOU JUST EAT MY CAKE...?
PET!
MUNCH MUNCH

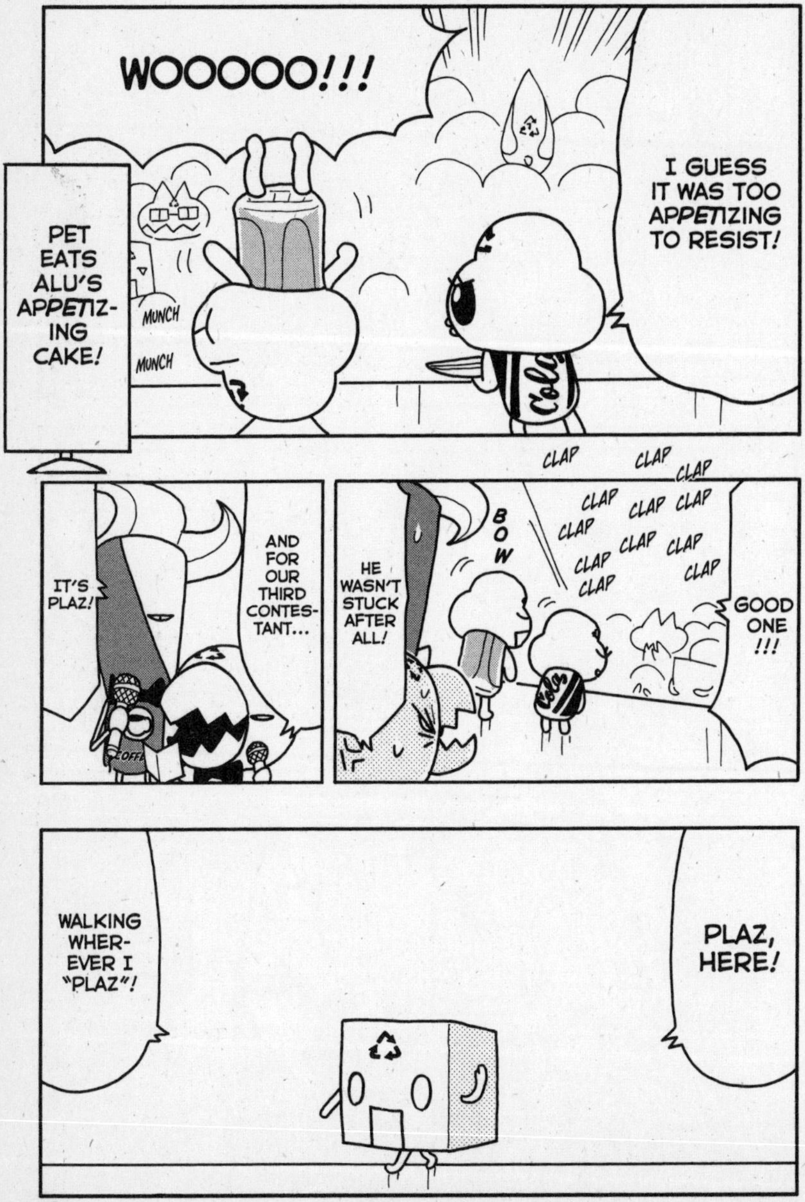
WOOOOO!!!
I GUESS IT WAS TOO APPETIZING TO RESIST!
PET EATS ALU'S APPETIZ-ING CAKE!
MUNCH
MUNCH
CLAP CLAP CLAP CLAP CLAP CLAP CLAP CLAP CLAP CLAP CLAP CLAP CLAP
GOOD ONE!!!
BOW
HE WASN'T STUCK AFTER ALL!
AND FOR OUR THIRD CONTES-TANT...
IT'S PLAZ!
PLAZ, HERE!
WALKING WHER-EVER I "PLAZ"!

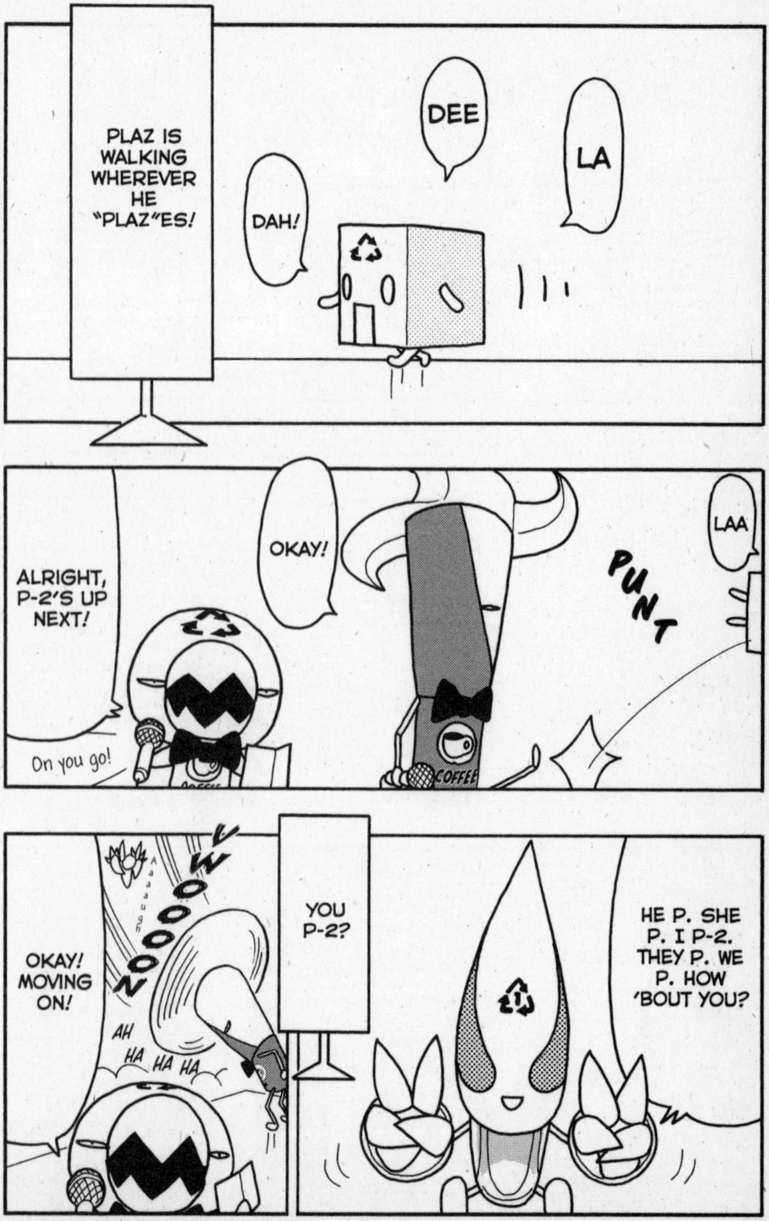
LA
DEE
DAH!
PLAZ IS WALKING WHEREVER HE "PLAZ"ES!
LAA
PUNT
OKAY!
ALRIGHT, P-2'S UP NEXT!
On you go!
HE P. SHE P. I P-2. THEY P. WE P. HOW 'BOUT YOU?
YOU P-2?
WOOOOOOOON
Aaaaaugh
OKAY! MOVING ON!
AH HA HA HA

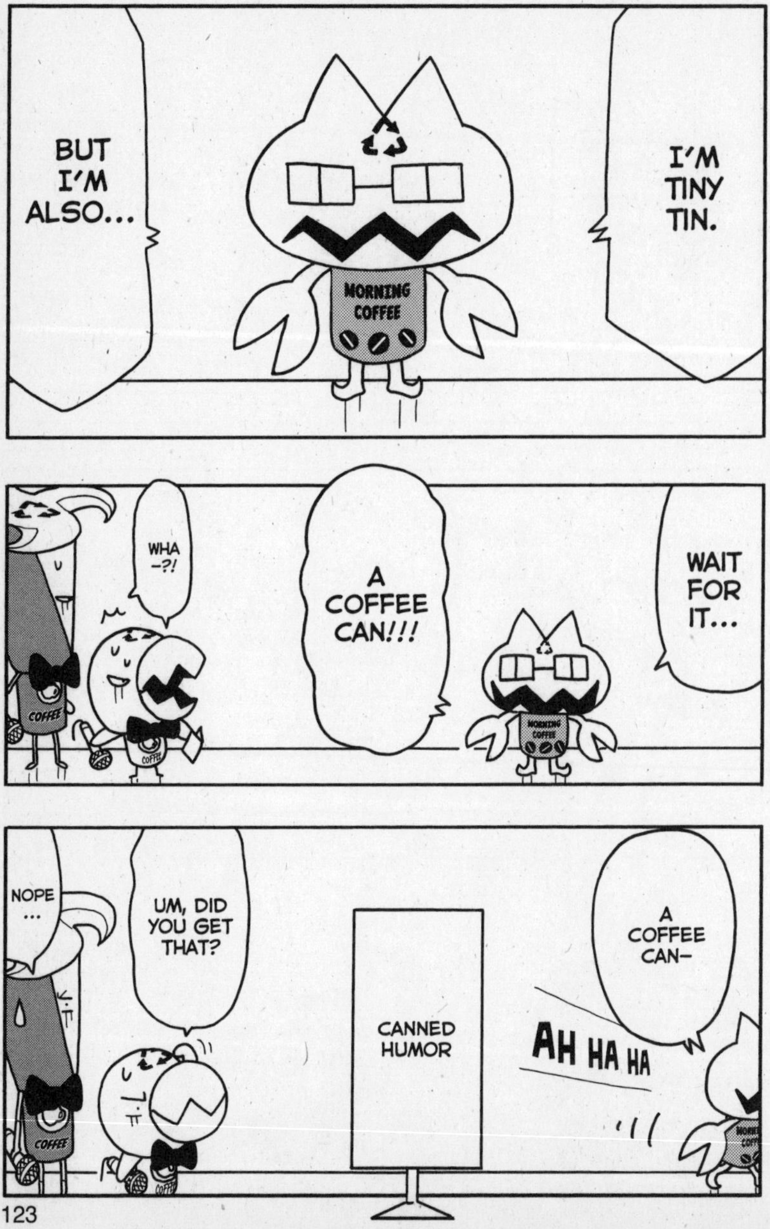
I'M TINY TIN.
BUT I'M ALSO...
MORNING COFFEE
WAIT FOR IT...
A COFFEE CAN!!!
WHA-?!
COFFEE
A COFFEE CAN-
AH HA HA
CANNED HUMOR
UM, DID YOU GET THAT?
NOPE...
COFFEE

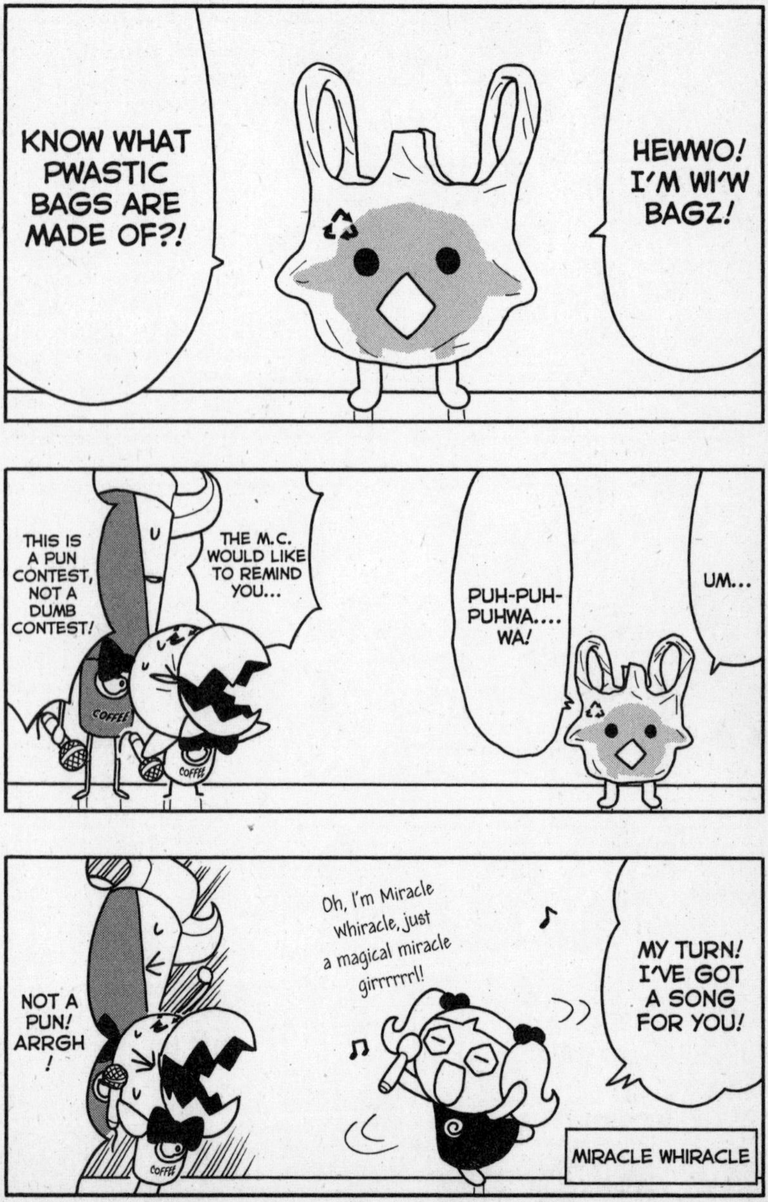
HEWWO! I'M WI'W BAGZ!
KNOW WHAT PWASTIC BAGS ARE MADE OF?!
UM...
PUH-PUH-PUHWA.... WA!
THE M.C. WOULD LIKE TO REMIND YOU...
THIS IS A PUN CONTEST, NOT A DUMB CONTEST!
MY TURN! I'VE GOT A SONG FOR YOU!
Oh, I'm Miracle Whiracle, just a magical miracle girrrrrrl!
MIRACLE WHIRACLE
NOT A PUN! ARRGH!

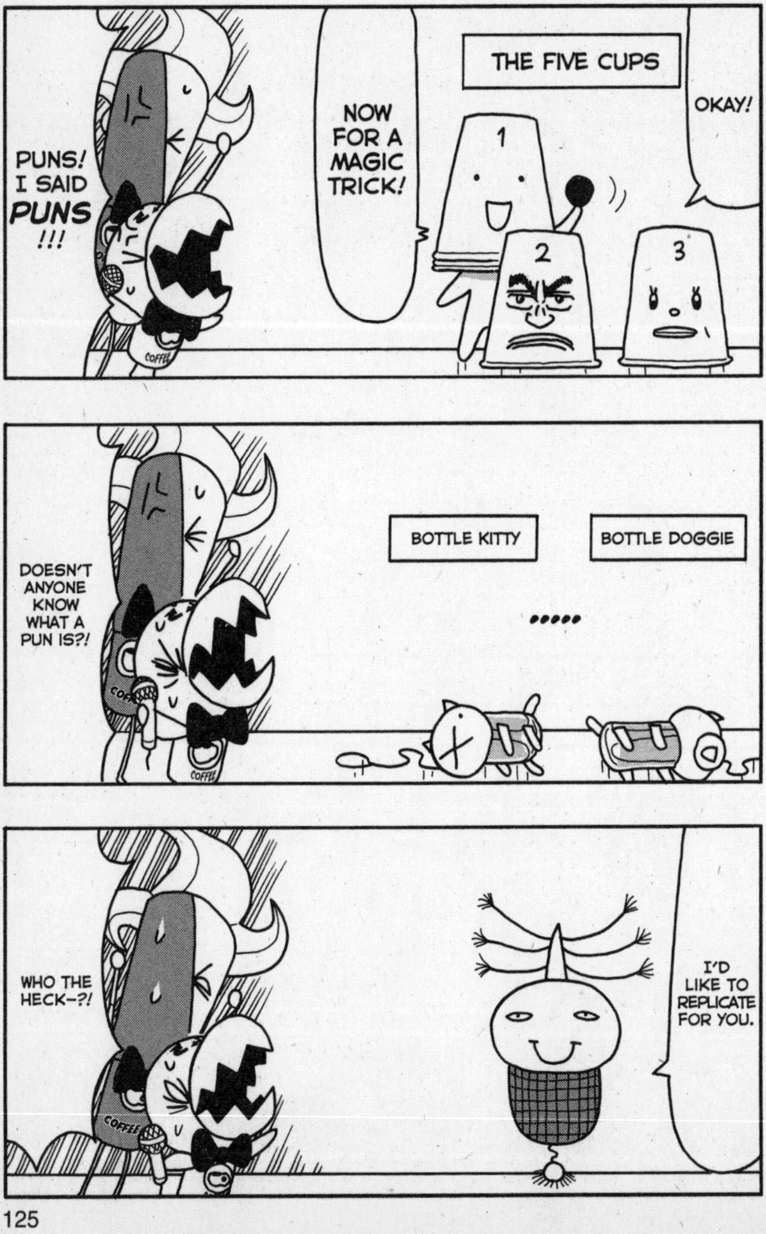
OKAY!
THE FIVE CUPS
1
2
3
NOW FOR A MAGIC TRICK!
PUNS! I SAID PUNS!!!
BOTTLE DOGGIE
BOTTLE KITTY
.....
DOESN'T ANYONE KNOW WHAT A PUN IS?!
I'D LIKE TO REPLICATE FOR YOU.
WHO THE HECK-?!

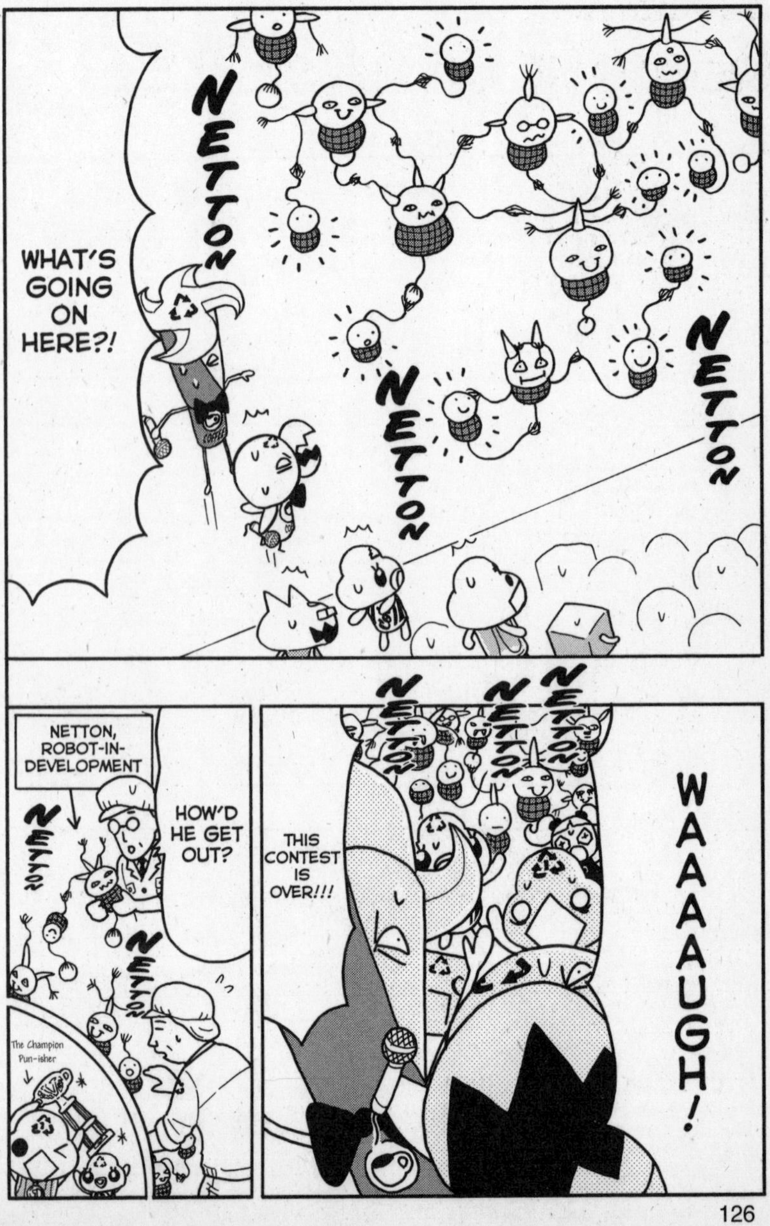
NETTON
NETTON
NETTON
WHAT'S GOING ON HERE?!
NETTON
NETTON
NETTON
WAAAAUGH!
THIS CONTEST IS OVER!!!
HOW'D HE GET OUT?
NETTON, ROBOT-IN-DEVELOPMENT
NETTON
NETTON
The Champion Pun-isher

CHAPTER 13

Remote Control PET

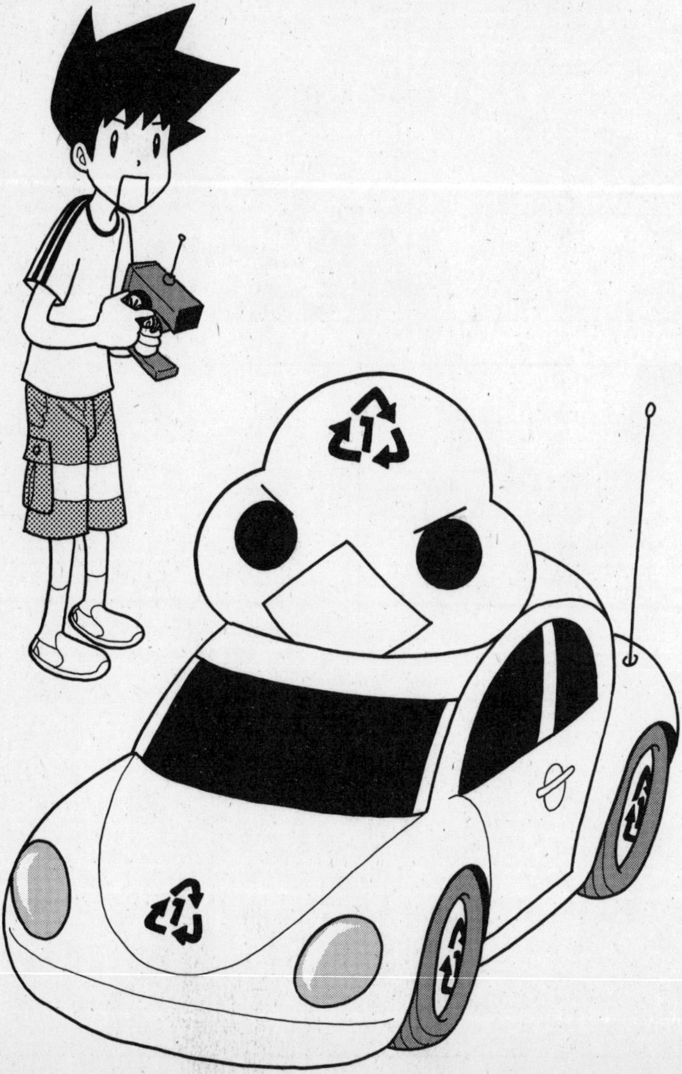

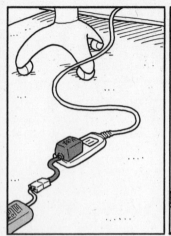

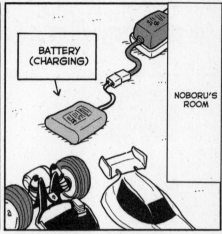

BATTERY
(CHARGING)

NOBORU'S
ROOM

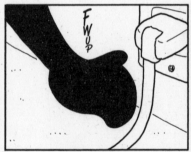

FWUP

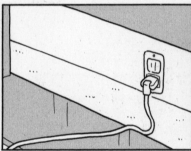

I'M
READY,
GUYS!

SNK

OKAY,
THE
BATTERY
SHOULD
BE
CHARGED!

YA

NK

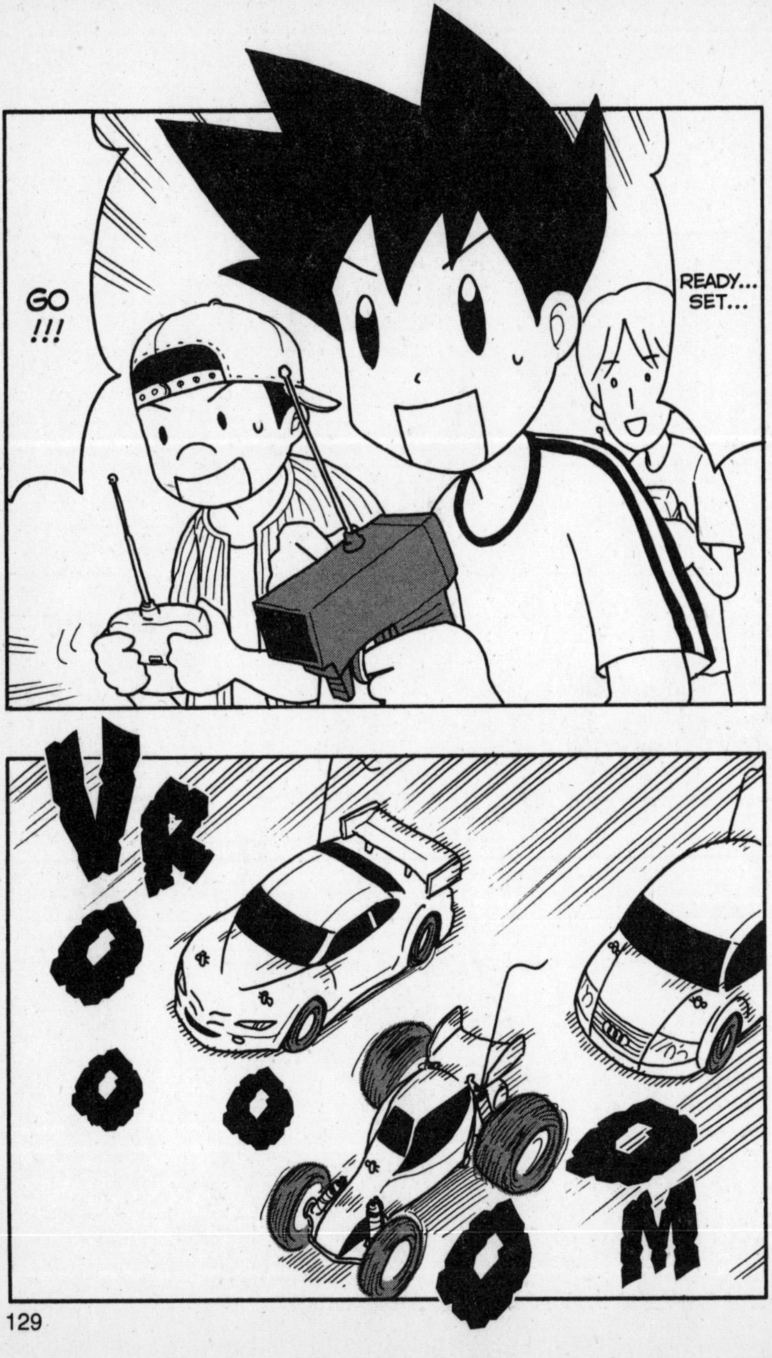
READY... SET...
GO !!!
VROOOOOOM

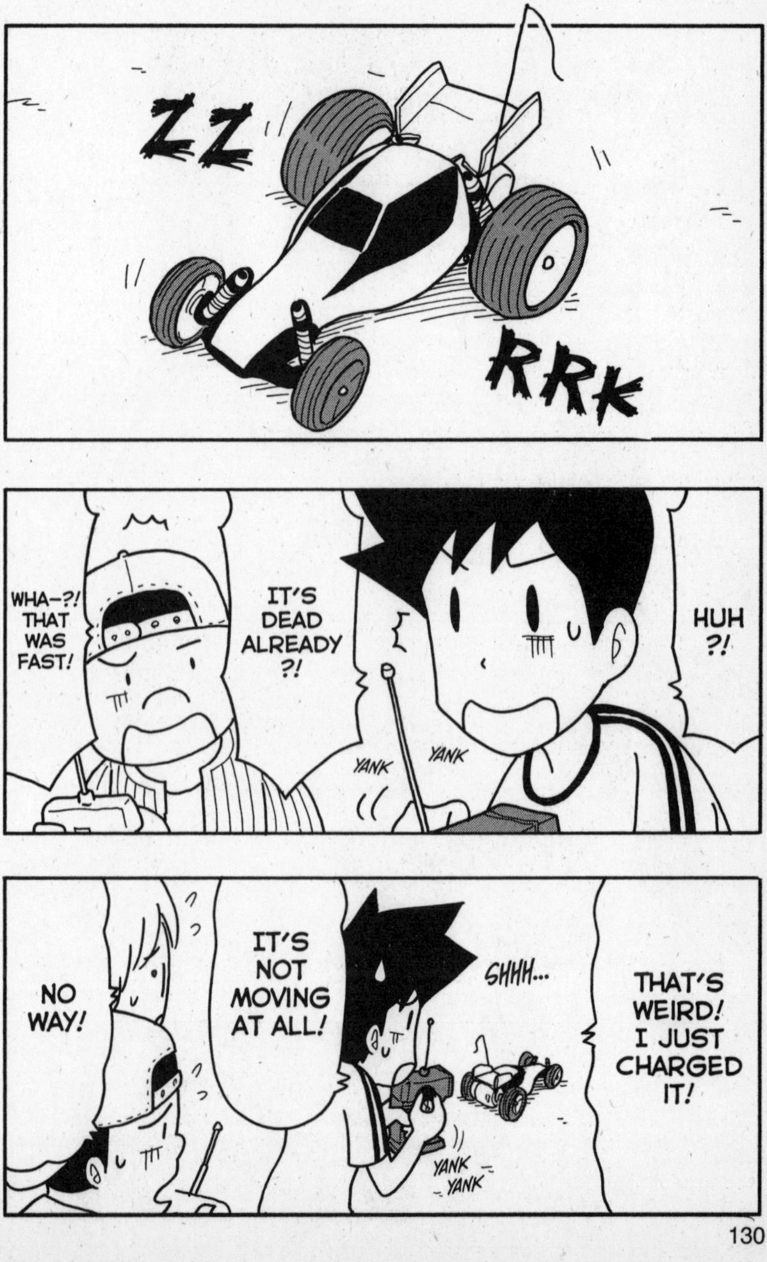
ZZ
RRK
HUH?!
YANK
YANK
IT'S DEAD ALREADY?!
WHA-?! THAT WAS FAST!
THAT'S WEIRD! I JUST CHARGED IT!
SHHH...
YANK YANK
IT'S NOT MOVING AT ALL!
NO WAY!

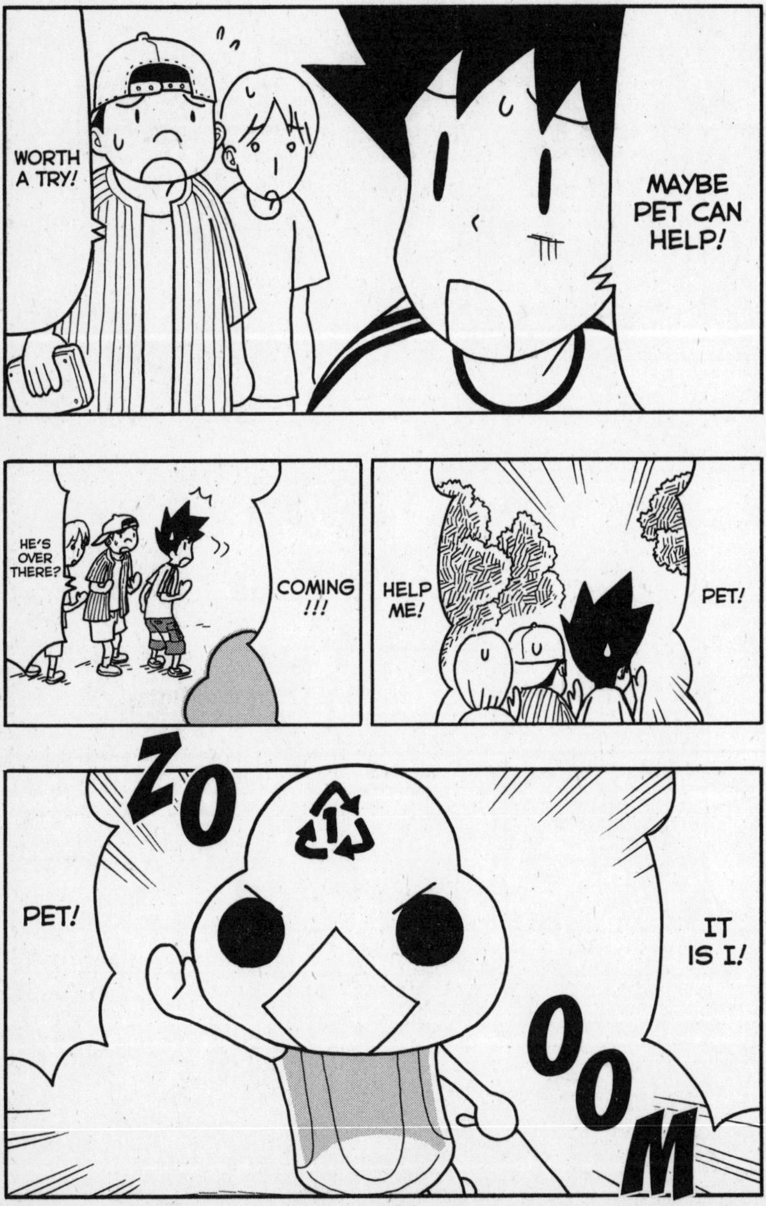
MAYBE PET CAN HELP!
WORTH A TRY!
PET!
HELP ME!
COMING!!!
HE'S OVER THERE?
IT IS I!
PET!
ZOOOM

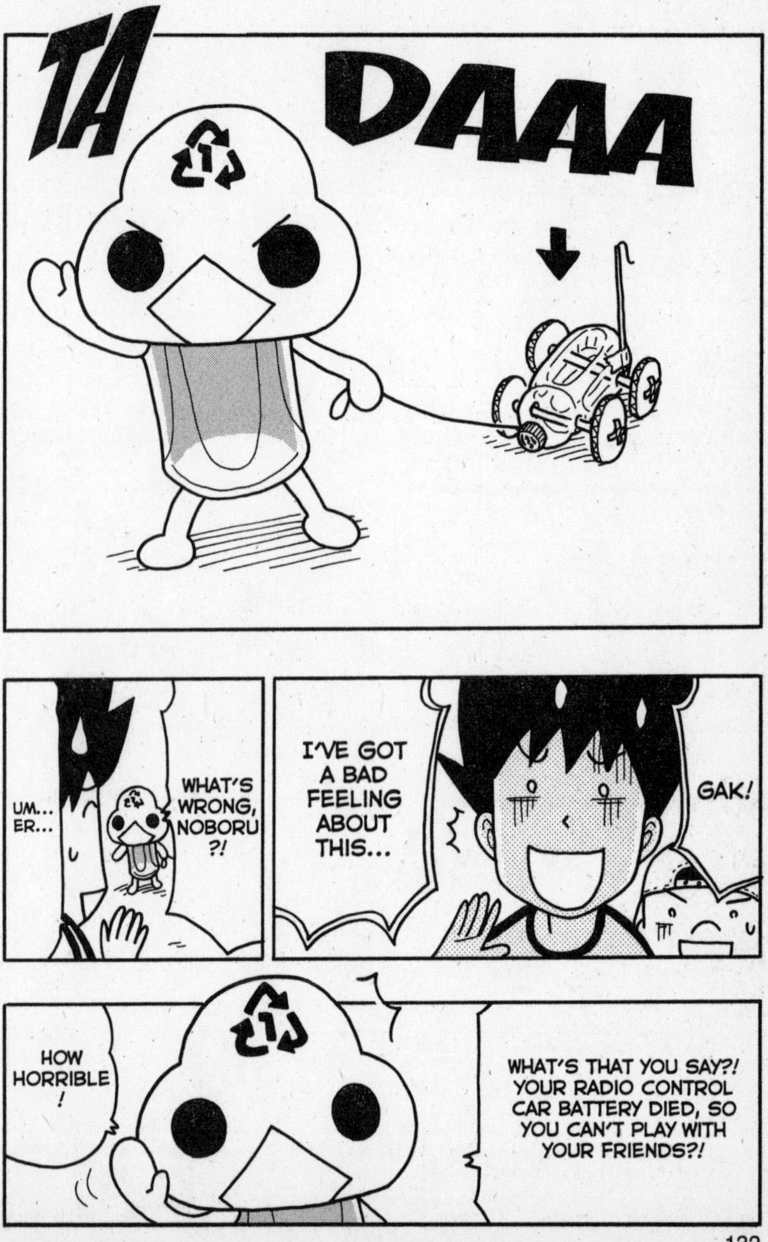
TA DAAA
GAK!
I'VE GOT A BAD FEELING ABOUT THIS...
WHAT'S WRONG, NOBORU?!
UM... ER...
WHAT'S THAT YOU SAY?! YOUR RADIO CONTROL CAR BATTERY DIED, SO YOU CAN'T PLAY WITH YOUR FRIENDS?!
HOW HORRIBLE!

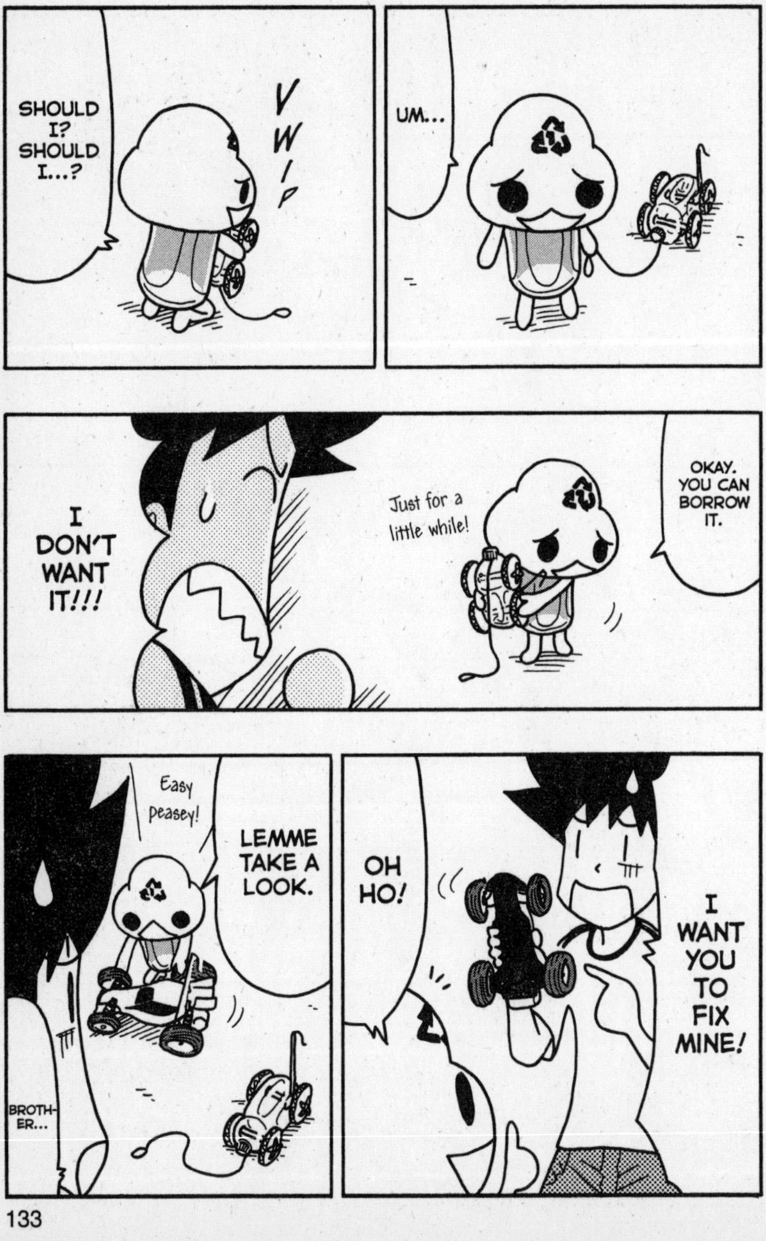
UM...
SHOULD I? SHOULD I...?
VWIP
OKAY. YOU CAN BORROW IT.
Just for a little while!
I DON'T WANT IT!!!
I WANT YOU TO FIX MINE!
OH HO!
LEMME TAKE A LOOK.
Easy peasey!
BROTHER...

WHEE! WHEE!
RATTLE
RATTLE
RATTLE
...THAT'S NOT WHAT I MEANT!!!
SLAM
YOU LOOKED LIKE YOU WERE HAVING FUN!

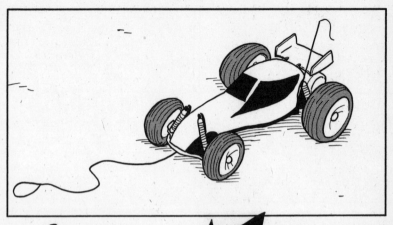

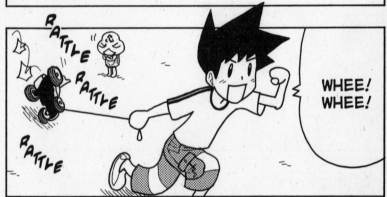

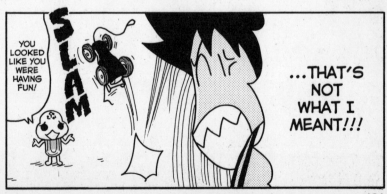

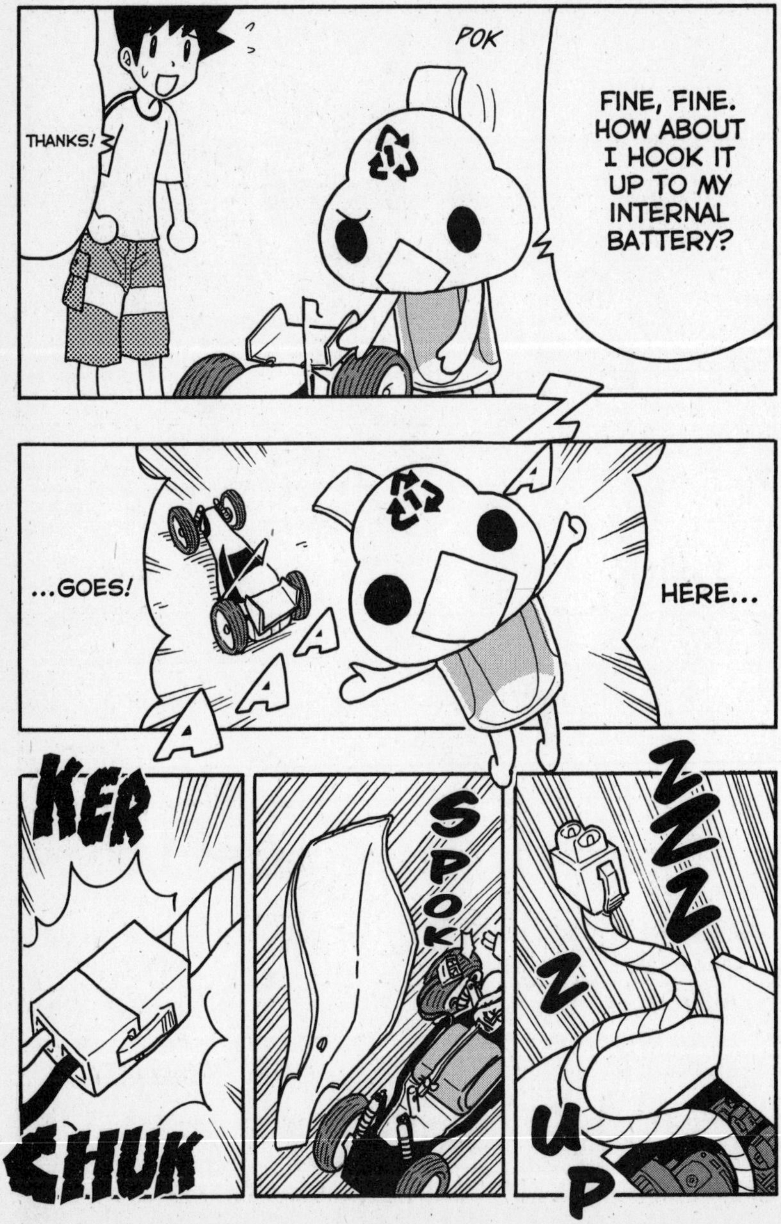
FINE, FINE. HOW ABOUT I HOOK IT UP TO MY INTERNAL BATTERY?
POK
THANKS!
HERE...
ZAAAAA
...GOES!
ZZZZUP
SPOK
KER
CHUK

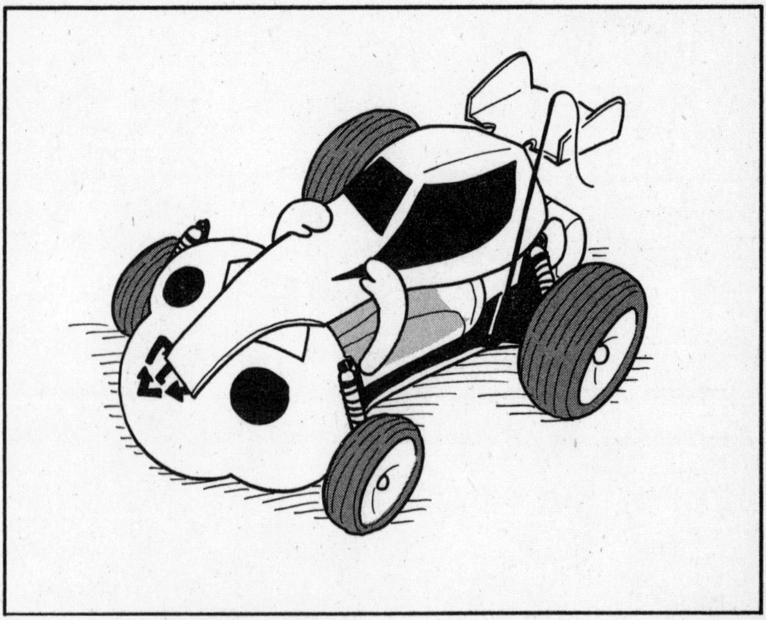

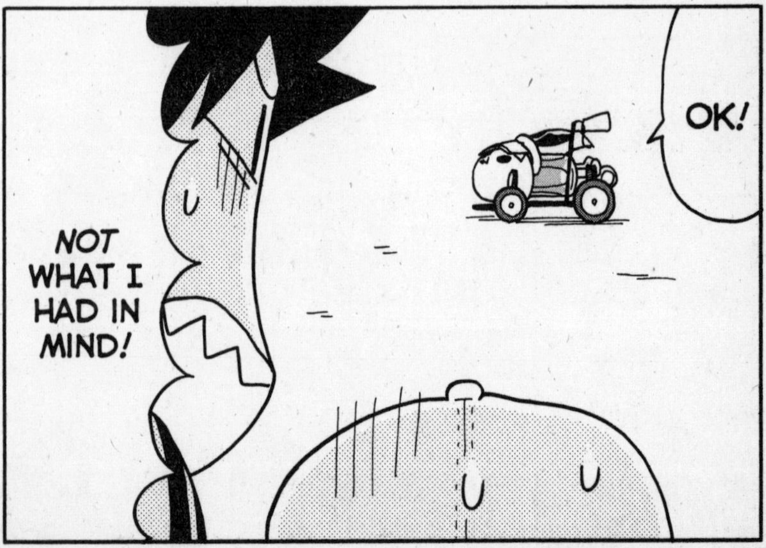
OK!
NOT WHAT I HAD IN MIND!

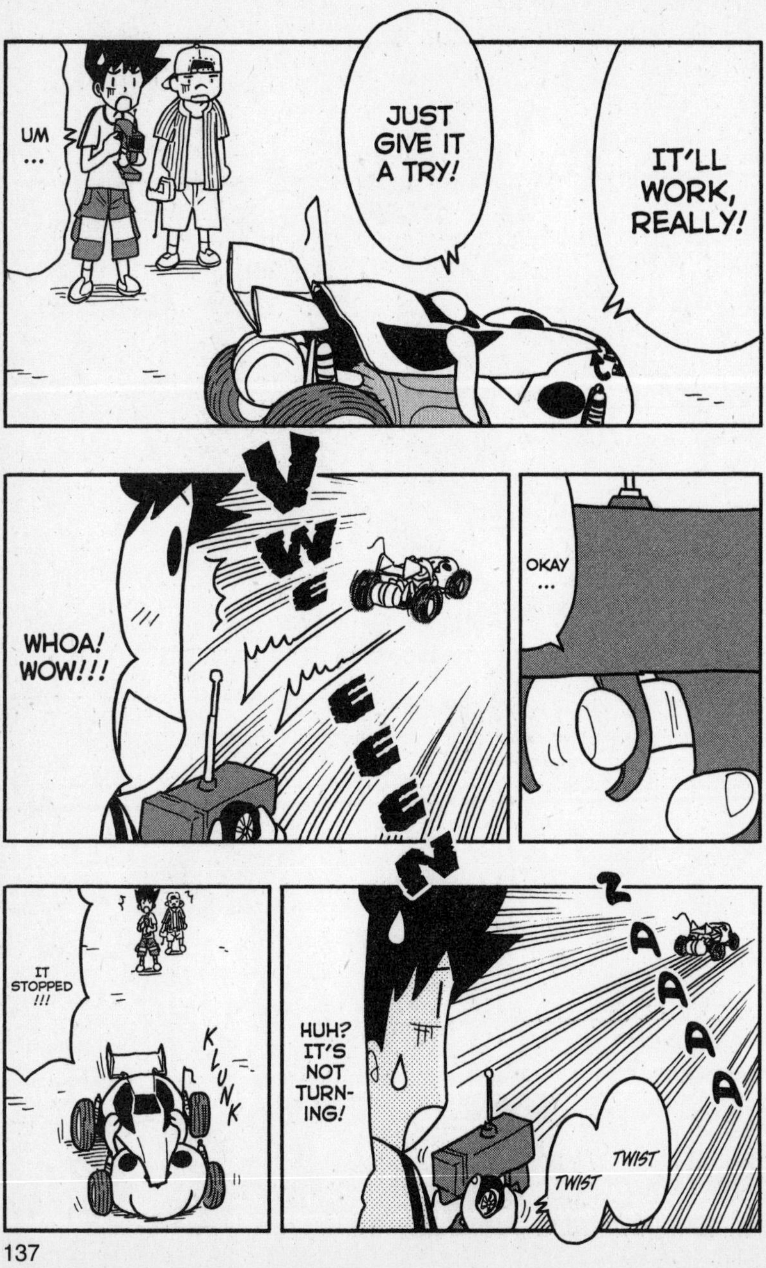
IT'LL WORK, REALLY!
JUST GIVE IT A TRY!
UM ...
OKAY ...
VWEEEEEN
WHOA! WOW!!!
ZAAAAA
TWIST
TWIST
HUH? IT'S NOT TURNING!
KLUNK
IT STOPPED !!!

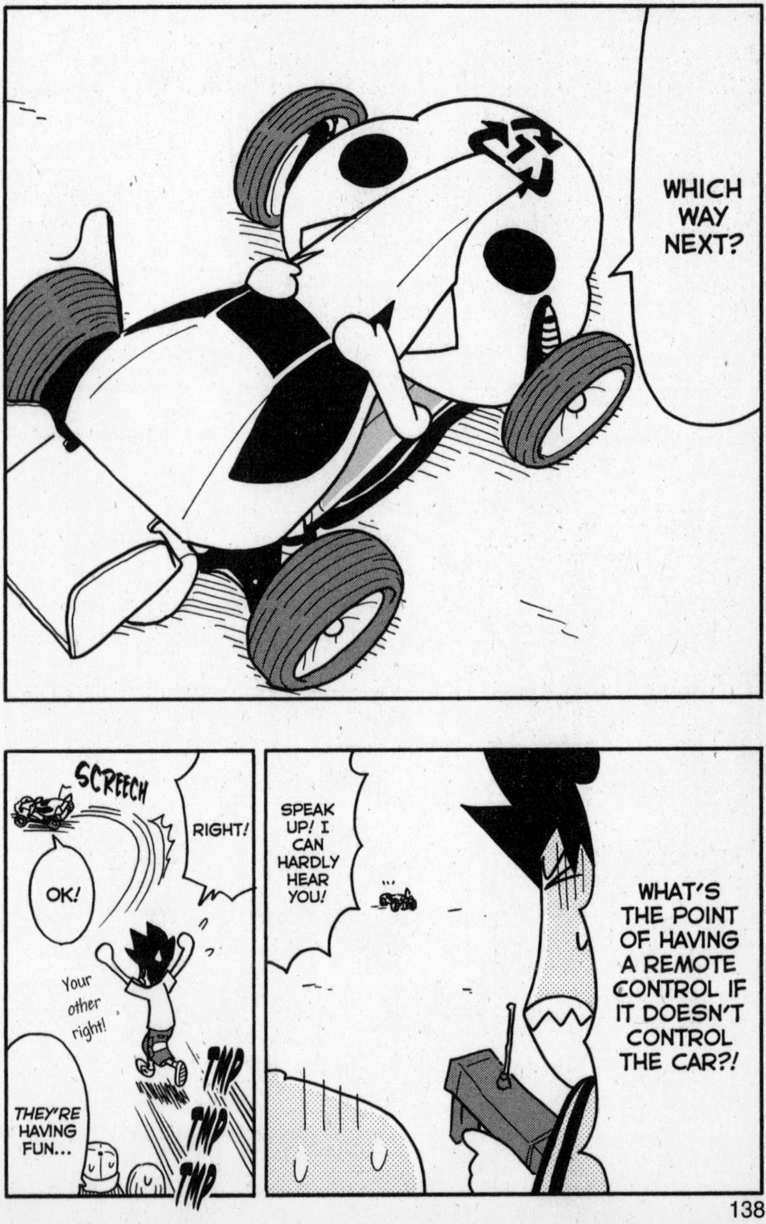
WHICH WAY NEXT?
WHAT'S THE POINT OF HAVING A REMOTE CONTROL IF IT DOESN'T CONTROL THE CAR?!
SPEAK UP! I CAN HARDLY HEAR YOU!
RIGHT!
SCREECH
OK!
Your other right!
TMP
TMP
TMP
THEY'RE HAVING FUN...

CHAPTER 14

The Secret of Netton

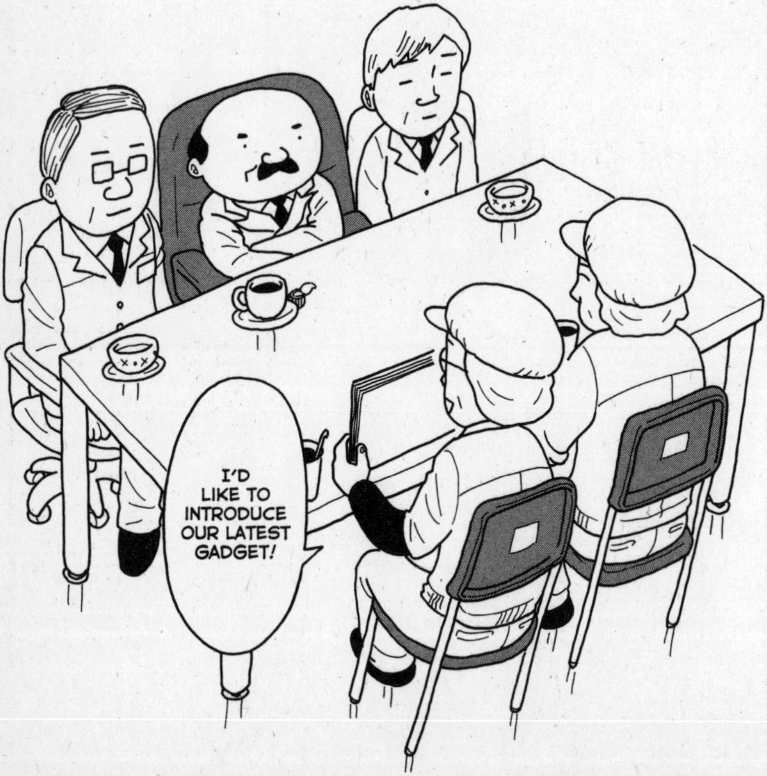
I'D LIKE TO INTRODUCE OUR LATEST GADGET!

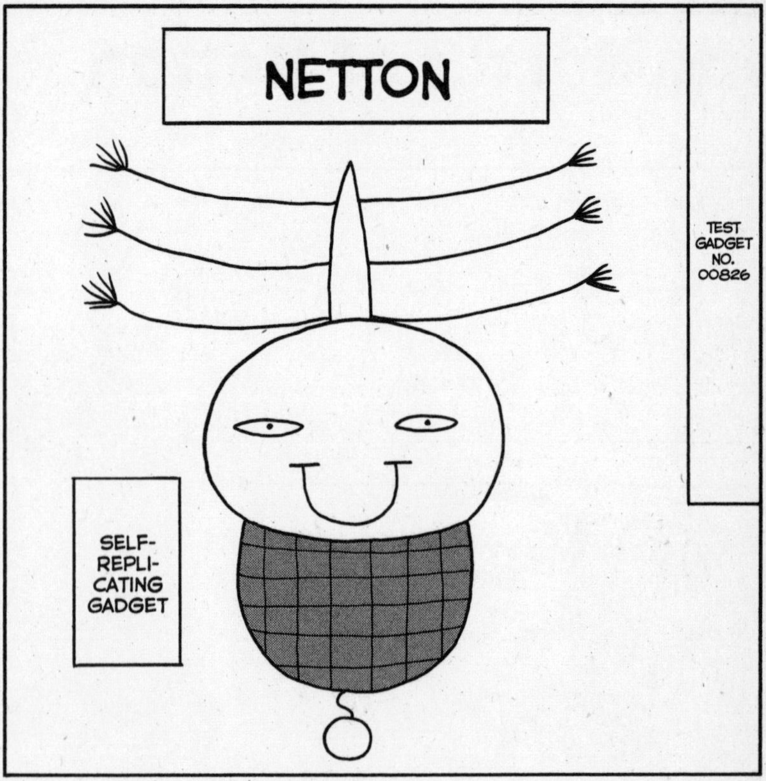
NETTON
TEST GADGET NO. 00826
SELF-REPLICATING GADGET

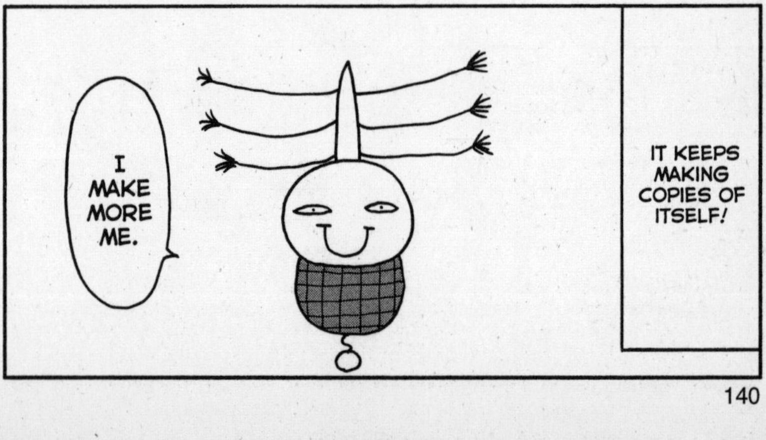
IT KEEPS MAKING COPIES OF ITSELF!
I MAKE MORE ME.

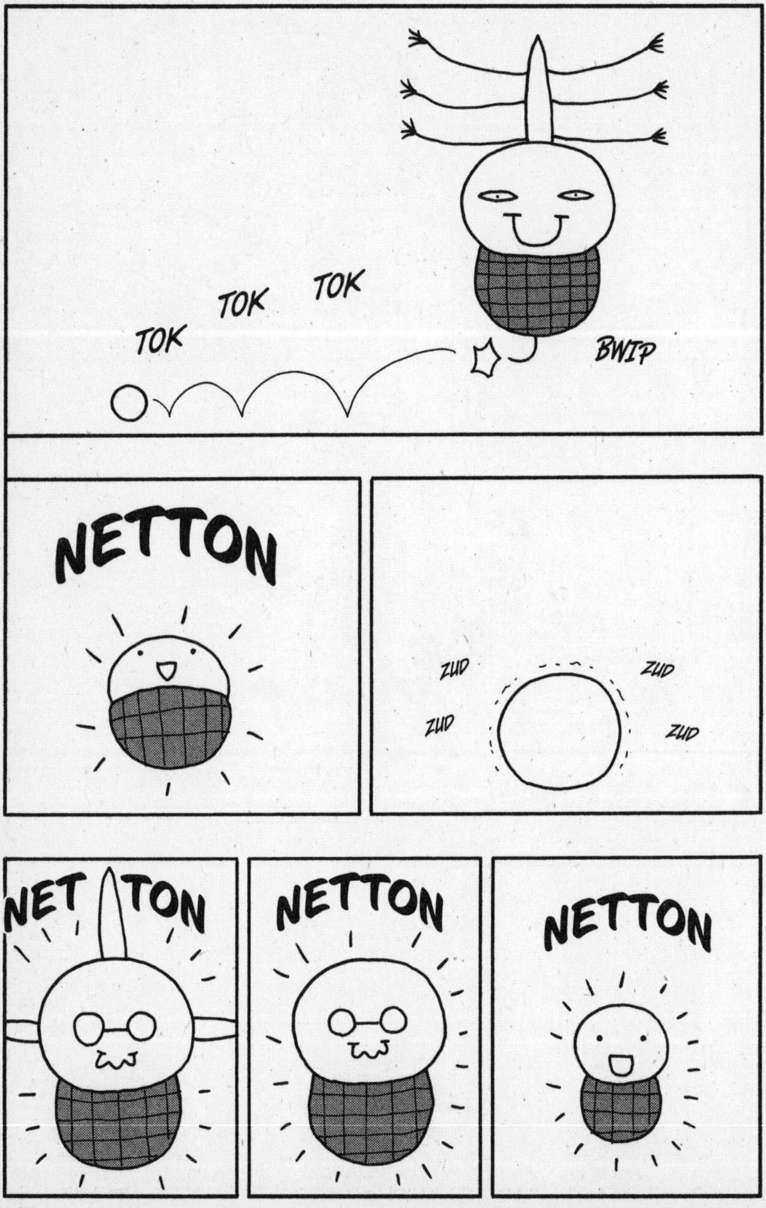

TOK
TOK
TOK
BWIP
ZUD
ZUD
ZUD
ZUD
NETTON
NETTON
NETTON
NET TON

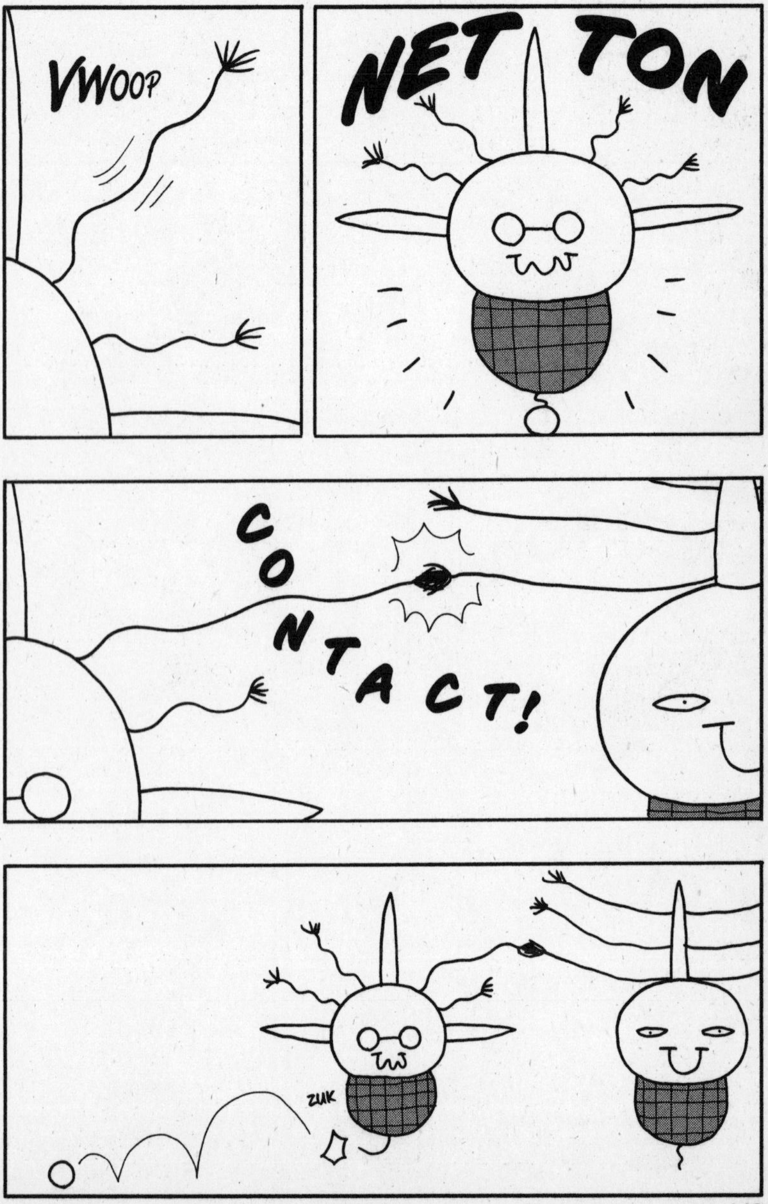
NET TON
VWOOP
CONTACT!
ZUK

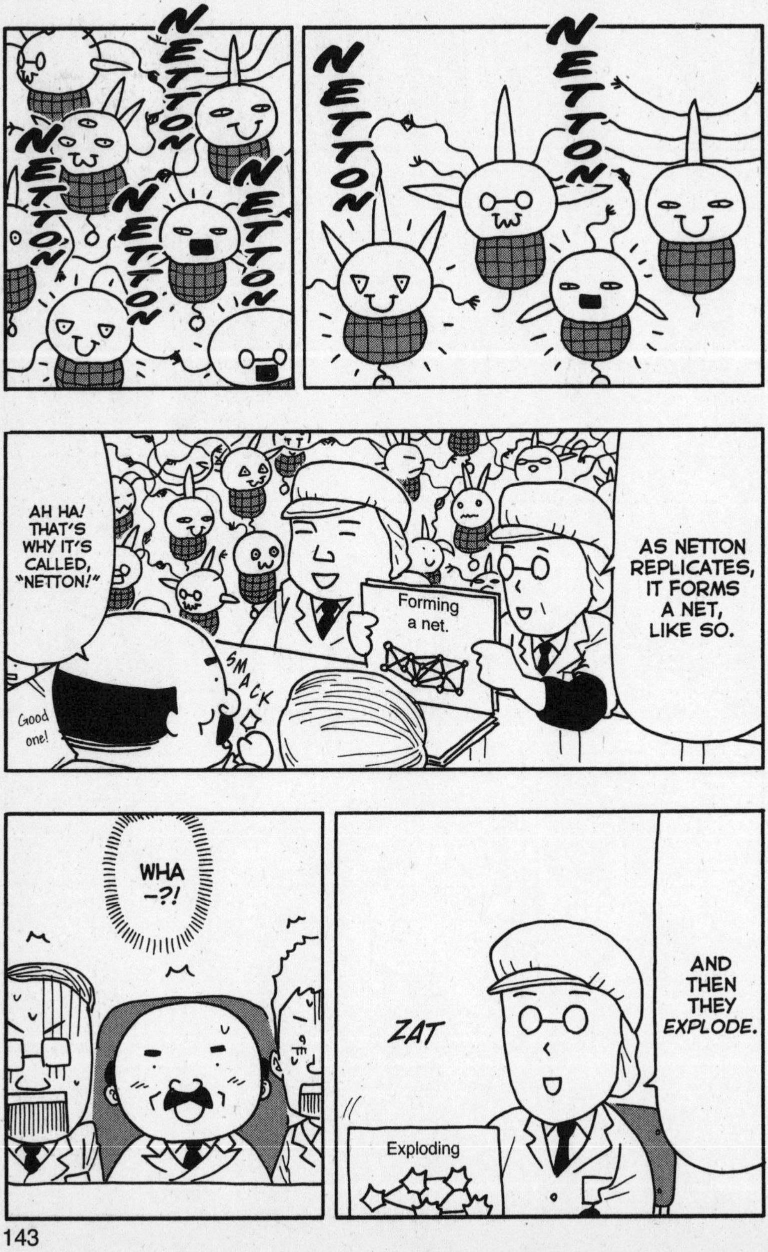
NETTON
NETTON
NETTON
NETTON
NETTON
NETTON
AS NETTON REPLICATES, IT FORMS A NET, LIKE SO.
Forming a net.
AH HA! THAT'S WHY IT'S CALLED, "NETTON!"
SMACK
Good one!
AND THEN THEY *EXPLODE*.
ZAT
Exploding
WHA-?!

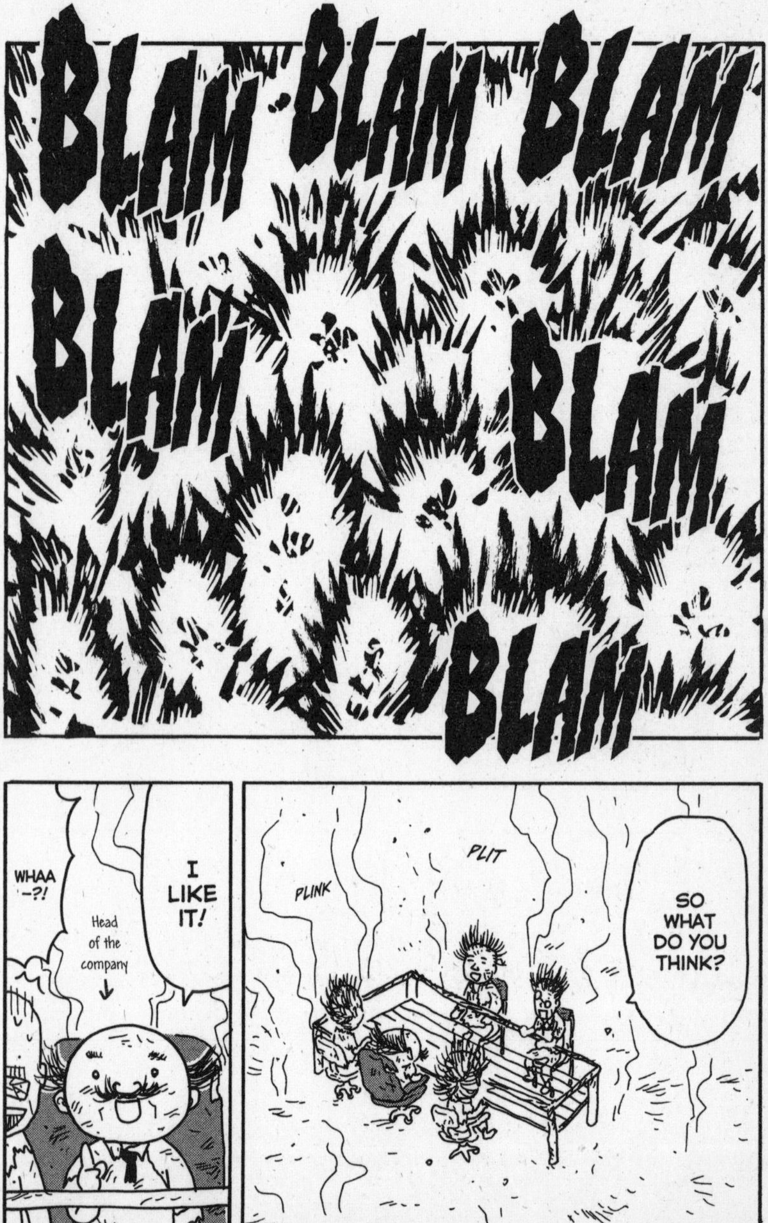
BLAM
BLAM
BLAM
BLAM
BLAM
BLAM
SO WHAT DO YOU THINK?
PLIT
PLINK
I LIKE IT!
WHAA—?!
Head of the company ↓

CHAPTER 15

PET-a-Doodle-Doo!

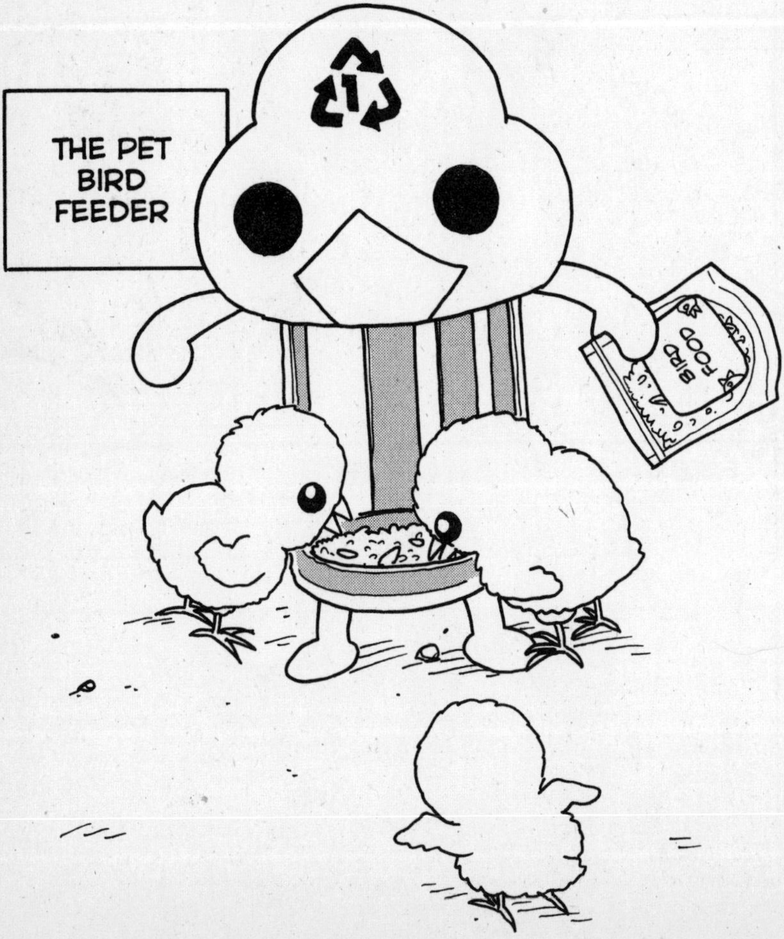
THE PET BIRD FEEDER
BIRD FOOD

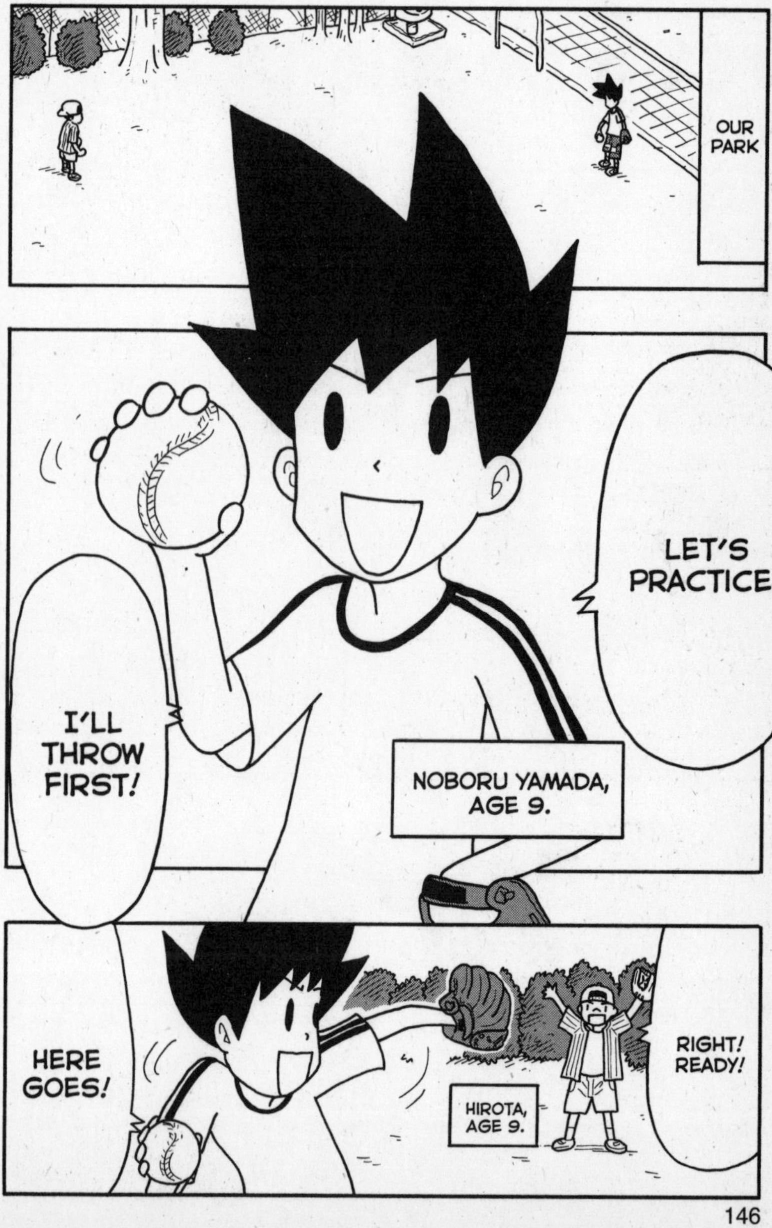
OUR PARK
LET'S PRACTICE!
NOBORU YAMADA, AGE 9.
I'LL THROW FIRST!
RIGHT! READY!
HIROTA, AGE 9.
HERE GOES!

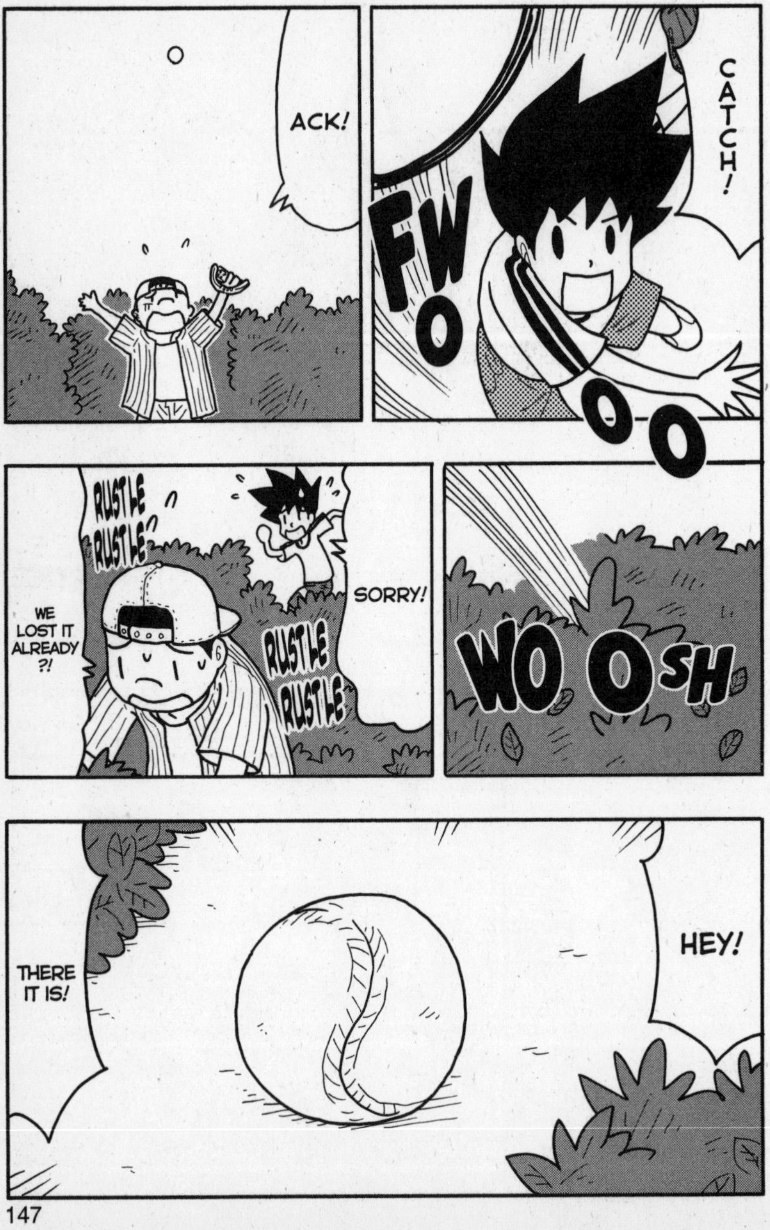
CATCH!
FWOOO
ACK!
WOOSH
SORRY!
RUSTLE RUSTLE
RUSTLE RUSTLE
WE LOST IT ALREADY?!
HEY!
THERE IT IS!

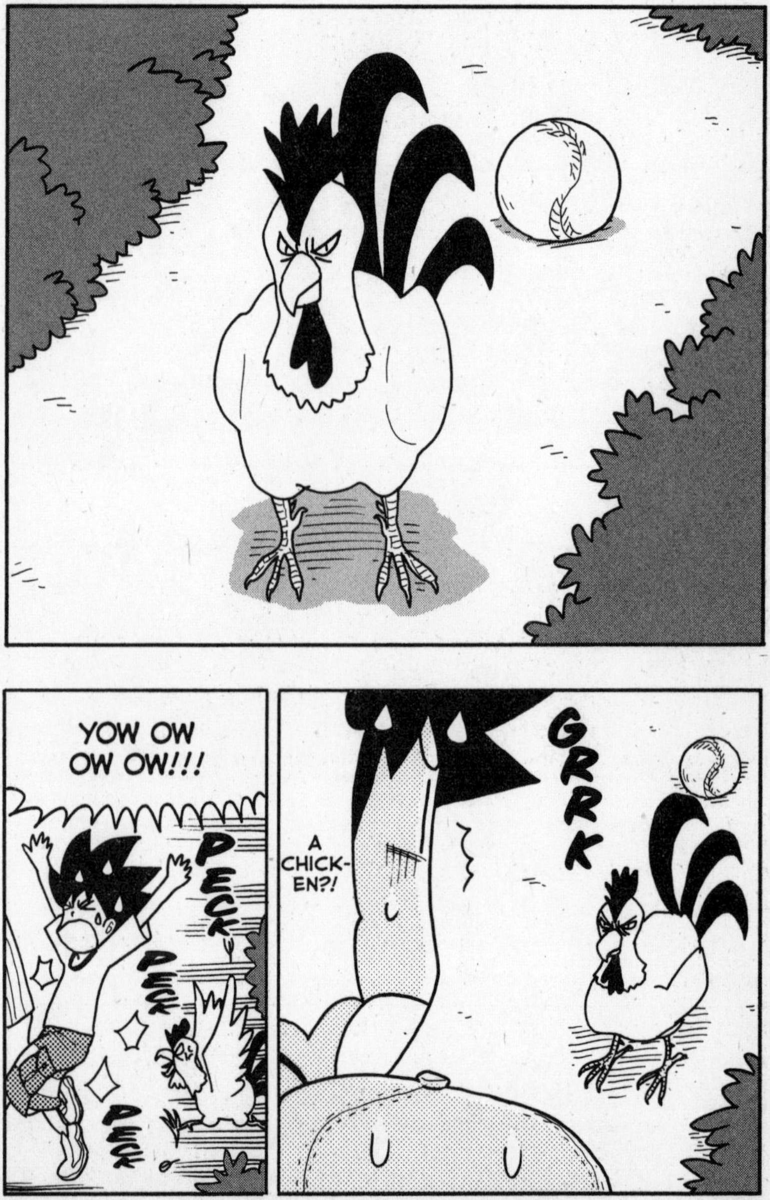
GRRK
A CHICK-
EN?!
YOW OW
OW OW!!!
PECK
PECK
PECK

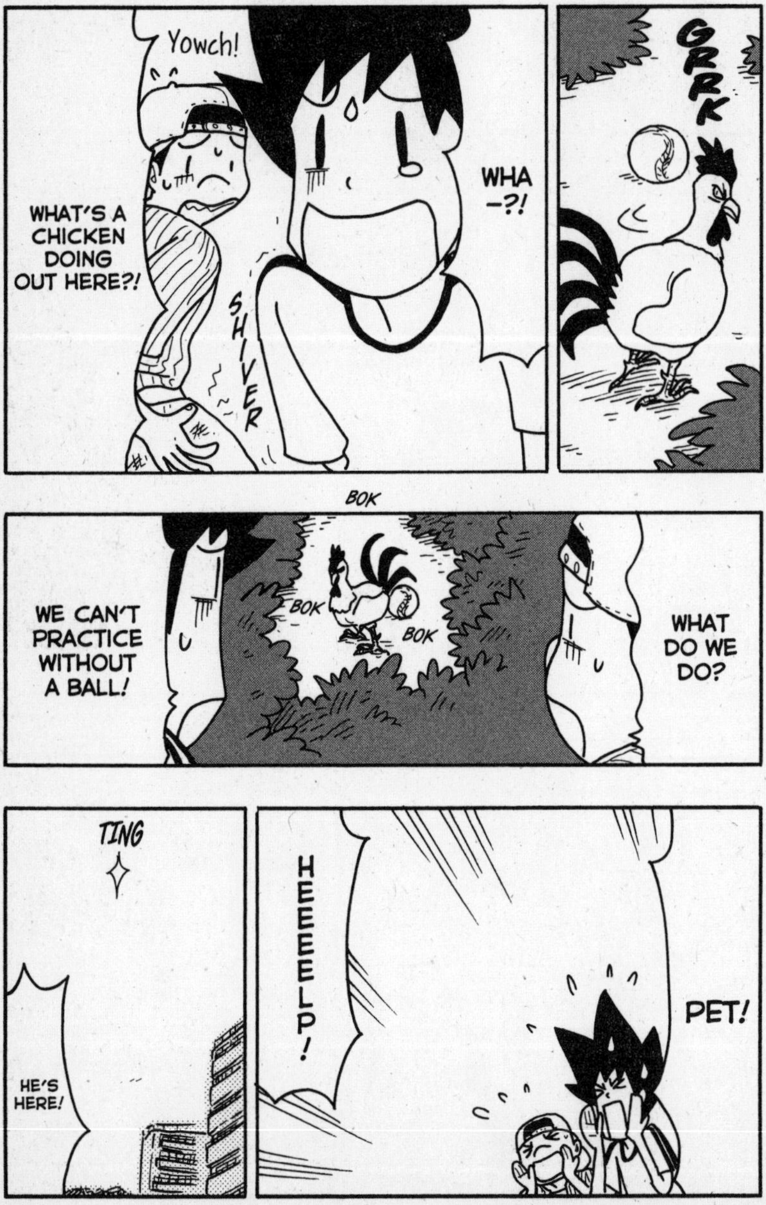
GRRK
Yowch!
WHA—?!
WHAT'S A CHICKEN DOING OUT HERE?!
SHIVER
BOK
BOK
BOK
WHAT DO WE DO?
WE CAN'T PRACTICE WITHOUT A BALL!
PET!
HEEEEELP!
TING
HE'S HERE!

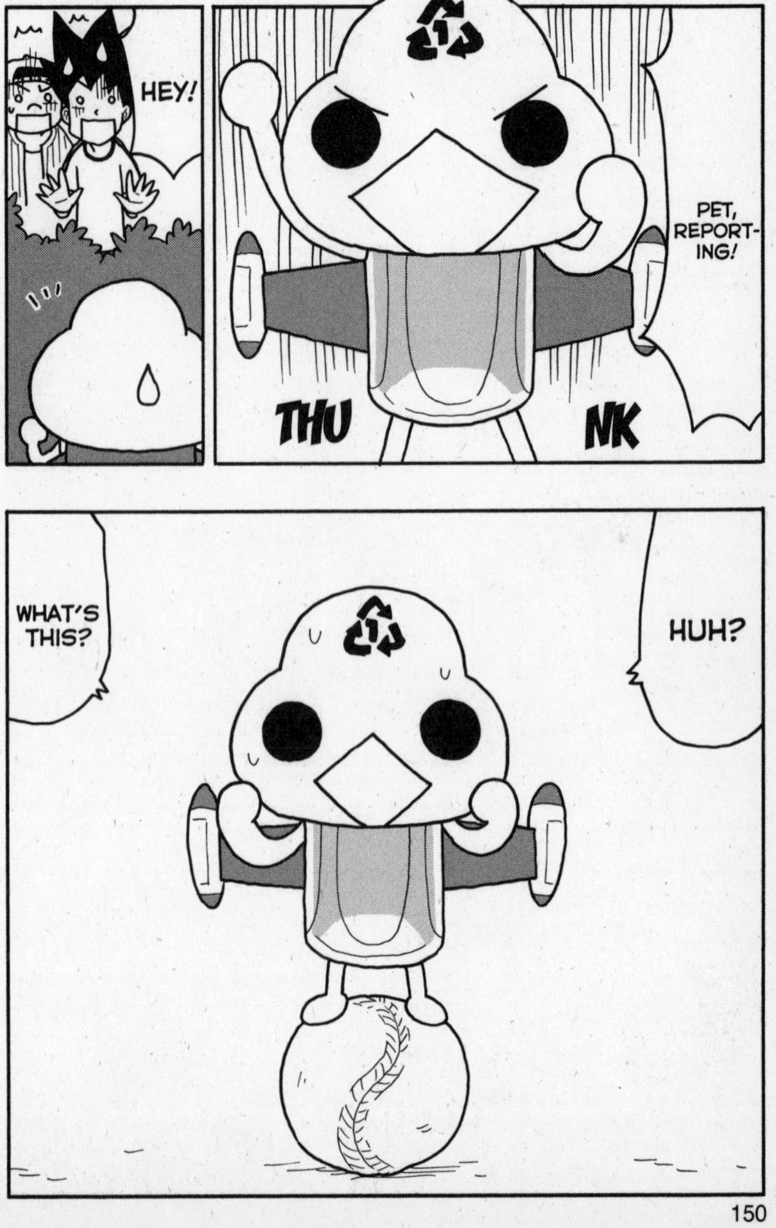
PET, REPORTING!
THUNK
HEY!
HUH?
WHAT'S THIS?

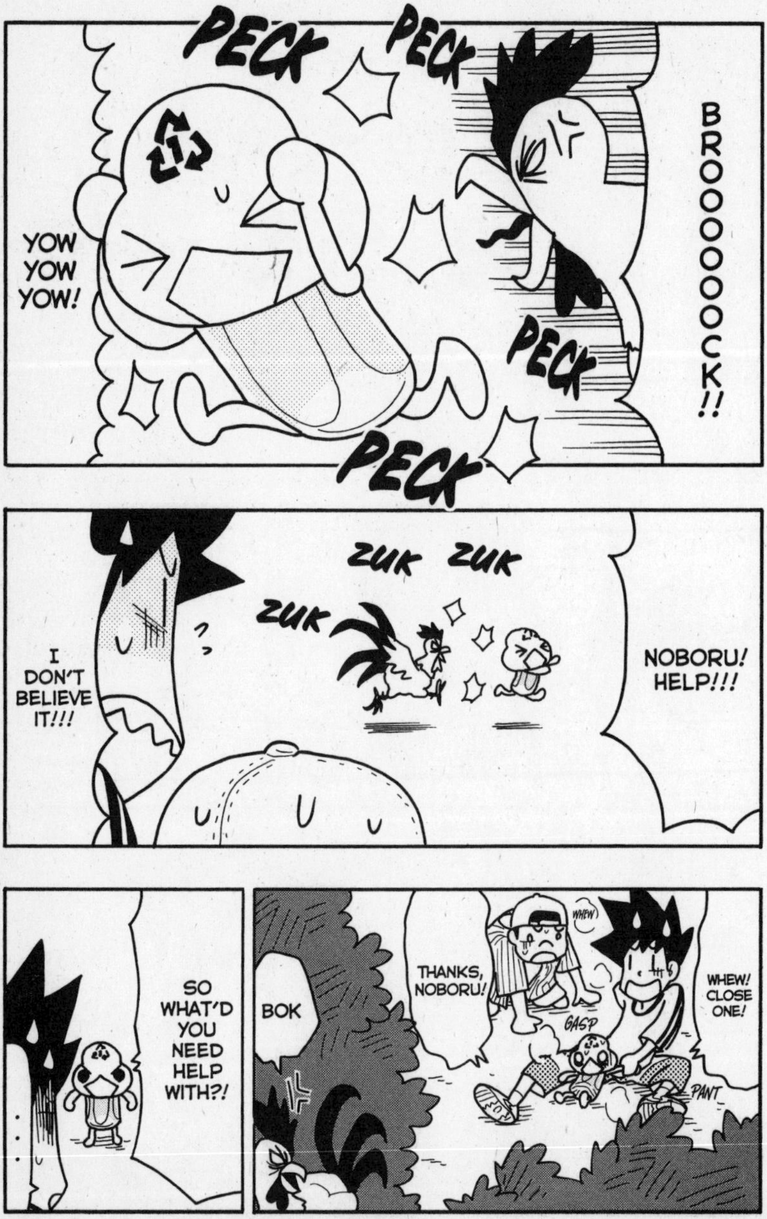
BROOOOOOCK!!
PECK
PECK
PECK
PECK
YOW YOW YOW!
NOBORU! HELP!!!
ZUK ZUK
ZUK
I DON'T BELIEVE IT!!!
WHEW! CLOSE ONE!
WHEW
THANKS, NOBORU!
GASP
PANT
BOK
SO WHAT'D YOU NEED HELP WITH?!

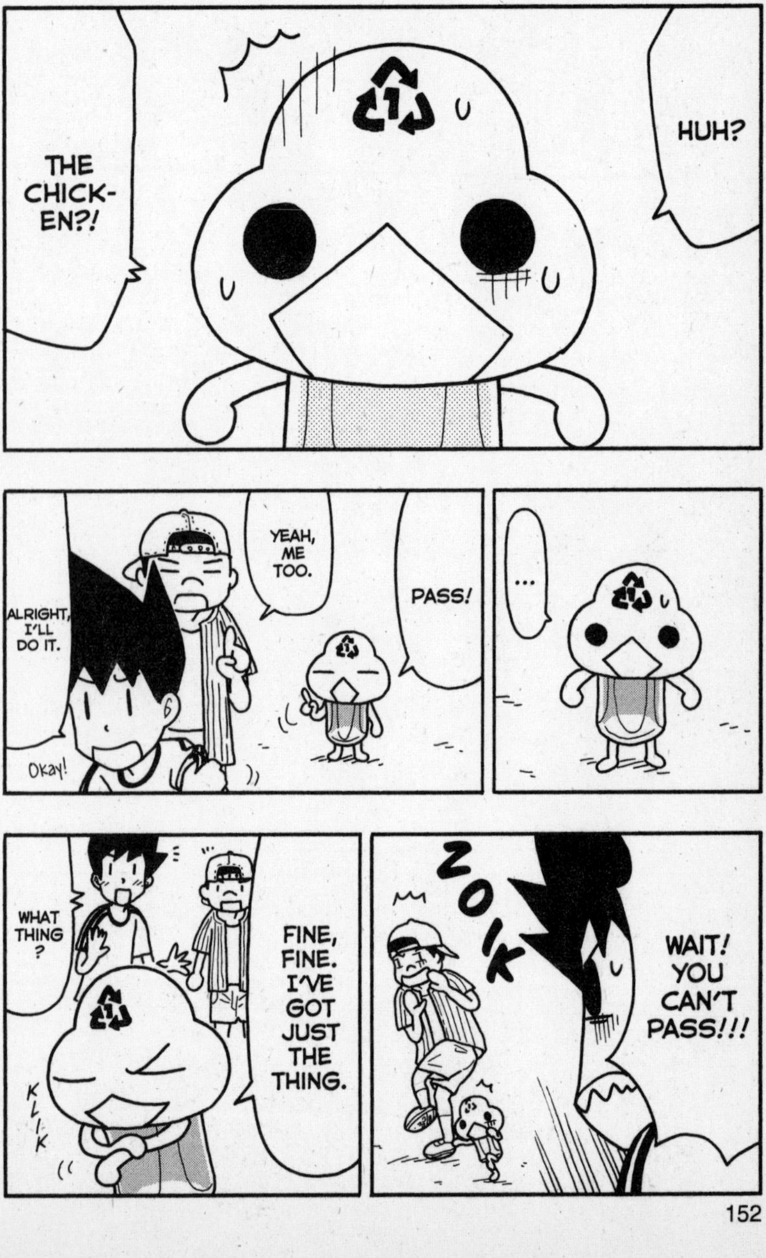
HUH?
THE CHICKEN?!
...
PASS!
YEAH, ME TOO.
ALRIGHT, I'LL DO IT.
Okay!
ZOIK
WAIT! YOU CAN'T PASS!!!
FINE, FINE. I'VE GOT JUST THE THING.
WHAT THING?
KLIK

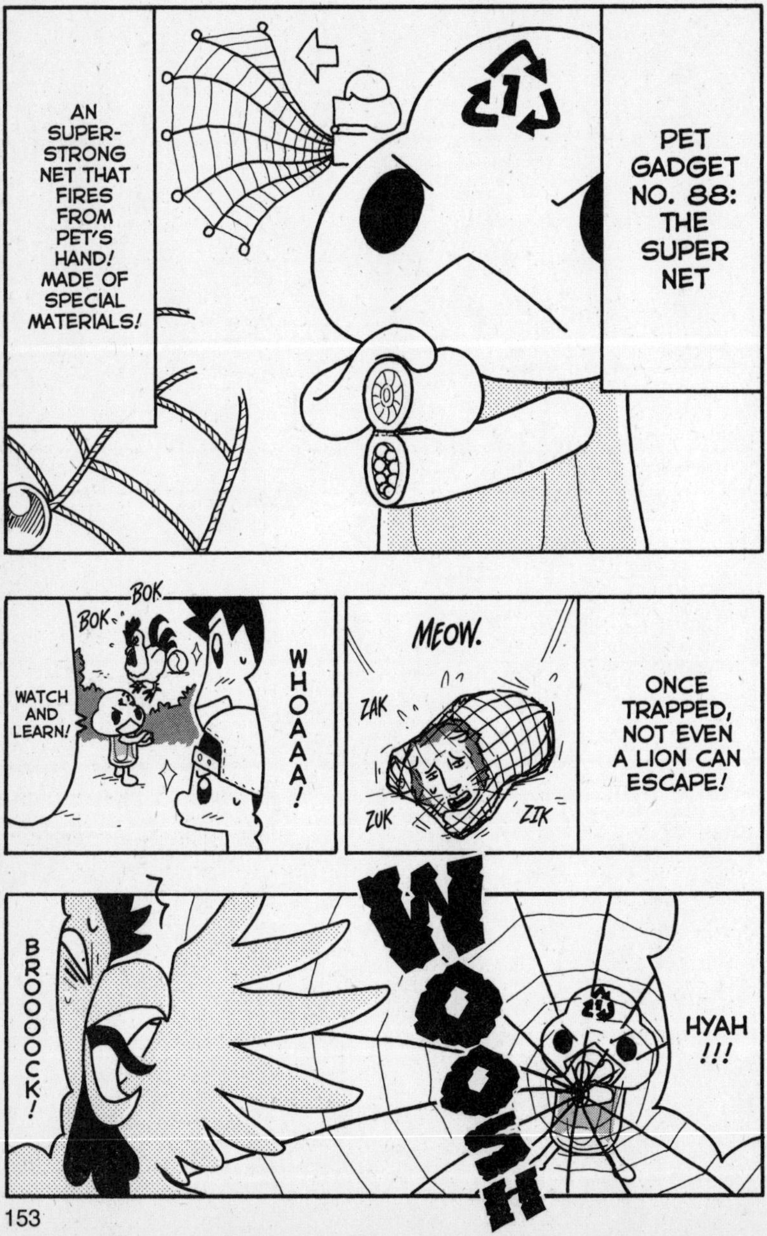
PET GADGET NO. 88: THE SUPER NET
AN SUPER-STRONG NET THAT FIRES FROM PET'S HAND! MADE OF SPECIAL MATERIALS!
ONCE TRAPPED, NOT EVEN A LION CAN ESCAPE!
MEOW.
ZAK
ZIK
ZUK
WHOAAA!
BOK
BOK
WATCH AND LEARN!
HYAH!!!
WOOOSH
BROOOOCK!

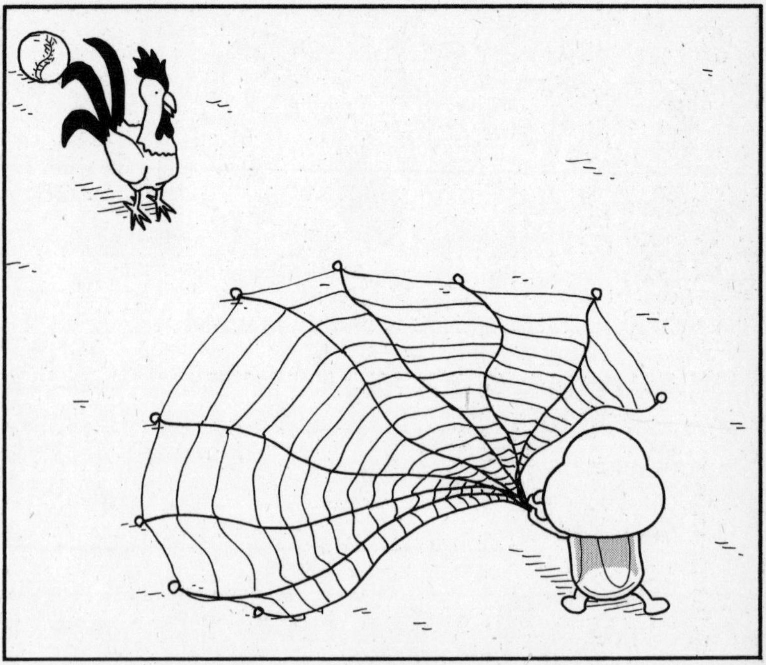

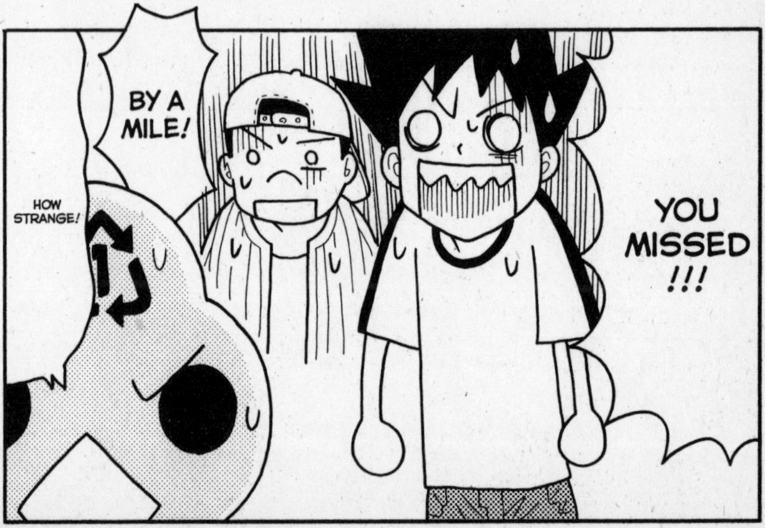
YOU MISSED !!!
BY A MILE!
HOW STRANGE!

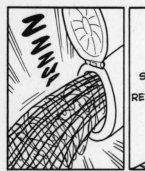 

ALRIGHT, ONCE MORE!

SUPER NET, RETRACT!

U S E L E S S !!

ZUB
ZUB
ZUB
ZUB

UNFORTUNATELY, IT TAKES OVER AN HOUR FOR THE SUPER NET TO GO BACK INTO THE LAUNCHER...

ALRIGHT!

?!

WOOSH

HAH! YOU FELL FOR MY TRICK! I'VE GOT ONE IN MY LEFT ARM TOO!

ZHUP

...

HMPH

BOK BOK BOK!

ZUB
ZUB

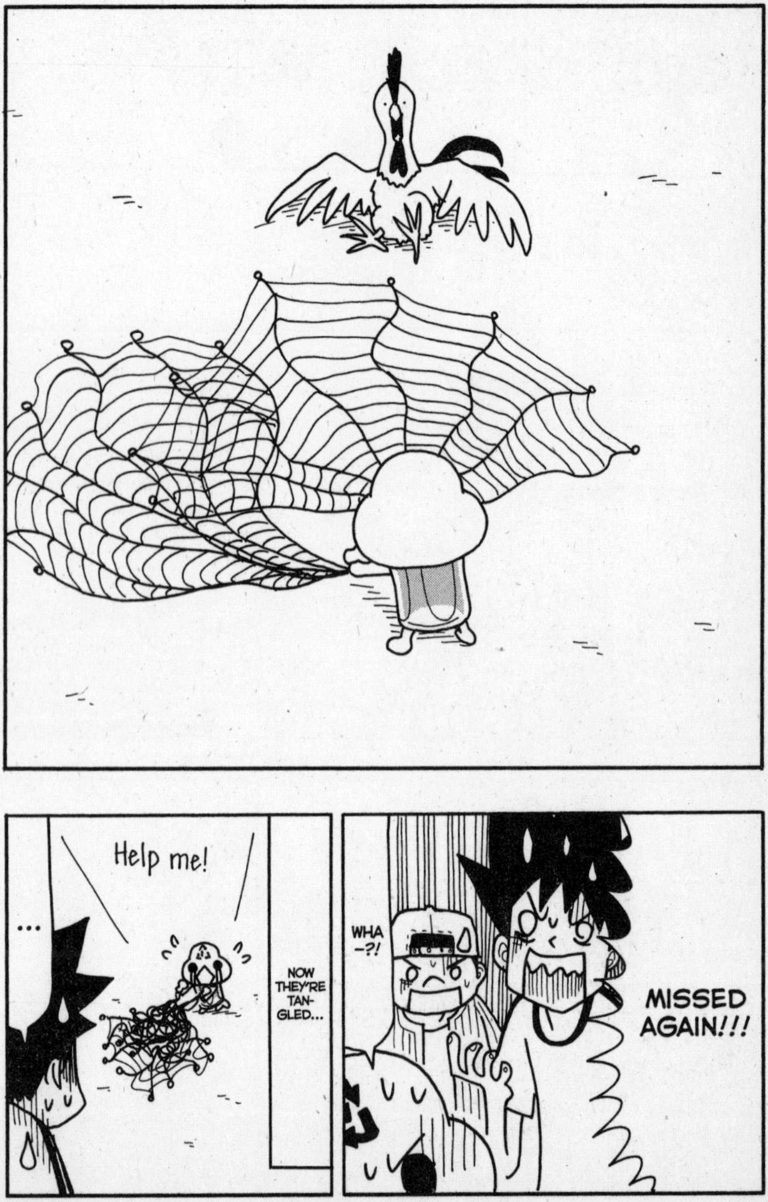
MISSED AGAIN!!!
WHA-?!
NOW THEY'RE TAN-GLED...
Help me!
...

Peep? Peep? PET!

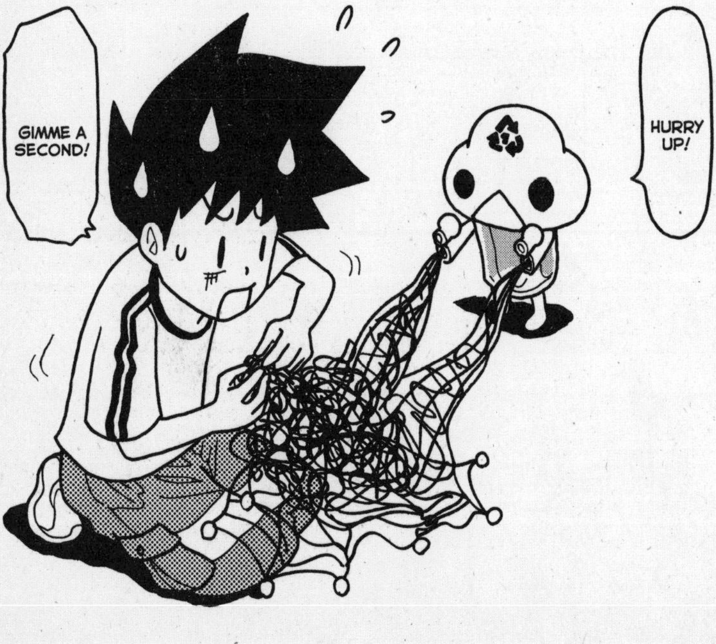
HURRY UP!
GIMME A SECOND!

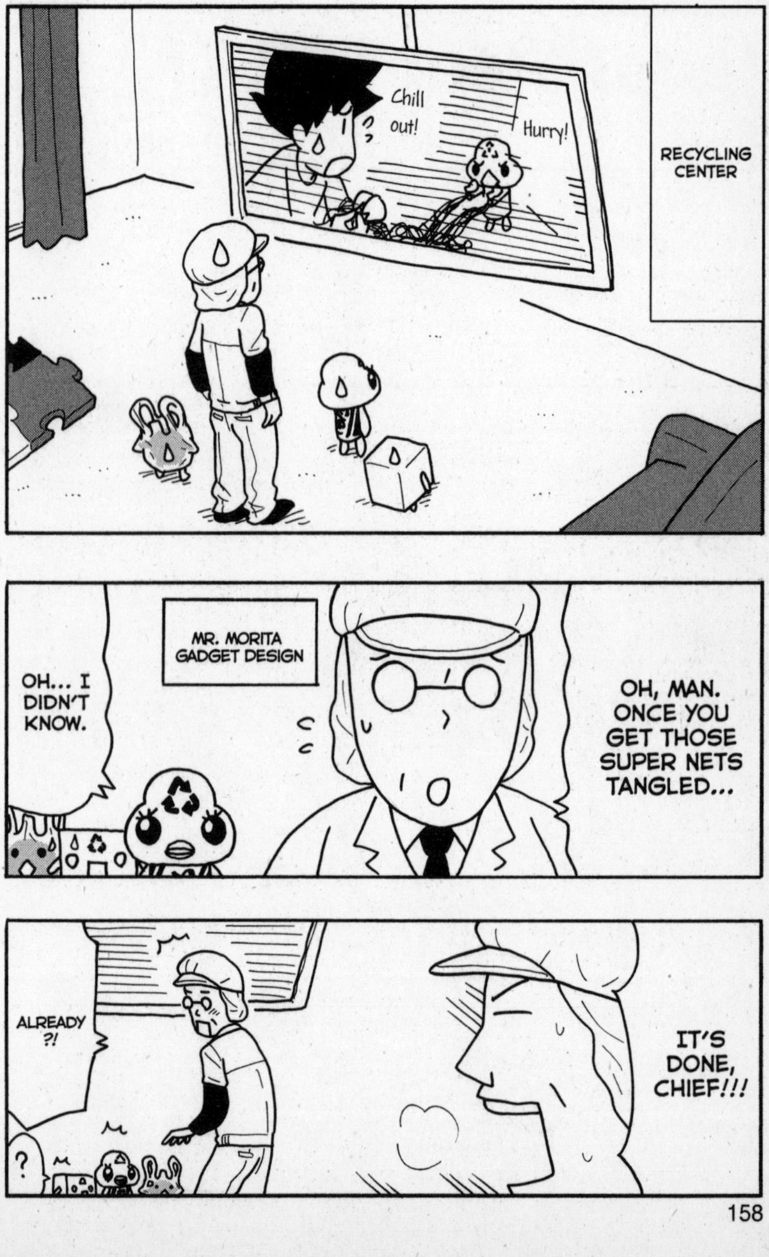
RECYCLING CENTER
Hurry!
Chill out!
OH, MAN. ONCE YOU GET THOSE SUPER NETS TANGLED...
MR. MORITA GADGET DESIGN
OH... I DIDN'T KNOW.
IT'S DONE, CHIEF!!!
ALREADY ?!
?

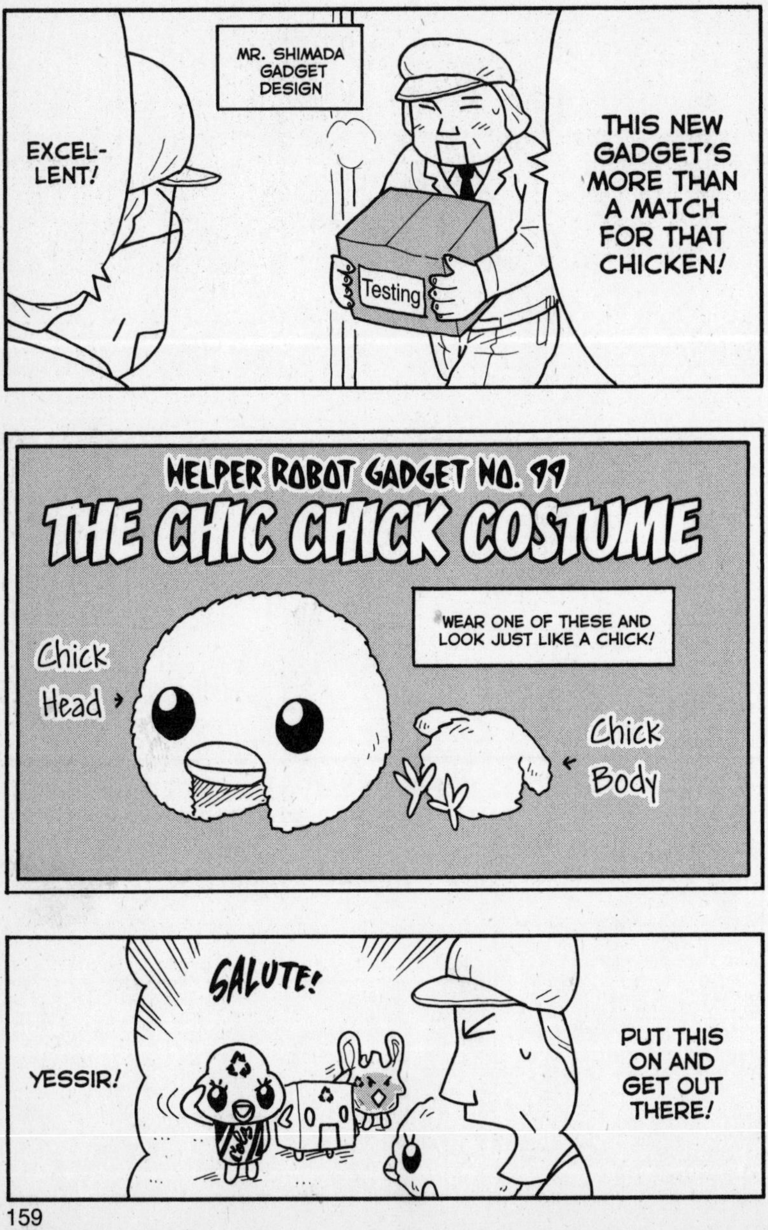
MR. SHIMADA GADGET DESIGN
THIS NEW GADGET'S MORE THAN A MATCH FOR THAT CHICKEN!
Testing
EXCEL-LENT!
HELPER ROBOT GADGET NO. 99
THE CHIC CHICK COSTUME
WEAR ONE OF THESE AND LOOK JUST LIKE A CHICK!
Chick Head
Chick Body
PUT THIS ON AND GET OUT THERE!
SALUTE!
YESSIR!

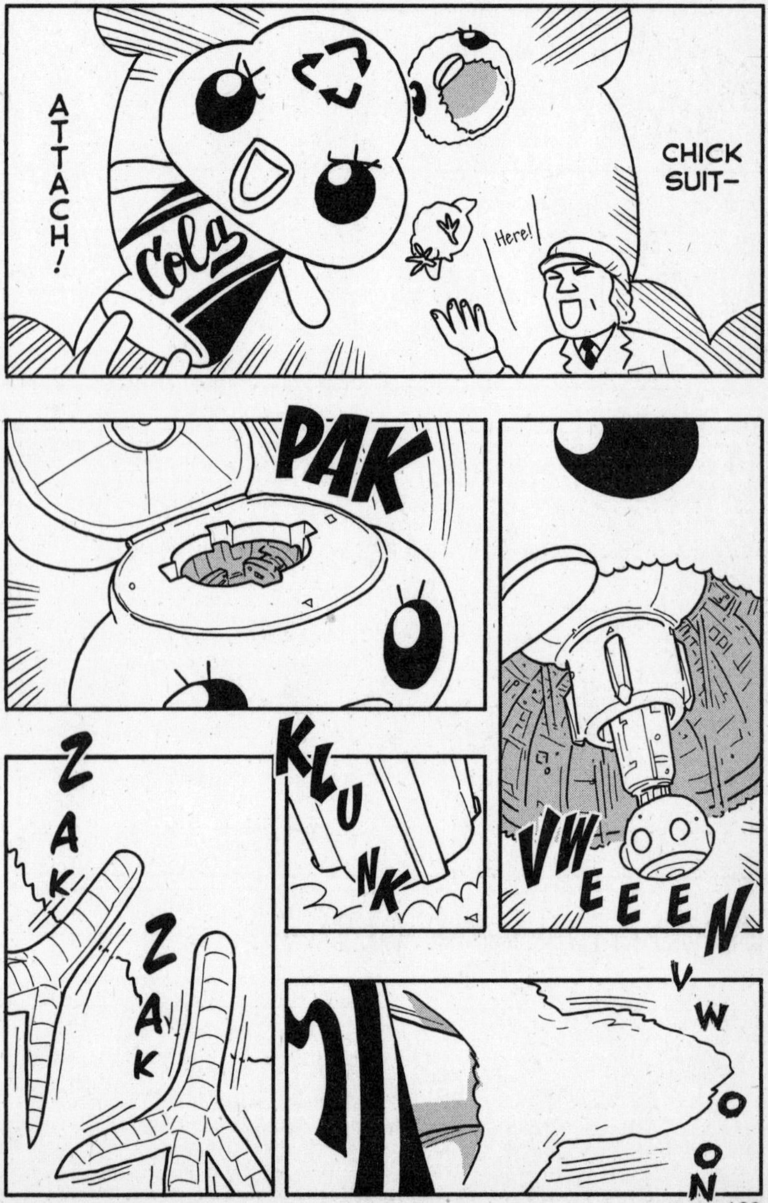
CHICK SUIT—
Here!
ATTACH!
VWEEEN
PAK
KLUNK
VWOOON
ZAK
ZAK

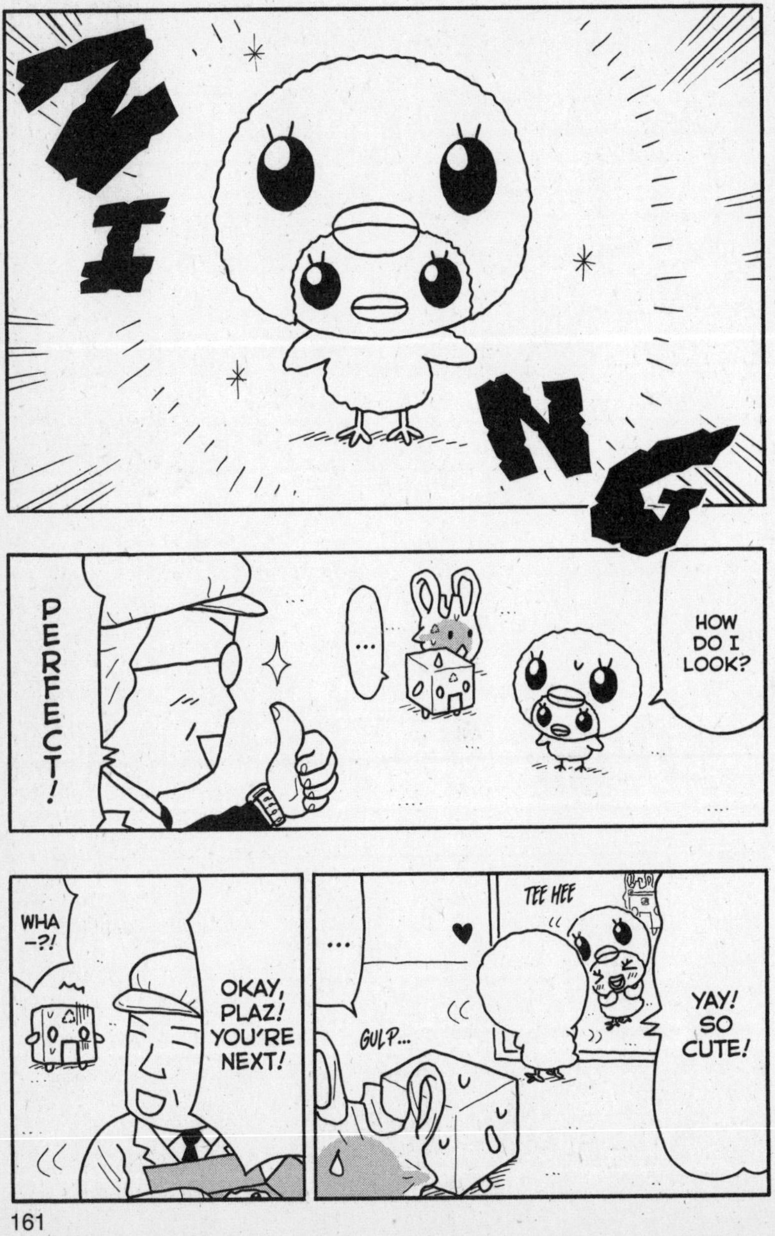
ZING
HOW DO I LOOK?
...
PERFECT!
YAY! SO CUTE!
TEE HEE
...
GULP...
OKAY, PLAZ! YOU'RE NEXT!
WHA
—?!

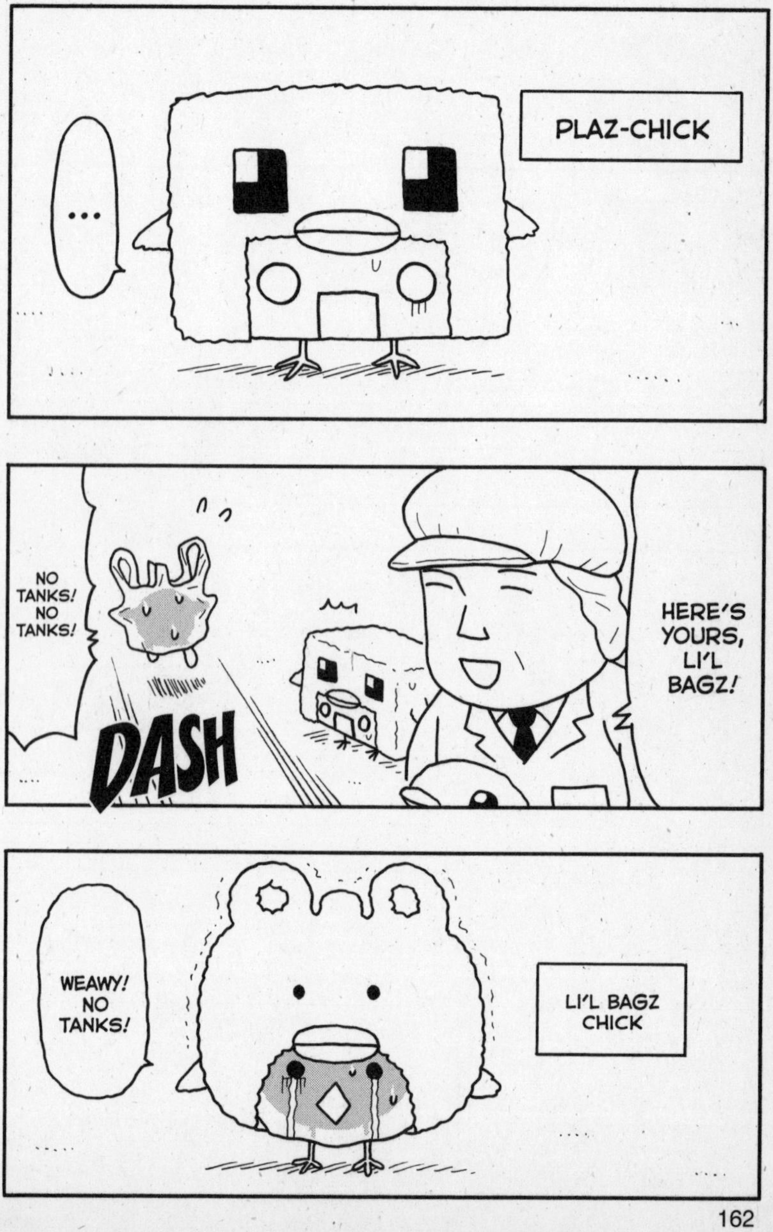
PLAZ-CHICK
...
HERE'S YOURS, LI'L BAGZ!
DASH
NO TANKS! NO TANKS!
LI'L BAGZ CHICK
WEAWY! NO TANKS!

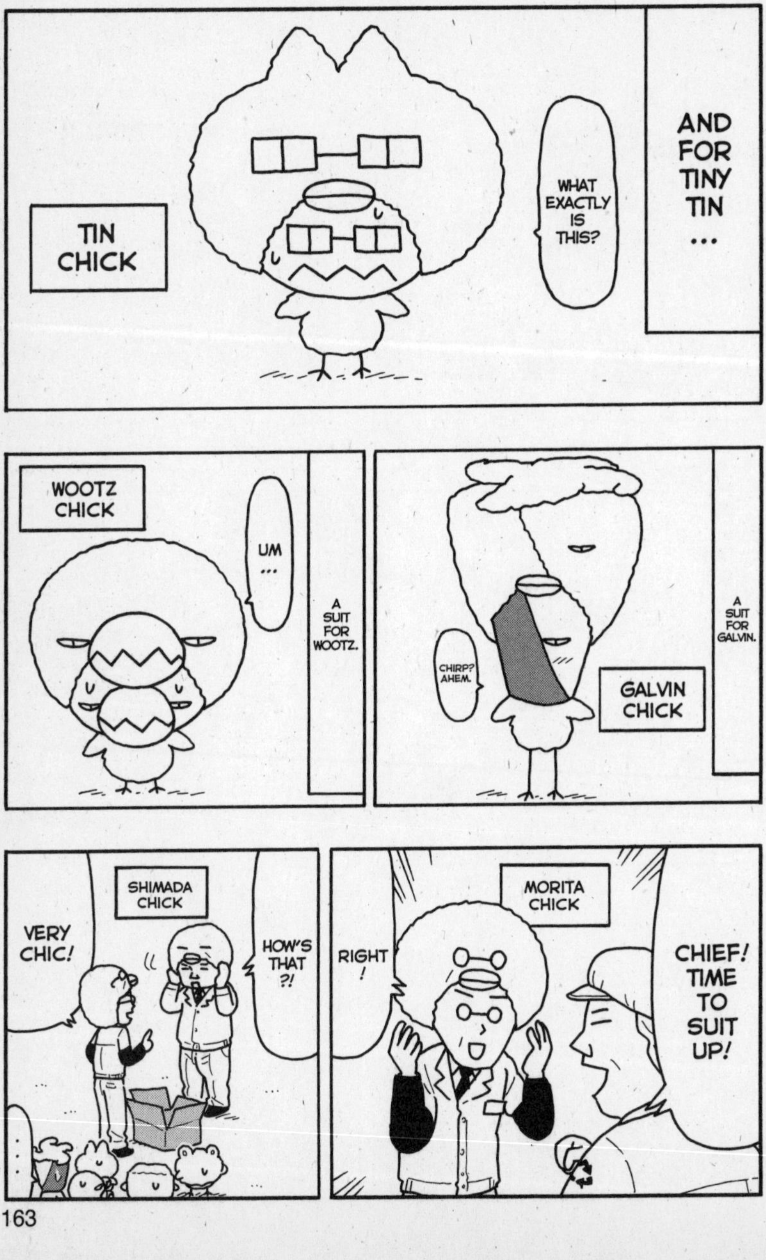
AND FOR TINY TIN...
WHAT EXACTLY IS THIS?
TIN CHICK
A SUIT FOR GALVIN.
GALVIN CHICK
CHIRP? AHEM.
A SUIT FOR WOOTZ.
UM ...
WOOTZ CHICK
CHIEF! TIME TO SUIT UP!
MORITA CHICK
RIGHT!
HOW'S THAT?!
SHIMADA CHICK
VERY CHIC!

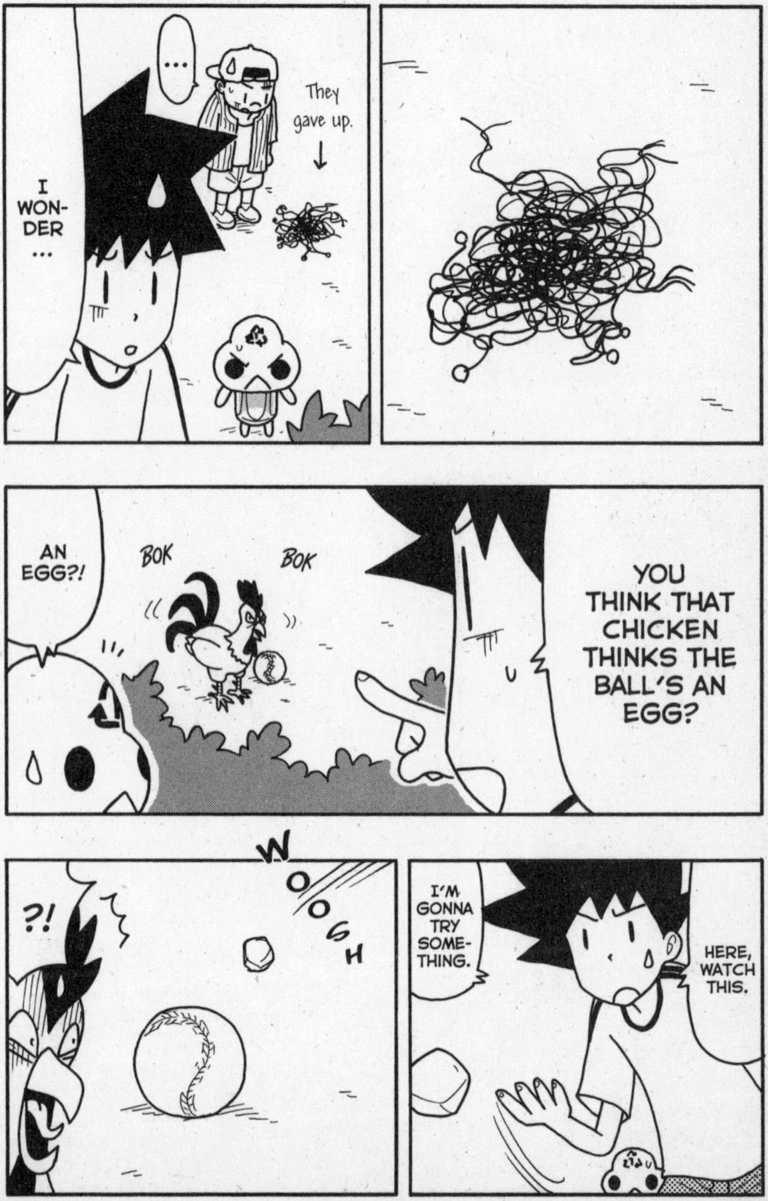
They gave up.
...
I WONDER...
YOU THINK THAT CHICKEN THINKS THE BALL'S AN EGG?
BOK
BOK
AN EGG?!
HERE, WATCH THIS.
I'M GONNA TRY SOMETHING.
WOOSH
?!

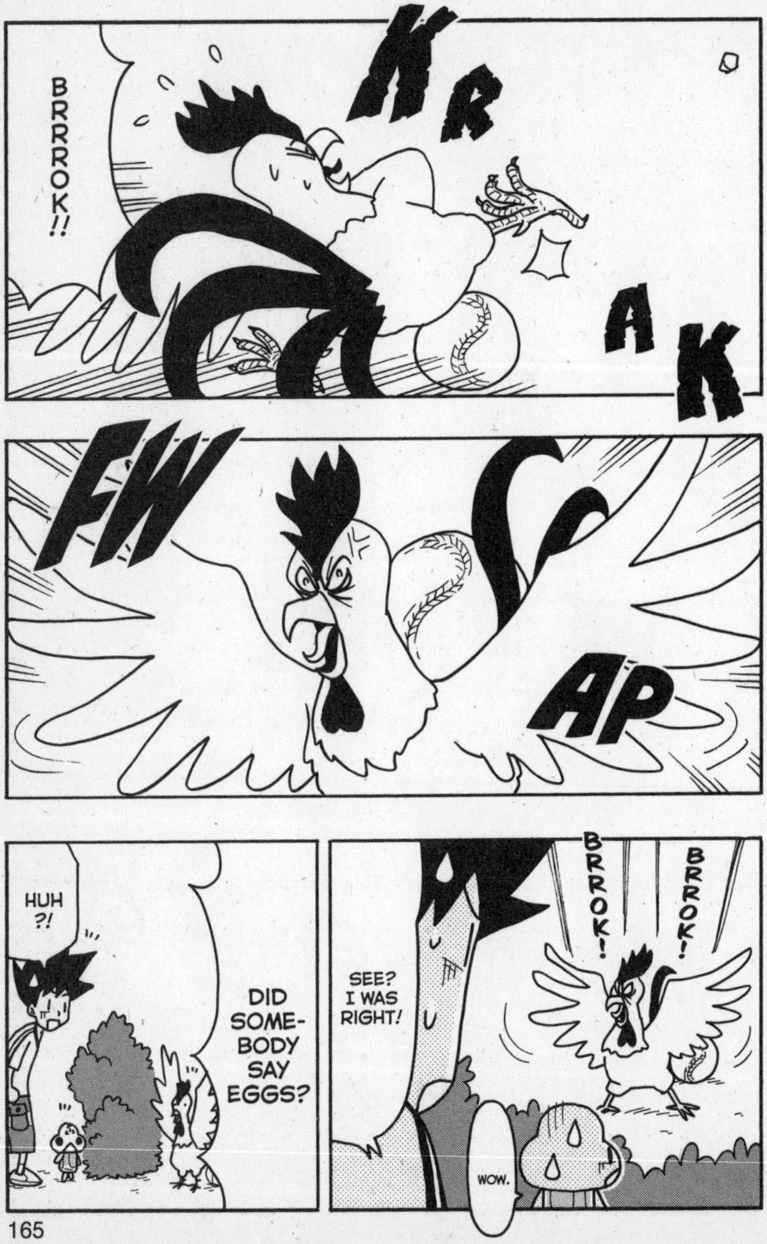
BRRRROK!!
KRAK
FWAP
BRROK!
BRROK!
SEE? I WAS RIGHT!
WOW.
DID SOME-BODY SAY EGGS?
HUH ?!

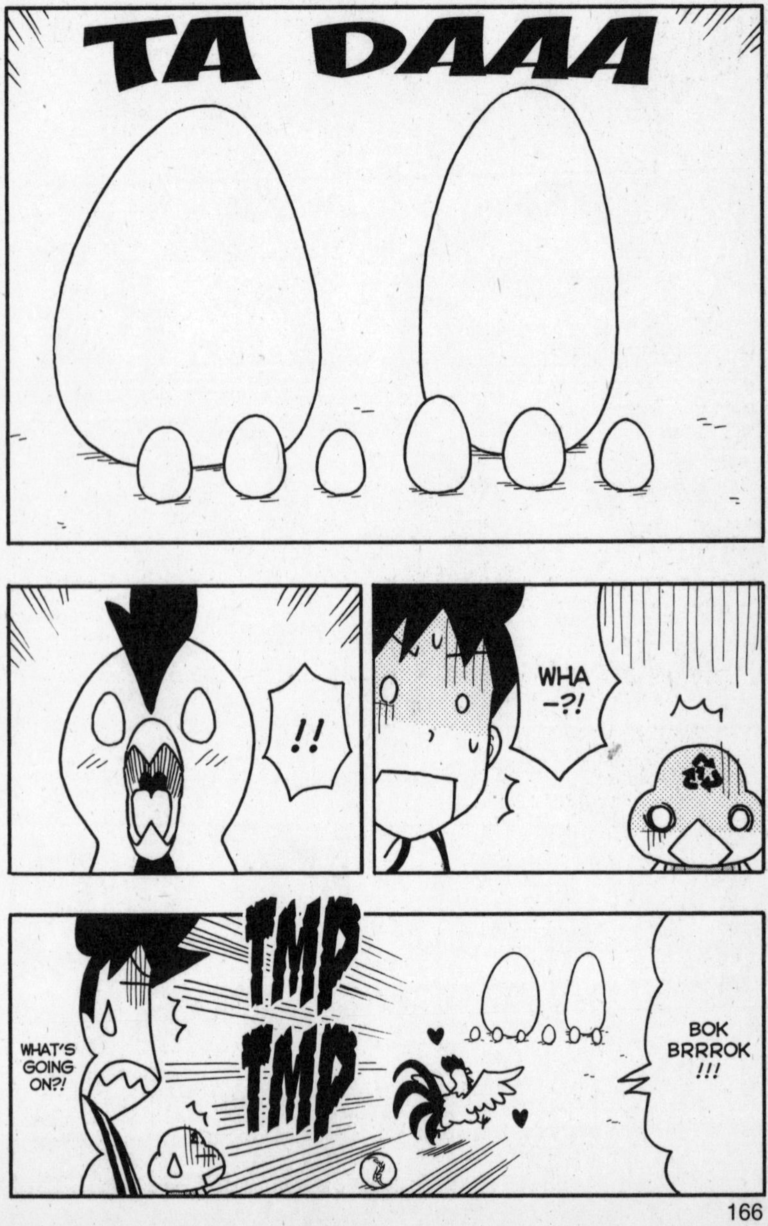
TA DAAA
WHA —?!
!!
BOK BRRROK !!!
TMP TMP
WHAT'S GOING ON?!

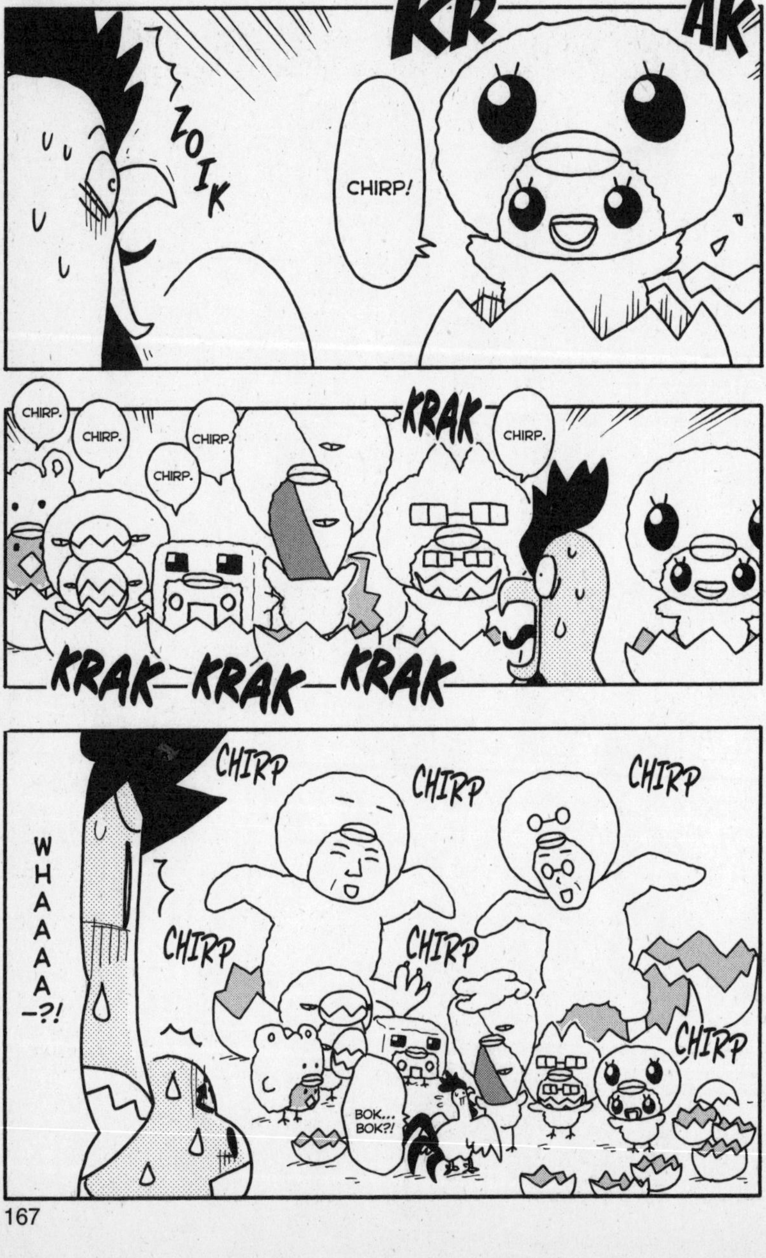
KR—AK
CHIRP!
ZOIK
CHIRP.
KRAK
CHIRP.
CHIRP.
CHIRP.
CHIRP.
KRAK—KRAK—KRAK
CHIRP
CHIRP
CHIRP
CHIRP
CHIRP
CHIRP
BOK... BOK?!
WHAAAAA—?!

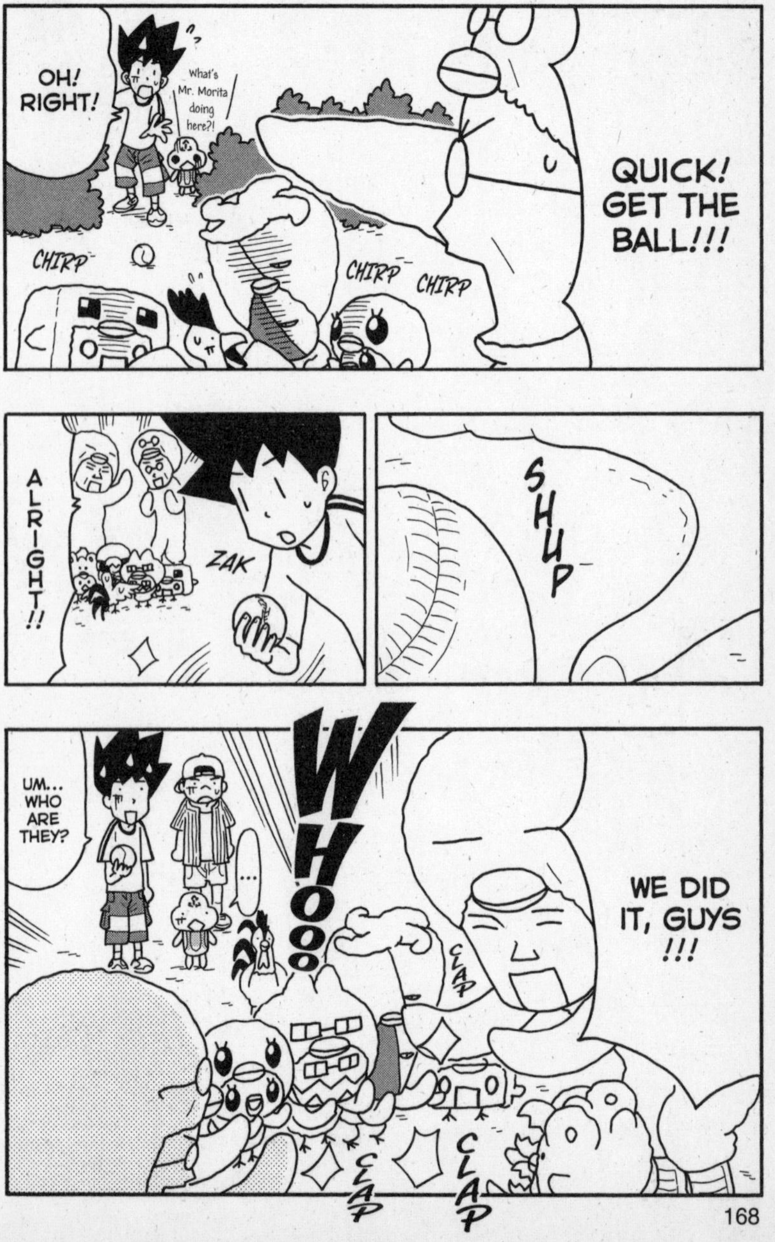
QUICK! GET THE BALL!!!
What's Mr. Morita doing here?!
OH! RIGHT!
CHIRP
CHIRP
CHIRP
SHUP
ZAK
ALRIGHT!!
WHOOO
WE DID IT, GUYS!!!
CLAP
...
UM... WHO ARE THEY?
CLAP
CLAP

CHAPTER 17
Revenge Is Tweet

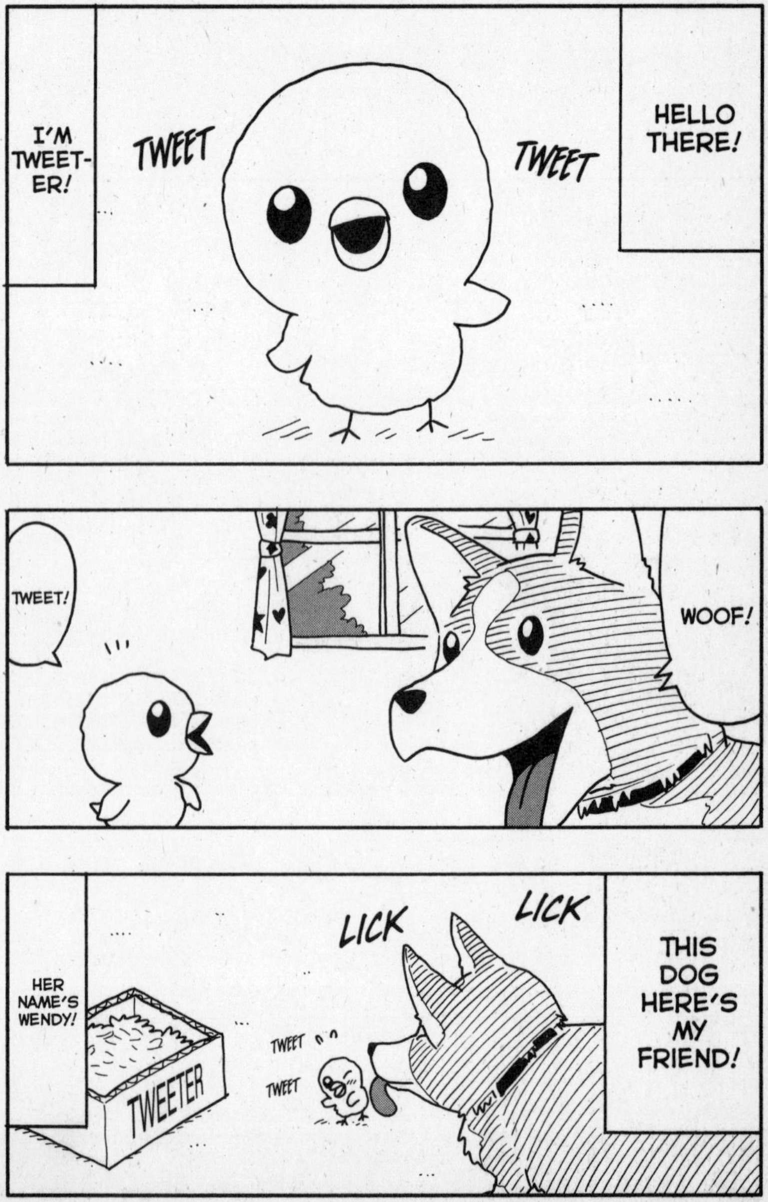
HELLO THERE!
TWEET
TWEET
I'M TWEETER!
WOOF!
TWEET!
THIS DOG HERE'S MY FRIEND!
LICK
LICK
TWEET
TWEET
TWEETER
HER NAME'S WENDY!

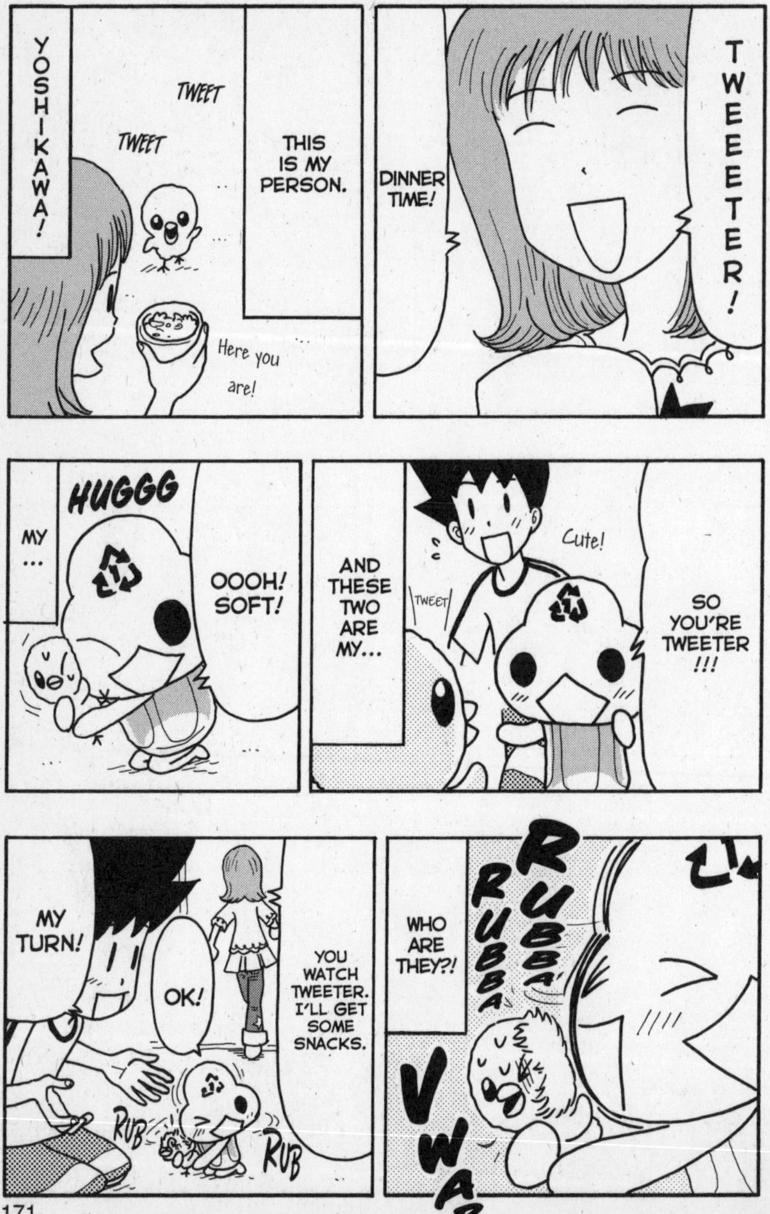
TWEEETER!
DINNER TIME!
THIS IS MY PERSON.
TWEET
TWEET
YOSHIKAWA!
Here you are!
SO YOU'RE TWEETER!!!
Cute!
TWEET
AND THESE TWO ARE MY...
OOOH! SOFT!
HUGGG
MY...
WHO ARE THEY?!
RUBBA
RUBBA
VWAP
YOU WATCH TWEETER. I'LL GET SOME SNACKS.
OK!
MY TURN!
RUB
RUB

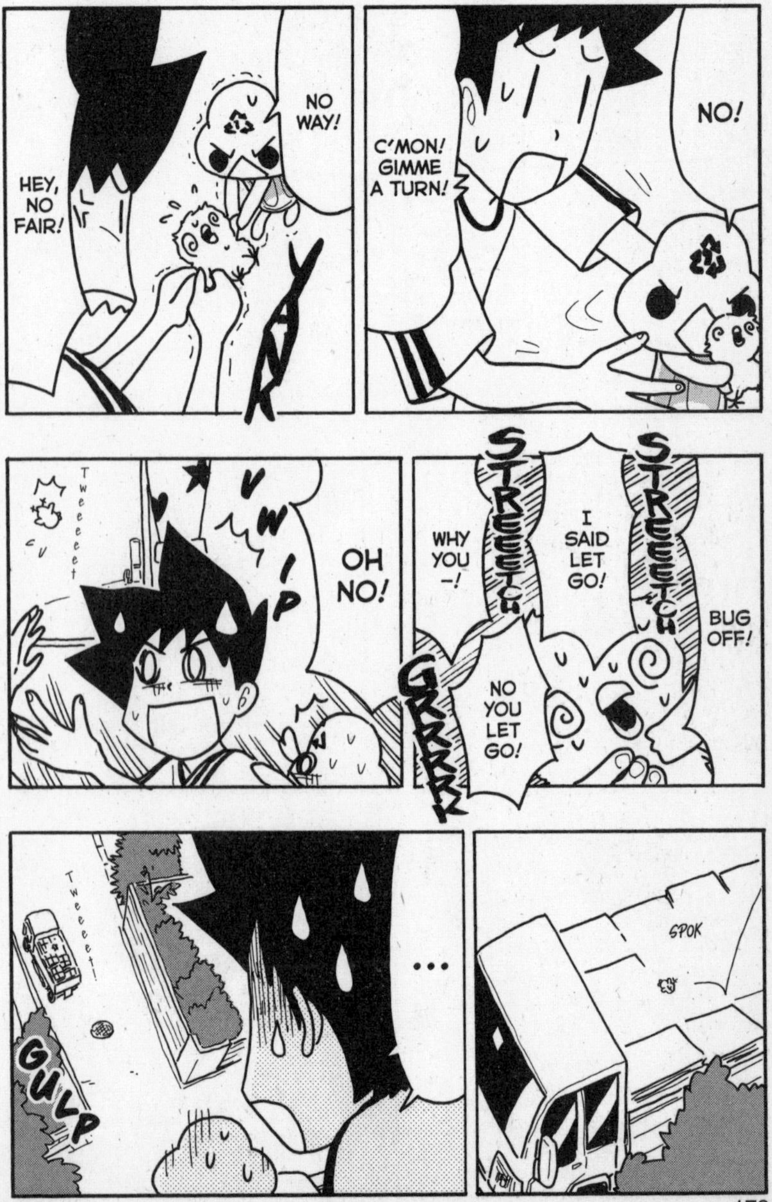
NO!
C'MON! GIMME A TURN!
NO WAY!
HEY, NO FAIR!
YANK
STREEETCH
STREEETCH
BUG OFF!
I SAID LET GO!
WHY YOU—!
NO YOU LET GO!
GRRRRR
OH NO!
WHIP
Tweeeeet
SPOK
...
Tweeeeet!
GULP

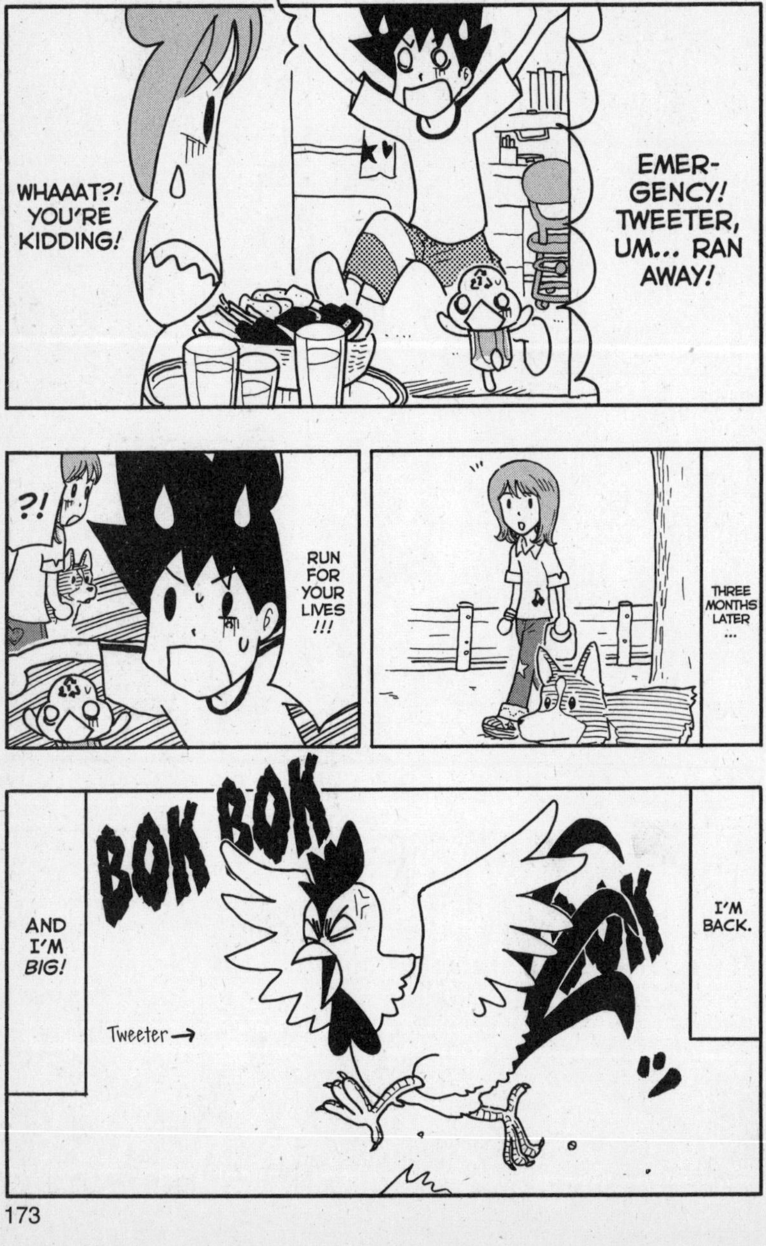
EMER-
GENCY!
TWEETER,
UM... RAN
AWAY!
WHAAAT?!
YOU'RE
KIDDING!
THREE
MONTHS
LATER
...
RUN
FOR
YOUR
LIVES
!!!
?!
I'M
BACK.
BOK BOK
AND
I'M
BIG!
Tweeter →

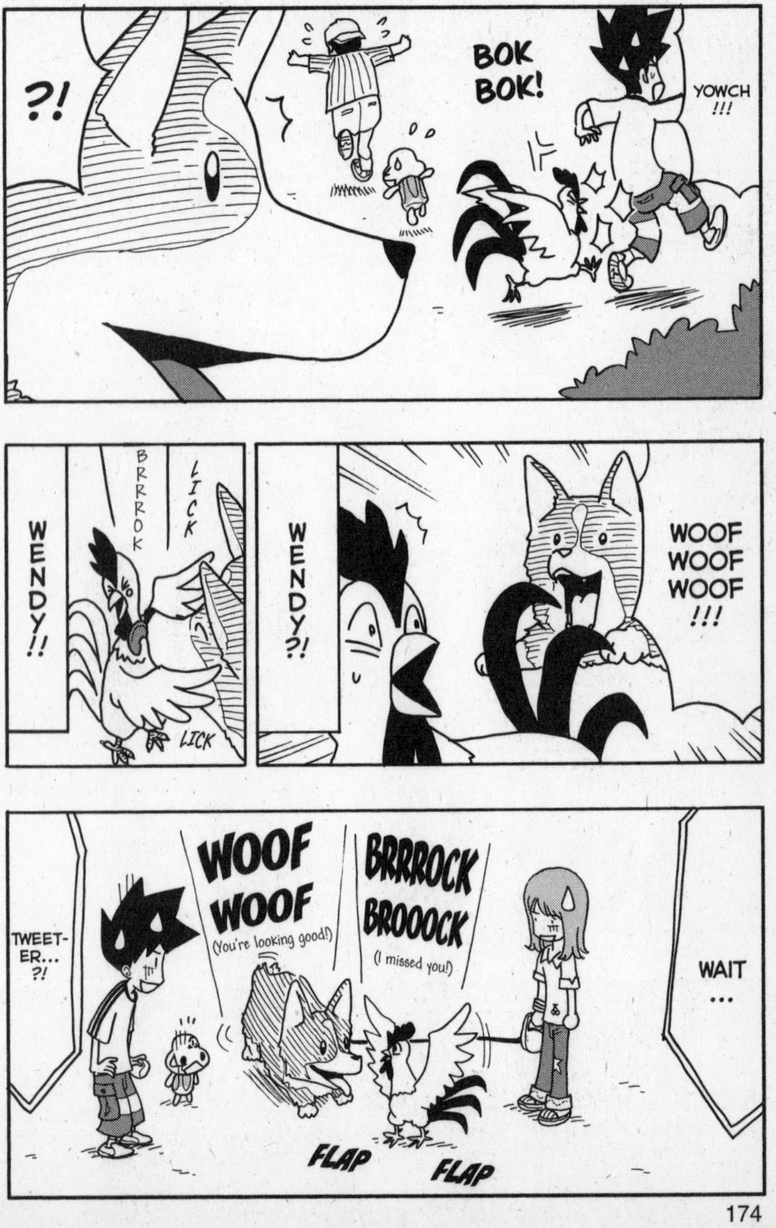
YOWCH!!!
BOK BOK!
?!
WOOF WOOF WOOF!!!
WENDY?!
LICK
BRRROK
WENDY!!
LICK
WAIT...
BRRROCK BROOOCK
(I missed you!)
WOOF WOOF
(You're looking good!)
TWEET-ER...?!
FLAP
FLAP

CHAPTER 18 The Need for Speed

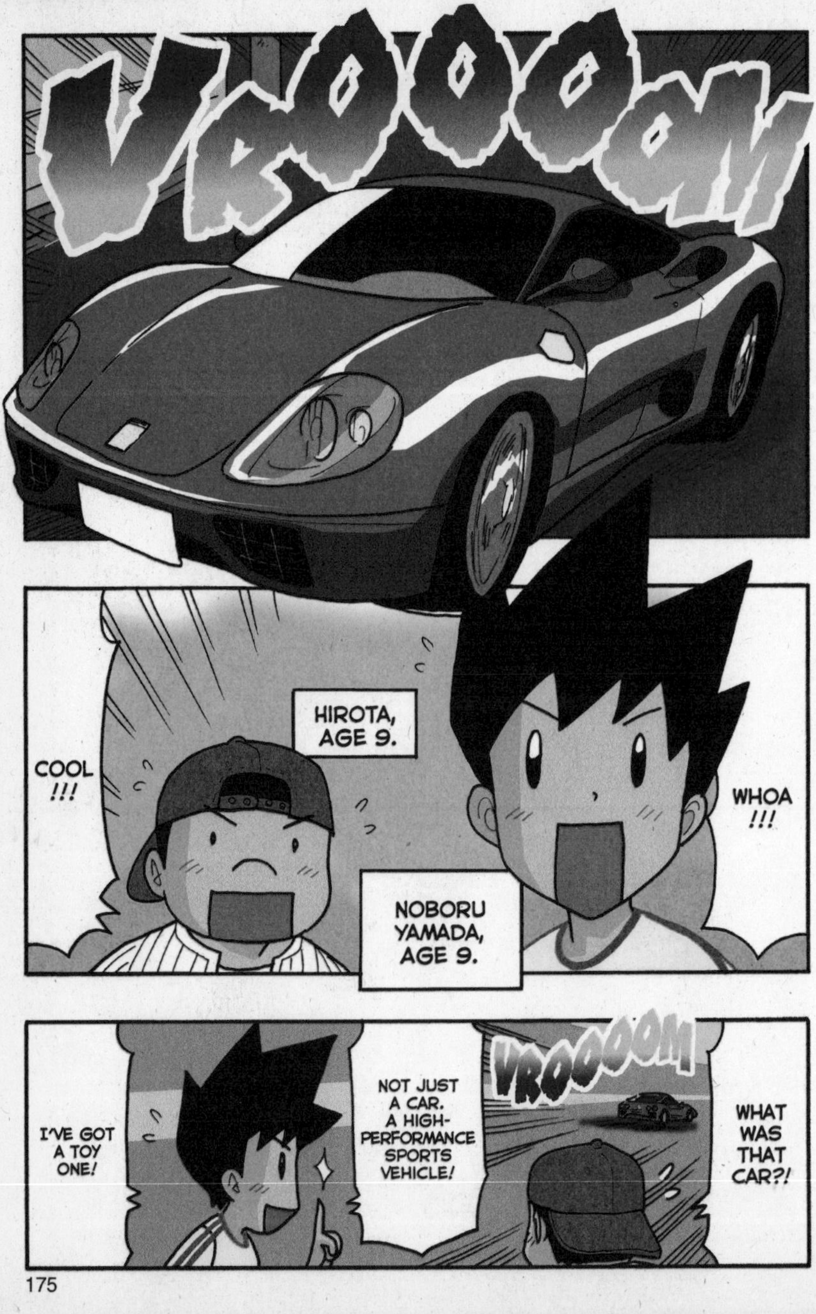
VROOOM
WHOA!!!
NOBORU YAMADA, AGE 9.
HIROTA, AGE 9.
COOL!!!
WHAT WAS THAT CAR?!
VROOOOM
NOT JUST A CAR. A HIGH-PERFORMANCE SPORTS VEHICLE!
I'VE GOT A TOY ONE!

CHAPTER 18
The Need for Speed

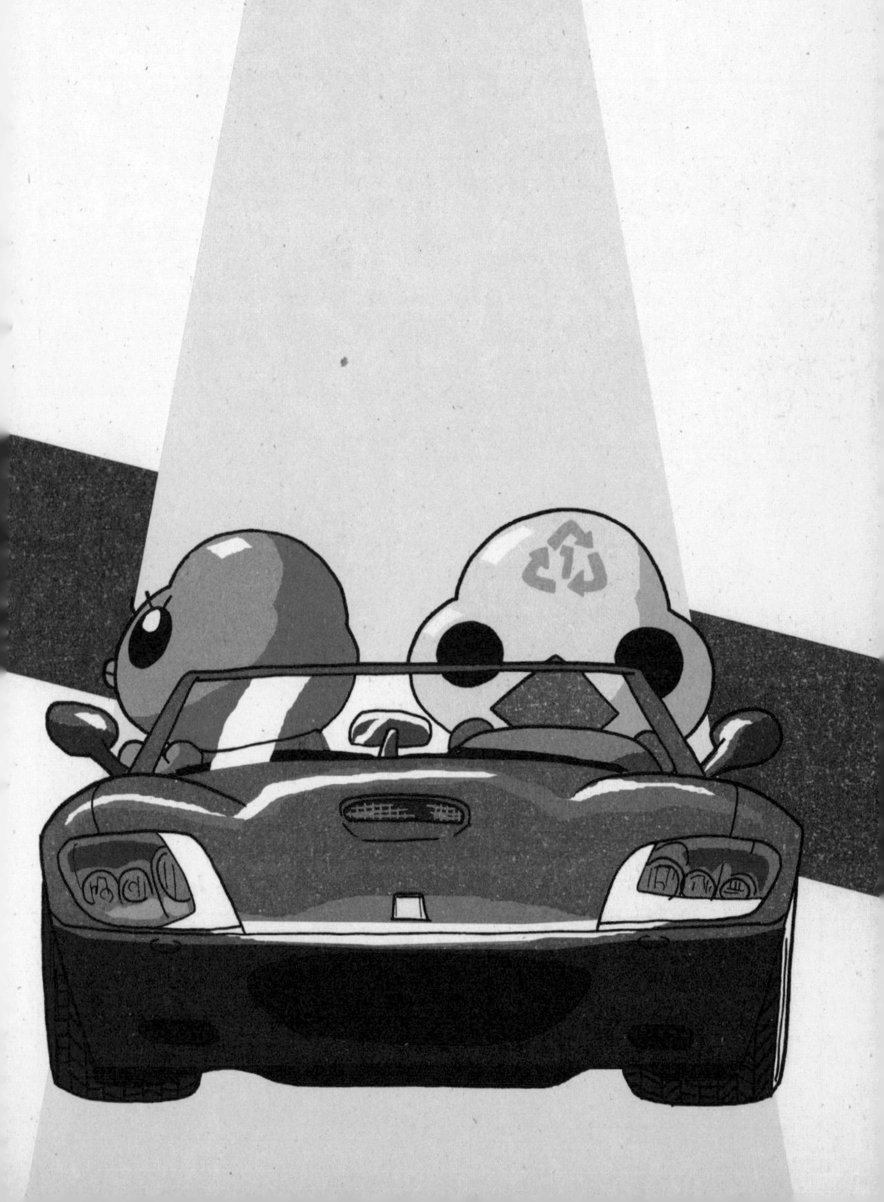

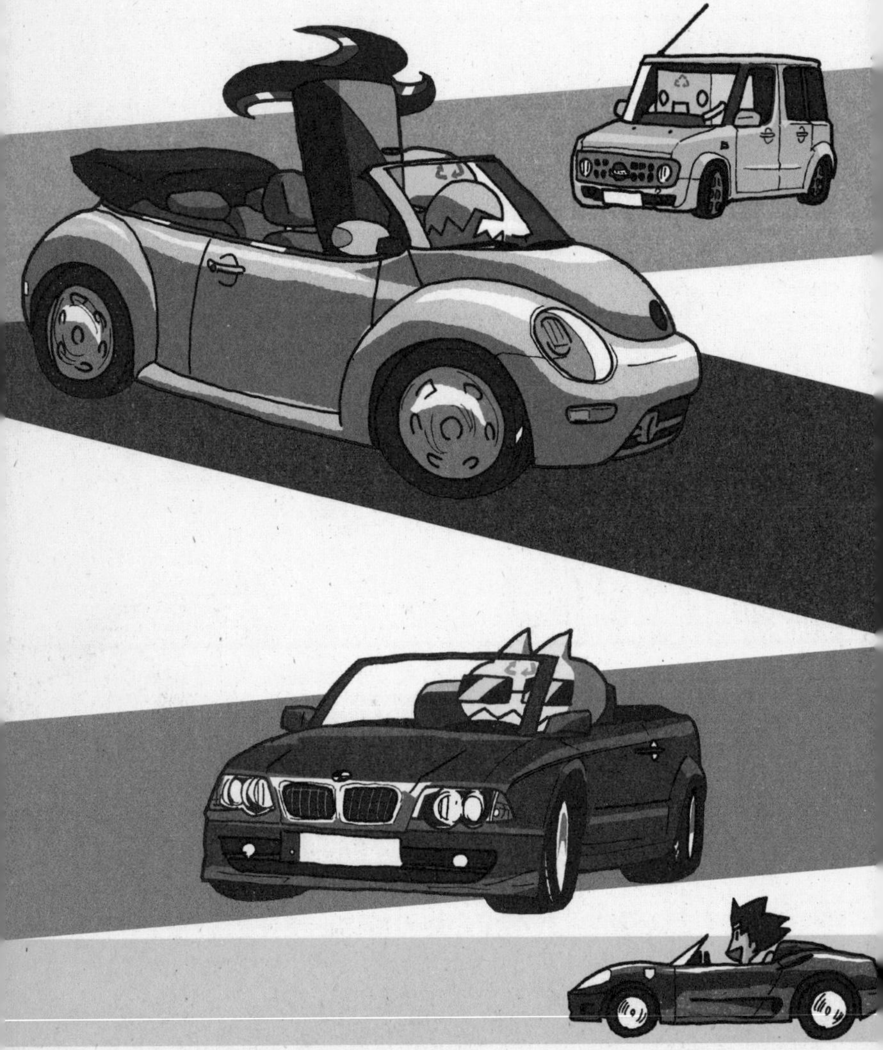

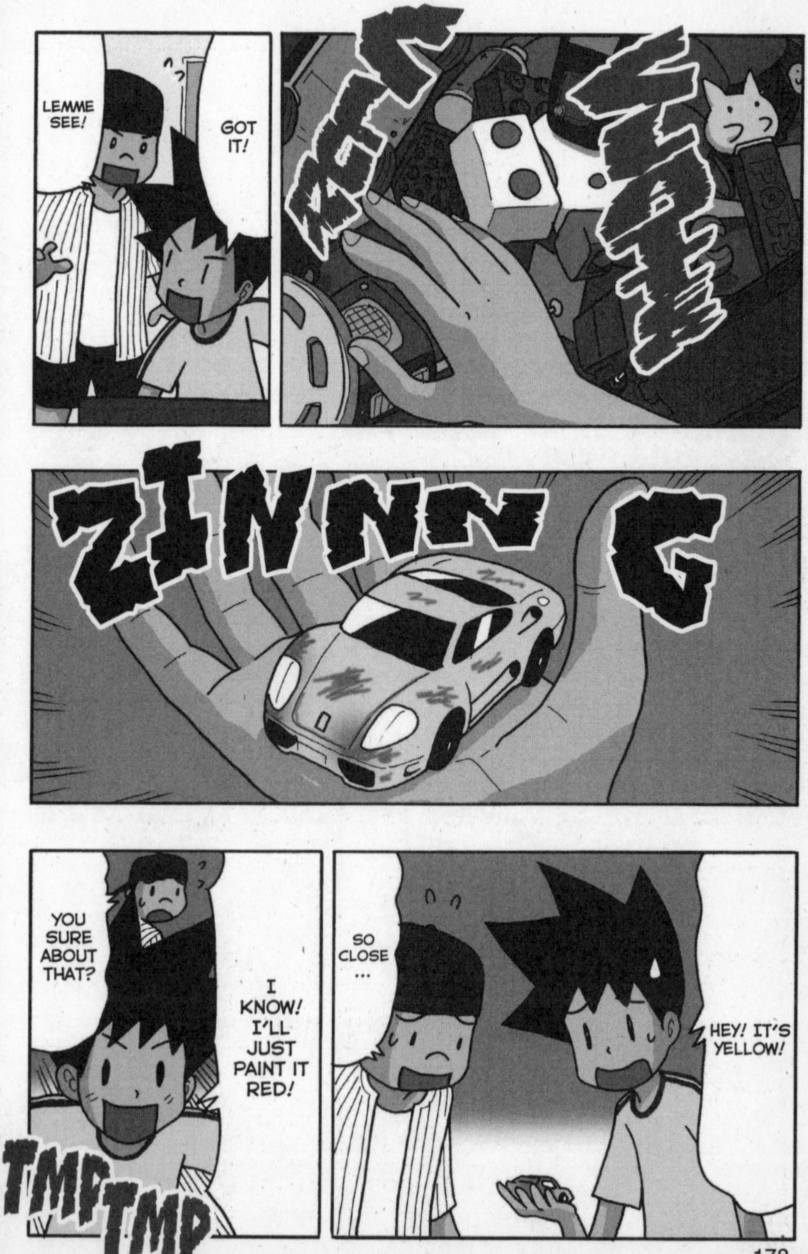
GOT IT!
LEMME SEE!
ZINNNG
HEY! IT'S YELLOW!
SO CLOSE ...
I KNOW! I'LL JUST PAINT IT RED!
YOU SURE ABOUT THAT?
TMPTMP

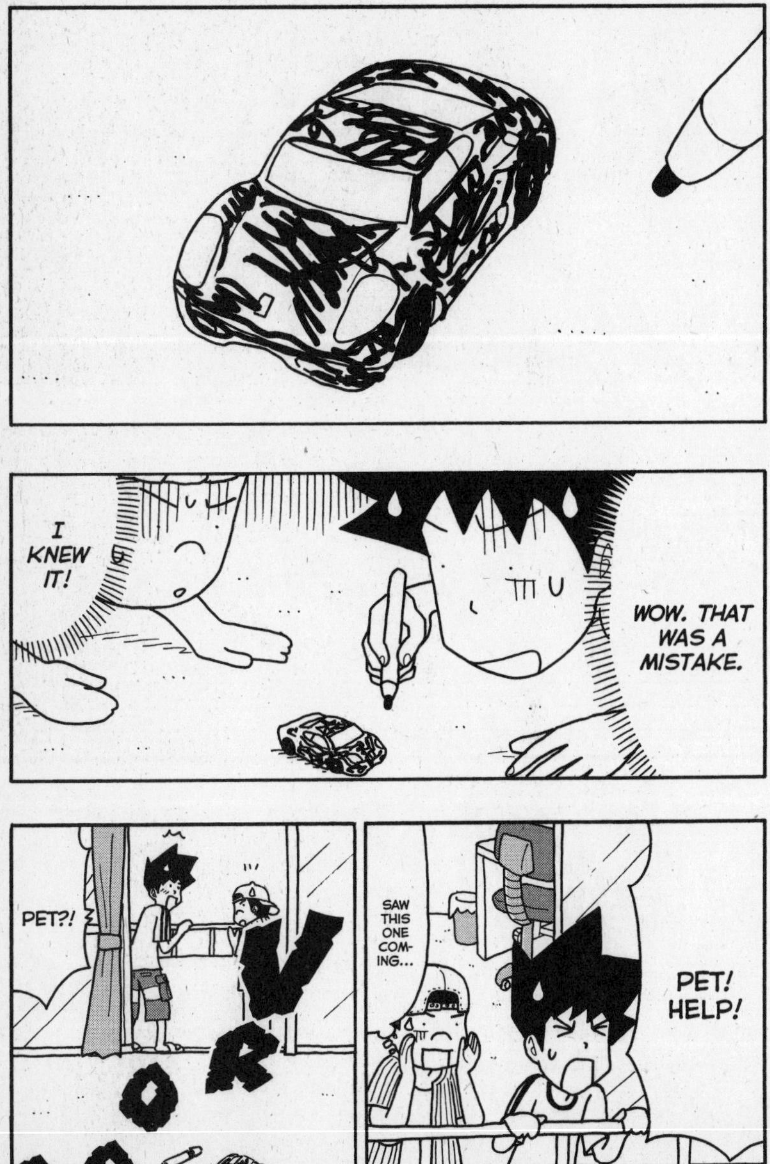
WOW. THAT WAS A MISTAKE.
I KNEW IT!
PET! HELP!
SAW THIS ONE COM-ING...
PET?!
VROOO

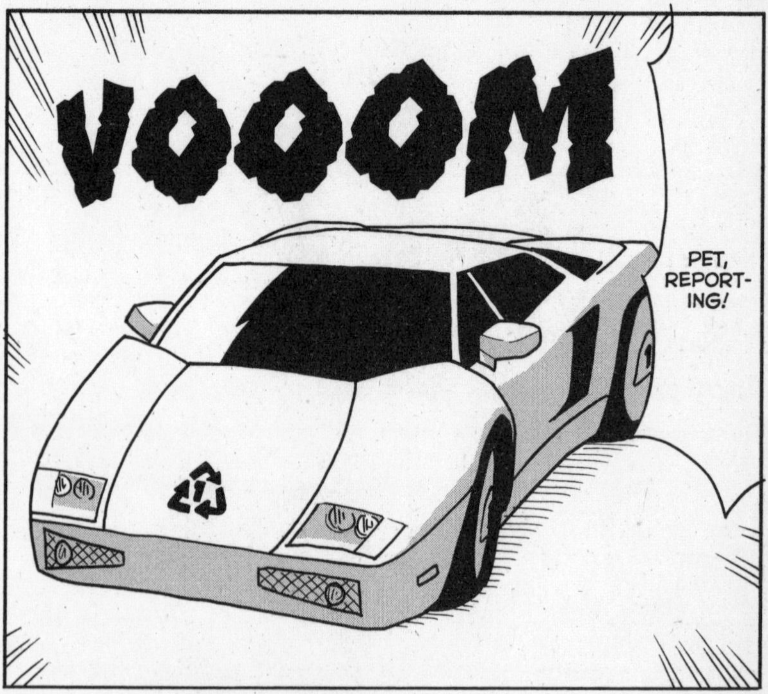
VOOOM
PET, REPORT-ING!

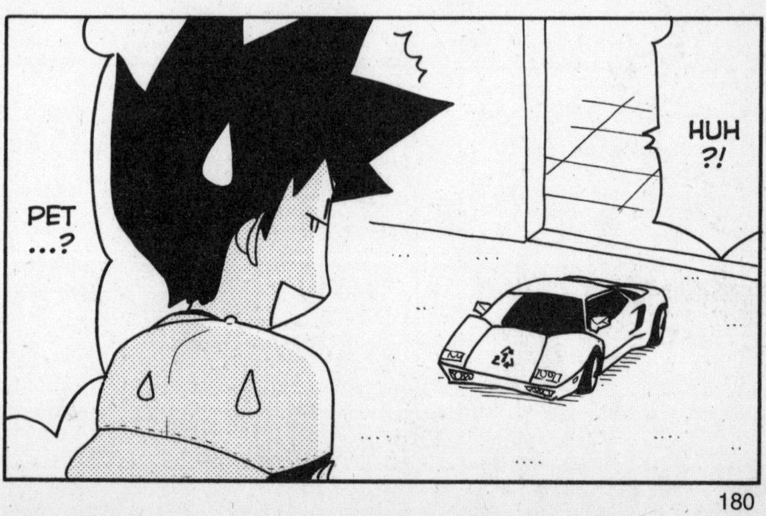
HUH ?!
PET ...?

THAT'S RIGHT! IT'S ME!
FULL TRANSFORMATION
ROBOT
SPORTS CAR
TRANSFORMATION
I DEVELOPED THE ABILITY TO TAKE THE SHAPE OF A CAR FOR THIS CHAPTER!
WHOA! COOL!!!
WATCH! I'LL TRANS-FORM BACK TO MY ORIGINAL SHAPE!
REFORM!!
ZWINNNNG!

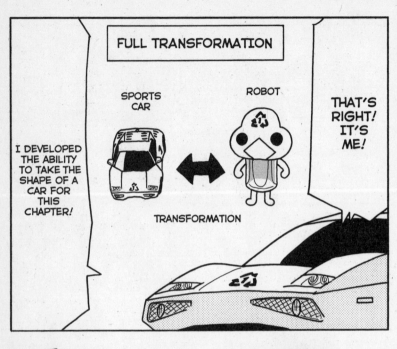

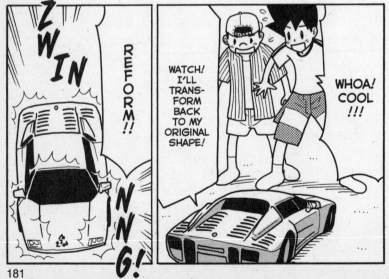

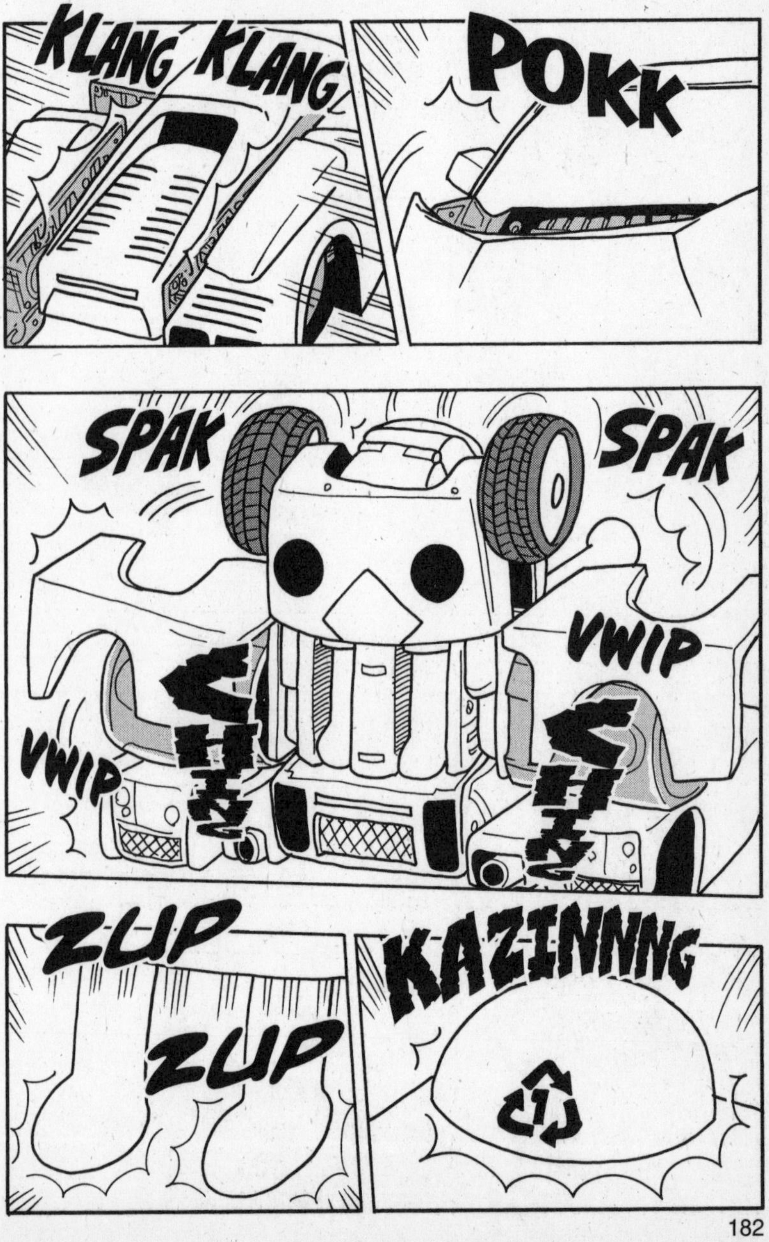
POKK
KLANG KLANG
SPAK
VWIP
SPAK
VWIP
KAZINNNG
ZUP
ZUP

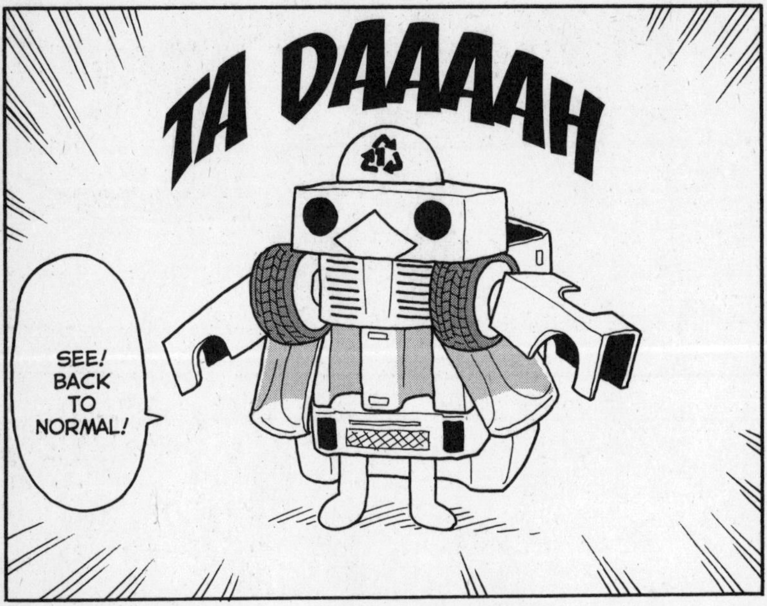
TA DAAAAH
SEE! BACK TO NORMAL!

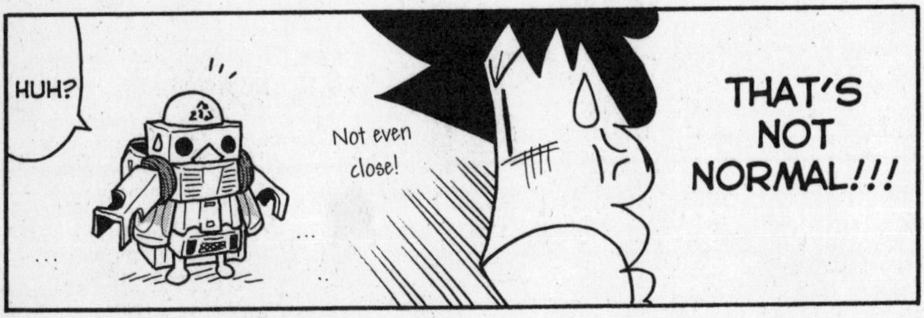
THAT'S NOT NORMAL!!!
Not even close!
HUH?
...
...
..

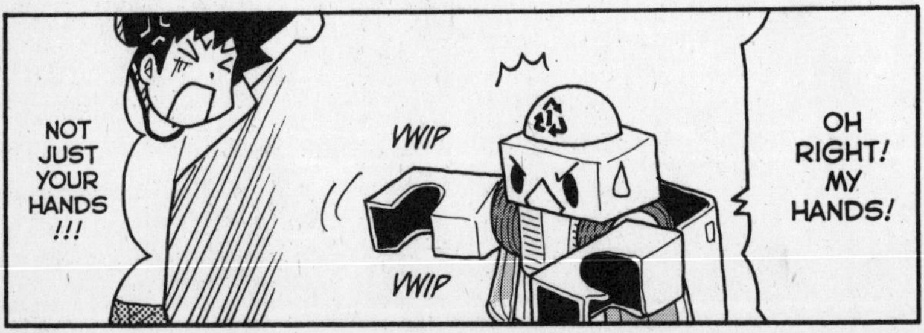
OH RIGHT! MY HANDS!
VWIP
VWIP
NOT JUST YOUR HANDS!!!

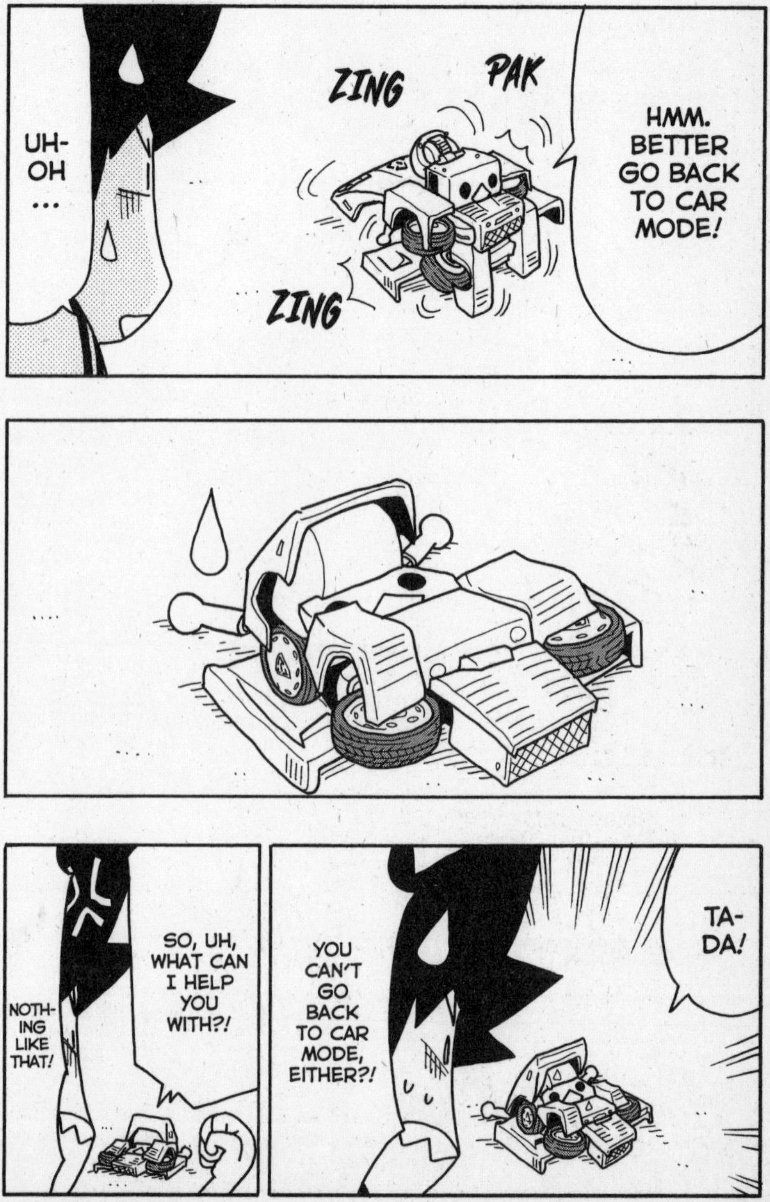
HMM. BETTER GO BACK TO CAR MODE!
PAK
ZING
ZING
UH-OH ...
TA-DA!
YOU CAN'T GO BACK TO CAR MODE, EITHER?!
SO, UH, WHAT CAN I HELP YOU WITH?!
NOTH-ING LIKE THAT!

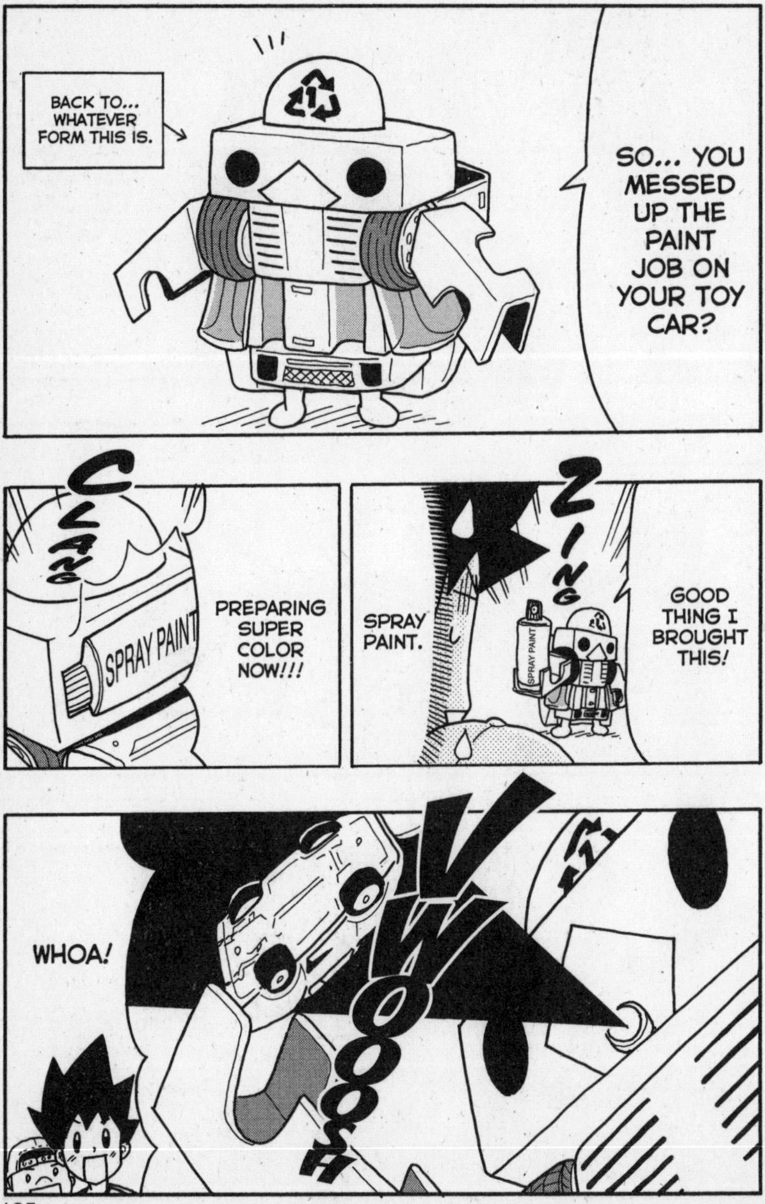
SO... YOU MESSED UP THE PAINT JOB ON YOUR TOY CAR?
BACK TO... WHATEVER FORM THIS IS.
ZING
GOOD THING I BROUGHT THIS!
SPRAY PAINT
SPRAY PAINT.
CLANG
PREPARING SUPER COLOR NOW!!!
SPRAY PAINT
VWOOOOSH
WHOA!

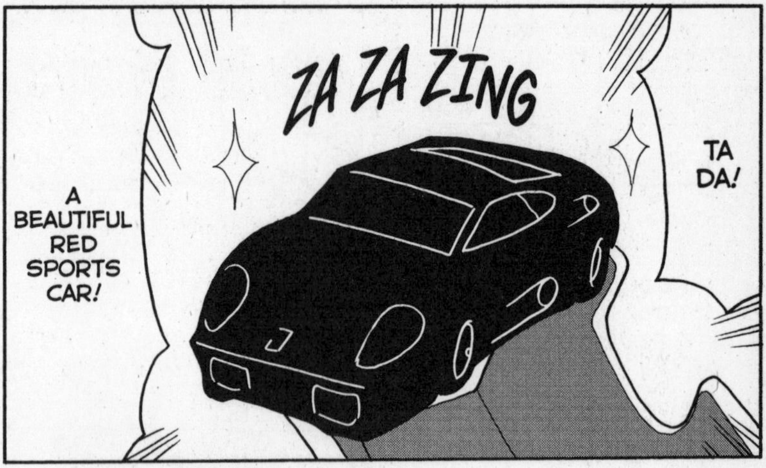
ZA ZA ZING
TA DA!
A BEAUTIFUL RED SPORTS CAR!

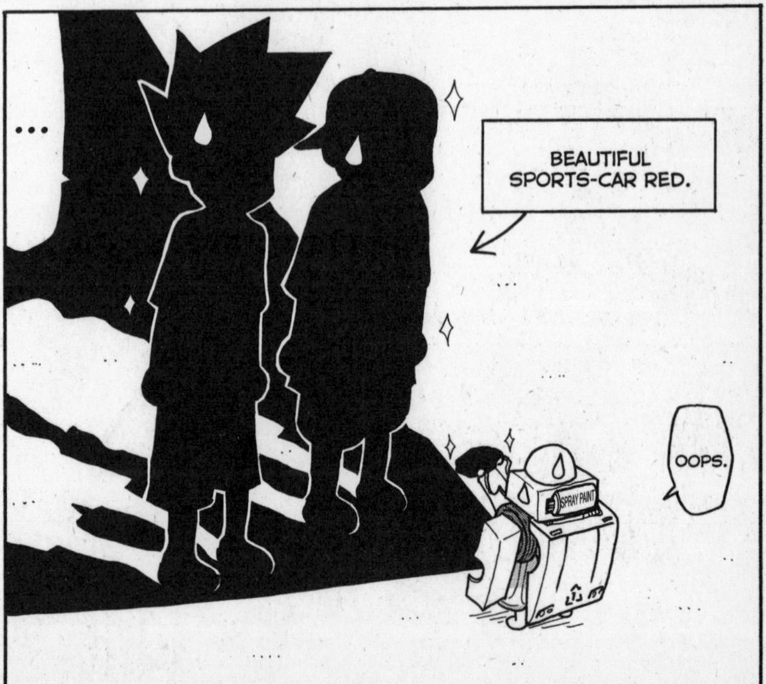
...
BEAUTIFUL SPORTS-CAR RED.
OOPS.

Special Bonus No. 1

Introducing new Recycled Robots sent in by our readers!!!

MILK CARTON ROBOT
RYOGA KAIDA, TOKYO, JAPAN.

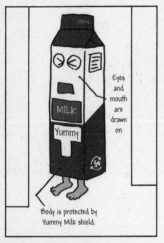

OPEN
MILK
Yummy
Eyes and mouth are drawn on
Body is protected by Yummy Milk shield.
MOO MOO MOO
COWS, ATTACK!!!
MILK
Yummy
THERE ARE 92 COWS IN ALL!
WHY?!
WAA

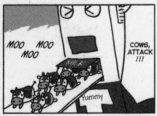

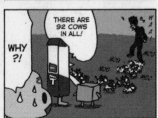

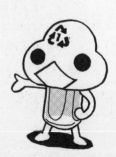

BET
KAZUSHI IMOTO,
YAMAGUCHI, JAPAN.

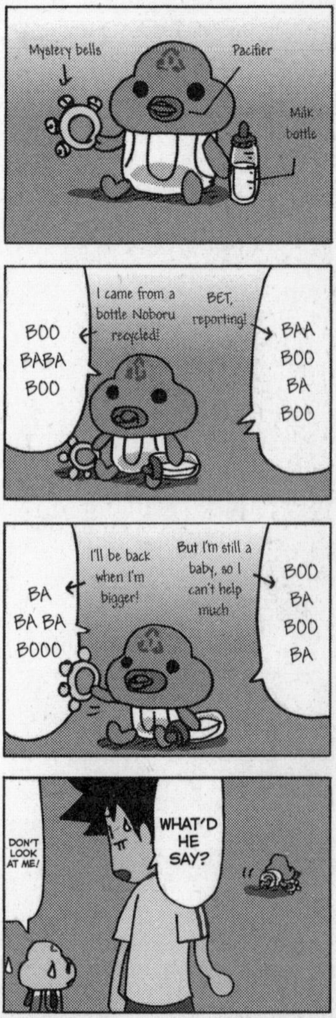
Pacifier
Milk bottle
Mystery bells
BAA BOO BA BOO
BET, reporting!
I came from a bottle Noboru recycled!
BOO BABA BOO
BOO BA BOO BA
But I'm still a baby, so I can't help much
I'll be back when I'm bigger!
BA BA BA BOOO
WHAT'D HE SAY?
DON'T LOOK AT ME!

PLASTIC BOTTLE RANGERS
YOHEI FUKUYA, TOKYO, JAPAN.

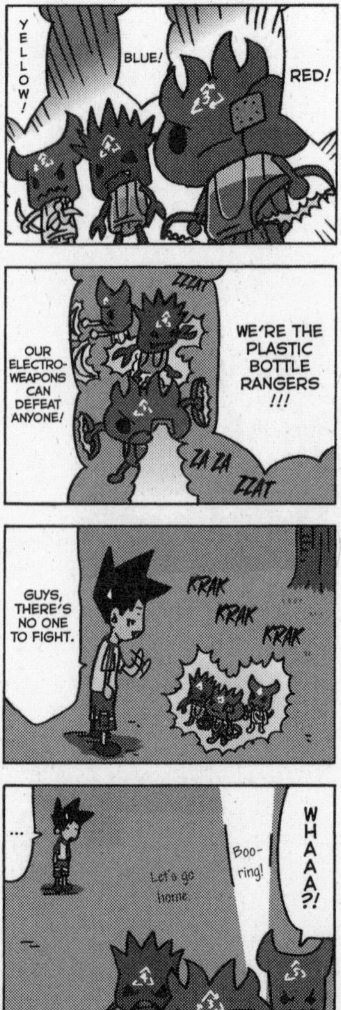
RED!
BLUE!
YELLOW!
WE'RE THE PLASTIC BOTTLE RANGERS!!!
ZZZAT
OUR ELECTRO-WEAPONS CAN DEFEAT ANYONE!
ZA ZA ZZAT
KRAK KRAK KRAK
GUYS, THERE'S NO ONE TO FIGHT.
WHAAAA?!
Boo-ring!
Let's go home.
...

ORANGE SODA
YUTARO YAMASHITA,
SAITAMA, JAPAN.

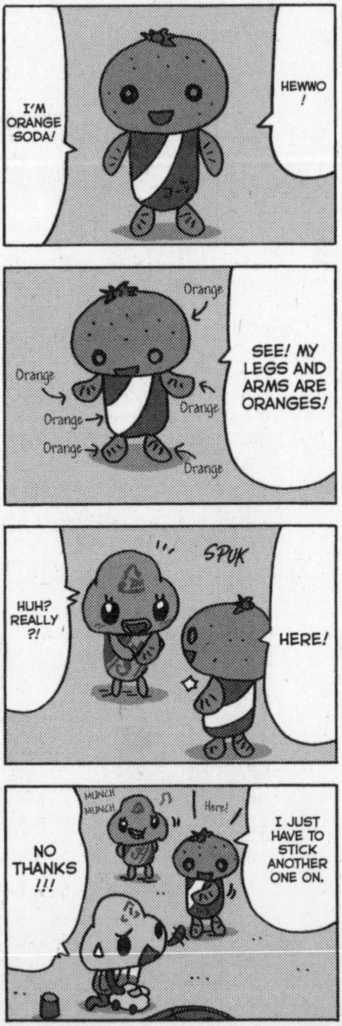
HEWWO !
I'M ORANGE SODA!
Orange
Orange
Orange
Orange
Orange
Orange
Orange
SEE! MY LEGS AND ARMS ARE ORANGES!
SPUK
HERE!
HUH? REALLY ?!
Here!
I JUST HAVE TO STICK ANOTHER ONE ON.
MUNCH MUNCH
NO THANKS !!!

RAINBOW CAT
AZUSA SAITO, TOKYO, JAPAN.

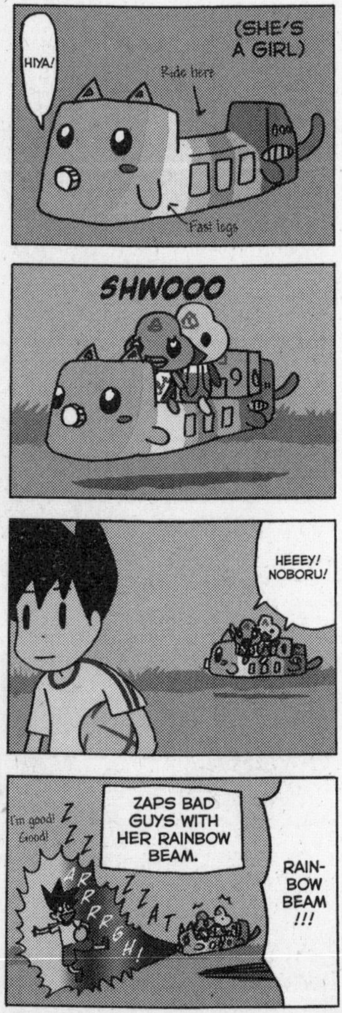
(SHE'S A GIRL)
Ride here
HIYA!
Fast legs
SHWOOO
HEEEY! NOBORU!
ZAPS BAD GUYS WITH HER RAINBOW BEAM.
RAIN-BOW BEAM !!!
ZZZAT
I'm good! Good!
ARRRGH!

SPECIAL BONUS NO. 2

PET'S MANGA LESSON

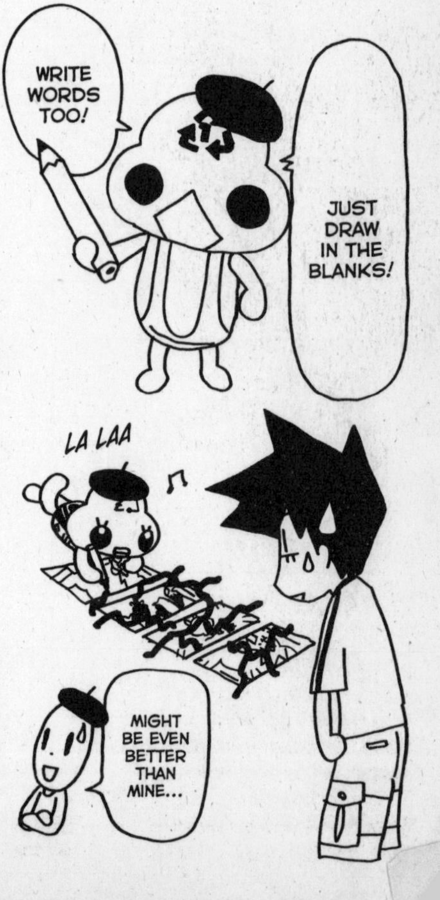
JUST DRAW IN THE BLANKS!
WRITE WORDS TOO!
LA LAA
MIGHT BE EVEN BETTER THAN MINE...

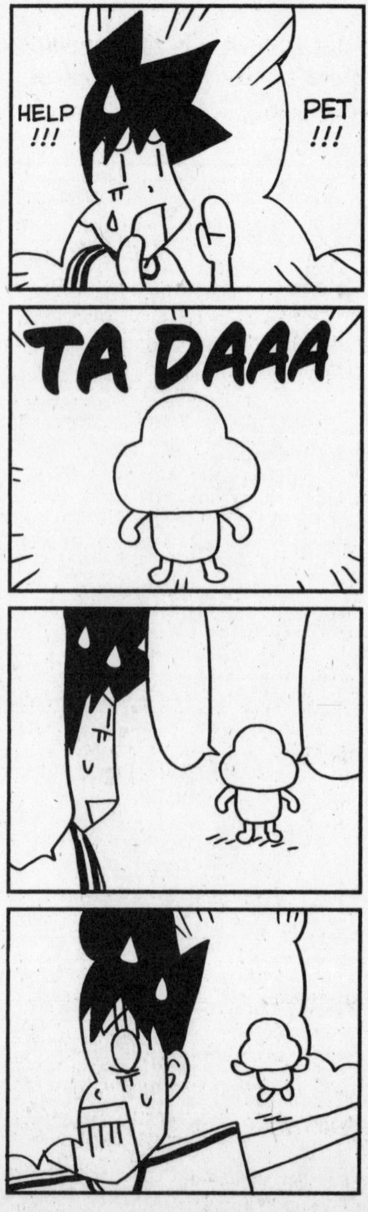
PET !!!
HELP !!!
TA DAAA

A Note About Recycling Symbols

In Japan, where ***Leave It to PET!*** originated, recycling is an important part of everyday life. While we only have one symbol ♻ that's used on most things that are recyclable in the United States, in Japan, just about every material has a symbol of its own. For example:

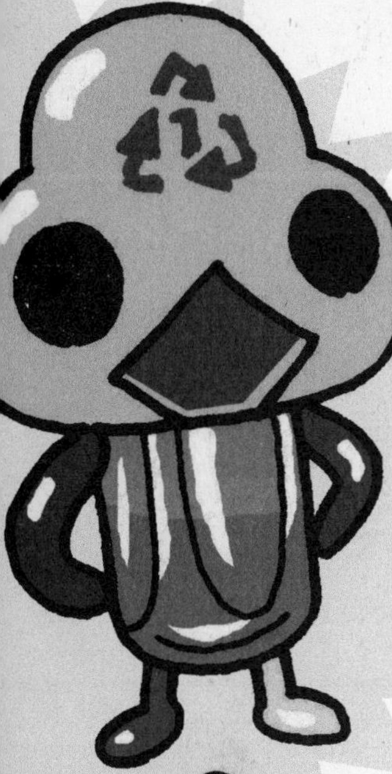

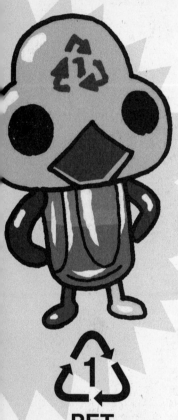

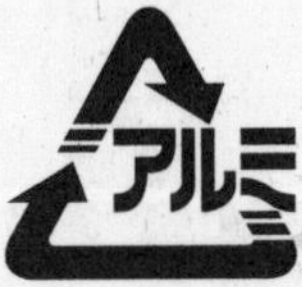
アルミ

This is the symbol for recyclable **aluminum**.

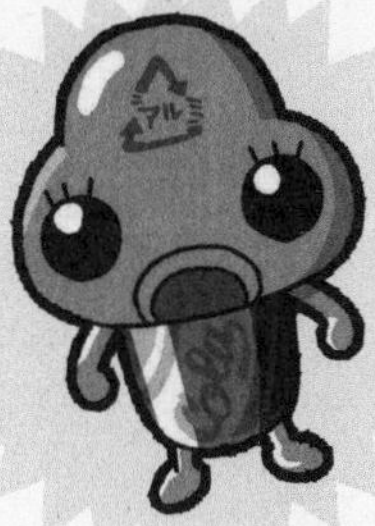

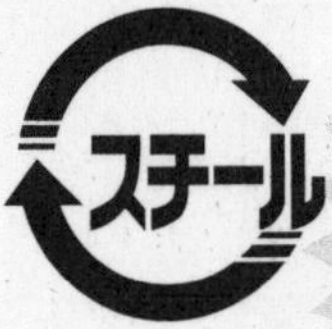
スチール

This is the symbol for recyclable **steel**.

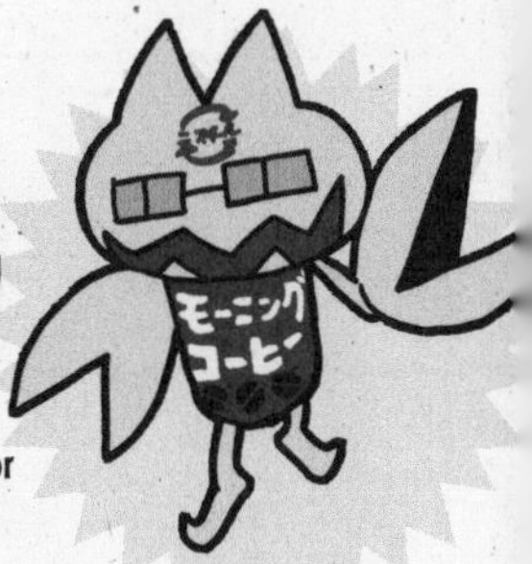
モーニング
コーヒー

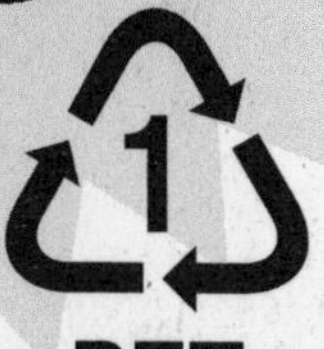
1

PET

The symbol for recyclable polyethylene terephthalate – the kind of plastic most plastic bottles are made of – can be found all over the world. Sometimes it appears with the word **"PETE"** instead of **"PET."**

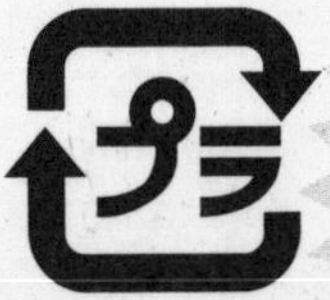
プラ

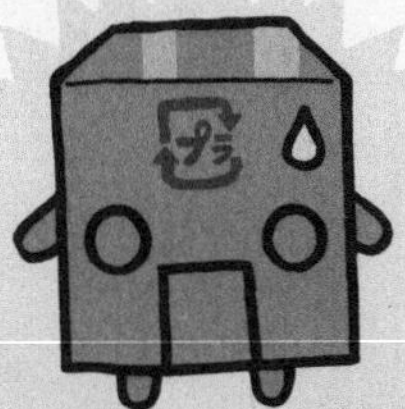

This is the symbol for recyclable **plastic other than PET bottles**.